Shard's Thugs

Dexter C. Herron

To: RICHARD
MAY THE ADVENTURE
NEVER END!

2/23/19

To; Hilary,
Dr. Jones, Lt. Patches, Gin, Brutus and Naga.

And…
Special thanks to Beth and Carlo.

Shard's Tactics

THUNDER ECHOED MADLY in the great hall, as feet, bare soles as hard as leather, pounded on the cracked and broken stone floor. Their voices growled and howled with panic and confusion as they dragged their broken weapons and wounded across the rotting drawbridge into the castle, into the darkness within.

He looked around desperately, his eyes quickly adjusting to the dim. Dilapidated, crumbling masonry, smashed furniture, mildew assaulting his sensitive nose, not at all what he had expected. He had used the sheer will of command to turn the rout into a retreat, hoping to escape with some resemblance of a military force in order to counter-attack the Humans. The Emperor would not accept defeat, and as long as Goblin blood still flowed in their veins, he would expect – no – demand they fight on.

They had outnumbered the Humans ten to one, but iron swords were useless against steel armor and great horses. Cavalry charged under the umbrella of arrows and ran down the Goblins caught flatfooted on open ground, and turned the great army of General Hookfang Rottingtooth into mincemeat.

"You three!" He bellowed. "Get up to the portcullis and shut those gates!" He looked around at the mass pouring into the hall. "Which one of you moronic fucks can count?"

One looked up, holding up both four-fingered hands. "I have seven and eight, Lieutenant." He pointed to his foot which was missing a toe.

"You brilliant running snot, take three non-lame twits to the wall and keep watch. Let me know if anyone followed us." The Lieutenant waved. "Go!" He looked around, trying to find anyone with rank. "You, Corporal! Take ten thugs and search the west wing. Make sure this place is empty!"

The Corporal looked uncertain. "Uh, how much is ten?"

"By Thrallic's furry balls! Where is your squad?"

"Dead. I'm the last."

"You fucking fuck!" The Lieutenant screamed. "You should be dead too! Kill yourself now!" He looked for someone else. "Can you count to ten?"

The Goblin who had been watching the Corporal try to figure out a painless way to stab himself looked up. "I know what ten thugs looks like."

"Good! You're a corporal! Search the west wing!"

The new corporal nodded then smacked the old corporal's arm, driving his short blade into his eye. While the old corporal howled, the new corporal snatched his baldric and put it on, tugging it into place as he shouted orders. Quickly a contingent, happy to be bullied around again, fell into a group and headed down the hall.

The Lieutenant nodded as he climbed up on a broken cinder block and shouted over the confused din. "Now hear this! I am Lieutenant Wiggletooth Shard! Who here thinks he out ranks me?"

Coming into the doorway was an ambling mass of shoulders with long dragging arms, a captain by his baldric. He shuffled forward on stout legs, standing as tall as Shard standing on a cinder block. "I am Ho Sheck Yek Yak, captain of the Black Raid Company. I am assuming command, Lieutenant. We will hold up here until General Rottingtooth sends reinforcements."

Shard nodded, stepping from his cinder block. He bowed submissively as he slipped his needler, a broken schlager blade with leather wrapped at the base for a grip, from his forearm guard and shoved it into the soft space under Yek Yak's jaw just as he prepared to climb up the cinder block to take command. Shard, with both hands heaved up, forcing the blade through Yek-Yak's palate, up into his brain and through the top of his skull.

Yek Yak looked mildly surprised and stepped off the block, unbuckling his turtle shell helmet. He pulled it off with a heave and peered into it, checking for damage. Satisfied it was okay, he pulled it back on, buckled it up, rolled his eyes into his head and died.

Shard had unbuckled Yek Yak's baldric and yanked it free during the monstrous goblin's helmet inspection and had it on before the big doof hit the floor. "We are preparing to counter- attack, ya gutless wonder." He shouted at the dead Goblin as he wretched free his needler. "The notion that we ran away to wait for reinforcements is an act akin to being a Hobbit!" He kicked the supine body in disgust, then looked up, his black mica eyes glistening. "Now hear this! Bind your wounds quickly for we will attack! Remember, we did not run away like Elves! We tactically relocated for an advantageous counter-attack! And we will counter-attack. Unless we counter-attack, then it's considered running away and that is unacceptable! Do you all understand?"

Uniformly, every Goblin eye looked back at him, blinking bewilderedly.

Shard sneered and muttered. "Close enough."

A Goblin in brightly polished armor marched up. "Lieutenant Shard?"

"That's Captain Shard!" he growled hotly.

"Ah, yes, congratulations on your promotion." He saluted. "I'm Tech Lieutenant Forring of the Emperor's Engineering Squad."

Shard squinted. "And what are you doing alive, you cowardly fuck?"

Forring motioned to the giant keg strapped to his back. "A dud. I ran around the field shouting, 'BOOM!', and it worked for a while but the enemy started catching on and those cursed Elves started using me as target practice."

Shard planted his fists into his hips. "And why the fuck didn't you run around to get them to use up their ammo? Even Elves have a fucking arrow expenditure budget."

"I was hoping to get a new fuse when I saw your detail running up here." He said looking around with a sniff. "So, have you seen any engineers around?"

"No, they all figured out how to explode themselves, you dumb fuck. Now go stand some place where no one will mistake you for a keg of ale."

He saluted, pounding his head with his fist. "Yes, sir!" He turned away, nearly striking Shard with the arrows that protruded from his explosive keg of Black Dirt That Blows Stuff Up, and then turned back. "Oh, uh perhaps I should mention..."

Shard rolled his eyes. "You are now fucking bothering me! Don't you see I have better things to do than talk to a walking bomb?"

He saluted again, wincing from the pain. "Sorry, sir, it's just there is a group of men amassing at the bottom of the hill."

Shard's eyes grew round as his heavy mono-brow bristled. "And just at what fucking point were you going to inform me of this?"

Forring looked offended. "Well, I was hoping that if I could get a new fuse I could run down there and take care of it."

Shard bit his lip, not wanting to encourage such a good plan. "Whatever," he mumbled. "How many are down there?"

Forring looked distant. "Uh, I'm not sure, I've only been trained to recognize what a group looks like."

Shard closed his eyes tiredly. "Scrounge up something to make a fuse." He opened his eyes and Forring was still standing there. "Now!" he barked. Then shouted up the stairs to the tower, "Hey! Up there! What's the status on those gates?"

From above, a head popped into view. "It's worked by a big chain. Nud is trying to chew through it." He answered brightly.

Shard shook his head. "Look for a machine, a Gnomish contraption, that when you turn the wheel the gate goes up and down."

"Oh, I guess that's what this thing is for." He looked back over his shoulder.

"Give it a try," Shard encouraged, then turned away before he did something rash and violent. In the crowd of the main hall, he spotted his PFC. "Private First Class Gralfange! Smiley! Over here!"

The Goblin ran over, his over-sized teeth gave him the look that he was smiling all the time. "Hey Corporal... I mean, Sergeant Shard." He noticed the Baldric. "Captain? You were a sergeant when you sent me to go check the east wing."

"Battlefield promotion. What do you have?"

Smiley smiled brightly. "East wing clear, Captain! The castle is empty, that it is."

Shard looked left, then right. "How is it I sent you to check the east wing and you come back from the west wing?"

Smiley looked down both halls, scratching his head. "Uh, well, the castle is in kinda circle shape." He outlined a square in the air with his fingers.

"Oh, then you saw the patrol I sent down the west wing."

Smiley shook his head. "Nope, never saw them."

Confusion flashed across his face. "So where the fuck is the squad I sent down the west wing?" He turned as the Goblin he sent to watch the walls ran up. "What do you got?"

"Sir, there is a group of men at the bottom of the hill. I count more than seven eights of them and less than seven horses, but more than four."

Shard leaned over to Smiley. Smiley whispered: "That's fifty-six men, we out-number them two to one, that we do. Perfect odds for an attack, sir."

"Are you fucking nuts?" he growled, holding up four fingers. "It takes this many Goblins to take out one Human." He held up his other hand. "And this many Goblins to take out a man on a horse." He turned back to the lookout. "You said more than seven eights. Can you only count as high as seven eights?"

The Goblin surveyed his fingers and toes to be sure he had them all. "Yes, sir."

Shard nodded, understanding. "So, when you say more than seven eights, is it almost double? Do you think you could get another seven eights outta that?"

The Goblin thought a moment, his ears twitching. "Yeah, I'd say that."

Shard held his breath. "And what are they doing?"

"Standing around."

"Are they forming up? Assembling to charge the castle?" When the Goblin shook his head, Shard hissed. "By Mumgerds smelly entrails, this is bad. They totally out-number us, the doors are wide open." He looked around at the rotted tapestries and sagging roof. "This is a perfectly good castle, empty of Humans. Wrong, wrong, wrong. Where are the people who live here?"

Smiley smiled. "Perhaps they're on holiday?"

Shard smiled brightly. "And they left the fucking door open so they could get back in, right? You stupid twit! There is something wrong with this castle and we've got to get out of here. Are there any other doors?"

Smiley thought. "There's a garbage chute in the kitchen. I think we could squeeze through, that I do."

Shard sincerely brightened. "Excellent! Where does it lead?"

Smiley frowned as he concentrated, trying to remember. "Uh, off a cliff."

Shard's mono-brow raised. "A cliff?" His mind reeled with the harsh memory of dragging his wounded men up the long-ass, narrow, rocky, winding trail to the castle. He could only conclude the cliff was both shear and a long, way down. "And what's at the bottom, water?"

"Yeah, and rocks!" Smiley smiled.

"Sharp, jagged rocks?"

"Yeah!"

Shard smiled warmly. "Well done! I'll send everyone off a cliff onto some sharp, jagged rocks. That way, their big pile of bodies will break my fall and I can counter-attack the enemy by my frigging self!"

"That's very brave of you, sir."

Shard cuffed him in the side of the head. "I'm being face-tious, you dolt!"

"Excuse me, Captain Facetious?" The goblin Shard sent down the west wing ran up. "I'm looking for Lieutenant Shard."

Shard spun hotly. "I am Lieutenant Shard!" He winced, correcting himself. "Captain Shard!"

"Oh, I thought you looked like him."

"Where the fuck have you been?" Shard growled.

"The west wing, sir. We're rich!" He chirped.

Seconds dragged as Shard stared at him, his face expressionless. "Come again?"

"We found a treasure room! There's a giant pile of loot! See?" He held up his hand showing the rings that were finely crafted for a Human's delicate finger crammed brutally on his thick Goblin fingers, quickly cutting off all circulation and turning his fingernails pearl white.

Shard turned hotly to Smiley. "Why didn't you tell me there was a treasure room, private?"

"Um, that's private first class, sir and we didn't see a treasure room."

Shard kneed him violently in the balls. "And you didn't see a back door either, private." He turned to the Corporal. "Show me," he growled. "Fast!" He trotted off down the hall with Smiley limping behind, uttering a squeak with each step.

Shard's permanent frown deepened as he passed the shattered furniture, broken statues and ruined rugs. A perfectly good castle, perfectly good furniture, and no one home. Suddenly, he stopped dead in his tracks as his eyes instantly teared. "Moxoly's favorite whore! That's a fuck righteous stench!" His nostrils burned from the acrid wall of stink. "Ugh, why didn't you warn me?"

The Goblin looked back at him. "What stench, sir?"

Shard tried to blink his vision clear. "The stench your mother has when she spreads her fucking legs. You don't smell that?" He glanced back at Smiley who was gagging.

"No, sir, not at all," the corporal responded, pointing to a door. "Here is the treasure room."

Shard wiped a tear from his face. "Of course, it all makes sense. An empty castle, door wide open, enemy at the front gates afraid to come in, the rotting stench of partially-digested Goblin and a big pile of treasure." He nodded, agreeing with his own logic. "We are so fucked." He leaned, peering into the open crack of the door.

Its scales glistened with a flash of scintillating color as the feeble light from the dirty window reflected off its ebony hide. Its belly was ivory, its talons were grey and its eyes were blazing crimson. Teeth flashed, fangs so big it couldn't close its mouth properly, making quick work of armor and bone as it shredded its Goblin meal. Chunks of Goblin meat dribbled freely from its maw as it chewed.

Shard leaned back, out of the doorway, beckoning the Corporal over with a jerk of his head. "So, let me get this straight: you spot a glint of gold through the crack of a door while running through a strange castle and find a huge mass of treasure, not noticing the giant black dragon sleeping on top of it?"

The Corporal looked confused. "What dragon?"

Shard nodded understanding his corporal was suffering from a bad case of 'Treasure Fixated Tunnel Vision Syndrome' or T.F.F.V.S. "You know this all belongs to the Emperor, right?"

The corporal's enthusiasm faded. "Oh, uh, of course, sir."

Shard rested a fatherly hand on the Corporal's shoulder. "But he doesn't need to know about every penny does he? If you catch my drift."

The Corporal nodded slowly, his enthusiasm returning. "Oh, right." He smiled dubiously. "Wink, wink, nudge, nudge."

Shard laughed breathlessly. "Yes, well here's what I want you to do: Run in there and grab a big box of gold and we'll split it 50-50, how's that?"

"Oh! Thank you, sir!" He saluted sharply, almost knocking himself unconscious.

Shard unbuckled the Corporal's baldric as the thug swooned. "And that gold's heavy. Here, let me hold this for you so you can carry that much more treasure."

"That's most considerate of you, sir."

"Run along now." Shard patted him affectionately on the head and slammed the door behind him. Smiley then shoved a chair against the door. "We are so fucking fucked," he said, handing the baldric to Smiley who wasted no time in putting it on. "Come on! We're getting out of here."

Corporal Smiley ran after him. "But how?"

He waved him off. "Don't fucking talk to me, you'll make me forget the plan." He shouted back, bursting into the grand hall. "Alright! Listen up, maggots! We're leaving!" He reached up to a rotted tapestry and tore off a wide strip. He picked up a broken chair leg and wound the cloth around the leg. "I need some oil." He looked at a Goblin treating the wounded. "Is that healing oil?"

The Medic nodded. "It's for the wounded."

Shard snatched the bottle. "The wounded will be left behind to delay a hungry black dragon coming this way," he said overly loud. He then shouted: "Anyone here wounded?" Everyone shook their heads as they clambered up to their feet, some balancing on stumps. "Excellent. Warriors all." He poured the oil onto his makeshift torch. "Hey, bomb boy, get over here!" Shard shoved the torch at him. "Take this and my flint and steel. Listen carefully: when I tell you, and I mean when I specifically fucking tell you, light this torch. Then, when I say so and not a fucking moment sooner, you shove that torch over your shoulder into the bung hole and complete your prime directive. You got that?" When Forring nodded, Shard slapped him on the back, then pushed him towards the gate, waving over Goblins with shields. Shard peered through the open gate at the long, winding road that snaked along the narrow spine of the rocky hill. At the end, the men mulled around in a loose, column-formation, three men wide. Shard pulled back, silently cursing himself. Even with Goblin shields to protect him from Elven arrows and perfect detonation timing, he would at best only blow up the first few ranks. He needed another plan.

It was leaning against the wall.

He ran over and picked up the Goblin banner, holding it aloft. "Listen, everybody! Here is the plan, we are going to pretend..." He stopped as the realized who he was talking to. "Everyone is going to follow this banner! Wherever it goes, everyone follows." He searched the faces in front of him.

"Who's a good runner? You? Good! Hold this." He handed him the banner. You stick to me like a booger, got that?" He grabbed Forring. "You lucked out, I'm not going to have to blow you up just yet." He peered up the stairs. "How's it coming up there?"

A head appeared in the trap door. "The Gnomish thing is busted. We found a hammer and were about halfway through smashing the chain."

"Thank Grumesh's rotting tusk. Stop that until I tell you. Is there a rope up there?"

"There's one attached to this warning bell."

"Tie it so you can climb down on the outside of the tower," Shard instructed. "When I tell you to, smash the chain, and when the gate drops, climb down that rope on the outside of the castle and run to the banner. Got it?"

He shook his head. "Nope, we don't have the banner up here."

Shard grit his teeth. "You'll figure it out." He turned as he heard the echo of a door smash from the west wing. "Okay, you shields, to the front!" He elbowed his way behind them, gripping the front thug's belt firmly. He then grabbed the belt of the thug holding the banner. "Forward, march! Double time, march! Run! Run!" At the run, he steered the Goblin column, four thug wide ranks, down the twisting road, peering through the spaces of the front shields. He could see the men readying their weapons, the thrice-damned Elves knocking their arrows. "Shields up! Shields up!" The air whistled with deadly shafts, striking on the upraised shields with a heavy thunk. "Closer! Keep your ranks tight!" Below, he could see the men ready to receive the charge, their spears at the ready. He could see the whites of their eyes.

Shard drew sharply on the shield in front of him, pulling him back. "Turn! Turn!" He drew the banner carrier around. "Run! To the castle, follow the banner!" He shoved the shield thug into the mass of Goblins running down the hill and plowed his way back up the hill, dragging the banner carrier behind him. Arrows rained down through the confused shields as the Goblin column reversed direction, stumbling over themselves, trampling each other, desperately trying to follow the banner.

Over the din of clanging armor and howling Goblins, Shard could hear the triumphant shout of men as they charged up the hill after the hapless Goblins, incensed for the easy kill.

Shard's heart pounded, his lungs blazed with fire and desperation. His feet throbbed from running on the stony ground and from being stepped on by the mass of Goblins around him. He charged on, up the treacherous hill, towards the open gates of the castle.

The black dragon stood on the drawbridge, its ivory belly exposed as it rose on its hind legs and roared like the drum of thunder, shaking Shard's body to the bone. He tugged on the banner-carrier's belt, shoving him off the narrow road and down the rocky hill before diving after him, rolling uncontrollably down the steep climb.

Lighting flashed across his eyes as his turtle helm struck a rock. Shard swooned, blearily looking up towards the road.

He could see the wings of the dragon, flapping to add speed to its run, chasing the men—the slow, soft and tasty men—down the hill.

He looked around the scattered Goblin bodies trying to rouse themselves from the fall. He crawled over to the banner carrier. "Give me that. I have a special mission for you. Come with me." He took the banner and passed it over to Smiley, then scrambled up the hill. At the road, he watched the slaughter below. The men tried to spear the armored hide of the beast, but the dragon slapped them aside with great sweeps of its wing. It vomited a torrent stream of fire, immolating those that tried to run.

Shard turned to his carrier. "Listen, you running cunt. I want you to stand on the drawbridge and when I tell you, start the Spring Festive Fever Fucking Dance. Then when the dragon starts to chase you, run into the castle, run all the way around and come back here. Do you understand?" The Goblin nodded nervously, gulping. Shard rested a hand on his shoulder. "Do as I say and you won't get eaten." Shard then looked to the tower. "Are you guys ready?"

A Goblin head pushed through the arrow slit. "We looked all over the place, but we can't find any banner."

"Just get ready to smash the chain that holds the gate!" Shard peered down the road at the dragon who was now stomping men into the dirt. He grabbed his runner and pushed him up to the road. "Dance! Dance, my little pixie! Dance!" Shard ducked behind a rock as the Goblin started strutting around on the drawbridge, hooting and thrusting his hips in a most provocative way.

Down below, the dragon looked up, a wriggling leg stuck in his teeth, at the little Goblin parading around on the drawbridge.

Its drawbridge.

It spat out the leg and roared with shuddering anger. Flapping its wings, it charged up the hill. Shard could feel the ground tremble as the dragon approached, a wave of stench rolling before it. He watched the brave Goblin turn and flee into the castle, driving the dragon to fury.

Shard scrambled up onto the road, waving at Smiley. "Get up here with the banner! Everyone, get up here." He turned to the tower. "Hey, tower! Smash the chain!"

The Goblin head looked down at him. "Uh, small problem, sir. Nud chewed through the chain when we weren't looking."

Shard felt his jaw opening and closing. "What the fuck is holding up the gate then?"

The Goblin's ears flexed, shrugging. "Dunno. Maybe it's rusted."

"By Masterly's slow dripping cock!" he swore. "Get down from there and follow the banner!" Shard looked around, grabbing Smiley's arm. "Take the banner down the hill, run! Kill any men you find. Now go!" He then looked for Forring. "Your destiny awaits! Come here, bomb boy. Hold out your torch." Shard took his flint and steel and quickly sparked the torch to flame. "Hold it up and away from the keg. Stand over here, right in front of the gate. Now when the dragon is about to bite you, shove that flame into the bung hole. Understand?"

Forring saluted, smacking himself in the head with the torch.

Shard slapped Forring in the head to put out his flaming hair. "Go, and may Quonte look upon you with contempt!" Shard turned and started trotting down the hill. He glanced back at Forring standing on the drawbridge, his legs braced, torch upraised, arm trembling. Echoing from the mouth of the castle, the dragon's chilling roar sounded.

Shard hurried his pace. Up ahead, he could see his Goblins attacking the half-dead Humans, stripping their steel weapons and armor from their dying bodies and shouting: "We're counter-attacking! We're counter-attacking!"

Suddenly Shard's runner burned past him. Shard turned, looking back up the hill and fear overflowed in his heart.

The dragon stood in the gateway, eyes burning, its oversized fangs dripping with blood. Forring stood before it, trembling, his shiny armor rattling, the torch in his hand.

Shard screamed. "Now! Forring! Blow it!"

Forring looked back over his shoulder, his eyes wider than a rabbit's, face frozen in terror.

"The prime directive!" Shard shouted. "The Black Dirt That Blows Stuff Up!"

Forring's lips silently mumbled, 'prime directive' as he turned and faced the dragon. He took a deep breath, held the torch high over his head and shouted, "BOOM!"

The dragon looked at him, reared back and let out a howling roar that shook the castle walls. Streams of rust rained as the portcullis gate dropped down, trapping the dragon within.

Shard looked heavenward. "Feckling's exploding zit! Pus be praised!" He waved at Forring. "Come on!"

Forring nodded, an absurd smile on his face as laughter built within his lungs, a nervous laughter that built to a painful shrill of delight. He tossed the torch into the dry moat with a wave, completely unaware that behind him, tendrils of flame curled around the dragon's toothy maw, building to a mane of white-hot fire.

Shard screamed at Forring to run for his life, but Forring only cupped his ear an instant before vanishing in a cascade of brimstone.

In that instant, Tech Lieutenant Forring completed his prime directive with a flash of lighting and thunder.

White smoke obscured the front of the castle. Chunks of stone fell from the sky. The gate, the drawbridge, Forring and the dragon were gone.

Shard wiped grimy sweat from his brow, his mono-brow knitting as he tried to figure out how they were going to get across the moat to get all that treasure.

From the moat, a massive, taloned paw reached up and grabbed hold of the edge of the drawbridge.

"By Thromgul's cancerous wart!" Shard swore as he turned and fled. "Everyone run! Go, follow the banner." He glanced over his shoulder as the dazed dragon's head cleared the lip of the moat and was looking around. Shard put on a burst of speed to get around the bend and out of the dragon's sight. Up ahead, he could see the Goblins amassing confusedly at a fork in the road. "Go left!" he shouted. As he ran up he watched as they suddenly split into three groups: one left, one right, and one back the way they came. Shard held out his arms to stop the group coming at him. "There, that way!" he shouted, pointing. He then ran to the right to catch up with that group and re-direct them, spotting Smiley in the crowd. "Come here!" he shouted, grabbing three other thugs with him. He pointed to a mile marker on the side of the road. "Here, Smiley, whip it out, hurry, hose it down. The rest of you, head down that way and wait for me." As they shuffled away, he turned back to Smiley who was looking confusedly at him. "What the fuck are you waiting for? Your schwankle, whip it out." Shard sighed tiredly as he remembered he hadn't explained the latest, twisted plan. "That dragon is going to run us down like it did those Humans. We're going to scent this side of the trail and lead him away from the army." He pointed to the mile marker. "Now piss! I need you to take the banner and direct the thugs to the muster point on the knoll we were at yesterday. Remember? I'll take these thugs and lead the dragon away."

Smiley nodded. "Yeah, I can do that, that I can." He looked at his schwankle in his hand. "But I can't piss."

Shard's mono-brow lowered. "I order you to fucking pee, right fucking now!"

Smiley's lip trembled. "You're making it worse!"

Shard relented, stepping behind Smiley and massaging the Goblin's shoulders through his padded armor. "All right, thug, just relax. Take a breath, close your eyes and think of a running brook." Shard launched his fist into Smiley's right kidney. "Anything?"

When Smiley stopped howling, he looked down through teary eyes. "Oh, I'm pissin' now, that I am."

"Good, when you're done, take the banner up there. You got that lieutenant's baldric?"

Smiley face flashed guiltily. "It was just on the floor. I figured you might need it later."

Shard snarled. "You conniving, treacherous fuck. You're promoted. Now lead the troops out of here. I'll catch up with you as soon as I get rid of the dragon."

Smiley tied up his pants. "Shard, you're the bravest Goblin ever!"

"Don't fucking suck up to me! I'm power-hungry. I have my own army and no fucking overgrown lizard is gonna take it from me!" He turned to the other thugs down the road. "You! Pee! There! Now!" After seeing what happened to Smiley, he had no problem soaking the post Shard had pointed at. Leading them in tow, Shard scented the trail leading up to an old farm. Shard ran up to the broken front steps, schwankle already in hand, and whizzed. "By Xoreckle's pimply ass!" he roared, writing his name on the steps. "That should do it."

The thug behind him pointed to the farm house. "Sir, someone here to see you."

Shard looked up the steps as he put his schwankle away. "What the fuck, can't a Goblin piss in peace?" Shard's vision focused on the pointed tines of the pitch fork aimed at his face. "Shit for brains, why didn't you tell me the farmer was coming out of the house?"

"I was watching you pee."

Shard nodded, looking up at the farmer, flashing a toothy, friendly smile at him. "Hey! You old fleshy bastard. There's a big fucking dragon coming to take a shit on your shack, hey?" The farmer only jabbed a warning with his fork. "Hey you dumb shit, run for your life! Dragon coming." Shard put his fingers against the side of his head making dragon ears. "He's gonna eat you!"

The thug behind him spoke up. "Sir, why are you warning the human? Let him be dragon chow."

Shard glanced back. "Because the dragon might chase him and then we can get away." He looked back to the old man. "Dragon. Understand, dragon? Grrr, Grrrr!"

The old man's eyes grew as wide as plates as his pitch fork lowered.

"He's getting it, sir," the thug cheered.

"Grrr, Grrr Grrr!" Shard chanted, prancing around. "Grrr! You old fuck."

The old man dropped his pitchfork and ran into the house.

"Fuck!" Shard planted his fists on his hips. "He was supposed to run out of the house."

"Sir?" one of the thugs called. "I think your plan to lead the dragon this way is working."

Shard spun hotly around. "I don't need your dumb ass to tell me how good my plans are." He blinked as the acrid stench of dragon teared his eye. He looked up to see the dragon sniffing at the post on the side of the road. Shard sprang up the steps, blindly charging into the gloom of the farmer's shack. Up ahead, he could see the silhouette of the farmer running with a chicken tucked under his arm and shooing a little sheep out the back door. Shard plunged on, through the back door, in time to see the farmer disappear into a storm cellar and slam the door shut behind him.

Shard pounded on the bulkhead, but could only hear the farmer bolt it from within. Shard turned and ran towards the barn, his thugs running after him. As he ducked behind the door, he could hear the dragon smashing his way though the house.

Shard looked up at the rusting farm tools knowing they would be useless against the dragon's invulnerable hide. The floor was strewn with hay and Shard contemplated setting it afire to mask their Goblin scent.

"I have an idea, sir," one of the thugs spoke up.

Shard was chipping flint sparks into the hay. "I don't know what's scarier: that dragon or you with a fucking idea." He blew on the flames.

"If we pee on the dragon's tail, he'll run around in circles chasing it and we can make a run for it."

Shard looked at him, waving the smoke away. "And what piss are you going to use? Have a spare bladder?"

"Actually, sir," the thug responded. "I've wet myself."

"Ah, no shit, maggot." Shard sneered. "You've been holding out on us." He stepped back from the gout of flame that shot up the tinder dry barn wall, suddenly realizing that setting fire to the barn while they were still in it was not the best idea. "And right now, I need you to piss on this fire before we all burn to death." Shard grabbed a rusted pick axe. "This way!" he shouted running to the back of the barn. He heaved the awkward tool and smashed easily through the back wall. He shoved through the new hole and could see a river. "Run to the water!" He shouted as he dashed down the trodden path. At the bank he skidded to a stop, looking back up to the barn, fully involved already, and the fire-proof dragon knocking it down with a negligent sweep of its tail.

Shard looked across the wide, fast flowing river and realized they were trapped. "By Allesive's spit soddened beard!" He swore as he looked back a the dragon. "He's following your piss scented pants. I think he's a little peeved at us Goblins right now." Shard looked around quickly and spotted a little dinghy in the water, tied to a sodden log. "Who here knows how to work a boat?"

They looked at him desperately. None of them could swim, let alone know the complexities of a man boat. Shard took his sword and cut the boat tether. "It's our only chance. Come here, diaper pants. You first."

The current grabbed the little boat and swept it quickly away. At the bank, the dragon roared in frustration, beating its wings harder and faster until it lifted into the air. The black dragon, an ominous shadow in the golden, afternoon sun, banked sharply, spiraling over the little boat and from its left nostril, snorted a fireball. In a fiery instant, the boat was nothing more than burning splinters.

The dragon circled once, checking for survivors. Then with a snort, flew off back to its castle and its treasure.

From a sodded log, bubbles broke the surface and slowly Shard's pointy ears breached the surface, soon followed by the rest of him. Assured the dragon was gone, he reached back into the water and, one at a time, fished out his thugs. Gasping, shivering, wet and alive, they clambered up the bank. One had a fish in his mouth.

Shard took the fish. "Private, get three more of these and you're a PFC."

The Goblin nodded and ducked back into the water. Shard started ripping the fish apart with his tusks.

"That was a brilliant plan, sir," one of the thugs spoke up.

"Shut the fuck up." Shard said, spitting partially chewed fish at him. "Mr. Bed-wetter, we would have been long gone if it weren't for your pissed soaked pants." He fished a bone from out of his teeth.

"I'm sorry, sir." he said dejectedly. "Um, when do I get my pants back, sir?"

Shard's mono-brow rose. "When you swim the fuck out there and find it among the burning pieces of boat." He watched as the fishing thug came up with another fish. "Now listen up, thugs. We're gonna have a bite to eat, wait till it gets a little darker, then run to catch up with the rest of the thugs before fucking Smiley makes himself a captain and tries to steal *my* thugs."

Shard's Mission

WATER DRIPPED RELENTLESSLY into an overflowing bucket, soaking the carpet to the point that it squished beneath Shard's feet as he made his way into the room. The office clerk looked up, his face pinched painfully by spectacles that weren't his and nodded, waving a rat-nibbled quill at him. "Captain Shard? Have a seat, the Colonel will see you momentarily. He's in the middle of his enema."

Shard nodded, his lip curled in a sneer, but relieved that he hadn't been summoned to hold the Colonel's shit bucket. He found a seat in a rickety chair and waited anxiously, mindlessly watching the rain cascade down the window pane. He had hoped that his existence would have gone unnoticed by command long enough for him to affirm hold on his company. In his rag tag march back to headquarters, his little group had grown to over three hundred thugs, all orphaned survivors of Hookfang Rottingtooth's army now united under the Black Dragon Company banner. Shard wanted them fit, well-drilled and, most importantly, to shout his name if anyone asked who their commanding officer was.

A Goblin wearing a leather apron and oversized black rubber gloves stomped into the room. "Ugh! Curse his exploding bowels!" He dropped a heavy canvas bucket on the clerk's desk. "He may want an officer to hold his bucket, but I'll be damned if I have to dump it."

The clerk peered over his spectacles at the Goblin, then resumed his work, ignoring him.

The Goblin hrumphed and picked up his bucket. He shoved the wretched thing at Shard. "You, thug, I order you to dispose of this!"

Shard growled. "What's about to happen is I'm going to kick you really hard in the balls, then shove your head in that bucket and watch you either eat or drown."

The Goblin's face wadded up with fury. "I'll have you fired from a catapult! Do you know who I am?"

"You're a thug carrying a shit bucket." Shard rose, preparing to kick him in the nuts.

The clerk timely and loudly cleared his throat. "Excuse me, Captain Shard?"

The Goblin looked sincerely surprised. "You're a captain?"

Shard thumbed his baldric. "Wipe the shit from your eyes, shit for brains, now spread your legs so I can get a clean shot."

"Captain Shard," the clerk insisted. "The Colonel is waiting."

"What are you, fucking psychic?" He glared at the clerk who only glared back with the message: 'Never, ever, fuck with the battalion clerk'. Shard relented, casting a side glance at the Goblin. "Go empty your bucket and get back here so I can knock your balls up out of your throat." Shard turned and stomped through the door.

Passing through the curtain of stifling heat, Shard paused at the door. There was a roaring fire in the fireplace and a gigantic silhouetted mass sitting before it, somehow withstanding the intense heat, reaching in with too short of a poker, prodding the flames hotter.

His left ear was bent at an odd angle, his right was missing entirely. His misshapen head had waves of ripples growing in size and thickness as they rolled down the back, making his neck look like a bundle of fat, bruised sausages piled on his sloping shoulders.

His enormous hand, the size of a hamhock, waved limply. "Fetch my toasting fork, would you?" His thick voice gargled as if he could hack up an oogie at will. Shard tried to shield himself from the blistering heat as he slid to the side the mantle to retrieve the long iron fork. The Colonel took it with a grunt as he leaned to one side. He then switched it to the other hand and poked at the gutted pig that lay on his desk, skewering a slab of fat. "Enemas always leave me gurglish. A bit of a snack settles me right out." He swung the slab over the fire and it instantly began to sizzle. "There are two ways a thug becomes an officer." He began without preamble. "One, they're born of royalty; or two, they're the offspring of a famous officer; or three, they murdered their commanding officer and swiped his baldric; or four, did something amazingly heroic; or five, sucked up enough; six, bribed his way; seven blackmailed his way; or eight, slept with Princess Hiroki." He examined his nearly charred piece of fat, touching it tentatively with his fingers before holding it back over the flame. "You are not blue blood, and you don't look like one of the general's bastard pups..." He squinted as he looked Shard over. "Your father. Who was he?"

"Longbrow Shard, sir, a sergeant in the Black Fist Battalion," Shard said quietly, obviously pained. "Killed by Elves. I never knew him."

The Colonel snorted. "Well, nothing there." He hummed as he thought. "Your heroic deed has just now reached battalion ears so that didn't get you promoted, and incidentally, you did a poor job of touting it. You don't cower like a suck up, you look too poor to purchase a captaincy and too stupid to extort one, and you're not scratching with a hell fire case of the pox which tells me you haven't banged the rose of the empire." He pulled his bit of fat from the fire and shoved it into his toothy maw. "So this leaves murder." His lips shone with dribbling fat as he squirmed around to get a better look at Shard. "So, tell me, who was your captain and how did he die?" The Colonel's one good eye was a blood red marble and glared harshly at Shard, filling his Goblin heart with ice. Shard tried to focus on the other eye, the pale, cloudy blue eye that seemed to roam, looking around the room randomly, occupied by other things. That didn't help either.

"Captain Thumper Padfoot the Fourth." Shard began quietly. "He was killed at the first charge. He took an Elven arrow through the neck." Shard pointed where the arrow had passed.

The Colonel nodded. "Your lieutenant?"

"Lukeweed Ripshod, sir. He was killed by Captain Padfoot."

The Colonel looked surprised. "Murdered his own lieutenant right before going off to battle?"

"Oh no, sir. It was right after he took the arrow through the neck. The lieutenant ran to his side and was leaning over him when the captain stabbed him."

"Ah, battle confusion, his mind addled by that thrice damned Elven arrow through his neck."

Shard thought about it. "He seemed pretty sure about it. He kept shouting; 'Ripshod! From the depths of hell I strike at thee! Die Mother Fucker! Die Ripshod!' Then he laughed and died."

The Colonel snorted. "All that with an arrow through his neck? A bit of history there, eh?"

Shard shrugged. "Hope so."

The Colonel nodded. "Sergeants? Corporals?"

"Trampled by cavalry, sir." Shard's memory flashed hot in his mind. The Humans riding their horses, not even bothering to swing their swords, letting the horses and their metal shod feet do the work for them. Shard's iron sword snapped clean as the horse stepped on it, the Human looking down at him, smiling triumphantly as the horse reared up, deadly hooves flailing. Shard ducked low and charged forward, swinging a furious fist into the horse's low hangers. The beast screamed, throwing his rider to the ground and the sword falling from his hands. He rolled out of the way of the falling horse, looking desperately for where his sword had fallen only to discover that Shard had found it, clenched in both hands. The Human's smug face was gone as his eyes grew wide with terror. Shard swung violently, determined to spill at least one Human's blood, a red smear on the field painted black by Goblin blood. "I called the re-group, looking for high ground to lead the counter-attack when, at that moment, the cavalry turned to trample us just as the Elves let loose a salvo, accidentally wiping out the cavalry. In the confusion, we pulled back to..."

The Colonel stopped him with an upraised hand. "The rest is history." He shook his head sadly. "So this means that you're a natural born leader and a hero." The pale, blue eye suddenly fixed on him. "Do you know what happens to such great Goblins?" Shard shook his head. "Two things. One, we get rid of them." He shifted in his chair as his cold blue eye found something else to look at. "Now there are two ways to get rid of an officer. One, kill him. Bad form. Two, send him on a suicide mission, always the popular choice. Three, send him on a mission that if he succeeds he'll be disgraced and if he fails he'll be disgraced, but those are few and far between."

"Lucky me," Shard mumbled.

"Four, give him an out of the way job like quartermaster. Can you count, Shard?"

Shard didn't like the idea of giving up his company, but it seemed to be the best choice available. "Yes sir, I can count. I have quartermaster experience as well."

The Colonel held up his hand, his pudgy fingers splayed. "How many fingers am I holding up?"

Shard winced. "All of them?"

"And exactly what did you do when you worked at the quartermaster's?"

"Swept the floor."

"So that leaves five, a commission. I send a warrant to Field Marshal Ribsplitter singing your praises and somehow convince him that you're an obedient, naturally-skilled warrior and not just a hot stick."

Suddenly the Goblin who had previously carried the shit bucket stormed into the room. His leather apron was replaced with a bright lavender tunic, highlighted by a captain's baldric. He dropped the empty bucket by the door and pointed at Shard. "Sir, I want that thug put on report! He is a disrespectful, foul-mouthed knuckle dragger!"

"I have a few bad qualities as well, ya dandelion muncher." Shard's mono-brow bristled.

The Colonel acknowledged him with a casual flip of his hand. "Captain Momoo, this is Captain Shard of the Black Dragon Company."

Momoo's face darkened. "What? I am captain of the Black Dragon Company!"

"Guess there's two now," Shard said.

Momoo shook his head slowly. "No, there is only one Black Dragon Company and I am its captain." His iron sword hissed from its scabbard. "We shall settle this in the tradition of battle! I shall have satisfaction!"

Shard palmed his needler, hiding it at his side. "Come get some," he growled.

The Colonel held up his toasting fork, pointing it at Shard. "What is that shinny thing on your tunic, Shard?"

Both Goblins hesitated at the Colonel's seeming irrelevant distraction. Shard straightened. "It's a fleck of a black dragon scale, sir. My chosen thugs wear them."

"Oh, yes." He nodded. "When you tangled with that black dragon and survived. Not many thugs can say that." His blue eye rolled up as he thought. "In fact, I don't believe there is a thug alive that can say they tangled with a black dragon and lived."

Momoo's jaw began to jack slowly up and down. "A dragon? A real black dragon?"

"A nasty one, I hear." The Colonel's fat hand pounded on the arm of his chair. "A fire-breathing one, is that right, Shard?"

Shard nodded. "Yes, sir. Unfortunately, it flew off before we could finish it." Shard glared at Momoo.

Momoo sheathed his sword. "Well, I can't see killing the good captain for such a slight." He tugged the hem of his tunic. "I'll let it go this time, Shard. Just come up with a new name for your company."

Shard lowered his stance. "Come now, ya spindly fuck. Your little honor was slighted and I don't think our Colonel could stand to have a slighted officer. Old thug rules: first thug who dies, loses."

Momoo turned to the Colonel, his face black with fury. "I will not tolerate this...this...this thug!"

The Colonel scoffed. "Oh never mind Shard, Momoo. He's still a bit kindled from his triumphant battle against the Human's." He looked at Shard. "What was it, Shard? You were outnumbered eight to one?"

Numerically they were even, but since it took anywhere from four to eight Goblins to kill one Human, that was about right. "We had the element of a surprise counter-attack." Shard could tell the Colonel didn't want them fighting, but Shard really wanted to skewer Momoo's nads. He decided that Momoo's time would come and left out the part about tricking the dragon into wiping out the Human company, leaving his thugs with a simple, yet motivating, mop up.

The Colonel smiled. "Counter-attacking!" He pounded the arm of his chair. "I think Shard's company was the only group to ever counter-attack in Goblin history. Look here, Momoo. Let Shard's thugs be the Black Dragon company. You've had the title long enough, let him have it awhile."

Momoo face sank. "But what will we be?"

"How about," Shard put in. "The Queer Purple Fuckers Company?"

The Colonel waved his hand. "No, already taken."

"The Colonel's Personal Shit Bucket Company?"

"I don't want to be involved." He snapped his meaty fingers. "I know! The *Other* Black Dragon Company."

Momoo shrieked. "But we were the Black Dragon Company first! How come he can't be the *Other* Black Dragon Company," he whined.

"Because it was *my* idea," the Colonel's voice lowered. "Don't you like my idea?"

33

Momoo blanched. "Oh, of course, it's a great idea. The more I think of it, the better it sounds," his voice thinned.

The Colonel banged his fist on the chair. "Splendid! I actually got past the introductions without spilling any blood." He leaned over, prodding the carcass on his desk with his toasting fork. "Now the reason I've brought you two thugs together is to explain your special, *secret* mission." He swung his fork into the fire, basting a slab of fat. "You have the honor of escorting Princess Hiroki back to port. There, she will meet a ship that will take her home to the Emperor." His slab caught fire. He blew it out with a puff, then put it back over the flame. "Not a tough assignment for my two finest officers. Momoo will be the primary, Shard. Let him do all the talking. The Princess has a scrotum collection, you see. If anyone remotely offends her, she whacks them off with this machine thing of hers. Not pleasant, not pleasant." He retrieved his sizzling slab and stuffed it in his mouth. "Avoid contact with the Human armies at **all** costs." He grated on the word, spitting bits of hot fat into the air. "The Princess is a most delicate flower and to be kept away from any ravages of war. Not so much as a hangnail or trench foot is to come to her awares." His blue eye swiveled, taking in each of them for a time before wandering off. "You do realize how important this mission is. Blue blood will not save you." He glared at Momoo. "And a hero would make a lovely addition to her testicle collection." He glared at Shard, before he licked his toasting fork clean with a nubby tongue. "Rest assured, castration will be the least of your worries if you two fuck up." His red eye looked at Shard while his blue eye fixed on Momoo. "If either one of you fucks up, remember, the Emperor has executions that go on for years!" He leaned back in his chair, glancing up at his candle-clock. "Now get the fuck out. Meet with the Princess's entourage an hour before dawn. They're bivouacked at the old plantation on the hill." The Colonel looked up as the company clerk wheeled in a shrouded cart. "Ah, my dinner is here! I'm rapacious." He took up his bib and tucked it about his collar as the two officers turned to leave. "Oh, and Shard?" he called him back. "On a personal note," he paused as Momoo stepped out of earshot, then whispered. "Don't you kill him, understand? Keep your fucking hands off Momoo." His blue eye leveled at him, searching his face carefully. "Are we clear on this?"

Shard's mono-brow raised as he slipped his needler back into his forearm guard sheath. "Aye, aye sir," he responded, disgruntled.

The Colonel poohed. "Oh, cheer up, Shard. Have faith. You'll be fine." He took up a giant bowl of broth and began to slurp loudly. Shard took his cue that the Colonel was done talking and left the room.

In the clerk's office, Smiley rose to greet him, dripping with water. "How'd it go, sir?"

Shard nodded, his face frowning hard. "The Colonel recognized my captaincy and gave us a very honorous mission."

Smiley smiled all the more. "Well, that's a step up. We thought the Colonel was just going to kill you, that we did."

Shard shook his head, glaring at Momoo's purple tunic descending the stairs. "I'm not sure if that's better or not."

Shard's Company

Rain. Cold, heavy rain fell from a colorless sky, pounding the clay earth with fat drops, filling the sagging gutters until the grey water cascaded, bubbling white into instant roaring rapids, carving gorges in the ground for the callused Goblin feet marching by to trip into, throwing the cadence askew and making openings for the Sergeant Major to fall upon the them with his horrifying bark, his yellowy, cracked tusks flashing, frothing, tearing with sound, a dull rusted saw on exposed flesh.

In the distance, thunder grumbled with hunger.

Captain Wiggletooth Shard listened to the thunder, its roll interrupted by the gruesome bellows of Sergeant Major Whoretwang Ribsplitter-Jones, legitimized, despised and un-loved bastard son of Field Marshal Whoretwang Ribsplitter. Ribsplitter-Jones and his father were old school thugs, when the sharpened rock was the field dominating weapon. Anger and guts and a good sharp rock was all a thug needed to crush his enemy. These Goblins were soft, spoiled, their swords of man-steel, ground down to Goblin size and edged wicked,

wicked sharp; extravagant and excessive. All they needed was a good rock! These Goblins had man-steel chain-mail, re-woven to fit their smaller bodies. In Ribsplitter's day, a thug had only the bristle brush of quill thick hair across his neck and shoulders to steal the brunt of a felling blow and a turtle shell to protect his melon. It was Ribsplitter's first promotion when he improved the turtle helms by taking the turtle out first.

Ribsplitter-Jones continued his cadence. The hard Goblin feet splashed in the grey water as one. The thugs were cocky, still excited about their triumphant counter-attack of the Humans, wearing the captured steel armor as trophies. Ribsplitter-Jones was there to remind them that they were thugs and they were going to die for the Emperor, and die horribly for best effect.

Shard found Ribsplitter-Jones on the long march back to the regiment. He lay dying, his tusks buried deep in a sorcerer's shoulder, Elven arrows had punched through his bristled hair, man-steel swords through his turtle shell, Dwarven axes through his tough his flesh. But he started the battle as any good thug should: with a plan to die. A good plan could carry a thug long after his death, if need be. His was to die with his teeth deep in a mage's body, taking the cursed soul with him to the long Walk of Fo, to stand before the Gates of Honmoia and be judged by Dru, the Lady of the Dead. It is said that if you bring another soul with you, you may exchange that soul to pay for some of your sins, to ease Dru's sentence and shorten your time in the Pyre before re-birth.

Shard's death plan was not to be reborn. His plan was to die with his hands wringing the neck of a thrice-damned Elf. His intention was to stand at the gate for all of eternity, un-judged, and each time Lady Dru came to check on him he would tell her, "Hold on, I'll be with you in a second, soon as I finish with this hamster packer." All of forever, choking the living shit out of some Elf, never going on for re-birth.

Shard hated Elves that much.

Ribsplitter-Jones, on seeing the mage, his lines already decimated beyond regroup, charged the Human lines, knocking them down like cards, ignoring the pain of the Elven arrows riddling his hide, and flung his ungainly body into the air, clamped tight on the shoulder of a bitch mage, closed his eyes and waited for Dru to ask: "So, Whoretwang, what'cha got for me?"

They rolled backwards down the grassy knoll, his jaw locked deep into bone. The Humans ignored the mage's shrilling pleas for aid because they didn't like her anyway. They splashed into a stream and were swept away. Drowning, bleeding, filled with blinding agony, only rudimentary spells could come to the mage's lips. She desperately reached out and snagged a branch and dragged herself on shore, inch by painful inch, casting healing spells on herself and, inadvertently, on Ribsplitter-Jones until exhaustion and pain weakened her spells.

They lay there, dying.

Ribsplitter-Jones was not at all happy at the idea of his death come true being interrupted when Shard came along.

His jaw had been locked so long it was frozen tight and it had to be pried apart with a iron bar, but Shard needed a good sergeant and Ribsplitter-Jones was without question the best. They readied to kill the mage, but she mumbled if she died, the magic lingering in Ribsplitter-Jones' body would leave and his wounds would kill him instantly. So the mage was bound, blindfolded, gagged and taken prisoner.

With spells still in his body and the Elven arrows yanked out, Ribsplitter-Jones recovered in a few days and was angrier than ever. Shard wanted him as angry as possible. He wanted his rag-tag troops drilled into form, into a company that when ordered would drive a thug-spike deep into Human lines, into the soft Elven archer companies, tear them apart, scatter their entrails across the battlefield and forever emblazon the name of *The* Black Dragon Company in Elven song, to be sung with dread and somber tones.

The chilling rain pounded. The sky was flinging its water down, hammering with force against Shard's helm. Water poured down his forehead and onto his mono-brow where it diverted from his eyes and into the deep furrows of his cheeks. There, it flowed freely down his gorget, inside of his armor, and into his scratchy burlap britches were it pooled.

Shard was miserable, but a good thug enjoyed misery.

As the temperature chilled, and Shard's breath curled about his head in fog, he fought to hide his smile as Ribsplitter-Jones turned his troops away from the mess hall, back to the center of the parade field for yet another go until they got it right. They were tired. Human armor was heavy, the padding soaked with rain and sweat, and they had been marching back and forth for hours. They were stumbling, screwing up their cadence, their alignment. Shard knew that Ribsplitter-Jones was no longer teaching drill. He was teaching discipline.

"Sing, ya rat bastards!" Ribsplitter-Jones bellowed. "E'rats! Sing ya fat, rat bastards!"

Low and spooky Goblin voices sang as one to the beat of the heavy footfall:

> *Momma, Momma why you cry?*
> *Your son is going off to die,*
> *Is it pride for future glory?*
> *All for the Emperor's Story.*

And so it goes.

"Well, they can march." Momoo said dryly. Shard peered back over his shoulder toward Momoo standing under the pavilion, out of the rain. "But can they fight?"

Shard looked back out at his troops. "See that little one? The one who has to run to keep up?" Shard watched her trip once again in the rivulet and roll desperately out of the way of being trampled by the rest of the formation. Her helm was too big and it hung over her eyes. Exhausted, scuffed, scrapped, covered in mud, save where black blood oozed to the surface to be washed away in the rain, and plagued by Ribsplitter-Jones screaming at her non-stop: "E'rats! Private Stalycks, yer fuggin' useless! I hates you, everyone fuggin' hates you!

You should fuggin' kills yourself. No, really, kill your worthless self right fuggin' now! 'Ats an order! Yer Momma asked me to see to it you kills yourself before you embarrass the clan anymore! I promised everyone double rum rations if you kills yourself. Please, I'm fuggin' begging you, lie the fuck down and die! Oh, just die for Groddard's sake! Common, for yer old sarge. Die ya useless Hobbit turd!" and all day long, without hesitation, she sprang back to her feet, skipped twice to get rhythm and fell back into formation.

Shard looked back at Momoo. "She could kick your ass so bad you'd cry like a Gnome."

Momoo sniffed. "Your company is that tough?"

"You're such a limp dick."

"Coming from a thug whose not the brains to come in out of the rain."

Shard watched his troops. "Coming from a gutless wonder afraid of a little water," he growled. "So where the fuck have you been anyway?"

Momoo folded his arms like an impatient professor with a slow student. "Shard, we are on a most salient mission. There is a certain amount of nose rubbing and networking to be carried out."

Shard's mono-brow twisted in confusion allowing the run off from his helmet to rain into his eyes. "What the fuck are you talking about?"

Momoo sighed. "There you have it. I now know why the Colonel needed me to help you so badly. Shard, are you going to send the officer who has the ear of Princess Hiroki to some shit job?" He went on as Shard's face relayed no hint of understanding. "I'm laying the stone work for our return! There are bragging rights to be had, choice jobs to line up, pick of new recruits, gifts from merchant traders looking for the Princess' favor on trade agreements! This is the opportunity of a lifetime!" He smiled, showing his yellowy green teeth, but it faded quickly as Shard's expression failed to change. "What part of this don't you follow?"

Shard's mono-brow dropped to a straight line again. "By Dodard's useless balls, the part about *secret* mission."

Momoo looked offended. "I haven't run out and blabbed to the Humans."

"Just the merchants and every ass-kissing officer in the regiment." Shard threw his hands up. "Every swinging dick is gonna know!"

Momoo put out a calming hand. "I told them to be discreet." He went on when he saw Shard wasn't believing it. "Our officers can be trusted and the merchants only look out for their long run interests, the last thing they're going to do is blab," Momoo scoffed, "Everything is well in hand."

"I should run you through for being a spy," Shard hissed. "I ain't worried about merchants, but if I know our own officers then this mission is already old news to the Humans. We're fucked." He pointed a stubby finger at Momoo. "When the Humans ambush us, my first thrust will be to run your ass through and whine 'I told ya so' while you're dying. Say 'Hi' to Dru for me; tell her I'll be along shortly." Shard turned and barked at Smiley who had been standing as invisibly as possible at Shard's elbow. "Fall them in." Shard looked back at Momoo. "And where the fuck is your pissant company?"

Momoo pointed. "There they are now. The finest thugs in all of Hookfang Rottingtooth's army."

Shard could hear the off-key notes of a flute as four thugs marched up from around the bend. One carried the banner, a faded purple flag outstretched by crossbeam. It bore the crest of a dragon sable in passant guardant to sinister trampling the heads of Humans beneath. The second thug was the flautist, and an amazingly poor one at that. The remaining two bore a sedan painted originally in white, now a very dismal grey.

Shard waited.

"*The* Black Dragon company are in formation!" First Sergeant Shiro barked at Lieutenant Smiley. Smiley nodded.

Shard continued to watch the progression of the *Other* Black Dragon Company, waiting for the rest to appear.

They never did.

The *Other* Black Dragon Company made their way and saddled up beside *The* Black Dragon company; the banner carrier in front, the flautist behind and the sedan carriers, with sedan, behind them. Shard's mono-brow was a wave of confusion. "What the fuck is that? By Gustin's nasty whore mother, where the fuck is your company?"

Momoo looked up, his tiny black eyes sparkling as they teared. "The bravest of the brave, they were, every last one of them." He held up his fist in triumph. "A most spectacular charge! We gave those Dwarves something to think about!"

A cold hand pushed through Shard. Dwarves? "What fuck nuts ordered you to attack a Dwarvish company?" In Shard's mind, he could see the Dwarves, heavily armored, shoulder to shoulder in an unbreakable front, with their ungainly battle axes and glaives that only they could wield, defying gravity with great masterful strokes that could turn a thug into a chunky, black, bloody smear with a single swipe. Shields and armor were like flesh and bone, flesh and bone were like nothing. Entire columns of thugs ground themselves into chicken feed and not even threatened the second Dwarven rank. Attacking Dwarves was worse than suicide. It was plain stupid. No one, Humans, Ogres, Giants, thugs, no one sane *ever* attacks a Dwarvish formation. "You're not that fucking brave," Shard determined, "And I'm surprised that you're that fucking obedient. So, who was the numb nuts who threw away a good company of thugs and then killed himself after he realized his error?"

Momoo was lost in the moment, reliving the instant his brave thugs drove into the whirling Dwarvish blades. "Hmm? Oh, my call. Mine all the way."

Shard blinked. "Oh, to slow their advance, to protect flanks then." Dwarves in formation didn't move fast, if at all. A trade off of mobility versus destructive force. That had to be it; no other reason to attack Dwarves.

Momoo shook his head absent mindedly. "No, not really. They were just standing there, not doing anything and my thugs wanted so much to get into the fight." He looked at Shard. "We were held in *reserve*. I'm sure you know how awful that is, standing around watching good fighting," he scolded. "My thugs aren't the type to stand around."

Shard's left eye was twitching violently. "So you attacked Dwarves? Dwarves in formation?"

He nodded. "A sharp looking bunch, but my thugs gave it their all."

Shard's square jaw was resting firmly on his chest. "Just up and attacked Dwarves in formation?" His voice was tiny and faint. "And how did you survive?"

Momoo scoffed. "Well, after the attack, I ordered my sedan carriers, banner bearer and musician to move along. I figured we'd be several ranks deep but when I saw the first rank still intact, I called to regroup. No sense in losing everyone." He smiled. "We did force them to rotate ranks. Even Dwarves can get tired."

Shard squeaked. Then he composed himself. "And this is all that's left? And you didn't kill yourself out of shame?"

Momoo laughed. "Be serious." He looked at the troops lined up. "Looks like we're ready. Let's address the troops." He stepped off.

Shard slipped his needler free, his feet building speed as his thrust aimed with deadly accuracy at Momoo's kidney. Shard's thoughts were racing in his mind. *Not the spine! He's gotta feel this!*

An armored body slammed into Shard's ribs, bowling him over. Shard twisted, fighting to get up but Smiley grappled him determinedly. "No, sir, you can't! The Colonel's orders!"

Shard finally pushed Smiley off and scrambled to his feet. He cast a glance at Momoo's back who was standing in front of the formation, babbling away oblivious while the troops watched Shard and Smiley go at it. Shard pouted as he put his needler away. Too many witnesses. He glanced up at Smiley nodding in agreement, relaxing his stance.

His fist suddenly launched full force at Smiley's face.

Smiley's face flashed total amazement as he saw the muddy fist suddenly grow in his field of vision. He closed his eyes.

And ducked.

Shard took three steps to keep his balance trying to recover from whiffing the air above Smiley's head. He looked at his lieutenant, his lips snarling at the audacity. Smiley realized his mistake and stuck out his jaw, closing his eyes tight and waiting.

"Uh, uh." Shard shook his head.

Smiley opened one eye, then the other. He stuck out his chest, turned his head, closed his eyes and nodded.

Shard shook his head.

Smiley let out a whimper as he squatted, spreading his legs.

Shard stepped back. Then took a light run and gave a gentle practice kick in the air. He went back to the starting point and made a mark in the mud with his toe and placed his foot firmly on the spot as he flexed his neck and rolled his shoulders. Shard leaned forward, shifting his weight for the perfect run.

Smiley stood stock still, legs spread, eyes tightly shut, teeth clenched, his hands in tight little balls.

Shard grunted, then snorted and turned, facing the troops as Momoo stepped away, his little pep talk done. Shard waited for the Captain to board his sedan and get carted off before he spoke. "Hey you fucks, listen up good. I'm your captain! Whatever that mouse fucker says you ignore, got that? Even if he says: Shard said so. You just nod your melon and ignore him. By Lormard's wife's surprisingly huge cock, I will lead you all to the Long Walk of Fo and I will see to it that each of you fucks has an elf in each hand to give to Dru at the gate. Are we all on board with that?"

Three hundred sets of cracked and yellowed teeth beamed back at him. "Sir! Yes, sir!"

Shard glanced over his shoulder at Smiley who was still in his squat position. "Break them for chow, no liberty tonight and reveille at two hours before dawn." He saluted limply. "Dis-fucking-missed." Shard was learning something new. Patience.

Shard's Allies

TEN BLACK PEARLS, glistening, peering down into the sun-swept valley watched the parade of colors make their way steadily along the trail. White horses walked abreast in the lead. Knights high in the saddle wearing heavy, well polished, sun-baked armor led the procession. Pikemen and shield-men in tight formation, grumbled from having to follow a horse's wake. Flighty Elves in visually painful tunics walked loosely behind them, their high-pitched, bird-like voices chirping echoes in the valley as they chatted incessantly away. Far behind them, their heavy footfalls sounding, the Dwarves trudged, obviously pissed they were not presently killing anything, proudly carrying their banner.

"About a hundred in all, sir," Smiley whispered.

Shard's mono-brow hung low over his eyes as he watched the small army make its way. "So, we're fucked, is what you're saying."

Ribsplitter-Jones wiped the foaming drool from his lower lip as he smiled. "E'rats! 'bout fugging time, it is. All this sneaking 'round, s'not right, no it's not. Time to take it to the blighters. Right up tha' poop shoot!"

Shard elbowed him in the side. "Keep your damned voice down." Shard huddled lower, beyond the lip of the knoll. "They're not moving. Just parading around because they're bored," he spat. "Fucking Momoo. Couldn't keep his flap shut. They know where we are and they're waiting for us to come walking right out into the open where they can fuck us but good." He sighed sharply. "They chased us here and now we're fucking stuck."

Ribsplitter-Jones snorked a laugh. "E'rats? Stuck wot? We've got the advantage! We've got two big factors in our pocket, we do. A surprise attack will catch 'em unawares. Full charge in column!"

Shard's lip curled. "What am I gonna do with their fucking underwear? You've taken too many shots to the turtle shell. What surprise is there in a full charge in column? We always attack that way."

Ribsplitter-Jones smiled with wizened evilness. "E'rats! We've got the sun to our backs, we do." He nodded, tapping his temple knowingly.

Shard rolled his black eyes. "Oh, right, those brave Elven bastards are gonna have a hard time picking us off as we're silhouetted coming over the hill."

Ribsplitter-Jones frowned dejectedly. "Well, hey wot? We outnumber them! We 'ave more than we need." He thumbed his chest. "I've been trainin' em!"

Shard nodded, conceding. "Smiley?" He looked back to his second in command. "What have we got?"

"Three hundred and forty seven thugs on full duty, seven Tech Lieutenants and a squad of Troll Rawque Chuquers."

Shard looked surprised at the last group. "Where the fuck did they come from?"

Smiley looked perplexed. "Didn't you recruit them?"

Shard looked at Ribsplitter-Jones who shook his head. "Are we feeding them?" Shard asked Smiley.

"I think so."

Shard shrugged. "Whatever. So that means?"

"We outnumber them by more than three to one."

Shard frowned. "We lose a bunch of thugs to Elf arrows, then battle it out with the Humans." He scratched his chin. "Then hope that Momoo can move the Princess across the valley before the Dwarves move in on us." He shook his head. "By the hairy back of Balstrad's Mother, we're fucked before we started. We'll lose nearly everybody. We can out-run the Dwarves, but the Elves'll pick us off before we reach reinforcements." Shard squinted as he watched Momoo pick his way up the rocky slope. "There's the bastard responsible for this fiasco."

Momoo looked up. "Shard, there you are."

Shard whipped a rock at him. "Keep it down!" he whispered harshly. "Ya brain dead Hobbit!"

Momoo crouched and settled beside him. "Sighted the enemy? Excellent! Her Highness has been itching to see His Emperor's Finest Black Dragon Companies in action."

He peered up at the ridge. "Scouted out a good observation point yet?"

Shard's mono-brow bristled. "Ya deluded fuck, we're all gonna die. I told you we should've moved the Princess at night; we might've snuck her by. I can only hope that I get to see you die first."

Momoo scoffed. "She's not into sneaking. Won't hear of it and I won't insult her by mentioning it. Come now. It can't be that bad. Let's have a look see." Momoo slithered up on his stomach and peered over the ridge. He harrumphed and retrieved a brass tube from his pouch and extended its sections. He looked down into the valley again. "Ah. Look at them down there. Blasted Dwarves, pompous bastards. I say we go attack them now, while they least expect it."

Shard scrambled up beside him. "What's that thing?"

"Hmm? Oh, it's a far-seer. A Gnomish device." He handed it to Shard. "The Colonel gave it to me as a present when I saved his life from a whore with a rat-tail comb." He pointed it into the valley. "Look through that small end."

Shard squinted. "I just see a blue blur."

Momoo pushed the big end down slightly.

"Whoa! Shit!" Shard hissed. "Look at that, he's scratching his ass!"

"Delightful, Shard," Momoo mumbled sardonically. "Now give it here before you break it."

Shard waved his hand away. "Shit, this is getting worse. Stupid worse! The Dwarves are carrying their war banner. Fuckers won't give that up for nothing!" Shard winced. "Wait,

wait." He continued to look. "By Terracoco's dog faced kids," he quietly swore. "That's it, we're beyond fucked." He handed the scope to Momoo. "Look down there, in the middle of the Elves. The guy wearing the dress."

Momoo squinted as he looked through the tiny hole. "They're Elves, they all wear dresses."

"The fancy dress."

"Oh, the tall one?"

Shard sighed. "Yes, the tall one."

"What about him?"

Shard hunkered lower, pulling Momoo's sleeve to get him to follow. "He's a mage." He looked over at Ribsplitter-Jones to check his sergeant's reaction. The Sergeant Major only ground his teeth trying to control himself.

Shard shot a hot look at Momoo. "This is all your fault, you dumb fuck. Enemy behind us and in front of us and we're trapped like rats. Why couldn't we go through the swamp where the man horses can't follow us? Why are we traveling during the day where the Elf scouts can see us for leagues? I told you to keep the Princess under wraps."

Momoo looked offended. "You primitive thug, you have no idea how to handle royalty. The Princess has been waiting for a battle! She wants to see one! She wants a parade of heads on pikes."

Shard sneered. "Well, she's gonna have ours!"

"But we outnumber them!" Momoo pressed and Ribsplitter-Jones nodded enthusiastically in agreement.

"And we have man steel, that we do," Smiley added, looking hopeful.

Shard looked at them as if they were mad. "The mage turns the ground to mud and we're stuck out there for the Elves to just shoot us." Shard frowned deeply as the image flashed in his head. The Humans watching the slaughter, laughing at the dumb Goblins dying in the muck. "The Humans have more than good steel. They're smarter, and they have allies. They've even picked the battlefield and all they have to do is wait for us to come out into the open. As for us? All we have is the Black Dirt That Blows Stuff Up, and rest assured our Tech Lieutenants will never get close enough with that mage casting spells at us." Shard rubbed his chin with the back of his hand. "I was hoping to attack the Humans as a distraction to sneak the Princess through, then sacrifice whatever was left to slow the Dwarves, but that blasted mage...," he spat.

"E'rats! Well, that's it then." Ribsplitter-Jones nodded. "The Black Dragon Company is fugged. Nothing left but to make a rip of it. Call the thugs and attack in full column."

Momoo nodded. "Finally someone with a plan." He started to rise. "I'll get the Princess." He looked over at a large flat rock on the top of the ridge. "I think that will make a lovely observation point."

"Shut the fuck up," Shard hissed. His eyes were dazed and distant. "I'm thinking." He looked up. "Allies," he whispered.

Momoo looked impatient. "What about them?"

Shard's left eye began to twitch. "That mage would be safer walking with the Dwarves, but Dwarves hate mages, magic and Elves."

"No news there, Shard."

Shard put his hands to his head, as if he was trying to stop it from splitting open. "They ally with the Humans 'cause they hate us more..." Shard unbuckled his helm and dropped it, rubbing his black spiky hair, his fingers sliding over the lumps and scars, face wincing in pain. He looked at Momoo. "Give me your far-seer."

Momoo was indigent. "I will certainly not."

"You'll get it back. Now give it to me or I'll gut ya."

Momoo sniffed. "Say please."

Shard rolled over and punched him in the nuts. He had the far-seer out of Momoo's pouch before he hit the ground. "Quit yer whinin', ya Hobbit. I only hit one nut." Shard shuffled back to the top of the ridge and peered down, watching the parade through the spyglass. "That guy, the guy on the horse with the gold helmet." Shard waved for Ribsplitter-Jones to take a look. "He's the chief. Look at him."

"E'rats full of himself, he is," Ribsplitter-Jones snorted.

Shard scuttled back down. "Damn right he is. He's out on a little field trip to get a bit of glory and some thug skins to carpet his new castle with. I'm gonna give him just that." He looked at Smiley. "Go get me the Trolls; all of them. Also, all of the *Other* Black Dragon Company, especially that flute player." Shard was rubbing his head with one hand and punching himself in the head with the other. "Get me a Tech Lieutenant and a hundred thugs, the rest will be in reserve. Form them up down there." He waved for Ribsplitter-Jones. "Get me this many of your biggest thugs." He held up all eight fingers. "Cut down some trees." Shard made a circle with both hands. "This thick, as tall as three of you."

Ribsplitter-Jones looked confused. "But we already have spears."

Shard ground his teeth and hit his forehead with the balls of his hands. "Useless against their armor." In his mind he could see the Human rider who had fallen, helpless on the ground, his heavy armor suctioning the mud. A turtle on its back. "You knock 'em off the horse, that's it. Let the other thugs finish them off." He grabbed Ribsplitter-Jones' baldric. "You get the big guy, you knock his ass off that horse, knock his ass on the ground, stomp on his head before he can get up and knock off the next one. I want all of those pompous bastards in the mud. When the ground troops come to the rescue, the rest of our thugs jump em'."

Ribsplitter-Jones nodded slowly, unused to such a complicated plan. "And what about the Elves and the mage?"

Shard squinted his eyes into little slits, his fists on the sides of his head. "You carry out your part." He tilted his head.

"Now?"

Shard punched him in the side of the helmet. "Not yet! Get the thugs and the trees first. Go now." He looked up at Momoo. "You get to lead the charge."

Momoo sat up, holding his swollen nut. "I can barely walk, you brute."

Shard sneered at him. "Bite me." He watched as a Troll, obviously the leader, scampering sideways as Trolls did, his massive multi-elbowed arms dragging on the ground behind him, made his way up the hill with Smiley close behind. Shard got up and walked down to greet him. "I'm Captain Shard." Shard saluted sharply.

The Troll's pearl white eyes shifted uncertainly as he took in Shard. His heavy lower lip pursed, and Shard almost thought the tall and amazingly ugly Troll would spit on him.

"Gidish, thorng ingas," the Troll said in a deep trembling voice. "Spliss whirrly gromph." The Troll put his hand under his left armpit and flapped his arm four times, making a wet, fart noise. "Piqurd," he said, with a final nod.

Shard only stared at him, having never dealt with a Troll. They were mostly elusive and entirely mysterious. The Human advance drove them from their holes, forcing them to ally with the Goblins for safety.

Shard tilted his head towards Smiley. "You catch any of that?"

"I don't speak Troll, sir. I thought you did."

Shard looked at him. "You rent out the unused portions of your brain, don't you? What made you think I spoke Troll?"

Smiley shrugged. "You speak Human, Elvish and Dwarf, that you do."

"I only know one phrase in those languages. 'Tell Dru that Wiggletooth Shard sends her another empty-handed soul.' And that's only useable when yer twistin' a blade in his guts." Shard faced the Troll. "Speakee Goblinee? Me, Shard. Big Chief here. You chief Troll? You got name?"

The Troll twisted his head and peered at Shard with one eye. He thumbed his chest. "Squiff."

Shard nodded. "Squiff? Great. I need your boys." He pointed to the flat rock at the top of the ridge. "Muster there and hide. When you see Dwarves in your rock range, you guys paste 'em." Shard peered up, hoping for understanding, he outlined a long double-braided beard. "Short hairy Hobbit. You throw rock at." The Troll only looked at him, then nodded slowly.

Shard smiled. "Great. I also need your best chuquer. He's gonna be with me."

Squiff thumbed his chest again and stood a little taller. "Squiff," he growled.

"You're the best? Okay. Stick with me." Shard looked at Smiley, pulling his second-in-command a little closer. "Get me the Chosen Thugs."

"So we are going to attack?" Smiley looked confused.

Shard smiled, showing all of his teeth at once. "We're going to counter-attack. Stick with your strengths."

Smiley looked even more confused. "But don't they have to attack first for us to counter-attack?"

Shard's coal black eyes sparkled. "Not when you have a plan."

Shard laid on his belly in the cold damp sod, peering through the tall, wispy grasses at the Human army slowly marching toward him. Through the far-seer, Shard noticed a detail of military sketch artists, sitting on folding stools with their easels and black sticks of charcoal, scribbling away. They were to historically depict the triumphant defeat of the Goblins and the capture of the Goblin princess. To portray the perfect triumphant march into battle, the banners waving, and the brightly colored tunics all in the right light, the commander ordered his company to march to one end of the field then back the other way, then forward again.

Shard snuck into position as they marched back.

Shard watched them intently, coming forward again. The troops were tired and pissed. After marching pointlessly all day, they wanted something to kill. The Dwarves were incensed, pushing and shoving each other, their heavy armor chaffing.

And in the distance, a bad flautist played.

Badly.

Shard hunkered down lower, his chin in the dirt, and waited.

The Human commander held up his hand and the company slowly came to a halt.

He listened.

Shard watched through the far-seer. The Human's face, his cleft chin dominating the view, smiled.

Slowly, in cadence, the *Other* Black Dragon company, their lavender banner catching the wind and unfurling proudly, entered the valley. The yellowy sedan rocked back and forth with the march, Momoo's face peering out nervously through the tiny window.

The Human cavalry sparked to trot. Drawing their swords as they entered the pass, a horn sounded attack sharply.

Shard watched them run by.

The foot soldiers followed at the half run, cursing, their formation slowly spreading apart.

Momoo was waving his arm and the *Other* Black Dragon Company turned and relocated for tactical advantage at the run.

The Human horsemen, sniffing easy glory, moved to canter.

The footmen at full run, unable to keep up, fell behind, their formation non-existent.

They ran past Shard.

The Elves chirping happily trotted after, the mage puffing to keep up. Falling further behind, the Dwarves ran, cursing.

The cavalry entered the pass, moving out of sight.

Metal clashed violently and horses screamed as thugs suddenly rose from the scrub. Goblins thrust with long, heavy spears, their blunted points smashing into the heavily armored cavalry-men, knocking them from their saddles. The second thug wave swept over the fallen horsemen and Human screams were quickly drowned out by Goblin war cries.

Their smiles gone, the Elves slowed to a trot, their fingers reaching for arrows.

"Now, Squiff."

The Troll rose up from the grass, his arm already lying over his back, his opal eyes wide and round. He jerked down suddenly and his arm whipped forward, slinging his unbalanced, misshapen rock with unerring accuracy, nailing the mage in the side of the head. The mage sighed and dropped.

No cries, no sounds, the Chosen Thugs sprang from the tall grass and charged into the distracted gaggle of Elves. Shard's man-sword, full length and wielded with both hands, slashed left, then right, and left again, each cut biting deep into soft, unarmored Elven flesh. He winced from the shrilling screams of the Elves as they scattered in terror. Those not killed in the initial attack ran in two directions: one group after the foot soldiers, the other group towards the Dwarves.

Shard barked at his thugs to chase the first group of Elves and leave the other group to the Dwarves.

The second group of Elves, their long hair trailing behind them, ran at the Dwarves who slowed to a march, their formation closing up and their shields locking together. The Elves screamed to be let into the safety of the Dwarven shields, but the Dwarves brandished their axes, fending them off. The Elves reared up sharply, pleading at them, cursing their stubbornness.

The Elves were the first to fall as the Rawque Chuquers began their bombardment of the valley. The Dwarves quickly raised up their shields for protection and only two of their number fell.

Their march was now reduced to a dead stop.

Shard watched as the footmen reached the pass in confusion. They paused aghast at the bloody sight of their cavalry, defeated, their bodies torn to pieces and a hundred battle-raged Goblins in formation standing before them. In that moment of hesitation, their flanks were besieged by thugs shouting their battle cry: "We're counter-attacking! We're counter-attacking!" as Smiley drove another hundred thugs from the woods while Shard and his Chosen Thugs attacked the rear a hundred strong, closing the trap tight. The panicked Human footmen found themselves surrounded and fell trembling to the thug company's steel. Each thug trained as a three Goblin team, attacked one Human, hitting him three places at once and killing him fast before moving quickly on. Sixty foot soldiers were instantly reduced to forty. A sergeant bellowed for lines to regroup but only thirty Humans made a cowering stand with nowhere to run. The remaining Elves ran to the Human formation who parted long enough from them to pass, but being shorter than the Humans their bows were useless behind the Human circle.

Ribsplitter-Jones' powerful voice sounded over the battle din and the Goblins instantly reformed and nearly a hundred strong fell upon the cowering enemy.

Shard ordered a quick mop up before turning his attention to the Dwarves.

Ribsplitter-Jones' domineering authority ordered the Goblins to stop looting the bodies and regroup. Looting would have to wait.

The Dwarves had slowly moved out of the Rawque Chuquer's range and watched with glinting eyes as the Goblins pulled into formation and marched towards them. The Dwarves tightened their ranks, their commander, buried somewhere in the center, ordered them to stay steady.

The Goblins were incensed, shivering with battle lust after the total destruction of the Humans. Unable to contain themselves, they were breaking rank, the march turning to a jog, the formation spreading apart.

The Dwarf commander shouted in Goblin tongue: "Look, it's a bunch of Hobbits!"

The Goblins howled as more broke rank, now running across the field.

Over the din, Ribsplitter-Jones' blood curdling voice bellowed with intent. "I said fuggin stop!"

The Goblins reared up over themselves, some rolling forward on the ground from the painful blast of the Sergeant Major's voice. The front liners, so close to their hated enemy, looked angrily at the Dwarves, so close they could spit on them, but after a quick exchange of jeers, retreated back to the Goblin formation.

"Cowardly Hobbits!" the Dwarven commander bellowed after them as the Dwarves laughed at the stupid Goblin formation. Their laugher slowly died away as the front row of Goblins brandished tree-sized spears.

From the front of the Goblin formation, one lone Goblin stepped forward, pulling a bright red shawl from his kit and wrapping it about his waist.

And began to dance.

The Spring Festive Fever Fucking dance.

And the Dwarves stared, never seeing a Goblin dance before, let alone the tantalizing Spring Festive Fever Fucking dance, unable to figure it out.

And on the hill behind them, Tech Lieutenant Gog Sliddermiser, bent over at the waist from the giant keg of Black Dirt That Blows Stuff Up strapped to his back, puffing, sweating, his eyes round black balls threatening to pop out of his head, ran with his arms pumping, leaving behind him a trail of smoke from the lit fuse.

The Dwarves were banging on their shields, keeping rhythm to the Spring Festive Fever Fucking Dance, hooting and throwing insults in both Goblin and Dwarf, completely drowning out the grunts from the Goblin running towards them from behind.

Gog was getting closer, closer. He looked up. The fuse was burned to nothing and a plume of sparks erupted from the bung hole. Gog looked ahead and the Dwarves were right there, he could see the glinting gold rings woven into their beards and hair, their fleshy, dirty sunburned necks.

Spittle frothed at his smiling lips, his lungs wheezed as he drew his final breath.

Gog shouted in triumph!

A Dwarf turned, his eyes growing as round as plates, his spear lowering from instinct as his voice charged to shout a warning.

Gog put on the final burst of speed, and leapt.

The Emperor's own Tech Lieutenants were carefully selected, specifically trained, well treated and respected by most thugs for their job was to deliver the Black Dirt That Blows Stuff Up unto the enemy and blow them up. They wore the shiny, silver armor that looked pretty and could stand up to most glancing sword blows and arrows. This, of course, was to enable them to get close enough to blow stuff up.

Against direct hits from Dwarvish steel, however, was another matter entirely.

Three Dwarven spears punched into his shiny armor, his momentum driving the shafts through his ribs and popping his lungs like balloons. Gog squeaked as the strength of his charge lifted him up on the spears and over the heads of the Dwarves. Not knowing what to do with him up there, more Dwarvish spear-men stabbed him.

Gog smiled as the last of the fuse burned away.

The Dwarf formation was knocked flat from the thunderous blast.

Blind, his ears ringing, his throat burning, choking from the smoke, the Dwarven commander scrambled to his feet, bellowing to regroup. He turned, brandishing his heavy war axe as the Goblins charged. He raised his axe, homing in on the horrendous battle cry of the enemy and poised to strike.

A tree-thick spear nailed him in the chest, knocking him to the ground. Something stomped on his head and kept going.

Shard screamed as he ran over the first rank of Dwarves, thrusting his sword forward, feeling it slide through, with only a brief resistance, Dwarvish mail and into the stringy meat beyond. Shard pulled and the Dwarf came with it, swinging his pole axe as he did, the haft catching Shard in the helm. Shard twisted his sword, planting a foot on the Dwarf's chest and shoving him off. The Dwarf took another swing, his pole axe blade sparking off of Shard's quickly blocking sword. The Dwarf staggered, then leapt at Shard. The Goblin side-stepped and watched the Dwarf bury his weapon in the dirt. Shard brought his sword down on the Dwarf's thick neck.

Metal flashed from the corner of his eye and Shard turned in time to see the Dwarven commander charge him.

Shard ducked forward into the arching sweep and drove his helmet into the commander's nose, smashing it flat. The commander stumbled back, rearing his axe for a blind swing when Ribsplitter-Jones stepped up from behind and took it from him.

As the Dwarven commander looked up, his fingers grasping for his ancestor's weapon, Shard drove his man-sword into the Dwarf's belly, just over the heavy *cuir-bouilli* belt and under the breastplate.

Shard could smell the Dwarf's sweat, feel his wet, sticky breath on his cheek as he leaned close and whispered to him in Dwarven: "Tell Dru that Wiggletooth Shard sends her another empty-handed soul."

The Dwarf commander, his face streaming in blood from his shattered nose, only smiled.

He violently gripped Shard's arms, stopping the Goblin from twisting the sword. He spun Shard and pushed him backward into the wild back swing of another Goblin. Shard's helmet spun as the blow hit home. Blinded by his own helmet, Shard only felt the world spin again as the Dwarf commander twirled him around, knocking him into Goblins to keep them off-balanced.

Shard drove his knee up and painfully smashed it into the Dwarf's armored groin. That failing, he planted his foot against the Dwarf's thigh and tried to push free but the powerful Dwarf held him fast. Panic began to creep into Shard's heart as he felt himself being spun around again. Shard threw his head back, heaving with all his might and let go the sword. He lifted his foot again and his heavy toes caught the quillion and shoved the sword the remaining hands-breadth of steel into the Dwarf's stomach.

The Dwarven commander gasped as his fingers slipped free of Shard's arm and they both toppled back away from each other. Shard quickly turned his helmet so he could see and scrambled to his feet. Panting furiously through his clenched teeth, he looked up to watch the Dwarf commander on his knees, his eyes bulging as he slowly, painfully began pulling the sword out of his gut. Shard screamed and ran forward, slipping free his needler. He kicked the Dwarf's arm, driving the sword back in and plunged the needler deep into the Dwarf's ear.

Shard stomped on the Dwarf's head as he wretched free his needler, then kicked the twitching body for good measure. Shard looked around, watching his thugs loot the bodies, holding aloft their treasures and hooting wildly. They had not only broken a Dwarvish formation, but kicked their asses as well.

"E'rats! He hads a bit of thug in him, ya think?" Ribsplitter-Jones stepped up, brandishing his new Dwarvish axe. "S'nice blade tho, s'nice," he said, admiring the ancient weapon, bright red Dwarf's blood oozing into the fine engravings. "Chops em clean!"

Shard finally caught his breath. "You could've helped ya know."

Ribsplitter-Jones looked offended. "Fuggin wot? E'rats a fair fights it woz. You'd be screamin' if'n I interfered, you would. 'Sides, now all the braggin' rights are yours now, ain't it."

Shard growled, grinding his teeth. The Sergeant Major was right, of course, but Shard had no intention of saying so. He looked around for Smiley and found the Goblin leaning heavily on the Dwarven banner. Black Goblin blood and red Dwarf blood stained the brilliantly embroidered flag. Smiley was panting, his permanent smile, faded. He looked up as Shard approached. "We did it, sir!" he said, mustering enthusiasm. "We broke a... Dwarf... formation, that we did! We kicked their... hairy ass!" He coughed painfully.

Shard's mono-brow lowered. "Yeah? And what the fuck's wrong with you?"

He shrugged. "Bit of... a leak, sir." He coughed and black spit frothed from his lip.

Shard frowned. "And you're getting it all over my banner." He kicked up a Dwarf spear with his foot and handed it to him, swapping out the banner as his makeshift crutch. Shard could see the black blood bubbling up though Smiley's chainmail shirt. Smiley was going to die.

Shard handed off the banner to Ribsplitter-Jones. "I need a count of the dead and wounded, both ours and theirs right away," he said to his Sergeant Major. "We also need to wrap up the looting and get the fuck out of here before the Human detail chasing us catch up and discover we're not dead. We've got to move the Princess now." He turned as Momoo's sedan trotted up. "Fuck me...," he grumbled.

"Blast you, Shard!" Momoo shouted, sliding down the window. "Blast you to Hel! May Dru spit on your soul!"

Shard stood silent, his mouth agape. He looked at the banner, then to the dead and dying Dwarves around him, then to Ribsplitter-Jones who was equally lost. He looked back at Momoo. "Fuck wha?"

"Of all the most idiotic, career-killing maneuvers I have ever heard of!" His face twisted in rage. "How could you do this to us? *To me?*"

Shard felt his stomach twitch as confusion and anger boiled within him. "You dickless Hobbit, what in Grizzy's revolting halitosis are you fucking talking about?"

Momoo was incensed. "You killed everybody!"

Shard felt the anger inside him begin to win over. "I'm thinking I missed one," he said, glaring at Momoo. "Will you fucking explain yourself?"

Momoo sagged, his energy depleted. "Shard, you thug," he sighed. "I should've stopped you. How was I supposed to know you would kill everyone?"

Shard felt the teeth in his head crack and pop as he ground them. "What the fuck are you talking about?" he bellowed.

Momoo leveled his gaze. "The Princess missed the whole thing!"

Shard's mono-brow twisted. "And whose fault is that?"

"Yours! You and your hyper-complicated plan!" Momoo shrieked. "With different parts and counter-attacking and what not. A simple attack in column was all we needed but no, not for mighty Mister Complicated Plan Shard. You had to do it your way and at no point did you say, 'Oh, and Momoo, make sure the Princess is in position', did you? No, you didn't. And now I'm left to describe our great victory to her Highness. This could have been a majority for me, Shard. And a stay of execution for you for all of your insults against her Highness." He shook his head sadly. "I'm going to have to do an amazing bit of talking to keep you alive, but I seriously doubt you'll keep your balls after this."

Shard's mono-brow bent with sympathy. "Oh, Momoo, I had no idea." Shard approached the sedan. "It must be so difficult for you to keep tabs on the Princess, and here it is, I screw up everything," he said softly. "I'm soooo sorry, Momoo. You're right, I'm just a big, dumb thug. How can I make it up to you?" Shard looked pensive, then brightened. "I know!" Shard punched Momoo in the face, then grabbed his purple tunic and dragged him out of the sedan through the window. "Ya Hobbit!" He kicked him violently in the ribs, then spun him around, smacking his head into the sedan. "This is all your fucking fault!" He threw him to the ground and stomped on him. "You better pray I don't lose my balls because I'm going to fucking smash yours flat before I bite them off." Shard opened the door to the sedan. "Smiley!" he ordered. "Get in here!"

Smiley limped forward, holding his side and using Momoo's unconscious body as a stepping stool, and climbed up into the sedan. Shard then handed him the banner. "Get this back to camp and tell them we're on the march." He slammed the door and watched as Momoo's sedan bearers trotted off quickly with fear adding wings to their feet. He then looked to Ribsplitter-Jones. "Let's pick up the pace."

The Sergeant Major nodded. "S'right." He jerked his thumb over his shoulder. "What abouts him?"

Shard looked over, surprised to see a surviving human sketch artist huddled on the side of the field. He was in shock, staring blankly at what was supposed to be a simple human victory. The other artists had either fled or were savagely killed.

Shard cocked his head as he thought, sheathing his man-sword and walking over to him. Shard's black eyes slowly looked him over, then took the pad from the man's limp hands and looked at the drawing of the Humans marching gallantly across the field. Shard nodded, then grabbed hold of the man's collar and dragged him across the field to where the Dwarves had stood their ground. There, in the grass, still warm and slick with Dwarf and Goblin blood, Shard drew his sword. The man cringed, whimpering, but Shard ignored him, instead posing over the dead Dwarf commander, his sword ready to deliver the final blow. The artist only glared in amazement until Ribsplitter-Jones cuffed him in the back of the head. The man quickly began to sketch.

"I may be nutless tomorrow," Shard said to no one in particular, "but by Lulox's oversized spleen, I will be the thug who broke a Dwarf formation and scarfed their banner."

Shard's Lover

IN THE DARK caves of the eternally snow-capped scapes of Mount Gah, the twelve-legged giant wooly spiders line their deep burrows with warm, delicate layers of silk. Goblin children, armed with harsh tobacco, send puffs of smoke down the burrows to rile the wooly spiders to the point they crawl out to see what's what. At the mouth of the hole, they rear back, red eyes glistening, holding aloft their razor sharp front talons and wave them about menacingly, showing that they are a spider to be reckoned with. The children stand their ground, for they know that the house cat sized wooly spider, armed with shooting quills and protected with a crusted, boney brow, the spookiest arachnid on the continent of Bratanich, is a wuss.

Once lured from its hole, the children only have to use a feather and gently tickle the spider's exposed belly to calm it down, then once its confidence has been won, they can pet it. When it begins to chirp and chitter happily, the kids can pick up the spider and take it down the mountain to the orphanage where the spiders hunt down the never-ending supply of amadil mice and the children harvest the spider's silk. Long strands of delicate thread are strung up around the children's barracks until dried. It is then combed, dyed, dried again, then carefully wrapped on wooden spools as part of their evening chores; the spiders perched on their shoulders supervising the operation. With enough thread, the Goblin children with fingers still full of youthful dexterity, can weave the most beautiful silken fabric and intricately detailed carpets, demanded on both sides of the world. If a child was good enough, they could buy their way out of the orphanage.

While the carpets were revered, fought over, stolen, and traded on the high market, the cloth was not. Goblin fashion designers demanded distinct hues like Phlegm Green, Inside Eyelid Pink and Swollen Left Nut Black, that every other race found not only hideous, but irritating to look at to the point of causing physical distress. The carpets, however, were filled with the colors that the children and their spiders liked. Colors like Old Forest Green, Sunrise Pink, and Deep Oblivion Jet.

Shard studied the carpet with a professional interest. Its weave, nape, and pile were of the most impressive quality. As a child, he and his spider, Mr. Whiffle, were most adept at weaving carpets, but lacked the imagination to create an interesting pattern. Shard bravely accepted the rejection as he watched the other boys leave the orphanage to weave carpets in the city. Whiffle bawled his eyes out. But they both accepted the cut when they found out that boys who were selected are castrated to keep them from maturing and their fingers small and delicate.

And now, so many years later, his nose pressed flat into a carpet of incredible design depicting the triumphant abduction of the young goddess Meka from the heavenly palace by the handsome and daring future Emperor Hchoak, his horn nubs of obsidian, his eyes of real flame and his sword of magic starlight upraised, running across the smoky plains with the kicking and screaming goddess dressed in dew gossamer over his shoulder, the armies of the gods in hot pursuit, all set against a background of the Misty Mountains of Anguish, the painfully gnarled trees of knotty chesterwood filled with puffs of pink, spring blossoms, Shard was once again moments from castration.

Ironically, Shard's carpet submission so many years ago was of the same tale, but Shard's design looked more like two stick figures trying to figure out how to fuck each other.

"This is all your fault, Shard!" Momoo hissed for the fifth time now. Shard stole a glance at his fellow captain. Momoo's face was pressed into the part of the carpet that depicted the de-flowering of the young goddess, as represented by the future Emperor taking a rose from her hair. "She's so pissed at you!" Momoo went on. "I've tried my best, Shard, but I can't see a way for you to keep your nuts." Momoo sighed. "And worse, I'll be remanded back to supply. A Momoo was born to lead thugs into battle, not issue kits to the little snots." Momoo shot a glance over to Shard. "Now let me do the talking, Shard, and perhaps the only thing you'll lose are your balls."

Shard wasn't worried at all. He wasn't going to lose his testicles. Under no circumstances would he stand before Dru without his beloved nuts. He resigned from the beginning that he was going to die, killed by the guards, but only after he took out Momoo. Although they took away his weapons when the Princess' guards came and arrested him, they failed to find his needler in their search. If Shard couldn't go to the Long Walk of Fo with an Elf in hand, then he'd see what he could get for a Momoo.

Tiny, fragrant petals of chesterwood blossoms filled Shard, and he realized it wasn't just the intricate weave of the carpet, but the room was filling with its perfume. Shard could hear the heavy plods of the guards dropping to the floor and banging their heads on the ground in respect. He could hear the jingle of the belled handmaidens and the nasal twang of the eunuch herald announcing the seraphic Princess Hiroki.

"I just want to know one thing," her delicate voice growled harshly as she flew into the room, her tiny feet suddenly appearing between Shard and Momoo, "Just how fucking dumb do you maggots think I am?" Her feet began pacing back and forth between them. "I want an answer! You clearly think I am as dumb as a fucking ball of spit, don't you?" The feet stopped pacing, one tapping. "Answer me!"

"You most angelic Highness," Momoo began smoothly. "We don't think you're stupid."

"So you're saying I'm wrong?" Her voice was low and deadly.

Momoo hesitated as he realized he was now in real deep. "Nuh, nuh, no."

"So then you do think I'm stupid! You think I'm a fucking idiot!" Her golden sandal slapped flat. "I am going to rip off your nuts one at a time!"

"Your Highness," Momoo squeaked in panic, "this was all Shard's doing! He's not even a real officer. I think he's a spy! He's been conspiring against you since we started. I've been trying to find evidence against him before bringing it to your attention, but your divine wisdom has already sniffed him out. And he's a coward! He runs from the enemy at every turn! And the things he says about you! I would rather rip the tongue from my head than repeat them!"

"Guard?" the Princess called, "bring my tongue pliers and rip Momoo's tongue from his head."

"Mistress, I speak true!" Momoo whimpered. "I ordered him to attack the Humans. I told him that the Princess wants to see us defeat the Humans, but he said we'll sneak her by at night, through the swamp. He told me to keep her under wraps. He's a bully! Always threatening people, and ignoring her Highness' wishes. He hits me at every chance. Really hard! I should have killed him when I had the chance, but the Colonel stopped me."

"Shut up, Momoo," the Princess said. "For days you have bored me with how fucking brave you are attacking Dwarves in formation, losing your entire company without inflicting a single casualty, and now you come skipping in here, with a command banner no less, and tell me how you brilliantly pulled off the impossible with only a couple hundred thugs and I'm supposed to believe that? Do you think I don't know what's going on? They packed me up and shipped me across the ocean to endure months of seasickness and a limited amount of suitors to entertain me, so I could be my father's witness to the destruction of the Human forces. Well, no banners have been taken, not an inch of Human lands claimed, and now I'm being shipped home empty-handed and you brainless idiots think that you can parade a bloody rag in here and tell me it's a Dwarf command banner? You must think I'm as dumb as you!"

Momoo turned his head, glaring hotly at Shard. "I told you this would happen! Why can't you listen!"

"Why are you talking to him?" the Princess barked. "Did you not tell me you were in command?"

"Technically, yes," Momoo pined. "The Colonel wants to give Shard, who is totally inexperienced by the way, a feel for command. I was to teach him the ropes, but he's such a rock head!" Momoo glanced at Shard.

"So you're saying that with this inexperienced rock head, you broke a Dwarf formation and took their banner? Goddess Meka! Thank you for these four balls to add to my collection!" Shard could feel the Princess' warmth as she leaned over them. "Are you that deserving of having your nuts ripped off?"

Momoo pleaded to Shard. "Tell her, Shard! Tell her it was I who lead the charge! Tell her the truth!"

Shard could feel her gaze across his neck. "Yes, Shard. The truth." Her soothing voice cut sharply.

"Your Highness, the truth is, he is totally deserving of having his nuts ripped off. However, if we can lure a musk-rat to take up residence in his ass, I believe it would be more entertaining."

"Shard!" Momoo shouted.

The Princess threw her head back and laughed, her voice the chiming of bells. "There's no reason we can't do both!" She clapped her hands. "Put him in the chair!"

"Shard!" Momoo screamed like a girl as the guards lifted him roughly to his feet. "Please! By Luklum's noble wart! Think of all I've done for you!" Shard could hear the metal buckles rattle as they strapped him to the chair. "I need my nuts! I haven't an heir! And I'm allergic to muskrats! I'll die!"

The word stung at the back of Shard's skull. He had figured that if he somehow survived this and had to stand before the Colonel, he would be faultless in Momoo's death if the Princess ordered him killed. But what could Shard say if he failed to so much as raise a finger to save the goon, but also suggested his mode of death? The Princess would be back in Bratanich and unable to save Shard from the Colonel who sounded like the type of thug who could very easily make life very hard for anyone. Shard tightened his lip as he swallowed the acrid bile building in his throat. He was damned either way. "Highness, it was Momoo who lead the initial charge against the Humans and their allies today."

He felt her gaze against his neck like a guillotine. "What makes you think you're out of the woods? Your part in this little conspiracy with Momoo has yet to be addressed."

"Highness is most noble and wise," Shard went on. "When the Colonel gave us our orders, he was confident that Momoo and I would get everyone killed if we encountered the Humans so he ordered us to avoid combat. He did not wish for your most beautiful self to fall into the hands of the Humans. However, an encounter was unavoidable, but by Braxt's contagious prickly rash, we were victorious."

Her sandal was tapping again. "Were you? You expect me to believe that this nibble brained idiot with a three thug company led the charge? And this bloody rag is your proof of victory?"

"And the Human," Shard finished.

He heard her sniff sharply. "Human?"

Shard nodded, rubbing his face in the carpet as he did. "Yes, an artist. The Humans brought him along to record their victory, but he recorded ours."

She clapped her hands. "Bring the Human!" she ordered.

"And his books and coal!" Shard added.

Shard could see the Princess' knee as she knelt beside him. "This had better impress me, thug, or I shall peel off your skin, tan it and wear it as a coat." Her breath was hot and tickled his ear. It smelled of honey. She rose and her sandals walked away. "Did I tell you to stop?" she ordered her torturer. "Rip his nuts off!"

"Owee, owee, owee!" Momoo whimpered. "You don't have to make it so tight."

"Yes, he does," The Princess said. "Do I tell you how to do your job?" She turned as the guard dragged the Human in and threw him on the ground beside Shard, pushing his face into the carpet, instructing him in the proper way to grovel. "Great, you have a Human. Does it do tricks?"

"His book," Shard said.

"Give me that," the Princess ordered the guard. Shard could hear her flipping through the leaves of vellum. Shard had seen the sketches, of the Human forces and their allies preparing for the battle, detailed portraits, and faces. There were rough sketches of the actual battle, notes written in Human tongue for more accurate and vivid works later. "And this is you? Delivering the death blow to the Dwarf commander?"

"Yes, your Highness," Shard said, trying not to sound too proud.

"And I'm supposed to believe this?"

Shard felt his mouth dry. "The Human draws what he sees." Suddenly, Shard lifted his head just enough to turn to the artist. He grabbed the artist and roughly pulled him up. Shard took the Human's pencil and put it in his hand, then pointed to the Princess.

The Human looked up, then picked up one of his books.

Shard watched the black coal flash across the yellow page. A curvy line became a pinched wasp waist flowing to a callipygian hip that plunged into a waterfall of long, long legs precariously balanced on tiny feet.

Stacked river stones became her flat stomach, two floating spheres became warship-like breasts, threatening to pop free from her silken bra, her swan like neck holding her regal head above it all. Her dimpled chin and strong, full lips were bent in bemused smile. Her sculpted cheeks held up her sharp, glinting eyes and her cutting brows. Her head, smooth and free of dents, growths or scars, was freshly shaved, save for a tail of shining wet tar that spilled from out of her golden crown and cascaded across her shoulder, hanging like a cape all the way to the floor.

Shard, like all thugs, had never laid eyes on the Princess. She was beautiful.

"By Malmaul's infected pinky toe," Shard whispered with awe.

The Princess snatched the book. "Let me see." She frowned at it. "Not bad, I guess."

"Not bad?" Shard scoffed. "The Princess' beauty shines through even the crudest of drawings. Now I know why we thugs must never look upon her Highness. Her beauty would blind us."

"Look at me," the Princess ordered.

Shard hesitated, his mono-brow bent. Slowly, he turned his head until he could see her tiny feet, her toenails like white opals, gem studded rings adorning them. Her gown, as little as there was, spun of spider silk, was the color of Infected Liver Maroon with Iron Pyrite borders. Her belt was linked doubloons with matching vambraces on her wrists. Her nipples, clearly outlined in thin, tight silk, were pierced with rings as thick as Shard's little finger. Shard could only stare.

"A little higher." Princess Hiroki prompted.

Heavy gold rings stretched her neck to royal proportions, her ears hung low with dangling jewels. Her dimply cheeks were pierced with studs, the left a pattern of a starburst, the right, the royal symbol of Spinecrack.

"You blind yet?" She asked after giving a few seconds worth of her radiant self.

"No," Shard said quietly, his eyes filled with wonder.

"At least blurry?"

Shard shook his head, unable to look away, his eyes drying out. "Oh no, wait; yeah, they're getting blurry."

She nodded. "Well, I don't have all day." She clapped her hands. "Gouge his eyes out!"

Shard nodded as the guard grabbed him from behind. "Fair enough." He scrambled to his feet and stood at attention. "I have looked at the resplendence of our Princess, broken a Dwarf formation and taken their banner. I've had quite the day." Shard gave a slight shake to his left hand, dropping the handle to his needler into his palm. If he faked passivity, he could catch the guards unaware and run to the Long Walk of Fo with at least one soul in hand and both eyes and both nuts intact.

Shard tensed as the guard took up a double-pronged eye gouger, black and crusted with dried blood from the work table. The guard smiled, showing toothless, grey gums.

"Stop," the Princess ordered. She was reclining on her throne, her face a little sad, a little tired. Her fingers gently slid over the Dwarf banner, feeling the weave and embroidery. "To answer my first question: No, I am not an idiot.

81

You two chuckleheads may actually be the only thugs to score against the Humans and I would be a fool to have you nutted just yet." She sighed as her evenings entertainment faded away. "Release them," she grumbled.

"Your Highness is most wise," Momoo squeaked as he was freed, clutching himself where he was clamped. He was bruised, but intact. "And noble, and smart. Not at all an idiot." He limped quickly from the machine, bent over and wincing with each step. "And beautiful! The rumors all fall short."

She looked up, her eyes sharp. "Did I say you could look at me?" She snapped her fingers. "Take his eyes out!"

"Eep!" Momoo squeaked.

"Your Highness," Shard spoke up, "please, I would then have to drag his useless, blind butt all the way back to battalion."

Her face darkened with anger. "Silence! Another word from you and I won't let you sleep with me."

Shard froze, his mono-brow twisted in surprise.

Momoo looked up startled. "What?"

The Princess waved at the guard with a sigh. "Give him two black eyes."

Momoo stood a little straighter, turning to Shard, his hands still clutching himself. "I'm primary, Shard. If there is anyone whose going to sleep with the Princess..."

Shard grabbed Momoo's tunic, hauling him up right. He cocked his fist and punched him in the eye.

Shard's Friend

BLACK, DISTRAUGHT TREES of mourning rose slowly, painfully from the thick, grey green mists. They picked their way slowly through the murky, shallow waters, slogging through the sucking mud, going about their business. Mosquitoes drifted easily on the thick air, moving in formation. The wolf owls stared blankly, eyes glowing softly, watching the Goblin company below.

Sergeant Major Ribsplitter-Jones hunched over the tiny glowing fire, stirring the boiling soup with his finger. He sniffed it, then poked at the tack to see if it had softened enough. He nodded and took up a twig of Harrow-toe, plucking the leaves. "He's looking for a little luv'n, he is. E'rats, a little Bunny Bug luv'n t'night." He snorked a laugh as he crushed the leaves in his hand, letting them drop into his soup. "Rubbing his big, fat belly with his legs, his little antenna waving and a wiggling. Calling for his girlfriend, he is." He stirred his soup. "His big ol' eyes glowing green, then red, then blue; then, when he's ready to make his move, he opens up his wings and starts a buzzin' and his eyes go all white then." He took his little pot from the fire. "And then he'll be singing, 'Ooo, ooo, oh, oh, ooo, uh chicka, chicka, chicka, mow, mow, wow.'"

Momoo took the wet cloth from his swollen, darkening eyes. "At first, I thought I knew what you were talking about, but now I realize that I have not a clue. What in Whipple's lumpy porridge are you bloody talking about?"

Ribsplitter-Jones hunched beside Smiley, who was curled up against the large roots of a stunted tree. "If'n the Captain gives a lissen, he can hears for himself." Ribsplitter-Jones pushed the soup at Smiley. "E'rats. Now you eats this here. Ribsplitter-Jones brewed you a little kick-a-poo joy juice. A little taste of some Harrow-toe leaves and you'll be feel'n all sorts of good."

Smiley made a face. He was pale, his eyes grey. "I'm not hungry."

Ribsplitter-Jones looked offended. "E'rats! Hey wot now? You're telling your sergeant wot's wot? You're forgettin' that you're just a thug with a stolen lieutenant's baldric. Ah yes, Ah's knows all 'bout that. Now you drink up 'n that's an order." Ribsplitter-Jones held up the spoon. "We patched up yer outsides, now we gots to patch up yer insides. Now eat up before I gut ya and get it over with."

Momoo fanned away the cloud of blood-sucking gnats that was swarming over his head and listened to the myriad of swamp noises that filled the heavy air. Razorquill bats shrilled before their final attack run on the slow moving cowbeasts. Rhino-toads hissed for no reason in particular.

Twitter bugs, twittered, howling hopper monkeys howled and the swamp itself periodically let lose with a foul smelling rumbling fart of methane, bubbling up from the mire. Momoo cupped his ear and over the din he could faintly hear: 'Chicka, chicka, chicka, mow, mow, wow.' "So, what exactly is that?"

Ribsplitter-Jones didn't look up as he scraped the congealing soup dribble from Smiley's chin. "E'rats the Bunny Bug a calling for his mate, it is. The most romantic bug in these parts."

Momoo spread another layer of cool mud on his privates, hoping the swelling would go down. "I didn't know you knew so much about bugs, Sergeant."

"I've been a thug as long as I can remember. Can't own a pet when you're a thug. Goin' from place to place 'n all. So I kept an eyeball out for the bugs, see. Bugs are everywhere. So, it's like hav'n a pet wherever I goes, see?"

Momoo laid back, covering his eyes again. "How cute," he said dryly.

"E'rats, they looks out for me, see? Like I know right now there's a beaver cricket somewhere between here and the Princess' tent. He's singing his little song: 'dweep, dweep, eep, eep, eep, dweep.' That's him say'n: 'Hey, it's a nice night out, right?' But he's a little shy sometimes, so he shuts up every time someone walks by. Like right now. Someone's coming from the Princess' tent."

Momoo sat up, startled, wincing a little from pain. "Guards?"

"Naw, guards make a racket," Ribsplitter-Jones said. "Beaver cricket shuts up for awhile when they go by. Probably one thug." Ribsplitter-Jones nodded. "E'rats. It's Shard."

Momoo was amazed. "The bugs told you it's Shard?"

"Naw, I can sees him right there." Ribsplitter-Jones motioned with his chin.

Momoo took the cloth from his face and watched as Shard picked his way through the soft marsh. "Well, you certainly took long enough," Momoo grumbled.

Shard sneered at him. "Rest assured, I was more than long enough." Shard looked over to Ribsplitter-Jones and Smiley. "How's he doing?"

"Just fine 'e is." Ribsplitter-Jones grinned.

"I'm dying, that I am," Smiley whispered.

"Oh, he'll be up and about in a bit, he will." Ribsplitter-Jones argued.

"Everything is so dark...," he said weakly.

"At's cause it's night." Ribsplitter-Jones stuffed another spoonful into him. "Eat more soup."

Shard snorted. "Just keep him quiet. Also, make sure the thugs are ready to roll in four hours." He looked up at the starry sky. "We bugger when the moon breaks."

Momoo looked up, his face darkening. "And do you think perhaps consulting me? I am a captain and your superior!"

Shard stepped over to him, his mono-brow hanging low over his eyes. "Be happy you still have your nads, let alone your baldric. The Princess figured out that you're as useful as a zit on her ass."

Momoo looked sincerely hurt. "I know more about being an officer than you, you overgrown thug!" he snapped. "And here it is, I saved you some fresh fish. See if I share it with you now." Momoo turned and took the lid off a bucket beside him and pulled out a wriggling fish. He sniffed it, smiling as he did. "Mmmm. Enjoy your hard tack, thug."

Shard stepped over and snatched the fish from him, sniffing it. "This is sea bass!"

"And you're a thief!" Momoo reached for it, but Shard pulled it away. "Give it here, Shard. You're a perfect villain. Just because you've slept with the Princess doesn't mean you can steal my supper!"

Shard's lip twisted angrily. "We're thirty leagues from any sea or river. Where did you get fresh fish?"

Momoo snatched the fish back. "Like any good officer, Shard. I am resourceful."

Shard swelled with anger. "You've been dealing with merchants!" Shard accused him, kicking him in the ribs. "I told you not too!"

Momoo scrambled to his feet, wincing as the mud pack at his crotch fell away. "If you were a proper officer, you would know that an officer has to have a certain finery," he huffed, tying up his breeches. "I cannot be expected to eat the same hard tack as a common thug. And I paid them well to be discreet."

Shard's face filled with anger. "With what? Pennies? Silver? By Ramboid's poisonous toe cheese! You're unbelievably stupid! The Humans have *gold!* We've probably been sold out already. They won't attack us in the swamp, but it won't take a brain to figure out that we only have one passage out of here." Shard pushed Momoo out of his way. "Lance Corporal Gample!" he barked. "Double the pickets! Then give the order to break camp on the double. Bury everything heavy, we'll pick it up on the way back. We're out of here now!"

As Gample punched a snappy salute and ran to carry out his orders, Momoo grabbed Shard's shoulder. "Now hold a minute, Shard. I'm in charge!"

Shard spun hotly on his heel and launched a fist into Momoo gut, doubling him over. He grabbed Momoo's shirt and held him up, whispering hotly into his ear. "I'm not surprised you haven't figured it out yet, ya fuck brained thug, cause I only figured it out myself. You and I are currently on a suicide mission. They want us to fail."

Momoo gasped for breath. "You're mad," he wheezed.

"Yeah, I'm fucking nuts. Think for once." Shard jammed him in the head with his finger. "What will happen when the Princess arrives home empty-handed. No banners, no loot or plunder, no slaves, nothing." Shard jammed him again. "Answer: General Rottingtooth and his cabinet will be ordered to gack themselves for their incompetence. Can't have that, so they send two companies to protect the Princess. One consists of two sedan bearers, a banner carrier and a bad flute player; the other is just a bunch of stragglers. When we all get whacked, they can say, 'Well, we sent two whole companies, but the boobs failed and the princess with all the loot got captured. Send us more thugs and maybe we can get her back.'"

Momoo shook his head. "You're the fuck brain, Shard. We don't have any loot."

Shard reared back and head-butted Momoo. "Fucking pay attention! The General says that because he needs a reason to explain why there is no fucking loot. We're the reason!"

Momoo opened and closed his mouth several times as his eyes searched Shard's face. He shook his head to scatter the gnats that lit on his exposed ear tips. He nibbled his bottom lip. "But they can't sacrifice me," he said quietly. "You're just a pumped up thug, but I'm a Momoo."

Shard shrugged. "You're a fuckrighteously stupid git who got his whole company snuffed and was too stupid to snuff himself. I'm a hero and nobody likes a hero. Makes everyone look bad."

Momoo began to wring his hands. "But, you've got a plan, right Shard? You're going to get us out of this, right? You can get us to the shore where the fleet can pick up the Princess and we'll be okay, won't you, Shard?" Momoo smiled. "You're getting ready to confuse the shit out of me with one of your plans, right?" A whimper escaped his throat. "A plan?"

Shard shook his head as he recalled the Colonel's list of how to get rid of an officer. Send him on a mission that if he fails he dies and if he succeeds he dies. "If we get the Princess to the shore, the admiral then has to sail back empty-handed. Think he's going to do that?"

"He can take up pirating. He could make a bundle." Momoo shivered in the warm, sticky air.

"He would have to go back empty-handed with the Princess. Now, what happens to the messenger who brings bad news to the Emperor?"

Momoo began to sob. "They rip out his entrails and hang him with it."

Shard's mono-brow rose with mild surprise. "Okay, I didn't think of that exactly, but yes, they'd fuck him up somehow. Now, the Emperor isn't going to snuff his daughter now is he?"

Momoo suddenly brightened. "He'll snuff the Admiral!"

"And what if the Admiral has two infantry thug captains to tell the Emperor the bad news?"

Momoo looked desperate. "But he hasn't got two captains, does he?"

Shard nodded. "He'll find two standing around scratching their collective asses on the beach."

"But I'm a Momoo and you're a hero!"

"You're the brain dead fuck who lost his entire company and I'm a pumped up thug."

Momoo put this fingers in his mouth. "By Quarsering's itchy hemorrhoids!" he cried. "What if we drop the Princess off at the beach and make a run for it!"

Shard beamed with pride. "Now you're thinking! We'll get right back to battalion where the General, who knows his days are numbered, snuffs us slow out of spite."

Momoo clamped his hands against his head. "No! This can't happen! This is not how it ends for a Momoo!"

Shard set his lips tightly. "We're not dead yet. First, we have to get out of the swamp and east without being seen by the Humans. There has to be another route through the swamp. I'm sure it will be rough going, but I think the Princess will go for it. Get out your map."

Momoo nodded as the image of hope flashed in his mind. He quickly dug through his field desk and took it out. As he set up his compass, Shard brought over a lantern. "We're here, Shard." Momoo pointed to an empty space on the map. "This is the direct route out of the swamp." He pointed to another empty space. "I think if we head a little southeast, we can cut through here and up to the plains. It's a straight shot." He smiled to himself. "This isn't so bad."

Shard scratched his head, fanning away the black flies. "Are you sure about this? There's nothing on the map."

Momoo stiffened. "If there is anything I can do, Shard, is read a damned map!"

"Hold it," Ribsplitter-Jones growled, setting down his little pot. "If'n I'ves ever heard worse last words than some officer armed with a compass say'n he knows where 'es at," He rose and stomped over. "'Ere, let's have a looks." He reached for it, but Momoo snatched it away.

"Excuse me, Sergeant." Momoo glared at him. "Your superiors are talking."

Ribsplitter-Jones threatened to slap Momoo with the back of his scaly hand. "And just remember you're talking to the unloved Ribsplitter." Ribsplitter-Jones pulled the map away. "If'n it wasn't fer Shard's little butt sniffer pal taking a liking to you,

I'd a geeked you an' dumped your body in the swamp fer the rats to choke on." Ribsplitter-Jones held the map at arms distance, squinting to see it clearly. "Here now, lets take a look." Shard held the lantern closer. "E'rats! It's not a proper map, is it? Where's the legend? All the squiggly lines?"

"Give it here, you bully." Momoo reached for it.

Ribsplitter-Jones raised the back if his hand and Momoo cringed. "Yer asking for it," he threatened, then looked back at the map. "Here, what's this now?" He squinted trying to read it. "It's not a Goblin map. In fact, s'not a map a'tall. It's a place mat from a local tavern."

"What?" Shard shrilled.

"Ere, look see." Ribsplitter-Jones showed him. "It shows all the places of interest. Like that rock that looks like a little boy takin' a piss. An ere's the waterfall 'at flows up. And this ere is the mountain of dung we passed." He snorted. "We've made a nice circle we have, visiting this lovely swamp. Look, were just south of the hole in the ground that farts."

"We passed that on the first day!" Shard shot a murderous look at Momoo. "Why didn't you tell me you didn't have a map?"

"That is a fine map," Momoo said defensively. "I found all those places, didn't I?"

Shard snatched the map looking at it. "That's 'cause we've been wandering totally lost!" He pointed. "You didn't even follow them in order!"

Momoo huffed. "Well, now that we have our bearings, URK!"

Shard's hands flew to Momoo's throat, throttling him. "I'm really sorry about this, Momoo." Shard spat through clenched teeth. "But if we're to have any chance to survive, I'm going to have to gack you. Nothing personal, ya fucking fuck!"

"'Bout frigging time," Ribsplitter-Jones grumbled. "We'll dump his body in the fart'n hole. We can say he fell in. I'll swear to that."

"No, wait," Smiley moaned piteously.

Shard looked over his shoulder. "Don't stop me, Smiley."

"The Colonel will know," Smiley moaned. "The eye..."

Ice pushed through Shard's belly as the image of the Colonel's sickly blue eye flashed in his mind. Shard imagined him standing before the Colonel, trying to find the words to explain how Momoo died while the eye looked right through him.

Shard let Momoo go, pushing him to the ground. "Blast you, Smiley."

Momoo coughed as he tried to breathe. "I deserved that," he wheezed. "Granted. I should have told you." He looked up, his eyes bent and pitiful in the shadowy, yellow lamplight. "I... I just wanted to do something right for this trip. I wanted to at least get us out of..."

"Shut up," Shard growled. "Now's not the time to get all mental on me. We'll all die in this damned swamp." Shard turned his back on Momoo, peering into the gloom. "We're lost in a swamp, the enemy hot on our trail and I'm saddled with a fucking idiot. I can't see how this can get worse."

Something moved in the mist, forming and swirling into a blurry silhouette of a Goblin. Shard peered into the dim, his mono-brow raising as the cloaked figure made his way deftly through the bog.

He was short for a Goblin, with a paunch that poked through his cloak. His bristling face whiskers were white, save for a ruddish dark strip that ran vertically down his chin. He puffed as he breathed, heavy from his exerting stroll. He seemed almost surprised to see Shard standing there. "Bloody brilliant!" He chirped with a sing song high-pitched voice. "I'm a bit amazed at your plan. You have everyone confused. Everyone." He waved a stubby finger at Shard. "You're either the smartest tactician on the planet, or an un-fucking-believably stupid git." He looked around at the clearing. "I'm a bit at a loss at what you'll do next." He peered up at Shard, the lenses of his glasses glinting in the swamp's bioluminescent glow. "I can't wait to see it!"

Shard glared at the Goblin. "And who the fuck are you?"

The Goblin seemed surprised that Shard didn't know. "Oh, didn't I tell you? I'm Major Bark-Bite. I'm to be your best friend."

Shard's Spy

BLACK MUD, STICKY and heavy as wet cement, clung to their feet, weighing on their legs, slowing them down. They marched in silence, heads down, watching for pitfalls in the dim, green, spooky glow that rose from the eerie mire. Ribsplitter-Jones marched beside them, leading the way with his chin, a frown etched on his face, his aura of discipline fanning out red and hot, keeping the thugs in line and moving by sheer force of will.

Bark-Bite moved like a cool breath in the hot, humid night. In and out of sight, leading them back the way they had come with astounding accuracy. He let the thugs catch up only when the gator rats hovered in ambush ahead. The Rawque Chuquers took them out quietly and quickly and then he moved on.

"Are you sure we can trust him?" Momoo trudged up to Shard, whispering. "The Colonel sent him."

Shard's mono-brow hung low as his eyes glared blood red into the gloom ahead. "What choice do we have?"

"But the Colonel wants us to fail!"

Shard shook his head. "He wants us to succeed. If the Princess makes it home and the Emperor finds out his generals are a bunch of fuck nuts and orders them gacked, the Colonel gets promoted."

Momoo made a small 'O' with his lips. "Well, what about this best friend business? I can't see you with a friend, let alone a best one."

Sharp sniffed. "He's got a map, knows how to read a compass and knows where the enemy is waiting for us." Shard sloughed mud from his foot. "That makes him my good buddy right now." Shard stopped and put up his fist to hold up the troops. In the darkness, Bark-Bite signaled. Shard crept quietly forward and crouched beside him.

Bark-Bite stooped and slowly parted an itchy-fern with his walking stick. He pointed out the dark figures of Elves, standing idle, swatting at the mosquitoes that grew fat and drunk off their sugary blood. Their bows were strung, but slung across their shoulders casually.

Bark-Bite signaled to back up.

"The enemy has left a rear guard," he whispered.

Shard nodded, expecting this. Bark-Bite reported that the main Human force was waiting for him to emerge on the east side of the swamp and trap him there. They left a rear guard just in case Shard attempted to double back. Shard decided then, since they were there anyway, to back track out of the swamp on the westside, take out the smaller rear guard and circle around the long way. They could deal with the Humans later.

Shard peeked out under the fern, then pulled back. He could hear their voices, high and shrill even in whisper. It plucked at the cord of nerves in his spine. Shard could taste their blood, thin and cold, pooling beneath his tongue. His mind raced with ideas of how to kill them slowly. He pulled back and hunkered beside Bark-Bite.

"They're just standing there. What are they supposed to be doing?" Shard asked.

Bark-Bite fished a pinch of snuff from a leather pouch. "They're Elves. They think they are so damned superior." He pushed a wad of tobacco into his lip, wiping the stray bits with his tongue. "I'd say they're so damned arrogant that they think they could hear and smell us in a swamp. Every thug knows that sound doesn't travel ten paces in a swamp." He spat. "Useless creatures, Elves. Unless you like your men soft, smooth, and boney." He peered at Shard. "Cowards, the lot of them. Would have cornered a company of them at Shaver's pass back during the Twelfth Invasion, but those little girl screams," he tsked. "We just had to let them go." He wiggled his finger deep in his ear. "The noise was simply horrendous."

Shard touched his knee to quiet him. "While there is nothing more fun than sitting around bad-mouthing Elves, they have bows and are really good at gacking thugs."

"I refuse to die by an Elven arrow," the Major went on. "Fought the blighters during the Eleventh Campaign; took four arrows. Not at once, you see. But each one festered, oh yes, it did. Betting pool was I wasn't going to make it three days. I won each pool. Once, my leg swelled up as big as a Tontor tail and turned the most peculiar color never before seen in medical history. They gave it a name: Survile. Sort of a yellowish, greenish, purple. The surgeons took a metal pipe and drained it out. Awk, the smell! Made one of the surgeons swoon. They gave the smell a name, too: Bleth."

Shard clamped his hand over Bark-Bite's mouth. "Begging the Major's pardon. But I'm going to take some thugs, sneak over and gack some Elves. You're more than welcome to come along." Shard turned to where Momoo was hiding and held up both hands asking for eight thugs. Momoo nodded. Shard then held up a 'C' for Chosen Thugs. Momoo nodded, less emphatically.

"I'd take an arrow," Bark-Bite went on. "If only one of those waifs would fight me one-on-one." He drew his short sword, a broad, heavy cleaver that glistened with a faint, magical dweomer. "Chop, chop, Lil' Elfie. Chop, chop!" He smiled, revealing amazingly straight and clean teeth. "That's her name: Lil' Elfie. Glows when Elves are around."

Shard grabbed his cleaver wielding arm. "Chop, chop later, Major. What's on the other side of the Elves?"

Bark-Bite nodded in agreement. "Yes, yes. There is a small camp of Humans. Sleeping away, comforted in the thought that their Elves will be able to hear anything for leagues."

Shard nodded, then slinked further into the bog, slipping quietly around to the left flank. He waited for his thugs to slip over to him and gave them final instructions.

They nodded and in the spooky swamp fluorescence, Shard could see their dark, bloodshot eyes smile with glee.

Shard shifted his huge man-sword across his back, tying it in place. He took slops of mud and smeared them over his shiny man armor, dulling the finish. His thugs were already covered in mud.

On their bellies, like sewer snakes, they slipped silently through the swamp.

Shard poked his head up, daring a risk at the Elves who scratched feverishly from the rashes of itch-fern that only inflamed in the gases of the swamp. Shard moved closer, slipping his needler free. He paused, daring not to breathe, timing his movements to the Elves' scratching. One hand, slowly, carefully placed as not to disturb the flora, Shard inched ever closer until he could hear the inane elvish chit chat. Closer, until he could see their pale, moon-bleached skin. Then closer until he could smell the sweetly sick perfume they bathe themselves in. Then closer still.

There he waited.

Shard watched the steam from their tiny nostrils curl about their heads like halos.

He waited.

He watched one pause and listen, then go back to chittering with his comrades.

Shard waited.

One rubbed his eye.

Shard coiled, pulling his legs beneath him, re-gripping his needler, flexing his fingers.

The elf yawned.

Shard was on his feet, moving quickly as he brought his needler in an upward thrust.

The elf turned slowly, his pale, star-filled eyes looked down at Shard in amazement, not really sure what it was. He then looked down with disdain at the shank of steel plunged into his ribs, lanced through his left lung, deflating it.

The elf's eyes, astral, sparking, grew wide as his mouth stretched to scream, but there was no sound. Around him Goblins leapt and swung steel, slicing the pretty but useless Elven mail with broad strokes. Elves fell with faces of horror and surprise, their screams piercing, teeth-clenching cries of pity and mercy, died silent within them, and the only sound was the cacophony of the dismal swamp.

Shard watched the elf's eyes, watched as each glistening twinkle faded out one at a time until only one remained. One tiny dot of life.

Shard sneered and leaned closer, until he could feel the elf's coolness against his cheek. "Tell Dru," he whispered in elvish, "that Wiggletooth Shard sends her another empty-handed soul."

And the elf's eyes of endless, sky blue looked at Shard, not in anger or confusion, but in recognition.

Shard twisted his needler and dragged it out, dropping the lifeless body into the fog.

Shard signaled to Momoo to move everyone forward, then slipped quietly to the edge of the swamp, hunkering down among the prickly bramble, peering into the Human camp. Nearly a hundred paces away, the Human guards stood around fires while the rest snored away in tents.

Momoo and Ribsplitter-Jones crept up beside him. Momoo peered with his far-seer. "I'd say we outnumber them six to one." He closed the scope. "I'll sound the charge."

Shard grabbed him by the back of the neck and held him still. "We sound nothing." He grumbled, then looked at Ribsplitter-Jones. "Line up the platoons. When they see me move, we all go. First platoon runs through and gacks all the guards; the rest kill everyone in the tents. No war cries, no noise."

Momoo whined. "Oh, come now, Shard. We have the advantage!" He watched as the Sergeant Major slipped off to give orders, then turned back to Shard. "Once, just once can't we have a proper fight? All this sneaking around and complicated plans." He looked around. "I say we ask the Major. Where is he?"

"He's as fucking crazy as you are." Shard grumbled, looking around. "Who the fuck knows where he's off to." Shard peered intently at Momoo. "Now you listen to me, you dumb fuck. My thugs, I'll run them my way. Because of your fuck-brained inability to keep your soup-suck shut, we've got a fuck load of Humans crawling all over the place looking for us. I'm not going to risk one thug so you can have a proper fight. You want a charge? Take your damned flute player, your brain-dead banner carrier and your two sedan bearers and lead the assault up your ass." Shard watched as his thugs took positions then looked back at Momoo. "I have to take care of these Humans, then somehow have enough thugs to battle my way to the shore with the Princess in tow."

"Where we'll be kidnapped by an admiral and taken back to the mainland and killed by a vengeful Emperor," Momoo concluded. "Seeing as we're going to die, we might as well make of go of it." Momoo adjusted his turtle helm.

"We might as well not."

Momoo shook his head. "Why are you so stubborn?"

"Because I have my orders." Shard slipped his huge man-sword from its scabbard. "Get the Princess to the shore and don't kill Momoo. Simple as that. And a thug follows orders." Shard turned away, watching his thugs move in the darkness, readying themselves. He turned back and watched the Humans in the open field. If Shard's thugs stayed low and quiet, they could make it halfway before they came into the firelight. By the time the Humans sounded an alarm and anyone could respond to it, the thugs would be in their midst, overwhelming them.

Simple as that.

Shard inched closer, lower, his chin nearly scraping the ground. A troop of armored Quill Ants marched in single formation right in front of his nose. The sounds of the swamp faded into the distance. Shard's pounding heart drowned out the throaty chortle of the Hallucinogenic Rhomboid Toad and the hum of the horde of Razor Flies that circled his head. Shard coiled himself, ready to spring, his eyes fixed on the guard showing off his new tattoo. Shard shifted his feet, feeling for solid placement. In his mind, he measured the distance. He could see himself, running across the field, his sword raised high. As the human turned, Shard would bring the steel blade down, cleaving the human from shoulder to nuts, a ridiculous smile entrenched on his face, laughing, the way they laughed when they rode his company down, crushing them beneath their monstrous horses, their steel-shod hooves dripping with black Goblin blood. It would be Shard's turn to laugh at them.

Shard curled his legs up beneath him. He glanced over at Ribsplitter-Jones as the Sergeant Major took a position. Shard nodded.

Ready?

The Sergeant Major looked right, then left. All around him were Goblins grinning like idiots, ready to run, ready to kill. Ribsplitter-Jones looked back at Shard with a nod.

Ready.

Shard turned his eyes back to his target, shifting up to his haunches, crushing the scream of blood-lust building in this throat.

An echoing cry shattered the night as Shard scrambled to his feet. The Razor Quill Ants took to the sky in panic as the Hallucinogenic Rhomboid Toads dove to the deep pools for safety. The Razor Fly Horde, poised to attack, fell on each other in a buzzing confusion and sucked their own blood while Captain Wiggletooth Shard, of His God Emperor's elite Black Dragon Company, tried to breathe pure swamp mud for several seconds with a muddy footprint on the back of his helm.

Shard peeled his face against the suction, jerking his head free from the bog and watched with growing horror as she ran across the field, her gleaming sword of pure iron pyrite held high, her shining butt cups barely covering her oh so smackable derriere. Her way-too-tight corset of brass and her helmet of pure and very heavy silver adorned with a Bat Falcon's wings gleamed in the torch light. Her legs shined with rippling muscle, her back heaving with breath. Her arm, lithe yet powerful, held aloft. Even from behind, she was enchanting.

As Shard blinked the mud from his eyes, he realized Princess Hiroki was attacking alone.

Momoo smiled, his dark eyes filling with tears. "Now she knows how to make a proper fight."

Shard lurched himself from the mud, from the gravity of swamp. His limbs where thick and unresponsive as he raised his man-sword, heavy and sharp, into the air. He bellowed his war-cry and found his lungs not loud enough. He could feel his feet thunder as they pounded on firm ground, but they were not fast enough. He flung his anger and desperation like a striking viper, but it fell short.

Around him he could feel his thugs, hear their unrelenting howl of fury as they followed him into the fray, into the Human camp, charging with reckless abandon, pumping up the speed to keep up with their commander who ran faster than the wind.

But Shard was too slow.

He watched Princess Hiroki, the beloved and only daughter of the God Emperor Spinecrack, skid to a stop at the first

Human she came too, took a stance, brandishing her sword and shield and waited patiently for the hapless, stunned Human to ready himself.

All of the Humans standing around the fire readied themselves.

And Shard ran like a madman. Screaming at the top of his voice, hoping to draw attention from the Princess to himself, but the Humans were focused on the Goblin beauty before them, especially around her prehistoric breast area.

They snapped from their brief reverie and scrambled for weapons and shields. As they all poised to attack her, she only waved her sword. "Ah, ah, ah..." She then pointed.

Just him.

She took her stance.

He took his, his eyes wild and round and desperate.

Shard poured on the speed. His limbs were suddenly light, his sword was magical, and euphoria surged in his mighty arms.

He watched as the Princess and the Human clashed. His steel sword was quick, and didn't even put up sparks as it chewed into her shield and sword. Shard could see the large nicks in her soft, metal blade as she wailed at the human in riposte. Her soft yet firm lips were turned down as she shouted her chi and pressed her attack.

The other Humans, not sure what to do with themselves, circled the Princess, moving to just grab her like an angry horse that needed breaking. They were smiling, laughing; entertained that this little filly had moxie.

Save one.

He turned. Hearing Shard's desperate cry his eyes grew round like a rabbit on the run as he watched more Goblins than his little illiterate mind could count charge down on him. He turned, holding up his shield in desperate fear.

Shard went after the guy next to him.

He turned, finally hearing the rumbling hobnail callous soles of Goblin's feet like a distant roar of thunder over the battle cry of the Princess, over the sound of her moon-sized breasts.

He said, in Human tongue, two of the few words that Shard understood: "Aw, shit."

The others turned to see what he was looking at.

Shard screamed. An indecipherable stream of desperation and fear which amazingly sounded in Human, Gnome and Goblin tongue as, "Black Dragon eats its dead!"

Shard brought his man-sword down. It was no longer steel, but starlight. His eyes were of real flame and his budding horns were obsidian. His sword passed without pause through the human with the new tattoo, from shoulder to crotch and beyond, slicing through cleanly to the ground at his feet.

Shard continued his whirlwind spin, his sword of stars leaving a trail of white iridescence in its wake as it came around again cleaving another surprised human, parting his shield, arm and body into two uneven parts.

Shard didn't pause as the panic-inspired idea overcame him that he was unstoppable. His sword took a life of its own as he lunged, his feet in the air floating gracefully over the fire pit, over the scorching tendrils of fire to attack another human. He watched the man's eyes, so clear and pretty, tremble as they filled with Shard's image, his sword filled with cold, pure moonlight streaking towards his unprotected chest with anger.

And the Princess kicked him in the head.

Shard tumbled out of control, his face slamming into the willowy grass so hard his ass hit him in the back of the head. He rolled ungracefully, sprawling like an overused whore, flat on his back, arms and legs akimbo, looking up uncertainly.

"Do you mind?" The Princess' image loomed over him. "I'm having a little... you know... fun?"

Shard blinked. The Humans were looking down at him, angry, insulted that he would interfere. The Princess was humiliated!

"Uh?" Shard said thoughtfully. "Um?" He said after a half beat of further thought. He then paused for another second and glanced quickly around. His thugs were making chum out of the sleeping Humans forces. Those Humans lucky enough to take a stance, clinging to a weapon, standing in their long underwear with woolly, toe-curled socks, were quickly hacked to bits by the Goblin triads, hitting them fast, knocking them down, and stomping on their heads as they ran by.

Shard looked back to Humans standing over him and smiled nervously. There were three now. Shard had killed two, the Princess, one. They seemed oblivious to the current events that Goblins were over running the camp. None of them had bothered to sound an alarm.

The Princess said something to them in Human tongue and they nodded and scoffed in understanding. One of them squared off against her Highness, crouching in a stance. She smiled and obliged.

The remaining two watched.

Shard reconsidered his original assessment. Humans were very good at attacking from a distance, or lobbing big rocks down from above, or riding down the enemy with horses, but when it came to a fair fight they blanched at the idea. They preferred to cut off supply lines instead of a head on confrontation, and enjoyed using ambushes whenever possible, except in the face of tactical superiority which was usually gained through some devious trickery of some such.

Shard propped himself on one elbow, watching the fight. The Humans were being quite chivalrous with the Princess, something he had never seen before in them. They talked chivalry all the time, but they were too victory-oriented to ever actually show any in battle. Shard had assumed they were going to surround and attack, but they were falling over themselves to offer up a honorable fight, or reasonably fair considering the Princess' soft metal ceremonial armor which exposed her, accentuating her boobs, her muscled midriff, and long, long legs. Yet despite these seeming gaps of armor, no one was even close to hitting her.

The Human was skilled in a brutal form of battle brawl which involved using only underhanded, surprise techniques, such as kicking, biting and low shots to the nuts. Shard watched as he lunged forward at the Princess. He seemed disjointed, distracted. His thrusts were weak, without commitment or follow-through. The Princess was a moving with collegiate precision, slapping down his weak thrusts then slipping her blade into armor gaps for a bloody score. With each pass the Human lost badly, the tendons to his shield arm severed, blood spewing from his side, his leg useless and stumbling around like a blind man.

As Shard climbed to his feet he recognized something in the Human's eyes. Hazel and warm, welcoming, trusting eyes that linked to a human soul. That tenacious, pit bull fervor soul that every race, every sentient being envied and only Humans possessed.

Those eyes of enduring courage, of faith, of unflinching determination, were locked, shackled and chained to Princess Hiroki's torpedo tits.

And with each pass she shrugged her shoulders giving them a little wave, a little, 'Hello!' A little, 'Look at me!' Breasts that could clean off a mantle with one quick turn or a writing desk in a pinch. Breasts that could shelter the homeless from a driving rain or table a round of beer at the local bar.

With a giggle they beckoned invitingly, clad only in a half moon of articulated links of brass, each stamped with a unique image of a vile sexual act. When she inhaled, so did everyone else out of sympathy. When she parried, dipping low, her cleavage, her entire scout-troop-losing-canyon, was plain for everyone to see.

And stare they did.

They said, *"If you defeat me, you can have me."*

The Humans weren't fighting to kill, but for the honor of bagging a Princess. The Princess was fighting for fun, and killing boob-blinded Humans was a fucking laugh riot.

The Human drooped from blood loss, teetering on his knees, his arms useless. The Princess leapt into the air, spinning and barking her chi and slamming her dulling blade into the back of the human's neck with a masterful stroke, smashing his vertebrae more than cutting it, and sending him to the ground.

Shard was on his feet, waiting for the remaining human's reprisal, but they only nodded, impressed by her Highness' technique, then played Paper, Scissors, Rock to determine who got to go next.

Shard sighed heavily. Humans and Goblins shared a common trait: they were suckers for a big pair of hooters.

Shard scraped the mud from his pauldrons as he looked around. The thugs were everywhere. The Human forces were scattered, their leaders strangely absent. The thugs were quickly losing their control, turning to blood lust. Shard let them go. They earned it.

He looked around for the biggest tent and headed there. He watched the last of the Human resistance taking a stand; a sergeant bellowing orders, commanding the men to hold their ground. Bands of thugs attacked and were repelled. Lance Corporal Gample called for the thugs to pull back, hoping to lure the Humans out of their line to a fight, but the Human sergeant kept them together, kept them alive.

Gample called for more thugs and lined them up. They were rowdy, howling and hooting, suddenly breaking ranks and swinging wildly only to be beaten back by the Humans, then beaten again by Gample.

Shard wandered over, catching the attention of one of the Trolls as he did. Gample turned and saluted sharply. "Sir!" he barked. "As soon as I get some spears up here we'll crush them!" He turned and bellowed at two thugs that broke rank to fall back in line.

Shard shook his head. "We can't wait any longer." He touched the Troll's arm and pointed to the Human sergeant, then he turned to Gample. "Prepare to crush!" He ordered, drawing his big man-sword. "Now! Crush!"

The thugs leapt at the Human line, moving as one, swinging furiously against their shields and using their sheer weight against them, breaking their line. Shard waited a single breath, watching the Human sergeant stumble back, blood streaming in his eyes from the Troll's flung rock. He then charged the line, driving his shoulder into the Human wall and opening it up enough to drive down his sword with a brutal two-handed strike. Shard felt the soft slice of meat and sinew, felt the splash of blood on his face, the scream of men in his ears. Shard drew back, swinging the back edge of the sword to hit something, anything, feeling the impact, then slashing forward again.

Suddenly they parted away from him, falling before his fury. The sergeant was before him, on his knees, dazed and blinded with blood. Shard swung fast, aiming for where neck met shoulder for a fast kill.

The Human ducked, dragging his shield up and blocking the blow. With a twist he thrust his sword, its deadly point keen and polished to a mirror, and sparked violently off of Shard's steel cuirass. The Goblin desperately reeled back to avoid losing his guts, stumbling from the surprise of the Human's trick. The Human quickly got to his feet, swinging fervently, forcing Shard to block the flurry of steel blows and back peddle out of reach. Shard shifted his footing, preparing to counter-attack, but paused when the Human suddenly lost interest, his eyes shifting their focus to a thousand-mile stare.

Shard squinted, ready for the Human's next trick.

The Human lurched as thugs swarmed him, stabbing him from behind again and again until he fell face first in the dirt. They continued their frenzy, prying open his armor to get to the soft meat beyond and ripping off parts of him. In seconds, the thugs scattered leaving nothing but a puddle of blood behind. All save Gample, smiling proudly, panting to catch his breath.

Shard wiped the Human blood from his eyes, his monobrow hanging low. "What the fuck do you want? A fucking medal?" Shard growled, sheathing his sword. "Just as I was about to take him out, by Hoargnick's inflamed rash, ya stab him in the back, leaving me standing around looking like a loser! Thanks a fucking lot, ya gamey assbag!" Shard turned away, ignoring the look of distress on Gample's face. "Now back me up while I check out this tent." Shard unshouldered his buckler and drew his needler. "Let's see what these mooks died for."

Shard crept slowly to the tent flap. He listened carefully and could hear humming, and "Mm hmmm." And "Interesting..."

Shard rose from his crouch as he parted the tent flap with the tip of his needler and peered in. Major Bark-Bite stood inside, leafing through papers, holding them up to the lamplight and checking for watermarks and secret writing, his eyes looking large through his spectacles.

Shard closed the flap and looked back at Gample. "Dismissed. Go have fun."

Gample saluted and ran off to join the growing chaos of Human slaughter. Shard sighed longingly, then stepped into the tent.

The Human commander lay dead in his bed, his face split halfway open. His eyes were still open, full of surprise, his mouth frozen in mid-gasp. Bark-Bite had slipped unseen into his tent, roused him, waited a half heartbeat for the Human to see him, realize it was a Goblin, then drove Lil' Elfie into his head the instant before he could scream, ensuring the Human died with a stupid expression on his face. Shard was impressed.

"Do you read, Shard?" Bark-Bite asked, not looking up from the papers.

Shard was putting his needler away. "I try not to make it a habit. Keeps me out of trouble."

Bark-Bite 'Humphed' as he looked at another bit of yellowy, withered page. "Shame, Shard, you're missing out on some amazing stuff."

Shard unbuckled his helm and scratched his prickly hair. "I'm sure." Shard dropped his helm on the bed and began to rummage through the Human commander's kit. "I never figured on living long enough to have to worry about something written on a piece of paper." Shard opened the commander's canteen and gave a sniff. He took a sip and smiled. "Ah yeah, that's what I'm talking about." He took a good swig, feeling the aged Dwarvish rum burn slowly and steadily down into his gullet. He offered the canteen to Bark-Bite.

"I was hoping you could help me with a word here." Bark-Bite took a sip from the canteen, making a face. "Oh, Dwarven Dark Fire Rum. This is a treat. You know, the secret is the Insanity Grubs that live in the casks where the rum ages." He corked it and handed it back to Shard who was going though the commander's laundry. "It's their excrement that adds the hallucinogenic qualities to the brew."

Shard held up a pair of silk britches to check for fit. "Thank Balick's nervous twitch for grub shit."

Bark-Bite bristled. "Fascinating history. The entire Wolf Claw Battalion conducted a year-long campaign against the Infected Groin Pull Ork army without ever leaving the barracks. Lost half their numbers. It wasn't for another year that they realized there never were any Orks." Bark-Bite went back to his papers. "Hmmm. Yes. There seems to be a bit of correspondence here. Some in Elven. Quite a bit about the Black Dirt that Blows Stuff Up. More than the typical 'Beware' notices. I wonder what this is all about?"

Shard found the commander's purse on the bottom of the chest and could feel the weighty coins through the leather pouch. "I'm sure you'll figure it out, Major." Shard cast a sly glance as he tucked the bag away for later.

Bark-Bite set the page aside and picked up a curled page, its wax seal broken. "Oh, I'll pore over it later, it's this dispatch that has me really perplexed. It's from the Elven magic council."

Shard was thumbing through a deck of cards with lurid Human poses. He squinted in the light. "The fucker, they're marked," he mumbled.

Bark-Bite looked at Shard. "The dispatch is a warning to this commander to beware the new Goblin captain."

Shard pulled the draw string of a cloth bag and sniffed inside. "Coffee!"

Bark-Bite's face was stoic. "It refers to the captain by name."

Shard looked up quickly, his mouth hanging open. "Wha, me?" Shard rose and peered at the indecipherable Elvish squiggle. "What the fuck does it say?"

Bark-Bite leaned toward the light, holding up the dispatch. "Woefully and frighteningly underestimate Wiggletooth Shard with sorry tragedy. Beware, the *Fated Ahborant* who shall haunt us. Already Daphne falls in irony." Bark-Bite looked at him. "*Ahborant*; this word I do not understand. Abhorrent means repugnant, but I can't imagine the magic council would spell something wrong and it is used in the title pretense. Why do they call you, *Abhorant?*"

Shard's mono-brow twisted. "Fuck should I know? Maybe it means: He who pisses on Elven parade." Shard shrugged. "Over-smart bastards. Can't they just say: Shard's a coming, lube up your holes cause he's gonna bone you but good?"

Bark-Bite shrugged. "I find it odd that they know you by name already. They normally don't refer to lower level officers by name."

Shard sneered. "That pansy fucking Momoo, probably blabbed my name all over the fucking place. I swear I'm gonna nail his nuts to a tree."

"I'd pay to see that." Bark-Bite nodded, then held up the document. "And look here, your name is written in Elven. Goblin names don't translate easily into Elven script. Someone did a bit of work to spell out your name in Elven."

Shard picked up his helm. "I can't decide whether to be honored, disgusted or just plain creeped out that the Elves have taken an interest in me." Shard pulled on his helm. "Maybe they'll invite me to their next freak march."

Bark-Bite sighed. "Don't take this lightly, Shard. This is highly irregular, highly irregular." Bark-Bite pointed to the last part of the letter. "Daphne is in the proper person tense. Do you know who this person is?"

Shard looked away, buckling up his helmet. "Nope. Don't know no fucking Elves. 'Sides, who can guess those mysterious fucks? I must've gacked her at some point. Yeah, I think I'm creeped out."

"Why do you say it's a she?" Bark-Bite's voice was level.

Shard didn't turn around. "Cause... cause they're all fucking little girly-girls, running around in fucking flowery dresses and wouldn't stand for an honest fight even if you nailed their foot to the deck," Shard growled. "I wouldn't give a Mule Rat's wrinkled left nut to know the inner workings of an Elf's tiny fucked up, little squishy brain and I don't know why you would give a drippy dick's worth a care either," He then added, "sir." Shard headed to the entrance. "I gotta check my thugs. I've left them alone for too long."

"You do that, Captain." Bark-Bite's voice was still steady. "Oh, and I'll expect my half of that purse you found." He held up the vellum to see its text in the light. "I think it's made from tanned Ogre scrotum."

Shard paused at the tent flap, then pulled it open.

He stopped, his eyes glowing yellow as he gazed into the sun.

The world was on fire.

Shard felt the burst of heat as he stepped out into the open. Thugs where running rampant, setting fire to everything: tents, barrels, rocks, and dancing in the warmth and glow with psychotic abandon.

Shard nodded to himself. They deserved a little celebration. He had driven them hard across dangerous lands and didn't rest until they were hidden safely in the swamps. Now, once again they tasted victory. It was time to kick back and enjoy a little wanton destruction.

One of the thugs ran past Shard. He stopped, skidding on his heels and ran back, hopping on one foot in front of his commander. "Burn!" he shouted. "Burn, fucking burn!" His tongue lolled out of his slobbering mouth. "Burn, yeah!"

Shard smiled proudly and slapped him on the head to put out the thug's burning hair. "Having fun?"

He did a back flip. "Burn!"

Shard nodded. "Yes, burn," he said patiently. "Find your squad leader. I want all the loot brought here so we can divide it up."

The thug's face of glee, drooped. "Burn!" he said insistently.

"Yeah, I fucking see that. Burn. Now hurry up, we've got to move this along. I want all the loot brought here." Shard pointed to the ground. "Pile it up here and we'll sort through it."

The thug looked confused. "Burn?"

Shard sighed harshly. "Enough burn. I want the plunder brought here!" Shard looked into the thug's vacant eyes. "The loot? The plunder? The stuff you took from the Humans?" Shard looked closely at the thug, hoping for a spark of recognition. "You did plunder, right? Before burn, you plunder, remember?" Shard felt the air in his lungs still. "Fuck," he whispered as his eyes rolled back. "Sergeant Major!" Shard bellowed into the air. "Sergeant Major!"

Shard could hear the rasping growl of the big Goblin coming from a nearby tent. "Who the fug wants his nuts crushed? E'rats, can't you see I'm fuggin' busy?"

Shard's lip curled, exposing his tusks. "Get the fuck out here!"

"Oh, so's ya wants Ribsplitter-Jones to stomp on yer 'eads?" Shard could see the tent shiver as the Sergeant Major flung open the flap, his face filling with surprise. "Fug wot? Burning already? Don't these thugs knows abouts a little footsie?" He looked up and noticed the tent he had been in was also on fire. "The Fuggers. I got to teach them abouts foreplay. Takes yerself a little time 'fore ya rapes 'em."

Shard's fists were in tight balls. "They skipped the rape part." His voice was low and deadly.

Ribsplitter-Jones looked a little surprised. "Wot! E'rats the best part! It's the whole reason fer being a thug! Getcher self a little battlefield commission." Ribsplitter-Jones gave a little hip thrust. He shook his head sadly. "Greedy bastards. Goin' straight for the loot."

"They skipped that as well."

Ribsplitter-Jones made a small 'oh.'

Shard jutted his chin and growled. "Get the thugs in line. Stop the burning. I need pickets set up and whatever is salvageable salvaged."

Ribsplitter-Jones nodded. "S'right!" He turned to go back into his burning tent.

"Now! We're beyond the raping part!"

Ribsplitter-Jones looked back, his big lower lip pouty. "But... She's... We're..."

"No more raping! Go!" Shard bellowed as the delicate aroma of Chesterwood filled the air.

"What's this about skipping raping?" The Princess walked up, her brass armor clanking loudly. The dented and gouged soft metal plates hung from frayed straps. Her sword of pyrite had snapped off at the quillions and she had to smother her last opponent between her boobs. He didn't put up much fight. Now, shivering from excitement and blood lust, her muscles glistening in the fire glow; she looked very desirable. Shard and Ribsplitter-Jones openly stared.

She planted her fists into her hips. "So here I am, waiting for the rape part to begin, and someone sets my tent on fire!" She glared at Shard angrily. "Is that anyway to treat someone who has a castration machine and a marked propensity to use it?" She stepped closer, her breasts like full moons rising over Shard. "Rape, plunder, burn? Isn't that how it works? How are we already at the burn phase while I am un-ravaged?" She tilted her head coyly, her anger subsiding. "What, you a little girly Elf?"

Shard suddenly snapped out of his wet dream. "Wha'? Fuck no! I...," Shard looked quickly over his shoulder at the Sergeant Major. "What the fuck are you staring at?"

Ribsplitter-Jones continued to stare. "My, have you grown," he said distantly. "Why, I remember you were this high," He held his hand by his knee. "And only this big," He held his hands in front of his chest. "Why, you're quite the woman now."

Her cheeks darkened as she blushed. "Sergeant Major."

Shard looked at him. "The thugs are burning shit!" Shard motioned for him to move along.

Ribsplitter-Jones stopped staring. "Ah, right." He bowed to the Princess. "E'rats. Duty calls, yer Highness."

Her thin eyebrows rose. "So formal? Come on sergeant, say it."

Ribsplitter-Jones' face tightened as he smiled. "Princess Twillter Buggy Boo."

Her face lit up. "Go 'wan Sergeant Major."

He bowed again and stepped off. Shard yelled at his back. "And find that dickless Momoo!" He turned back to the Princess. "Your Highness, I'm sorry, the thugs..."

"Burned everything?" she finished. "I'm beginning to see why there is no loot for His Majesty."

Shard looked away. "Actually, we've never made it to this phase before. The thugs are unaccustomed to victory." He looked up. "I went to clean out the command tent and next thing I knew..."

"Blah, blah, blah, Shard. I am standing here still unravaged." She motioned to the command tent. "Let's go. That one's not on fire. I do have a little modesty."

Shard looked at the command tent. "Wait, that's the..."

She cut him off. "No wait; fuck now." She said tersely. "I don't know about you, but I'm still in the rape mode." She pulled open the tent flap and looked back. "You have heard Ribsplitter-Jones's class on foreplay, right?"

Major Bark-Bite stepped out of the tent. "Twice."

Her eyes narrowed and Shard could see tiny flecks of ice fling from them. "It's you."

Bark-Bite's whiskers bristled and his eyes loomed big from behind his spectacles. He slowly reached out and gave a gentle squeeze to her left boob.

She slapped his hand. "What did I tell you about that?"

He addressed her left breast. "I'm sorry, what was that?"

Her soft, kissable lips hardened as her knee reared up and nailed him in the crotch.

The Major bent forward, a small whine escaping from within him. "Now I remember why I came out here." He gasped, looking up at Shard. "I have something I want you to see." He rose, shaking off the effects of the groin shot with a shudder.

Shard's face was a little desperate. "Can it wait?"

"Yes, it can." The Princess said grabbing Shard's arm. "He has to rape me now."

Bark-Bite shoved a parchment in front of Shard's face. "A detailed map of the area and the latest troop movements."

"Boring!" the Princess shouted. "Now, Shard, come bore me." She went to pull him into the tent when she noticed Momoo trotting up. "Ugh! This is getting better all the time," she moaned.

"Shard!" he called. "Shard, what's this about already being in the burn phase?"

"Not all of us," the Princess grumbled.

"Well, Shard, I'm looking out for you." Momoo smiled proudly. "I've put aside some rapes for us officers."

"Hello?" The Princess slapped Momoo in the head. "I'm standing right here!"

Momoo bowed. "A thousand pardons, your Highness, but you told me not to look upon you, or speak to you, or breathe your air."

"Yes, but I didn't say to ignore me! And you're still breathing my air! Stop breathing!" She planted her fist to her hip. "Shard will not require any rapes." She looked at Shard who was staring intently at the map. "Put that away and let's go."

Shard took the parchment from Bark-Bite. "How the fuck are we gonna get out of here?" Shard pointed at the map. "This smudge here is, what, troops?"

Bark-Bite nodded. "We are here, this group we just destroyed. Here is the swamp. Here are the main Human forces on the other side of the swamp. Now down here are two units that have chased you for several days. I imagine they will be hot on your trail again, once the survivors from this battle reach them."

Shard looked at Momoo. "How many survivors?"

Momoo's eyes were bulging, his cheeks puffed and darkening as he held his breath.

Shard gave a hissing sigh. "When we attacked, it's a good assumption that some of the Humans looked up and saw a fuck load of thugs running at them so they turned tail. Probably mostly Elves. No way we can catch them. If they are not amassing for a counter-attack, which is unlikely for Elves, then they may meet up with the other Human forces and tell them where we are."

Momoo's eyes rolled.

Shard turned to the Princess. "Please, your Highness, tell him to breathe."

She cocked her head. "Not unless he brought his own air with him."

Shard sighed and looked at the map. "The main forces are waiting for us on the other side of the swamp. That leaves this way to the north. What are these triangles?" he asked Bark-Bite.

The Major's whiskers bristled. "The Old Grey Mountain range. This is the mountain pass here." He pointed. "This is the citadel that blocks off the road. Old Gourd Head. High walls, rooks and a company of Humans with a contingency of Elves. Any attacking force coming up the pass gets rained on by catapults, arrows and insidious weaponry before coming to a dead stop at the gates."

"By Philbert's rancid pudding mold," Shard swore. "We are the living embodiment of fucked!"

"What do you mean *we*, Halfling." The Princess growled.

Shard punched himself in the head. "There's got to be a way out of this."

Bark-Bite leaned close to him, his eyes looming large. "Yes, Shard, there must."

The Princess scoffed. "We fucking attack!" She shouted at him. "We just kicked their asses! Why are we worried?"

Bark-Bite touched her arm. "Your Highness, each victory we've had has been using sneak attacks and superior numbers. We'll be slaughtered in a head on fight."

She looked horrified. "So! You mean we fight like Elves instead of dying like *thugs*?" Her eyes filled with fire. "Hogsthpth's Flying, Flaming Razor Shit! If Shard won't attack, I'll appoint someone who will." She looked to Momoo. "Get ready to attack!"

Momoo eyes were crimson, his face black and glistening beads of sweat dotted his brow. He was trembling violently, convulsing as his body pounded for air.

The Princess frowned. "What the fuck is wrong with you?"

Bark-Bite peered at him. "He's suffocating. You told him to stop breathing."

Her eyes widened with curiosity. "Think he'll die?"

"Doubt it," Bake-Bite answered.

Momoo squeaked as his eyes rolled back and he fell with a painful thud.

"Oh! He's dead!" the Princess chirped happily. "How cool! Now, that's discipline! I've actually ordered someone to die! Now who can say that?"

Suddenly Momoo gasped for air.

"What!" the Princess roared. "He's alive! And breathing my air!" She reared her foot back and began kicking him in the groin. "Stop breathing my air!" She punctuated each word with a kick to the nuts, alternating left and right.

"Your Highness!" Bark-Bite pleaded. "He's unconscious. He doesn't feel a thing."

"He will when he wakes up." She gave him a final kick. She sneered at his still body, then looked up. "All right, that was mildly amusing." She looked at Shard. "Okay, I've crushed nuts and now I'm feeling very randy. Let's go." She motioned to the burning tent with a tilt of her head.

Shard stood, punching himself in the head, grunting in pain with each punch.

The Princess leaned towards Bark-Bite. "What is he doing?"

The Major studied him. "Thinking."

She nodded, partially understanding. "About raping me?"

Shard stopped punching himself as his eyes blossomed wide, his breath holding still in his lungs. He looked at the Princess. "You speak Human tongue, your Highness?"

"Duh!" She mocked. "How was I supposed to rule the subjugated masses you were supposed to subjugate if they can't understand me?" She squinted at him askance. "Why?" She smiled seductively. "Does that turn you on?" She slinked closer to him. "Want me to talk Human?"

Shard shook his head, turning to the Major. "And you speak Human?"

"Oh, yes; yes indeed," the Major answered. "A most peculiar language once you get the hang of using so many words to say something. Such as Humans say, 'Would you be so kind as to hand that to me' where a thug would say, 'Gimme!'. Human words aren't hard on the palate, but it does require a lot of lip flapping. And the grammar! Insane! It's a literary mugging."

Princess Hiroki slapped him in the back of the head. "Shut up." She looked at Shard. "Why do you care? And you better not be thinking what I'm thinking, because if you are I'm setting up my nut ripper."

Shard looked to the ground, scanning the dirt, then he dropped to his knees. He quickly grabbed a stick and began drawing lines in the dirt. He sat back, looking his drawing over and scratching his groin. He added a line, then a circle, then looked at it. He punched himself in the head, then erased the line and drew another. He looked up with the eyes of a wild-man. "Momoo," he whispered.

"Momoo?" Bark-Bite and Princess Hiroki said simultaneously.

Shard quickly scrabbled on his hands and knees to the supine Momoo. "Wake up." He patted Momoo's cheek. "Hey, buddy, wake up." He hit him a little harder and Momoo stirred. "Wake the fuck up," Shard growled impatiently.

Momoo's eyes popped open, looking blearily around before focusing on Shard. "What? Oh, Shard. I was having the most pleasant dream. I was..." His voice trailed off as his face bent drastically in horror. Suddenly he grabbed his crotch and began screaming furiously, thrashing around. "Arrgh! This is the worst pain ever!" He howled as tears spewed from his eyes. "Gibergit's double-stubbed toe! Kill me, someone, fucking kill me! Oh, my frigging, fucknutted fuck balls! I'll fucking pay you to fucking kill me!"

The Princess roared. "Nobody fucking kill him, ya hear!"

Shard slapped him in the face. "Come on, Momoo; I need you!"

Momoo began wailing long, trembling off key notes like a haunting ghost. "Oh, this hurts worse than when I got my dick caught in a desk drawer!" He looked down as if he could see himself through his britches. "One's flat! Oh, Malitit's lactating wart! One's flat!"

The Princess glowered. "Just one?"

Shard grabbed Momoo by the collar and shook him. "You dumb fuck! Pay attention! She's going to come over here and do it again if you don't fucking listen! I need you to go get those rapes you were saving. I need you to bring them over here!"

"The rapes?" both Momoo and the Princess said.

"Yes!" Shard growled. "I want you to put them in the command tent!"

Momoo tried to catch his breath. "Both of them? Aren't you being a little greedy?"

"No, I think I see where this is going," the Princess said. "Okay, I'm up for a little group action, but Momoo and Bark-Bite are out."

"What?" Bark-Bite wined.

Shard grabbed the front of Momoo's cuirass, pulled it open and grabbed his nipple with a sinister twisting pinch. "Just fucking do it!"

Momoo's face was shining with tears and snot. "Okay, okay, I'll do it, I'll get them," he whimpered. "I, I just can't move my legs."

Shard's mono-brow hovered low over his eyes. "The Princess is going to fucking kick you in the fucking nuts until you fucking die!"

She smiled. "I'll make it last. With bathroom breaks, it'll take about a week." She looked down at her hip, hiking her butt up. "It's a great exercise for your glutes and calves." She patted her firm rump, then noticed Bark-Bite was staring at her shapely bottom. She slapped him, sending his glasses, glinting with firelight, off into the night.

"Ooo," he said, then plodded in search of them.

Momoo was crawling frantically away and Shard stood up, brushing his hands together in satisfaction. "Okay, here's the plan." He looked up and realized only the Princess was there.

She was frowning. "No, no, no. I have a better plan. Yours is getting too kinky." She reached over and grabbed Shard's ear and dragged him over to the tent which was now only smoldering and consisted of four walls of canvas. "Let's stick to the basics: you're going to have your way with me. You're going to savagely and, incoherent with blood lust, bang my skull into the headboard and drill me until I'm bow-legged. You will do it with uncontrollable furor and passion which will include: pawing, groping, biting, and speaking in tongues." She stopped at the tent flap. "Wait." Her eyes fell distant and blank. "Oh, by Lady Chudd's Needle Point Pattern of Death, it's past." She looked at Shard. "It's too late. Sorry, Shard, the moment's past. The battle rage has ended." She shrugged. "I'm not in the mood anymore." She sighed, then blinked. "Ah, no. There it is." She smiled. "Let's go!" She dragged him into the tent and closed the flap.

Shard's Ruse

THE TATTERED MAN stood tall and gaunt over a sea of soft green, forever waving hello. He turned slowly, lazily, following the faint breeze, his empty eyes keeping watch over his charge. When the wind changed direction, he waved goodbye.

Black Jon-Crows glided easily in the lazy air over the vast green pasture. They swooped, homing in on the fat, pulsing kernel pods swelling with golden early morning sun, their black talons extended, their eyes glowing with glee, only to veer off at the last second. Angry and frustrated, they circled the tattered man and settled on his shoulders, squawking obnoxiously in his empty ear.

He ignored them.

Furious, they hopped along his extended arms, flapping their hairy wings. *Don't you see? There are intruders in the kernel field! Aren't you supposed to do something about that?*

But the tattered man ignored them, as he always did, happily waving hello, or goodbye.

With their enraged, gleaming, vengeful eyes, they tore open the tattered man's head with their serrated, hooked beaks and ripped out his brains, sending flurries of moldy straw down on Momoo who sat below the tattered man's feet.

Momoo cursed and pitched a rock up at the Jon-Crows for the twentieth time that morning. The rock sailed past the birds by a wide margin and vanished somewhere into the field.

"Ow!" someone shouted. "Who the fuck keeps throwin' rocks?"

"Sorry," Momoo mumbled, noting the birds were now ignoring his attempts to scurry them and continued to dig into the tattered man's head. Momoo sighed and brushed the hay from his hair. He looked over at Shard. The Goblin captain was contentedly pulling a bone needle and thread through a baldric. They had marched through the night before Shard hid his company in the midst of a tall kernel field, losing them in the towering green stalks. As dawn ringed the horizon, he ordered the troops to get a few hours of precious sleep.

Momoo sniffed. "So, Shard...", he began.

"I'm not going to fucking explain it to you again," Shard growled, not looking up from his task.

Momoo watched him, impressed by his deft needlework. "You have to admit, it's your most confusing plan to date."

Shard looked up, his mono-brow level, and studied Momoo. The idiot had a point. Shard nipped off the thread with his teeth, then balled up the baldric. He paused and scratched himself, then leaned back and called over his shoulder. "Gample!"

"Sir?" came a response from the kernel field.

"Get your sorry ass over here." Shard stashed the baldric behind his back as he heard the Goblin make his way through the stalks. Gample broke from the line of tall plants and popped to attention, sharply punching himself in the head.

"Lance Corporal Gample, reporting as ordered, sir."

Shard eyed him carefully. "What the fuck was that last night?"

Gample looked confused. "Uh, well, sir, I was trying to attack the enemy with strength in numbers like the Sergeant Major said."

"And you did a piss poor job at it." Shard pulled the baldric out and threw it at him. "Well you fucking better figure out how to do it or the thugs will tear you a new asshole."

Gample caught the baldric, fumbling with it before he held it up. A corporal's baldric. Seconds passed as it slowly dawned on him that he'd been promoted. He looked up. "Thank you, sir!"

Shard shook his head. "It means you're gonna work your fucking ass off. Now go report to the sergeant and stand by to have your ass kicked."

Gample punched a salute so hard he staggered. "Yes, sir! Thank you, sir!"

Shard barked. "You disobedient little fuck, why are you still standing here?"

He punched himself again and stumbled, a little dizzy. "Right! Yes, sir!" He wobbled off.

Shard carefully put his needle away, scratched himself with both hands, then looked at Momoo. "Alright ya dumb fuck, I'm going to explain this ruse to you one more time." Shard picked up a stick and began to draw in the dirt. "I will put this so simple that even you will understand." Shard pointed to his impromptu map. "This was the swamp we were in. To the east of the swamp are the main human forces blocking our way to the shore. Here is the camp we raided. This is the command tent here. To the south and west are more human forces hunting us down. This line here is the road north. This circle is the citadel blocking the road. You with me so far?"

"Where am I on the map?" Momoo asked expectantly.

Shard sneered as he glowered. "I'm gonna shove this stick in your eye. Fucking pay attention!" Shard drew a little stick figure outside the command tent. "Here. This is you."

Momoo frowned. "Why am I hunched over like that?"

"'Cause you're holding your fucking swollen balls. Now, back to the big picture. Humans to the left of us, Humans to the right of us and Humans coming up from below us, Humans blocking off above us. Now, where do we go?"

Momoo stared at the map. He pointed south. "We hit them here and break through."

Shard growled. "Wrong. These are rolling plains. The Elves will see us for miles. These west and south units will combine and they will be twice as big by time we meet them which means we won't stand a blood tick's chance in Mama Ogley's boney ass." Shard pointed at the swamp, scratching himself with his free hand. "If we go into the swamp, we'll be stuck there. If we attack the main forces, we'll be killed.

We have no choice but to go north. Now north is a heavily guarded citadel. So, how do we get them to un-guard? We use a ruse."

Momoo nodded. "Okay, I'm good with this part."

"Now, you put the rapes you were saving in the command tent which is not on fire. You with me so far?"

Momoo nodded emphatically. "Yes."

"Good. Now, Major Bark-Bite and the Princess stand outside the command tent and talk very loudly in Human tongue, that her company of thugs and the Major's company of thugs are going to meet up with our companies of thugs, then all four companies will go north to storm the citadel."

Momoo nodded at alternating speeds. "Okay, I think. But where do we get the other two companies of thugs?"

"There aren't any. This is a ruse, remember? Now, we leave the rapes in the tent, pretending to forget them there and go north. When the south and west units show up and find the rapes in the tent, the rapes will tell the commanders what they heard. The commanders will wonder why the Goblins are speaking their plans in Human tongue and conclude that it's a ruse. They will assume that we're not going north, but east to surprise the main Human forces and take them out with four companies of Goblins." Shard's eyes flashed with the cleverness of his plan. "Now, the Humans will send word by magic to the main forces that they are about to be attacked. They will in turn call for reinforcements from the citadel, the closest place. The citadel will send everybody leaving only a skeleton crew to watch the place. We then storm the citadel. See?"

Momoo rubbed his temple where a painful throb developed. "Uh, yeah." He squinted at the map. "Yeah, I see. You're making the Humans think we're going east, by telling them we're going north, and then going north," his voice trailed off.

Shard beamed. "Exactly! They will dismiss our obvious trail going north as part of the ruse to fool them."

Slack jawed, Momoo nodded. He closed one eye as his brain sucked more power to think. "Okay, this is a ruse within a ruse, right?"

Shard nodded. "Yes. Now I imagine the rapes have already been found, and the Humans have all contacted each other by magic, so all we have to do is wait for the citadel to clear out."

Momoo wiped the drool from his lip. "There's just one thing I'm a little foggy on." He looked up at Shard. "How are the rapes going to tell the Humans the plan?"

"What do you mean, how?" Shard's mono-brow tilted. "They're just going to say it."

"Well, that's just it. How are they going to say it?"

Shard's mono-brow tilted more. "What the fuck do you mean, how? They're going to go up to the commander and say, 'Hey, I overheard the Goblin battle plan.' That's how."

Momoo nibbled his fingers. "Well, I guess if you say so." He nibbled more. "It's just that..."

Shard leaned forward. "What?"

135

Momoo looked perplexed. "It's just that I didn't think that sheep and goats could talk."

Shard's mono-brow twisted painfully. "What the fuck are you talking about?" He scratched. "What sheep and goat?"

"The ones in the command tent."

Shard blinked. "There were no sheep or goats in the command tent."

Momoo stopped nibbling his fingers. "Yes, there were. You told me to put them there."

Shard reached up with his hand and straightened out his mono-brow. "What in Calli's fetid armpit sweat-soup are you talking about? What fucking sheep and goat?"

"The rapes," Momoo insisted.

Shard sagged and rubbed his temples. "Momoo, you're making no fucking sense. You mean you put a sheep and a goat with the rapes in the command tent?" Shard looked up, stopped in mid-scratch, his eyes round as plates. "The rapes?" he said in a hollow voice. "The rapes you put aside, were a sheep and a goat?"

Momoo nodded. "Um, well, yeah," he said meekly.

Shard's face darkened. "You were going to screw a sheep and a goat?" he screamed.

"Don't be absurd!" Momoo's head jerked back, indigent. "The goat was for you."

"For me?"

"I figured your personalities matched better."

Shard blinked. "You screw farm animals? What the fuck is wrong with you?"

Momoo nibbled his fingers again. "Well, this may come as a bit of a surprise, Shard, but I'm not very confident with the ladies, you know."

Shard put his hands to his head. "Oh, fuck me up the ass with a horned melon," he moaned.

"Well, if I knew your preferences before hand..." Momoo admonished.

Shard felt his teeth grinding. "Momoo, shut the fuck up! You have the brains of snot!"

Momoo looked offended. "What? Is this now my fault? You said put the rapes in the tent. I did. You didn't say to make sure they could talk. If you had, I would have taken the extra time to see which sheep could talk." Momoo folded his arms. "How am I supposed to figure out your ruse within a ruse? An ordinary ruse isn't good enough for you, is it? How am I to follow that? And I was under a lot of pressure at the time. If you recall, I had just had my nuts kicked up my throat and I was trying to swallow them back down. And here I was, thinking of you. How about: "Thank you for rustling a goat for me, Momoo?' If I'd known you'd be buggering the Princess, I wouldn't have bothered. And another thing, don't you think it's time I get a turn? Here I am, bringing you goats and I bet you haven't once mentioned to the Princess that I'd might like a go at her? You selfish bastard!"

Shard had his fists to his head. "Shut up, Momoo. By Mitzganor's dyke girlfriend's butt plug, fucking shut the fuck up!" Shard looked at him, his eyes as red as rubies. "We are one fuck beyond fucked!"

Momoo threw his hands up. "Only one fuck, Shard? I must be slipping."

Shard was hunched forward, staring at his drawing. "Yes, you diddling git, only one," he grumbled. "Of all the fuck wonder stunts," he said quietly. "Sheep?" A laugh escaped him. "And the goat was for me?" Shard looked up. "Was it a nice goat?"

Momoo watched him carefully. "Yes, a rather fine goat," Momoo answered. "You, you're not mad?"

Shard beamed. "Strange, isn't it? We're quite fucked and yet, I'm not mad." His eyes looked up at the Jon-Crows pecking at the tattered man's head. "I wonder why that is?"

Momoo looked nervous. "Uh, perhaps it's because you've already thought of a new and better plan. A ruse within a ruse within a ruse?"

"Hm?" Shard thought about that. "No, I don't think so." He shook his head, dismissing it. "You see, it's like this." He made some scratches in the dirt. "Without the rapes to tell them anything, they will simply follow our trail north. That puts the northern trail blocked by a fully garrisoned company in the citadel, and two pissed off companies of Humans blocking us off from the south." Shard artistically added the kernel paddies etched in the steppes of the mountain. He then looked up at the tattered man, mindlessly waving goodbye. Shard nodded to confirm his bad luck. "And the wind is blowing to the south which means those damned Elves will smell us for leagues." He looked back at his sketch. "I don't think I've missed anything. Fuckrighteously fucked." He looked up, smiling.

Momoo shivered. "And yet you're happy." Momoo slowly slid back on his butt. "I bet you're anxious to attack the citadel. Just a straight run, in column. Hi-ya!" Momoo looked hopeful.

Shard looked at the end of his stick, checking its point. "Nope, it's not that."

"Then charge the companies from the south and breaking through?" Momoo slid back a little more.

Shard mused, pursing his lips as he thought. "Now that's a plan. We will all die running down the narrow trail. Just a few good mage zaps; you know the one that streaks out and fries you? No way to duck out of the way, we'll just watch them come and roll us over." He snorted a laugh. "We won't get to bloody one human. We'll all get to see Dru empty handed."

"And yet you're smiling," Momoo squeaked.

"And yet I'm smiling." Shard smiled brightly.

"You're going to kill me, aren't you?" Momoo bumped against the tattered man's post.

Shard weighed the idea. "Not right away. I figure we have a couple hours."

Momoo glanced around nervously. "Oh, I see. Well, I guess we should get started then." Suddenly he pointed over Shard's shoulder. "Oh, look! It's the Princess!" Momoo spun around and, on his hands and knees, quickly scrambled away, hoping to hide in the tall stalks. Lightning flashed across both eyes as he felt Shard's heavy elbow crash into the back of his skull, knocking his face into the cool, black earth. Shard's full weight landed on him, pinning him, forcing scraps of air from his lungs. "It's not my fault!" Momoo wheezed.

Shard pressed one hand into the back of Momoo's neck and lifted him up high enough to drive a knee into Momoo's kidney. "So?" He cuffed him in the side of the head. "It's not like I need a real reason to gack you, other than I've fucking had enough of you." Shard straddled him and began punching him randomly along his spine. "I'm just wondering if we have enough time to stake you down and have all the thugs walk up and bugger you before we march off to die at the hands of the Humans."

Momoo gasped. "Wait! Wait! I have an idea!"

Shard paused, relaxing his grip. "Excuse me?"

Momoo shifted so he could breathe. "Yes, yes, punching me in the head gave me an idea!" His eyes shifted back and forth as the concept swept over him. "I can take the Other Black Dragon Company down the trail, and, and uh, when the Humans see us, run away." He panted. "Yes! Run away. Uh, up the trail, up to the citadel, see... and then they shoot at us, and when they shoot at us, we duck! Then all the arrows hit the Humans behind us and kill them! Brilliant, isn't it?"

Shard punched him in the kidney. "No, it's fucking stupid." Shard leaned to the other side so he could get a few shots on the other kidney. "Cavalry will run you down. And your plan still leaves the citadel intact. The point is to get on the other side of the mountain."

"Yes, but they will feel so bad killing their own that they'll gack themselves out of guilt."

Shard grabbed his hair, trying to rip out clumps. "And maybe they will leave the gates open too."

"Ugh!" Momoo grunted as Shard ripped out a lock. "We could dig a tunnel..."

Shard hit him harder. "Oh, just shut up and let me beat you to death."

"No, Shard!" Momoo pleaded in-between poundings. "I can pay you."

"Momoo, there is nothing that will stop me from killing you." Shard grabbed the fine, wispy hairs on the back of Momoo's neck and began yanking them out. "Here's my new plan. I can go to Dru with you and say, here's the stupid sheep fucker who wiped out two companies of perfectly good thugs. I'm sure to get something for you."

"Help!" Momoo whimpered. "Major Bark-Bite! Princess!"

Shard pulled out his needler, eyeing its wicked edge. "Bark-Bite's vanished and the Princess fucking hates you. There is no one to save you." His lip curled savagely as he aimed the point into Momoo's ear.

Gample pushed his way through the wall of kernel plants. "Uh, excuse me, sir?"

Shard looked up hotly. "Gample, can't you see I'm busy killing Captain Momoo?"

Gample winced as he punched himself in the head. "Yes, sir. Sorry, sir, but you wanted to know the moment the citadel bugged out."

Shard's mono-brow arched as his head jerked back. "What? How many? Is it just a patrol?"

Gample pointed into the field of plants. "Here's the runner now." He turned. "Hey! This way!"

A goblin pushed his way through. "This shit goes on forever!" He looked around at the little clearing and popped to attention when he saw Shard. "The citadel's on the move, sir." He punched a salute. "Seven eights and a little more." He held up two fingers. "This many more." He was panting and wiped the sweat from his face with his other hand.

Shard's mono-brow flatlined as he tried to remember how many seven eights was. He recalled it was a platoon size. "What did they consist of? Was there a banner?"

The Goblin nodded, still catching his breath. "Humans, mostly. Bunch of Elves and this many Dwarves." He held up eight fingers. "There was this many horses." He held up two fingers. "This many mages." Two fingers. "And a banner." He thought. "There was a cart and some mules. I didn't count them. There was a contraption in the cart with some Gnomes with it. I didn't count the Gnomes."

Shard blinked. Bark-Bite had tossed a bunch of numbers at him, but Shard could only understand that the citadel would have little more than a platoon and if the Goblin was right, then they had just marched out of the citadel leaving a small rear guard.

Slowly, Shard climbed off the whimpering Momoo, his mono-brow was in a slow wave of confusion. "How far?"

The Goblin tilted his head as he thought. "I got a few minutes run on 'em. They wasn't moving too fast on account of the Dwarves."

Shard nodded slowly. "Find the Sergeant Major and tell him. Then tell all the thugs to take clumps of dirt and rub it all over themselves." Shard picked up a clod of the manure rich soil. "It'll mask our scent. We'll need to be real quiet when they go by," he spoke slowly, quietly, taking in both Goblins. "Tell the pickets to keep themselves hidden. We're gonna let them just walk by." Shard looked up at Gample an then Seven-Eights, searching their eyes. "Understand?" When the two thugs nodded, Shard tilted his head. "Go. Spread the word. Hurry."

They saluted and vanished into the green.

Shard sat back on his heels as Momoo picked himself up. "Un-fucking-real," Shard said distantly. "It fucking worked."

Momoo was holding his head. "Oh, no! This is awful!"

Shard shook his head, staring at his drawing in the dirt. "But how? How did it work?"

Checking for where he was bleeding, Momoo pleaded. "I'm done for."

"Shut up!" Shard hissed at him. "You're going to be fine, ya baby."

Momoo looked at Shard, his eyes wild and desperate. "Shard, this is worse than death! My reputation!"

"What the fuck are you talking about?"

Momoo's hands clutched the air before him, his face warped in horror. "The plan? It worked! Do you know what this means?"

Shard shook his head. "What?"

Momoo leaned close, his mouth agape. "THE SHEEP TALKED!"

Shard punched him in the chest. "Shut the fuck up, you flaming idiot!"

Momoo winced from the punch, but went on. "Shard, don't you understand? There are sheep who know things about me," he whispered. "Intimate things."

Shard was looking at his dirt sketch. He rubbed his chin, mumbling to himself. "They wouldn't just up and abandon the post. It's not a raiding party, not with Dwarves." Shard scratched. "There would be more carts if the unit was being relieved."

"I should have killed them," Momoo said. "Turned the carcass over to the mess." Momoo buried his face in his hands. "Now there are sheep all over the country..." He looked up startled. "What are they saying about me?" He looked desperately at Shard. "How was I to know?" His gazed leveled. "Shard, I need you to kill me. Something quick though, not that death by nut kicking, okay?"

Shard looked at him, letting out a harsh sigh. "By Zcronklin's broken cock bone, Momoo, the friggin sheep didn't talk. Sheep don't fucking talk!"

Momoo eyes searched him as the light of realization slowly flickered across his face. "Of course, you're right. How stupid! Sheep don't talk." He laughed to himself, breathing relief. "It was the goat."

Shard's eyes rolled then looked away, ignoring Momoo. He looked back down at his sketch. He drew another box next to the command tent then tapped it with his finger as he thought; lines deepening in his brow.

Momoo smiled, tentatively touching the swelling lump on the back of his head. "Ow, that did hurt." He checked his fingers for blood. "And you know what?" he asked brightly. "You owe me an apology." He took out a kerchief and dabbed the spot where Shard ripped out his hair. "I didn't fuck up after all. The goat blabbed, just not as you intended." He reached over towards Shard's kit. "Let me have some of that Dwarf rum you were drinking last night."

Shard's hand was a flash as it locked on Momoo's wrist. With the other, he pointed to his sketch. "Here." He pointed to the box he drew. "This is the tent were Ribsplitter-Jones was. He had a rape in there." Shard looked up at Momoo as he released his wrist. "The Princess and I then went into the tent. The rape must have hid somewhere. She must have been hiding in there the whole time."

"And you didn't see her?"

"I couldn't see around her Highness' boobs."

Momoo thought, disappointment crawling over him. "So it wasn't the goat?"

"No, it wasn't." Shard sneered. "So no medicine for you."

Momoo's bottom lip quivered. "But I didn't fuck up. You beat me for no reason. I should at least get a couple swigs."

"You fucked up." Shard wiped his map clear with a sweep of his hand. "We lucked out. No medicine for you." He picked up a clod of dirt and crumbled it in his hand. "So you sit there and fester." He started rubbing dirt on. "And dirty up." He looked up, his eyes glinting red. "Don't make me do it for you."

Shard's Siege

HIGH ON THE narrow, winding and poorly maintained road, where the mountains pinched themselves, Old Gourd Head Citadel, a massive fortress carved from the rock of the mountain itself with lines chiseled into its façade to look like brick work, stood proud watch. Built by Dwarves, back before building permits or environmental impact statements were needed, it was originally named Au' Groureded F'trell which in Dwarven meant Fort on Hill of Heart Attacks, since many of the builders would make it to the top of the mountain, the long ass hill of no reprieve, have a heart attack and die. It had not been built for strategic reasons since at the time there wasn't any threat of invasions coming over the mountain, but for marketing reasons; it simply made darn good sense to build a fort up there. It was a space begging for a fort. Six Halflings and a sling shot could hold off a hundred-man unit with mage complement in the pass, imagine how tough a fort would be? It would be stupid not to build a fort there.

Dwarven units used to saw the handle off their toothbrushes to cut down on the weight they had to lug up the hill.

Pack animals chugged painfully up, unable to pull but the lightest of carts and equipment. The Dwarves soon gave up the fortress since it was such a pain in the ass to maintain and sold it to the Humans at a time when Humans were into a major military build-up and bought anything Dwarvish, or even sounded Dwarvish. They changed the name to Old Gourd Head because that's what it sounded like. This also turned out to be a great marketing ploy because very few soldiers would ever volunteer to go to Fort on Hill of Heart Attacks.

From its vantage point, it proved to be a most formidable bastion. The commanders bragged that its gates had never been breached, that no foe had ever scaled its haunting walls, and there was much sooth to the boast: no foe had ever bothered to climb the long ass hill to even try. The lower passes provided much easier access with flat, maintained roads and complimentary maps with marked points of interests provided by the Elves of Nor-Ster, who inherently were a collective bunch of pains in the asses, but were masters of distraction. They didn't like visitors in their fabled and legendary lands and launched a massive marketing campaign to illustrate all of the better places to go rather than their home turf and distributed the maps to anyone who passed by.

Old Gourd Head was not on their list of 'Better places than where you are now' list.

The impenetrable fortress of technological wonder and miraculous, engineering design went untested. Its most formidable features were not its high pressure hoses that spewed flaming Squick T'r at 50 yards, or the Shok Tong Strike blast which emanated a furious wave of static electricity. Nor was its terrifying, horrifying, send-the-kids-to-bed-with-nightmares, Efriam F'k-em Ghod Go Gun, a device banned by the Collective tribes of The Down Right Creepy Ngath, outlawed under penalty of death by the Council of Dark Evil Dwarves, and rated Best Buy by the Masters of the Northern Army under the class of 'When you're going to violate a treaty with an open and obvious war crime, here's the way to go about it' list. A one hundred and nine millimeter, crank-operated, belt-fed, air-cooled, crew-served, turret-mounted weapon capable of launching a hive of pissed off, queen incited, White Fang Horror Hornets at an area target of up to one hundred yards at a maximum cyclic rate of four hives a minute, each hive having an effective area of ten yards (unless used against Elves who are, of course, allergic; then twenty yards). The only weapon to be classed as a biological, terror, fauna weapon of mass destruction. These formidable, intimidating and very illegal weapons were all second to the fact that the citadel sat staunchly on the top of the perilous, winding, and unforgiving Hill of Heart Attacks.

And nobody, nobody sane at least, would march a siege force all they way up the cardiac inducing hill only to lose them all against the impregnable, unbreachable, unbreakable walls.

"And that's why, Shard," Momoo reached down and plucked a thistle, rolling it between his fingers. "we are all going to die. Worse than throwing yourselves against Dwarves. We are all going to be running around screaming with our heads on fire, our clothes clinging to everything and pissed off horror hornets chasing us until we all die, and die stupid." Momoo sniffed the dark purple flower. "That's why we do it, you know." His whole face sagged as he frowned. "That's why we Momoo's have always sent their companies against Dwarves." He darkened as the thistle twirled between his fingers. "Because a Momoo must not die stupid." He sighed. "We mustn't. Or we won't get laid." He looked up at Shard, but the Goblin was busy, laying on his belly at the crook of a large boulder, peering through the far-seer. Momoo looked back to his thistle. "Like any good thug, getting laid is imperative, but for a Momoo getting laid by a proper wench, and by proper I mean wealthy, is crucial, and to do it we need some sort of boasting right. You see, it's not victory, by Varium's triple nostril it's not, but by the thugs you command and their dedication to you. That Shard, is the gauge of an officer. How many thugs can he inspire to follow his command unto the death and what is a better way than to put them against Dwarves? Order a bunch of thugs to their death and the girls go wild. I mean, only an idiot could not get laid with that kind of backing." He bit off the thistle head and mused on its bitter taste. "Now if you send them in waves, grind up the first platoon while the other two watch, then send in the second while the third watches, then send in the third and those dumb, brave, bare ass bastards attack at full charge and get collectively hacked into pieces; if you could order that, then describe it graphically at any proper function, like a lady's bunion picking..." His eyes rolled up into his head as he happily thought. "Orgy! Oh, oh, oh!"

Shard blinked, as he took his eye from the far-seer. He scratched his chin as he thought, then rubbed his eye and re-focused the far-seer.

Momoo peered up at the Goblin captain. He then looked down at the ravine where all the thugs laid clinging to the rock face, hiding behind shrubs, and waiting for the command of attack.

Momoo sighed. "Momoo, you nutless sheep fucker," Momoo growled, "shut yer fucking pie hole before I garrote you with your flappy tongue." Momoo cringed and whined. "But surely, Shard, you don't expect me to figure this one out by myself? You're putting the Princess in danger!" Momoo sneered. "We wouldn't even fucking be here if it wasn't for your stupidity." Momoo cringed. "It's always my fault, isn't it Shard? If you ever did anything like a proper thug, proper meaning respect for your superior officer, then we would have finished this mission long ago." Momoo frowned deep-ly. "Finished meaning getting every one killed so you could get laid." Momoo pouted. "You and your clever plans, haul-ing us all up this damned hill so we can die stupid. At least attacking Dwarves does not first involve trudging up the bloody Hill of Heart Attacks. How you talked the Princess into this suicide mission is beyond me." Momoo looked up at Shard who only squinted through the far-seer and scratched himself. Momoo nudged him. "This is the part where you explain everything to me."

Shard didn't look away. "This is the part where I call you an assbag and you shut the fuck up. Assbag."

"Humph." Momoo mumbled and scrambled higher up the ridge to peer over the crag. Shard reached over and pushed him back down. "Shard!" Momoo hissed angrily.

Shard sighed tiredly. "Alright, sheep fucker, I'll explain this one time." He motioned with his head. "Come up here and take a look down there."

Momoo smiled like a thug on Red Meat Day as he slithered up the crag and propped up on his elbows. He peered down the narrow trail at the haunting, black rooks towering over the stone cobble path. Two tiny figures, swathed in dirty bed linen, trudged their way along the poorly maintained road. One was a crippled hunchback; the other was dragging a lame leg.

Shard handed him the far-seer. "Look down there. We can't ram those gates, not with that fucked up road. The doors are Dark Elven Iron Wood with Dwarven steel reinforcement brackets. Impenetrable. So, the only way in is to make them open the door. The Princess and Tech Lieutenant Mobly are pretending to be pilgrims on a sojourn to the legendary ancient mountain temple."

Momoo looked back. "What mountain temple?"

Shard shrugged. "There's always a monk's hideout in some stupid inaccessible place. It doesn't have to exist, hence the term 'legendary'."

Momoo nodded. "And when they notice the pilgrims are Goblins?"

Shard smiled. "They won't. The Princess will keep her hood down and tell them they have Hole in the Head Disease and are en route for healing from the mountain monks. The Humans won't look."

Momoo made a face. "Ugh, why Hole in the Head?"

"Because it's hideous and non-contagious. That's why the Humans won't look."

Momoo nodded peering down at the road. The guards were standing at the giant doors, watching the two shrouded figures approach. "Okay, what happens once they're in?"

"The Princess walks ahead, while Mobly stumbles on his crutch right in the doorway. He lights a fast burn fuse under his robes and moans 'Oh, I've hurt my ankle!' That's the Princess' cue to take cover. Five beats later, Ba-Boom! We charge the blown up gates, kill everybody and take the pass."

Momoo squinted through the far-seer. "Your most brilliant plan to date," he said approvingly, watching the shrouded Princess engage with the guard. "She's at the gate now."

Through the blurry, trembling glass, Momoo watched the guard recoiling in disgust, his hand going to his face, shielding himself, his other hand, shooing her away. The Princess insisted, but he pointed back down the mountain angrily, waving her off; that failing, he pushed her.

Shard squinted. "What's happening? Has Mobly stumbled yet?"

Momoo pursed his lips. "No, but their disguises are working."

Shard nudged him. "Let me see." Shard took the brass and glass Gnome *machina* and peered through its tiny hole, down its long, dark tunnel, a smearing view coming into focus.

The Princess had flung off her robe, her gleaming brass cups sparking in the sun, her globes of wonder, spilling over, had the guard's eyes riveted, growing just as big and oblivious to the fact that she was raising her foot to kick him in the head.

"Shit!" Shard screamed. "By Mother Hammerwhipple's gas-powered vibrator!" Shard looked down to Momoo. "Plan's gone to shit! Get everyone for a full assault! Attack!"

Momoo looked up startled. "Attack what?"

Shard kicked him. "The bloody gates, ya sheep fucker!" Shard turned as he rose, peering down the scope, watching the guard stumbling into Mobly, the Tech Lieutenant holding him up as the Princess spun around, swinging her crutch with both hands at the second guard.

Shard bellowed over his shoulder. "Now! While they are distracted!" He turned to see Momoo arguing with Gample.

"Yes, you doof!" Momoo bellowed. "Attack the gates!"

"Attack!" Shard's scream ripped a harsh echo through the pass as he drew his man-sword and held it aloft. "By Onestro's lethal hernia! Attack!"

"Attack the gates!" Gample repeated the order as he scrambled from his hiding place.

"Attack the gates!" Everyone shouted, rising from the scrub.

Shard turned, and pointing his sword like a lance, barreled down into the pass. Glancing up at the walls, he saw they were un-manned; no warning horns had sounded. He fought the urge to smile as the reckless thought of success flashed across his mind. Up ahead, Tech Lieutenant Mobly struggled with one guard to stop him from shutting the heavy doors while the Princess drew her new steel sword and began her attack, hacking brutally as the guard desperately tried to defend himself.

Shard felt his heart race as his feet pounded on the uneven trail. This was going to work! He was going to add Old Gourd Head to his collection of victories and his captaincy would be assured! He could hear the thunder of his company running after him shouting their war cry: *"We're counterattacking! We're counterattacking!"*

The Human guard reared back and head butted Mobly, stunning the Goblin and dropping him to his knees. The guard then turned and leapt onto the Princess' back, grappling with her. A third Human guard appeared, wandering out of the guard shack wearing only his britches and a look of bewilderment.

His eyes grew wide as plates at the image of a whole world of Goblins running down at him.

Gawking, he stood there. In the entire time he was stationed at Old Gourd Head, no one had ever sounded an alarm, ordered General Quarters, or even held a fire drill. Now, as the attack that everyone was sure would never come had arrived, he had no idea what he should be doing.

Shard poured on the speed.

Tech Lieutenant Mobly flung back his robes exposing the giant bomb strapped to his back, the tiny fuse in the bung hole spewing a stream of smoke, just as the half-dressed guard decided he should close the doors.

"Oh! I've hurt my ankle!" Mobly screamed as he stuck his fingers in his ears. More guards scrambled out of the guard shack and wrestled Princess Hiroki to the ground, dog piling the ferocious Princess.

Shard ran faster as the doors began to close. Stone chipped and splintered as Elvish arrows rained down on him, but he ignored them as he focused on the narrowing gap of the doors, Mobly trying to stick his foot in the way, sparks spewing from his bomb. Human hands were grappling with him, pulling him back into the citadel, prying his fat Goblin fingers from the door.

Shard suddenly reared back, his feet skidding and ripping open on the rocky surface, desperately trying to change direction as the idea that he was running full tilt towards a lit casket of Black Dirt That Blows Stuff Up, came to his mind.

Shard turned, his feet thumping away from the gates and into the rushing wall of the Black Dragon Company. Shard felt his lungs collapse as he crashed badly into the oncoming shield wall. The world spun quickly into darkness, but Shard dismissed it with an angry will. He looked around only to find the tide of Goblins was carrying him back to the doors, the open gap turning to a slit, Mobly's desperate face, his eyes bloodshot, bulging.

Shard had yet to recover his breath when he was smashed into the heavy, black, oaken doors, then held there by the rushing tide of thugs.

Mobly finally exploded.

To Shard and the Black Dragon company, there was only a sudden whoosh of air and a slight rattle of the door.

Shard looked around curiously, amazed that the doors had held. He lifted his feet up against the door and pushed the thugs pinning him back so he could breathe. All around him, thugs were hacking at the door, their steel sparking against the hard, hard wood. He could see Gunnery Sergeant Glenkar pointing up at the citadel, directing the fire for the Trolls to hurl their rocks. While that was helpful, it was only a matter of moments before they would all crackle with static, burn with Squick T'r and swell up with hornet stings. "Retreat," Shard whimpered, still gasping desperately. He tried to shout to Ribsplitter-Jones, but couldn't even hear himself.

The sky flashed polar white as the static machine warmed up.

Shard kicked a thug in the gut, doubling him over, then climbed up on his back to get enough height to see over the ruckus. He peered into the mass until he spotted First Sergeant Shiro. "Retreat!"

Shiro began bellowing the order, causing Ribsplitter-Jones to look from his task. "But we just fugging got heres." He shrugged as he drew breath. "Re-frigging-treat!" the Sergeant Major shouted.

Shard felt the wave pull back as the thugs began to change direction. He climbed off his thug, grabbed him by the belt and desperately pulled him along. Above, gouts of flame vomited from the tower walls and Shard could feel intense heat on his exposed cheeks. Shard pulled the thug around and pushed him ahead, just as hornet's nests began raining down.

Shard gritted his teeth as ice began to fill his spirit. He had failed to take Old Gourd Head, killed the Princess and was about to lose his company to a stupid, painful, fiery, electric, stinging death; un-laid. His only hope was to find Momoo and kill him so as not to arrive at Dru's empty handed.

Suddenly, a huge hornet nest crashed ahead of him, breaking open and sending a thick cloud of fat, black and green Horror Hornets into the air. Shard slashed with his sword, hoping to disburse them, kill some, at least die fighting. He continued his run, squinting, swinging, his teeth locked, a growl of anger at himself for failing utterly escaping his lips, as he ran into the cloud of hornets.

He grunted as a dull thud of a nest struck him in the back, between the shoulder blades, and sent him crashing hard to the ground face first. Stars exploded painfully across his vision as his sword clattered away from his stunned hand.

Shard moaned as the world swam beneath him. Slowly he opened his eyes, shaking the fog from his brain and trying to clear his vision. Furry hornets, green and black checkerboard patterns across their fat bellies, surrounded him, laying supine, their sharp, poisonous talons reaching skyward.

Dead.

Shard dismissed his first thought, which was that he had killed them all with his flashing sword. He then dismissed that they had been stunned on impact and would at any second wake up and sting the crap out him because some had broken wings and legs, and even bodies. Shard peered into the cracked open carapaces. They were dried out, their guts turned to dust. The hornets had been dead for a long time.

Shard got to his feet, looking around. Millions of dead hornets littered the walkway. Shard turned back to the citadel. Fire was spewing urgently into the sky. The Human operators, with their heads aflame, ran back and forth along the length of the wall carrying buckets of water to the flaming Squick T'r thrower and dousing it down, hoping to put it out, but only spreading the flaming Squick T'r all over the place.

Lighting flashed from the main rook and a Human was flung into the sky, arms and legs wind-milling and when he fell, he simply stuck to the outside wall as if it were coated with glue. He grunted, trying to push himself off the wall and slowly he peeled himself free only to flop back at a really awkward position and stay there.

So many years, Old Gourd Head went untested. The hornets inter-bred, became genetically defected, and eventually died off. The gaskets from the Squick T'r thrower dried out and rotted so when ignited, it splashed flaming Squick T'r everywhere but forward. The static electricity machine was a victim of Gnome cannibals. A transistor borrowed, the spare capacitor needed, a few yards of copper wire absconded, nothing ever returned as promised.

Shard scanned along the wall. The few Elven defend-ers that had been left behind were either killed by Rawque Chuquers or set on fire when the flaming Humans running along the wall bumped into them.

Shard turned to his troops hiding in the scrub. "I need this many Tech Lieutenants." He shouted, holding up four fingers. There was a murmur about the bushes, and after a minute, five Tech Lieutenants, their armor painfully bright in the direct sun, made their way up. Shard nodded and waved them to follow him to the front gate. "Hurry!" He ordered, trotting back to the huge oaken doors. "Here! Set your charges, we'll blow the doors!"

The Tech Lieutenants nodded urgently. Slack jawed and nervous, they huddled together with flint and steel and sparked their torches to flame, then reached back and touched the fuses to their bombs.

They closed their eyes tightly and stuck their fingers in their ears.

Shard shook his head. "No, you fuck wits!" He grabbed one and pulled his finger out of his ear so the thug could hear him. "Take the bomb off your back! Then, take cover with me and hurry!"

They nodded and quickly began to un-shoulder their bombs. Shard turned and hustled up to the ridge to take cover. He could hear the footfalls of the lieutenants behind him. Heavy footfalls.

Shard stopped sharply and spun around to see five Tech Lieutenants carrying their bombs in their arms. "You're fucking kidding me!" Shard screamed. "Stop! Leave the bombs!"

They stopped dead in their tracks and set them down, then watched the fuses burn.

Shard hit himself in the helmet with his hand. "No! Put the bombs back! We are blowing the doors!"

"But you said..."

Shard's mono-brow bristled as the fuses burned lower. "Don't fucking argue! Put the bombs in front of the doors, leave them there, then run up here without the frigging bombs." Shard pointed at the door. "Now, fucking go!" They nodded, picking up their bombs and lumbering back to the gates.

Something whipped past Shard's ear. He looked up and saw troops gathering at the walls. Ignoring the smoke and fire, they were lining up and throwing rocks, broken plumbing, and casks of nails that exploded on the walkway, sending iron pieces all over the place. Shard un-shouldered his buckler in time to deflect a porcelain tea kettle. At the doors, the five Tech Lieutenants stood, watching their fuses.

Shard blocked a copper gravy boat. "Leave the bombs there and come here!"

Their black pearl eyes shifted down, saddening, nodding slowly at their orders. One looked up. "I'm sorry, sir, when you say leave the bombs, you mean, leave them?" he shouted.

Shard waved his arms furiously. "Yes! Fuck nuts, leave the bombs!" The Tech Lieutenants looked at each other despondently, hesitating. "I'll get you all new bombs!" Shard shouted, ducking an angry, fluttering chicken. "Bigger bombs!"

They smiled, nodded and turned to catch up with Shard.

Thunder cracked as the kegs exploded, knocking Shard down with its furious force. Dust and smoke flooded the pass and bits of shiny, Goblin armor rained down, tinkling on the rocky, uneven road. Shard shook his head as he stumbled to his feet. He felt his eyes tear from the thick, oily smoke as he squinted trying to see, brushing rocks, debris and Goblin bits from his pauldrons. He had to regain momentum in the attack. They had wasted too much time and what chance of the Princess still being alive was quickly running out.

"Attack!" he bellowed, choking on the smoke. He thrust his sword into the air and charged, listening to the thugs behind him, shouting their battle cry. Shard plunged into the cloud at a full run.

Shard felt his teeth rattle violently as he smashed into the heavy oaken doors.

Blinking, bleary-eyed, he looked around trying to see if this was yet another set of doors. He sheathed his sword and touched the dark wood. It was hot, and the blast peeled back several layers of varnish, but the doors themselves were unscathed.

Shard waved away smoke as he tried to think. There were no trees to make a battering ram, and if his thugs tried chopping their way through, he could resume his attack in a week or so. And speaking of thugs, he was five seconds away from them trampling him in their charge.

Shard bellowed and kicked the door, neatly breaking his toe.

From within the citadel, Shard could hear the locks of the door click open, one at a time and the thick bar being moved. Shard stepped back as the door slowly pushed open. He grabbed its edge quickly and pulled hard desperately, panic tinting his vision as he threw his head back and heaved it open, then leapt aside.

Three hundred thugs in a frantic avalanche stormed by, howling triumphantly. Shard bellowed after them. "Kill! Go! Kill! But no burning! Don't burn anything! Ya hear! And find the Princess!" Shard watched them rush by, then drew his sword. He wanted desperately to kill something, anything, but it wasn't likely to happen.

Momoo casually stepped over. "This was your plan all along?"

Shard re-gripped his sword, his eyes hot and red.

"A bloody mass of confusion," Momoo snorted. "How did you open the door? And where is the Princess?" Momoo looked at him. "Just as I was starting to think you were some sort of genius," Momoo shook his head. "Well, your lucky streak has run out. At least we won't have to worry about the Emperor killing us. I think the hard part will be to decide exactly where we should all fall on our swords in disgrace."

Shard limped closer.

"I knew it was a bad idea to send the Princess into danger," Momoo went on. "Bad, bad, bad. But it's Shard's masterwork plan, surely it'll come out all right." He shook his head sadly, looking down at the human remains killed in Mobly's blast. "You will do the right thing and take the blame for this fiasco, right?" He nudged something with his toe, making a face as he did. "I distinctly told you not to do this. I said, I don't know how many times, not to waste time and risk the whole mission trying to take this obscure and obsolete military post, but you had to have your glory." He sighed, slumping on himself. "No matter, Shard. No one will remember your name. They'll all remember how a Momoo killed his Majesty's favorite daughter, the gem of his eye." He looked up at Shard, his face filling with pallor. "What are you doing?"

Shard stalked closer, raising his steel sword. "Helping you fall on your sword, ya dickless gerbil!"

Momoo trembled, his eyes growing with fear, then suddenly joy. "Look! It's the Princess! She's all right!"

Shard grit his teeth. "By Longhee's weeping butt sores, Momoo, I didn't fall for that before, what makes you think I'm gonna fall for it now? I'm only trying to decide whether to gut ya or brain ya. I think if I gut ya it'll last longer."

Momoo pointed frantically. "No, really! Look, it's her!"

Shard smiled, evilly. "Good for you. Let her beauty be the last thing you see." Shard drew his sword back, ready to thrust as Momoo shielded his eyes, choosing not to watch.

"Don't you kill him!" the Princess shouted.

Shard felt her voice like an icicle between his shoulder blades and spun around. Princess Hiroki was walking over, stumbling as she picked her way through debris. Her left breast-cup was missing, her modesty protected by a helmet she found and suctioned into place. Black blood trickled from a gash on her shoulder. "Leave him alone," she commanded. "Not until I've had a chance to harvest his nuts can you touch him."

Shard stammered. "Your Highness! You're alive!"

She tilted her head towards him. "What's that you say?" She looked around. "Ugh, will whoever is ringing that bell please stop?"

Shard wanted to hug her, but remembered his place. He sheathed his sword. "But the explosion?"

"Butter is blow John?" she repeated, confused. "What are you babbling about? Did you take a shot to the helm?" She then looked up at the thugs running on the walk above. "Stop with the bells!" she shouted, looking for the culprit. Not seeing him, she shrugged, stuck her finger in her ear and wriggled it about. "So anyway. The Humans seemed to think Hole in the Head disease was contagious and wouldn't let us in. I might have lost it in the translation. Anyway, that lowly Human puke dared call me a wretched creature. The insolent dog ate my sandal leather." She nodded, her soft lips in a hard sneer as she peered at the bottom of her sandal. "Look, see? Right there! Incisors. I bet that hurt." She put her foot down. "Then they jumped me. Their unworthy hands were groping and pawing and squeezing my breasts and ass like animals." She rubbed her offended derriere. "It's nice that there are some people that can appreciate a fine ass like mine." She hiked up her hip, trying to look back at her bum. "It's overlooked sometimes. Can you imagine that?" She pouted, looking up at her two transfixed captains and four thugs who stopped in mid-loot. Hiroki smiled, then frowned. "Then that idiot Mobly went and blew himself up! Just as things were getting interesting." She let out a hissing breath. "All those dirty, smelly Humans, rubbing, caressing my royal skin." She shuddered. "I could've handled them." She muttered.

Momoo clamped a hand on Shard's shoulder. "Well, looks like your blasted luck held up. She was protected from the blast by all the Humans coping a feel." He threw his head back and laughed.

Shard spun around and kneed him in the groin.

Momoo yelped and doubled over. "And I bit my tongue," he groaned.

The Princess barked. "Hey, I told you I want those nuts!"

Shard bowed slightly. "Just tenderizing them for you, your Highness." He spoke loudly to make sure she heard him.

She smiled. "Now that's sweet. Now go find someplace you can rape me. And make sure no one sets it on fire this time. The ambient lighting is nice, but the fumes gave me a headache." She wriggled her finger in her ear again. "Oh, and find the moron ringing that bell and put him to death, please."

Shard bowed. "As you wish." He turned and limped his way deeper into the citadel.

Ribsplitter-Jones was standing in the middle of things, bellowing at everyone. "Bloody 'el, ya miscreants! E'rats! Don't forget yerselves! Stick together! Roust 'em outta there!" He turned, looked down at Shard and saluted. "E'rats looking good so far. No real resistance coming in. Some of the thugs got a little of the lust going and fell on each other when there weren't enough Humans to go around. We did find a group holdin' up in the chow hall." He smiled. "So we puts 'em on the menu."

Shard nodded. "Have you found the Human commander yet?"

The Sergeant Major shrugged. "Eyah, the fugging coward's probably holdin' up in that round house theres." He motioned towards a massive two-story stone blockade tucked back beneath the mountain outcropping. It looked much older than the rest of the citadel. Shard presumed it must have been part of an earlier construction. It had only a few arrow slits for windows and one heavy, dark wood door. "Permission to blow it, sah?" the Sergeant Major asked.

Shard shook his head looking at the indestructible door. "I don't think we have any Tech Lieutenants left. Put guards around it. Secure the rest of the citadel and then we'll figure what to do with it." Shard eyed the foreboding roundhouse, its thick walls and narrow windows, then spat at it. "Fucking Dwarves."

"E'rats the truth it is." The Sergeant Major agreed. "Only those fuggers would put a fuggin fort inside of a fuggin fort." He squinted and peered at the second story. "E'wot? Looks like the fugger's up there."

Shard had seen the flash of a dark green, mud-splattered cloak move past the thin window. He shook his head. "Why would he be covered with mud?" Shard stepped closer. "Bark-Bite! Are you up there?"

Bark-Bite peered down through the window and Shard could see half of the Major's face. "Shard?" He shifted and peered down with his other eye. "Oh, you've made it. Come in, there is something you should see."

Shard limped over to the door. He pulled up the latch and the door swung open easily. He looked back at his Sergeant Major. "Still want to blow it?" he asked sardonically.

Ribsplitter-Jones gave a half shrug. "E'ya, just to be sures."

Shard growled. "Wait here." He stepped into the dark room just as Bark-Bite made his way down the spiral stairs. A Murder Splatter Red carpet with Stolen Gold edging, greeted Shard at the doorway. By its weave, Shard could see it was an old carpet, and the Dwarves with their harsh boots had disrespected it and tromped on it for centuries. Sunlight spilling lines of white fell from the narrow windows. Candle wax was splattered in the corner. Gruel or soup stained the other corner. There was a copper spittoon, green from age, sitting in the center of the rug to catch an incessant drip from the ceiling. The incessant drip missed. There was a marsh of roof strained water pooled in the center of the carpet, beside the pot.

The Human commander lay dead beside the copper pot, his helmet and sword beside him. A Lil' Elfie blow put a part in his hair and split him open and flies were already feasting on the soft, squishy bits inside. Whatever bled out of him, vanished into the rich color of the carpet. All those years of abuse, it was still a horrific red.

Bark-Bite grabbed Shard's arm, pulling his attention. "This way!" he whispered urgently, moving quickly and lithely down the last steps and across the room. "It's in the basement."

Shard gave a last look at the well made carpet, then down the dark stair. "How did you get in here before us?" Shard asked, following down the narrow passageway. Tiny stones jutted out from the wall, forming crude steps vanishing into deeper shadows. Shard peered into the darkness, feeling the cold which seemed to rise from the pit, trying hard to follow the Major who seemed unabated by the dim, moving further and further away from the daylight above. While a Goblin could navigate easily on the darkest of nights, he still needed some ambient light, even the faintest of starlight, to see.

The basement of Old Gourd Head was a dark, cold tomb.

Shard couldn't even hear the footfalls of the Major moving further ahead. He could make out the cubbyholes dug out of the stone and the ash grey bones of the dead, shelved and neatly filed away for eternity. As they made their way deeper, the shelves grew shorter as the dead seemed to shrink from Human to Dwarf.

"Bloody slow down!" Shard called into the darkness. "I can barely see my hand in front of my face! Where are you going?"

"Move your hand out from in front of your face and you'll see better," the Major whispered back. "We're following these fresh footprints."

Shard couldn't see his feet in the inky darkness and his broken toe was throbbing painfully, swelling and probably changing color. Survile, more than likely.

"Right here," Bark-Bite suddenly said. Shard walked into him. "You're having a little difficulty in the dark, aren't you? You should eat more Gysin Berries."

Shard could no longer make out anything. "Hold on, I got a candle in my satchel." Shard reached in with one hand, while finding his flint and steel in his other pouch.

Bark-Bite seized both his wrists. "Please don't."

Shard sighed, exacerbated. "Begging the Major's pardon, sir, but it's frigging dark!"

Bark-Bite leaned close and Shard could smell the nasty, mentholated tobacco he chewed. "Shard, your tactical awareness is immeasurable," he whispered. "I imagine it would have taken Momoo three tries to guess that it's dark. They want it dark down here for a reason. A horrible reason. Shard, we may be fucked, we as in every thug one of us, fucked." Shard tried to pull back, but the Major held firm. "I am speaking of Kamehameha fucked." The Major pulled Shard's hand forward. "Shard, I need to share this with you, but you must keep this an *oath secret*. Swear it!"

Shard jerked his hand back as if he'd been burned. "I am not putting my hand in your pants!" Shard's voice was harshly loud in the dark crypt.

"What are you talking about, Shard?" The Major stopped whispering.

Shard shook his head quickly, violently, disbursing the ghosts of his childhood at the orphanage and the headmaster on a warm Sabbath day when he was held back in class for *special* tutoring. "Uh, nothing, sir. Forget it," Shard mumbled, heat rising from his cheeks.

Bark-Bite put his palm to the side of his head and pushed against it, popping his neck with a crisp, quick staccato. "Hand in my pants?" the Major scoffed. "I haven't bathed since the occupation of Ghan-Sun by the Drunken Hornac Monks. It's a little bit of a protest, you know." He sighed. "I wouldn't shove my hand in my pants either and let me tell you I've needed a good scratch for six years now. You know the kind: the sinful 'eyes rolling up into your head almost like sex' scratch." He shivered, then calmed again. "I'm sorry, remind me why we're talking about scratching in a dark tomb?"

"The Kamehameha fuck," Shard said.

"Oh, right, right, right." He leaned close to Shard, whispering in his ear. "Shard, we may be fucked, as in every thug one of us fucked."

"We covered that part."

"Oh, so sorry." Bark-Bite took his hand. "Did you swear secrecy yet?"

Shard nodded, hoping to speed things up. "Yeah, sure, whatever." He could hear wood scraping against wood and the foul stench of rotting eggs filled the still air. Bark-Bite pulled Shard's hand forward, and then pushed it down.

Dirt. Dry, gritty dirt.

It poured liked coarse sand, clumps breaking up easily. It felt light in his hand. "Kamehameha fucked," Shard mumbled.

"Yes!" Bark-Bite's was a harsh, forced whisper.

"Sir?" Shard paced his words carefully. "It's dirt. You have found a bucket of dirt."

"Yes!" His voice echoed in the crypt.

Since meeting the Major, Shard was torn between respecting a superior officer, discovering a potential mentor, or skiving another incompetent boob in the back. It was at this particular second that Shard struggled anew with his dilemma. Shard could feel his foot throb in pulse with his quickening heart.

"You're not getting it, are you?" Bark-Bite asked.

"Nope."

"Smell it."

Shard sniffed his hand. "Stinks."

"Mmmmm," Bark-Bite hummed. "Now, Shard. Put it together. There is a reason I brought you down here. There are very few smart thugs in his Majesty's army. You're smart, yes you are, but don't know it yet, no you don't. I have to work that brain of yours, Shard." Bark-Bite nudged his arm. "Figure it out."

Shard sniffed the dirt again. He'd smelled it before. He wished he could take a look at it, but it was dark and Bark-Bite wouldn't allow him a light.

Shard felt the air in his lungs still.

"Yes..." Bark-Bite whispered. "Very simple now, isn't it? Most things are if you take a moment to put them together."

In the history of time, the Dwarves were the first to smith metal and never letting go of that title, mastered it, and wrought magic into metal to create Mithral which they sold by contract exclusively to the Elves. Dwarves mastered weapons and armor, shaping their battle prowess on being indestructible and wielding really sharp things.

Elves are flighty, unpredictable and cowardly, preferring to fight from afar than risk their delicate looks. They were the first to discover and master archery. Every Elven child learned to shoot a bow; their individualized, handcrafted weapon issued as they descended the birth canal. Their accuracy was unerring, raining deadly shafts from the sky.

Gnomes are smart. Punch them all in the face, annoyingly stupid smart. Hyper, too. Annoyingly, too much caffeine might make them explode, hyper. They could build a widget for all occasions; from torches that burn underwater to enormous bladed contraptions of glistening brass and dark wood, puffing steam and black coal smoke that could cut down a battalion of thugs like overripe wheat.

Hobbits are affable, and cute. Real cute. They were lightning fast with a belly-rolling joke and always ready with an engrossing story. Every Hobbit, *every* Hobbit, carried a small valise that contained the rarest, most delectable spices, and they were fast to pop it out and fry up something exquisite, or boil something mouth-watering. A Hobbit could roll a turd in sugar and serve it on a toothpick and everyone would wait in line for seconds. No one on the planet could say a bad word about a Hobbit until, of course, with great intent and effort, they pissed one off. Hobbits were useless in battle, incapable of standing in ranks, unless pissed; and then, once angered, unstoppable. Historically speaking, it had been done before. A legendary event, really, that could have been solved with the quick purchase of an ale; for what Hobbit could remain slighted over a pint? None! But the unrepented slight of a Hobbit is a misgiving that invokes that dark, forgotten Hobbit tenacity. Like an angry badger, they are unyielding! Unrelenting and unwavering, they know not the meaning of surrender, regardless of how many times you show it to them in a dictionary. And because they are all related, there is no such thing as a Hobbit orphan, to piss one off was to piss them all off. To somehow cross that line is tough, but once crossed, your new battle cry becomes: 'Oh, have I erred?'

Humans are crafty, clever like a fox with far-reaching imaginations that can think outside of their race. They were the first to concorporate Dwarves and Elves, who really don't like each other, to battle against a common enemy. Humans can build unshakable alliances, make oaths that would sucker anyone no matter how many times they screwed them before. They are strong; not as strong as Dwarves, but strong. They are agile; not as agile as Elves, but agile. They are smart; not as smart as Gnomes, but smart. They are steadfast; not as steadfast as Hobbits, but steadfast. They are wholly unremarkable save for their thrice-damned, glad-to-meet you, smile.

Goblins are stupid. Goblins are ugly. Goblins only fight when they think they can win, which is most of the time on account of how stupid they are. Save for carpets and textiles they are unskilled; forging iron swords that snap with a killing blow and armor that is good only against rabid turtles, which are surprisingly common, but useless in a real fight. They only have numbers on their side; vast, uncountable numbers, turning landscapes into black, seething, chanting masses, driven murderous by their ghostly, spooky drums, their eyes glowing red with rage, thinking nothing of sending divisions and regiments into slaughter to simply prove that they could.

It was an old Elven adage: *to kill a hundred billion goblins means you only have nine hundred trillion to go.* As if there was a Goblin that could count that high.

The Goblins have one advantage, slim as it may be, above all the races; one trump card to play that could strike disheartening fear into even the most cheesed off Hobbit ranks. The Black Dirt That Blows Stuff Up. No one could say how they got it, what Goblin thought of it, or more likely, what drunken Gnome gave up his discovery without a proper patent, but the Goblins had the technology and they clung to it tightly. It was the secret of secrets, and only when some pumped, berserking thug, adorned with good, shiny armor, with a keg of Black Dirt that Blows Stuff Up strapped to his back with a smoldering, sparkling fuse burning, suddenly rushed the line, did anyone else know of its existence. At that moment, when the thug lunged from his shield wall, tongue lolling from its grinning maw, giddy with mad glee to finally fulfill God Emperor Spinecrack's prime directive, running hell bent at formations, regardless of the intimidating walls of shields, bristling spears, swords, and lances, unafraid, it was too late for the Humans and Dwarves and Elves and Hobbits and Gnomes to do anything except watch themselves blow up.

Shard felt his mouth dry, his voice cracking as he spoke. "They stole it from somewhere."

"Hardly," Bark-Bite said sadly. "I know my Black Dirt. This is a consistent grind. Better than anything we've ever produced." He sniffed. "I can't place the composition, but it is fresh."

"Alright then!" Shard brightened. "We just took out their factory!"

"Hmmm, doubt that." Bark-Bite sounded tired as he pushed past Shard, making his way out. "You'd smell a factory for leagues. Besides, who'd want to haul supplies up this bloody, murderous hill?"

Shard followed, longing for sunlight again. "Well, big frigging deal!"

Bark-Bite stopped, turning back. "End of the world as we know it isn't a big deal to you?"

Shard pushed past him feeling for the stairs. "Only a thug has the nads required to strap on a big frigging bomb."

"That is true," Bark-Bite followed, "but a Gnome could invent something to make delivering the Black Dirt via Tech Lieutenant obsolete."

Shard stumbled as he found the stairs, but made his way quickly up, limping. "Well, we got their stash, now. Don't we?"

"Perhaps," Bark-Bite stumbled on the same step. "I hope that was their whole stash, but I doubt it is. They were making their way along a secret path, that's the only reason to come up this cursed mountain trail."

Shard focused on the light falling from the doorway above. "Yeah, whatever. It's ours now. This changes nothing. We are still getting the Princess home." A silhouette appeared in the doorway peering down into the gloom. "And here she is now," he whispered.

"Shard?" She called down. "What are you doing down there and who are you talking too?"

Shard made it up to the top floor, resisting the urge to grab the Princess' boob for a hand hold. "Ah, Bark-Bite had some junk in the cellar he wanted to show me."

Princess Hiroki peered down into the darkness. "Where is that little creep?"

Shard looked back. There were only stairs leading back down into oblivion, back down to a horrible secret. "He, uh, went back down to desecrate a corpse." Shard felt for a fleeting instant he had imagined the whole thing.

The Princess frowned. "That's not like him to pass up a chance to leer at me." She tapped her sandal. "Remind me to slap him upside the head next time I see him. What could be so important in some dumb Dwarven tomb?"

"Nothing, your Highness," Shard said quietly, looking down.

Shard's Loot

TINY, DELICATE LINES of white frost etched the thick, uneven panes of glass, casting branches of mist across the blurry image of the opulent moon. Shard watched as the pudgy god of night slowly rolled across the blue velvet sky. His naked body glowed with an eerie light, his muscles lined sharply in its distinct shadow. The Princess' mane of jet hair spilled like wet tar across the river stones of his stomach, her head nestled against his chest. Her breasts were pressed up against him like pillows. He could hear his thugs roving around in the citadel below. Murmuring, suddenly bursting in laughter, then hunkering down into quiet again, mindful of Shard's orders: keep quiet, move whatever loot from the lower holds, grab what weapons and armor there was from the foundries, and get ready to move again.

Goblins not assigned to a detail sat wrapped in cloaks, hunkered below the walls and rolling yellow elf bone dice to amuse themselves on watch. They had been ordered to stay low, in case of returning Human patrols. They had amassed all the heavy, dropable stuff they could find and piled them at the bottom of the stairs. A huge kettle of oil was simmering on the south rampart, wafting heavy steam into the cold air. Several thugs stood around the boiling cauldron, frying up bits of meat and soft dough and burning themselves as they tried to eat it while it was still too hot. At the base of the cauldron was a network of gutters. When the cauldron was tipped, a river of scalding oil filled the gutters and a hot, golden shower then rained on invaders. It was part of the original citadel design, but it had been abandoned in favor of the more complicated flamethrower apparatus.

From the outside, nothing appeared amiss, save but one Human, shivering, whimpering, stuck to the outer wall by static charge. He had surrendered countless times and the thugs, unable to figure out a way to peel him off, only laughed and teased him until they bored of that game. They ignored him for a while until his incessant surrendering became annoying and they pelted him with manure until he shut up.

Bark-Bite interrogated him. He wasn't forthcoming with information until the sun set and the brisk mountain air settled in the pass. Bark-Bite offered him a bit of hot broth lowered down in a bucket. Bark-Bite also dropped down a blanket which, the moment it touched his charged body, clung to him instantly. Grateful, he talked. He went on until Bark-Bite was certain he knew nothing interesting, and then left him.

Smiley, sweating in the cool air, sat in the open sedan, watching as the thugs loaded the loot they found into carts. He was a little tipsy from a brew that Ribsplitter-Jones came up with by mixing distilled sugar cane with lotus honey, rose hips and paint stripper. Smiley was counting on it finishing him off and was quite annoyed when he realized it wouldn't.

Momoo was assigned to stand around and remind the thugs that an officer was keeping tabs on them and they were to be carrying out their tasks with a proper military gait.

Meanwhile, Shard, bonked the Princess. Shard watched the sun set below her mountain range, dropped crumbs in her valley as he ate his supper, and without missing a beat was able to carry her over to the iron stove, spark flint to steel, start a warm fire, and return her to bed all the while keeping her thoroughly entertained.

The fire had burned down to angry coals and the thugs had settled down and Momoo found himself a place to hold up. Shard stared up at the shadow-swept ceiling.

"I can hear you blinking," the Princess said, not moving. "You're keeping me awake with you incessant blinking." Her voice tickled him. "You had best be thinking of me if all you're going to do is lie there and keep me awake with your stupid blinking."

"Yes, your Highness," Shard said honestly. "I was think-ing of you."

She purred. "That's sweet. Are you thinking of anything kinky, like tying me up again?"

Shard's voice softened. "No."

"Mmmm. What then?" She squirmed tightly against him. "What fantasy of me is keeping you up?"

He sighed. "It is only a few days to the shore. Unless the Humans are really fast or have already cut us off, it should be a straight shot."

She sat up. She was a silhouette in the darkness, the frost moon glinting off her breasts, like silver crescents. "What? You're sad to see me go?" She laughed softly. "I think you have it too good, thug. You should remember the wonderful time you had and how happy you are to have kept your nuts."

"Yes, your Highness," Shard said.

Slowly the darkness deepened within her silhouette. "There is something else? You're not missing me already, are you?" Her voice threatened.

Shard dismissed it with a shrug from his mono-brow. "I am going to miss you," he said flatly.

Hiroki shifted, rising a little higher. "And yet there is something else." She determined. "What is distracting you from thinking entirely about me?"

Shard's eyes sagged as he glanced out the window. "We've found a few trinkets here, but nothing of any real worth, at least to present to the Emperor. When we have no loot to take back, the Admiral will take us to the Emperor to explain why. We will then be put to death."

Hiroki nodded in agreement. "Well, that is true." She arched slightly, rolling her shoulders back. "What are you thinking of now?" She took a deep breath, expanding her lungs.

"How fucking incredible your boobs are in the moon light," he answered.

"You're going to die horribly at the Emperor's hands," she announced, shrugging, making her boobs swell. "Now what are you thinking of?"

"Are those nipple rings heavy? You carry them so easily."

She nodded. "Excellent." She cuddled beside him. "Just checking." She lay her head against his chest and within a minute was annoyed again. She sighed stiffly. "You're still blinking."

"Yes, your Highness."

She flexed her fingers, her polished nails like steel in the moon light. "If you, 'Your, Highness' me one more time I will gut you right here and now." She propped herself up on her elbow and looked down at him. "Isn't dying at my father's hand good enough for you?"

Shard's gaze was flat. "No."

Princess Hiroki sat bolt upright. "No? Did you say, no? Why, you miserable thug! I'll drain the blood from your body, fill a vat with it and drown your miserable, wretched self in it! What an honor it is to die at the Emperor's hands!"

Shard sat up. He could see half of the Princess' face in the harsh light, her lips set in a hard frown. "I want to die destroying your father's enemies." He matched her frown and her rising anger. "I have three hundred able-bodied thugs with steel weapons and armor. I have Non-Commissioned Officers and Staff NCO's, to include the best Sergeant Major in his Majesty's army. We have discipline and high morale!" His eyes flashed with passion. "I want to kill for his Majesty. I want to paint the landscape in Elf blood! I don't want to die when there are Elves left to fuck up! I'm going to have the great throng of Yarl Stonebiter fall on their swords when I surround the great Dwarven bastions with my captured Elf slaves, buck naked, their glowing white arses pointed to the sky like a field of lilies, my thugs armed with brass-tacked paddles, spanking those toilet white asses until their horrible screams drive the Dwarves frothing mad and make them all leap from the high tower onto their flat, little heads! I'm going to weave the most horrid carpets from their scalps! Drink Gnome mead from their bloody craniums! String their nuts like tiny pearls for you to wear! I'll watch the soft golden glow of your magnificent breasts lit from the fire light of their burning temples! Obliterate any trace of them!"

Hiroki was leaning back, holding the bed sheets to her bosom defensively. "I see you've given this some thought," she said, quietly. "Okay, first you back up." She shooed her fingers at him. Shard hadn't realized he had been creeping closer during his rant. "Don't you yell at me," she scolded when Shard scooted back to the far side of the bed. "You'll be yelping three octaves higher next time, understand?" Shard nodded, abashed. "Good." She softened. "Look, I know you're a great warrior and an adequate lover and I can appreciate that. No one has broken a Dwarven formation before and you captured Old Gourd Head." She glanced out the window at the black mountain walls. "Ugh, this miserable place doesn't even have a view." She shrugged. "But you

captured it anyway and I'm sure that counts for something."
She pursed her lips thinking. "Tell you what, I'll ask father to
let you kill Momoo before he puts you to death."

Shard looked down, defeated. "Thank you, your
Highness," he said despondently.

Princess Hiroki threw her hands up and slapped her thighs.
"E-YA!" She shouted. "We are back to 'Your Highness' again."
She waggled a finger at him. "Look, it's not my fault there is no
loot. All this time you officers are standing around with your
collective thumbs up your asses while your thugs are burning
everything! You're supposed to be showing me the future site
of my new palace, not shuffling me home empty-handed." She
shuddered. "Ugh, disgusting ships! And sailors make the worst
lovers! An entire fleet of lame dicks. Big masts, tiny dicks." She
shook her head. "Explain something to me: If you're going to
bugger the cabin boy, why not just hire a cabin girl? Wouldn't
that make things easier?" Surprise flashed on her face. "That's
it!"

Shard jerked back as if stunned. "You want us to gang
bang a cabin boy?"

She waved her hands frantically. "No, you idiot! The loot!"

Shard's face lost all expression. "The cabin boy has loot?"

"Didn't take your smart potion today, did you?" Hiroki's
eyes narrowed shrewdly. "We get some loot!"

Shard's first response was far more insulting than what
he actually said. "Where do we get it? The Loot Store?"

Her lips tightened. "How the fuck should I know? You're
the one with the great army. Find a castle that looks rich and
storm it!"

"A few days march out of our way," Bark-Bite said quietly, "is the Clan of Leopolis the Hungry."

Shard's head swiveled quickly. "Bark-Bite? Where the hell are you?"

The Princess began searching under the pillows. "I am going to slap him up side the head with a crowbar!"

"Oh, and speaking of buggering the cabin boy," he went on, "Admiral Arthgoth married his boy – made him wear dresses for years. Divorced him when he reached puberty."

"He's under the bed!" She roared.

Shard dove over the edge of the bed, hanging upside down and moving the bed skirt out of the way.

A feeble shaft of moonlight cast across the well-fitted masonry. There was a fat dust bunny sorting lint into piles and a large, chipped chamber pot with ivy growing from it. Shard reached under and moved the chamber pot. No Bark-Bite. Shard sat back up on the bed and shrugged.

The Princess had wrapped herself in the bed sheets. "You find Bark-Bite and you bust him in the teeth," she ordered.

Shard nodded weakly. "What if he's right about this Leopolis?"

She snorted. "Of course he's right." She waved regally. "Now go! Fetch me some loot!" She kicked Shard with her tiny foot and sent him off the bed. She then rolled over, wrapping herself tightly in bed sheets and pretended to sleep.

Shard quickly wrapped his jock after a good scratch, then pulled up his britches and picked up his sword. He took his baldric from the bedpost and slipped that on. He yanked on the heavy iron ring and pulled open the door, tripping over Gample who was crouched with his ear to the door. Shard clambered to his feet. "Just what the fuck were you doing?" He pulled the door closed.

Gample looked at the glass in his hand, then tightened his lips and saluted, inadvertently smashing the glass into his head. "Cheap thrills, sir!"

Shard looked at his bleeding corporal; it was hard to fault honesty. "And how long have you been here? Has anyone else passed through this door?"

Gample thought, scratching a tiny sliver of glass from his eyebrow. "I got here when the Princess was baying like a sheep and screaming: 'Take me, Sheppard boy! Milk me! I'm a baaad little sheep!' No one came in or out since then."

"Too bad. You missed the best part." Shard looked around. "Where are the Princess' guards?"

"Downstairs. I think they overheard the best part and were afraid they were next."

Shard agreed. "Yeah, that could have happened. And how the fuck did you get up here?"

"They let me up," he replied simply.

"They just let you sneak up here to eavesdrop on her Highness?"

Gample snorked. "Not for free,"

Some little voice in the back of Shards head told him to let it go. "Where is Momoo?"

The Corporal shrugged. "Last I heard, he was inventorying the captured livestock."

Shard swallowed a bit of vomit back down. "Get some thugs together and sack this building. Stay out of the Princess' room, her guards will take care of that." Shard found his chainmail and, after slipping off his baldric, pulled it over his head. "And I want that red carpet from downstairs." He shrugged to get the mail to fall into place, then pulled on his heavy belt. "Roll it up nice. It's gonna go with my kit." Shard shouldered his baldric back on then found his helmet and tucked it under his arm. "Oh, but before you do that, go find Momoo."

Gample saluted. "And tell him what, sir?"

Shard shook his head. "Nothing. Just find him. And bring another glass with you." Shard turned and headed down the stairs. The Princess' eunuchs leapt to their feet, and Shard ignored their squeals and fawning and headed for the heavy door. They chased him with atomizers, spritzing his wake with perfume.

The cold, damp air welcomed him. The moon, huge in the sky, prepared to set below the saw-toothed, jagged mountain. Most of the thugs had found a place to settle in for their well-deserved nap, leaving only guards to watch the place and the three piles of inventory, precariously stacked in the courtyard. There was food: flour, sugar, jerky and tin cans of condensed milk. Next to that were weapons and armor. Last was miscellaneous.

"Captain Shard!" Smiley called trotting over. "Is it still captain?" He peered closely at the baldric. "Huh, so it is." He smiled genuinely happy, his trademark as vivid as ever. "Your slowing in your old age."

Shard's mono-brow rode low over his eyes. "Ya useless Hobbit!" he barked. "I thought you were supposed to be dying, you lazy fuck. Give me that baldric you fuck brain so I can give it to a thug that I can abuse."

Smiley clutched his baldric tightly. "I've been working, sir, that I have. I have all this tallied up." He held up a hand-carved wooden plate. "And here, I took some flour and fried you up a doughnut."

Shard looked at the golden circle of dough frosted with brown sugar. His mono-brow hung lower. "What the fuck is this?" He picked it up, sniffed it and took a bite.

"Mmmm, good, eh?" Smiley said.

Shard gagged and spat it out. "You can't shiv me in the back like a real thug, you have to poison me?" Shard spat several more times. "Ugh, it tastes like fucking dirt!"

"Oh, that's cause I dropped it in the sand on the way over," Smiley answered brightly.

Shard looked at Smiley carefully. His smile was unwavering, but the rest of him was. Smiley rocked as if he was standing on the deck of a ship and his eyes were sloshing about with the tide. Shard held up the doughnut. "So this isn't brown sugar, is it?"

Smiley thought. "You want one with brown sugar?" Smiley fetched a basket from beside him and pawed through. "No sugar ones." He held up one, scrutinizing it. "Here's one that looks like it has chocolate chips on it."

Shard punched him in the face, then mashed the doughnut into his forehead. Smiley's smile didn't falter. Shard's mono-brow lifted in surprise, then arched with curiosity. He cuffed Smiley up side his head. Smiley didn't blink. "Alright thug, what gorilla-fuck juice are you on?"

Smiley mused, then giggled to himself. "Sergeant Major found a healing potion, that he did."

Shard watched as the hulking, stooped frame of the Sergeant Major made its way from the shadows. "Ribsplitter-Jones!" Shard called to him.

The Sergeant Major's long, jutting neck rotated. "Ah, there's you fuggin got off too." He stomped over. "You're nots done with yer treatment," he said to Smiley. He paused and nodded to Shard, knuckling a salute. "Begging your pardon, Captain."

Shard sighed. "I know I don't have time for this, but I have to ask: What in Nucilo's carnivorous dandruff are you doing?"

Ribsplitter-Jones smiled brightly, his yellowy jagged teeth looking nastier than usual. "E'rats a good question. I'm just fixing up the executive officer with a little medicinal brew." He held up a silver flask. "Founds it in the watch tower." Shard took the flask and with his skeptically look, he uncorked it. Ribsplitter-Jones quickly put his hand over it. "If'n I may, sar." Ribsplitter-Jones took the cork and waved it quickly under Shard's nose.

Shard felt the fine hairs in his nose stiffen, petrify and fall out as his eyes welled up with tears. "By Klaysiron's rusted drool cup!" Shard chocked, trying to breathe. "That's a fuck wrong stench!"

"E'rats true," the Sergeant Major agreed. "Cleaned out my pipes and bowels in a fuck beat."

Shard sneezed. "Are you fucking mad? You drank some?"

Ribsplitter-Jones licked his dry, cracked lips. "'Ere's I had to test it before givin' it to the Lieutenant."

"And that aged dwarf piss is going to heal a belly wound?"

The giant thug shrugged. "E'rats, or kills him. I figures I could make it a two-step program. "Step one, soften him up so he doesn't feel step two." Ribsplitter-Jones suddenly seized Smiley's tunic and drew the tails over his head, blinding him. He then shoved Smiley into the pile of flour sacks. He deftly tugged open Smiley's bandage and poured the rest of his flask directly into the pus-swollen wound.

Smiley wrestled with his shirt, pulling it down then watched with interest. "Ooo, great idea!" He chirped. "Saves me the trouble of having to drink it."

Shard held his nose. "And that is going to heal him?"

Ribsplitter-Jones shrugged. "E'rats should kills the infection... or kills him."

"Bbbbbbrrritzzz!" Smiley exclaimed.

Shard grabbed Smiley's baldric to sit him up. "Don't you fucking keel on me yet. What have we salvaged for loot from this place?"

Smiley pointed to the piles as he scrambled to his feet. "Lots of food and weapons." He stumbled over to the third pile, struggling to pull his shirt down and straighten his baldric. "I found us a war banner." He held up a swath of cloth.

"Smiley, it's black." Shard informed him.

Smiley brightened. "It's a black dragon sinister rampant on a sable field!"

Shard wasn't sure what that meant, but it seemed to mean it was a black flag. "Got it. Anything shiny?"

Smiley winked. "This!" He pulled out a gold wand. It was one outstretched hand long, very ornate and delicately carved. Its butt was an emerald chip and its head was a curled, ten fingered hand as wide as both of Shard's thumbs put together.

Shard took the short wand, rolling it in his finger tips. "And what the fuck is this? A back scratcher?"

Smiley shook his head. "It's too short and the fingers are blunted. I think it's a Dwarven Nasal Nugget Extractor."

Shard handed it back to him, then wiped his hand on his pants. "I see them lining up for this," he said sardonically. "Can't they use their fingers like everyone else?"

"I don't think it would do as good job." Smiley started wedging the device up his tiny nose.

"And did you think it might be a nad scratcher for obese Gnomes?" Shard asked. "Give me that before you extract your brain." Shard took the handle and pulled. Smiley came with it.

"Weee!" Smiley giggled, stumbling into Shard. "I dink ids stug."

Shard pushed him off, sending him into flour sacks. "Enough fucking around. At first light, I want all the wagons this place has loaded up with all the food there is. Everyone who does not have steel armor and weapons gets some. Just leave me two wagons for some stuff I found in the cellar of the command tower." Shard looked at Smiley who was yanking on the wand with both hands and both feet. "Assign two thugs to keep him out of trouble." He sighed, turning to Ribsplitter-Jones. "And get that thing out of his nose before he starts feeling pain again."

As the sky brightened with dawn, the mountains silhouetted with shadow, the Black Dragon Company and the *Other* Black Dragon company marched chanting, their deep rumbling drums metering cadence, out of Ol' Gourd Head and down the other side of the Hill of Heart Attacks. Their eyes were red with delight, their steel weapons glinting in the feeble light, their smiles sinister. The Goblins struggled to keep their loaded wagons from rolling uncontrollably down the slope, constantly chucking the wheels, first with logs, which kept rolling down the hill, then with misshaped rocks. Heels dug in, backs against gunnels, creaking ropes, slowly the wagons made their way along the back side of the slope and down to the plains. Shard opted not to leave a force behind to hold the citadel, they'd only, somehow, fuck up the indestructible fortress. It could not be burned and the Black Dirt That Blows Stuff Up he recovered from the cellar was not enough to bring down the walls, so Shard ordered the doors bolted, Goblin snot smeared on the locking beams on the off chance that Elves climbing over the wall to open the doors would touch it and die from ickies, and march his company out of the ancient, Dwarven citadel. To the east and just out of sight was the ocean, where the Goblins tenuously held the peninsula and the lifeline of supplies and reinforcements. It was there that Shard was to deliver the Princess.

Shard turned to the northwest, following Bark-Bite's instructions, moving his thugs along the lowlands and valleys, away from the outposts and spying eyes. They raided a few farms, pillaged a bit for practice, and made their way undetected to the steppes of Glambin-Sur, the lands of Leopolis the Hungry.

Shard took ten thugs on a reconnaissance mission and low crawled through the tall grass to get a good look at the fortress. In campaigns of the past, Glambin-Sur made a great first conquest. Close to the shore with an inviting bay for ships to land, anyone would be hard pressed to find them a better spot to launch an invasion. After disembarking and amassing troops to the north, Glambin-Sur with its gentle slopes and poor defenses, lay tantalizing to the Goblin invaders. In full regalia, Rhino Hawk horns heralding their approach with its mournful cry, the haunting goblin tornado drums drove the Goblin armies into blood lust. Banners of delicate weave and startling colors were held aloft proclaiming the names of the Goblin battalions: The Black Cobras, The Black Tigers, The Black Ostrich.

A slow, black stain crept across the earth, a rising tide of terror. Formations in neat, broad columns, moving with assurance toward its destination: the lands of Glambin-Sur. Its earth work defenses were easily overwhelmed as the charge set on and an unbelievable number of Goblins swept across the providence. The small bastion of Human defenders were quickly and easily conquered. It was there that the Goblins established their first fortress, a wooden palisade that peered from the high scope.

As the Goblin army marched ever forward, Glambin-Sur continued to swell with more invading forces. They quickly established farms in the black soil, raising grain to feed their troops and captured cattle. When the Humans finally organized an army to force the Goblin horde back to the frozen wastes of Bratanich, Glambin-Sur was a productive farming community not only supplying the army, but exporting mass quantities of food back to Bratanich. Crop rotations re-invigorated the sweet soil that gently rolled beneath the Goblin plow. As the Human defenders marched over the horizon and the last of the great Goblin army shrank beneath their steel weapons, the Goblin farmers harvested their final crops, spread manure, and retreated quickly, leaving the soil ready for their next invasion.

Years would pass and the Humans would build some sort of fortification or watchtower, which the advance Goblin troops would destroy and the process began again.

"Until recently," Bark-Bite mused. "Hmmm, I'd say the last twenty years, give or take. Oh, they built bigger and better forts, but after we'd discovered the Black Dirt That Blows Stuff Up they stopped doing that." Bark-Bite had appeared at Shard's elbow during one of the company's march breaks, striking up a conversation somewhere in the middle. "But now? Now they seem to know when we will attack." the Major went on, as Shard got over his fright. "They'd amass an army and plant them right there. They even built a garrison just for that." Bark-Bite spat in the dirt, wiping the dregs from his chin with his cuff. "It's too expensive to just keep an army on hand big enough to stop us," Bark-Bite explained. "The Humans just got good at predicting when and where we were going to attack, recruit, train, and then plop them right in front of us. They simply fended us off ten years ago. Bloody annoying. They hid from the advance units, then marched up as the rest of the army came to shore. An entire force buggered! Mages stood with their white dressing flowing in the breeze, casting giant balls of purple fire and burning our transport ships." Bark-Bite sniffed. "All those good, young thugs, sank right to the bottom." Bark-Bite shook his head sadly, remembering. "If they had only stood up straight, we would have saved the taller ones. Bay wasn't that deep."

Bark-Bite sighed as the memory weighed on him, sagging in on himself. "I was with the advance unit." Bark-Bite's dark eyes flickered in the white moonlight as they gazed back through time. The road they stomped on had been only a goat trail then. Moving quietly and quickly under the cover of night, they moved across the shore. Carrying the kegs of Black Dirt That Blows Stuff Up on their backs, they made their way into the forests, across the steppes and through the tall grass, making a long, looping, surprise flanking maneuver to the newly-built fortress of Glambin-Sur. A tactical strategy not by design but because of the newly-issued iron housed compasses were less than useful. Quickly digging, they sapped below a stone and mortar rook and planted their charges, rigged the fuse and buried the lot.

Bark-Bite huddled low on a grade, flint and steel in hand, and waited for the dawn. Watching the tiny black sails in the distance, a smear on the horizon, Bark-Bite waited, risking the revealing light of the sun, waiting until the human watch-towers had surely seen the fleet and would sound an alarm before sparking his fuse to light. Hissing, writhing, it quickly burned up the slope and into the mound of earth where the bombs were hidden.

Bark-Bite put his fingers in his ears and hunkered down for the massive explosion.

And explode it did.

The entire bastion disintegrated into dust.

Bark-Bite looked up curiously. Even the cheapest Human fortification would have withstood better fare, the bombs knocking out the support structure allowing the tower to fall under its own weight leaving a pile of rubble; yet Glambin-Sur was gone. Nothing left but a grey, rumbling cloud.

On Bark-Bite's hip, Lil' Elfie began to throb. He inched it from its sheath and its eerie glow threatened to give away his position.

Hissing dust settled, giving way to the rolling tattoo of snare drums. Suddenly, the painful high-pitched shrill of Elvish flutes filled the air, making Bark-Bite wince from the sharp twang that seemed to drill his back teeth and driving his squad to blood lust. Bark-Bite squinted through the set-tling dust.

Arrows ripped invisibly through the air, finding targets in the lightly armored Goblin unit. Enraged by the wailing Elvish throng, the Goblins charged from their positions, drawing their iron swords from scabbards, ignoring Bark-Bite's screaming orders to fall back.

A playful wind snatched away the curtain of raining dust to reveal the marching mass of Humans in shield wall formation. Bark-Bite stared wide-eyed as impossible numbers moved in cadence out of the remains of the garrison. They had to have been crammed in, standing shoulder-to-shoulder, chest to back, waiting for this moment to spring their trap. A rampart had been dug to protect them from the blast.

Bark-Bite turned and ran as his squad reached the Human lines. They plowed into the wall with a crash and bounced off, quickly falling beneath the flashing, razor-sharp Human steel.

Feet pumping, Bark-Bite ran in a desperate sprint as Elvish arrows sprouted in the tall grass all around him. As he reached the edge of the sloping downhill roll, off in the distance, through a break in the trees, he could see the ocean, dark blue in the early morning, and the tiny black tatters of cloth of the Goblin flotilla silently making their way across the still waters, unsuspecting that their blitzkrieg was about to be counter-blitzkrieged. Bark-Bite ducked his head. With his lungs sputtering, rattling with hot coals that burned holes in choice, tender spots, Bark-Bite forced his body—short, overweight and soft—to run.

An Elvish arrow ripped into his back violently, right beneath the left shoulder blade, hurling him forward. He face planted, skidding nearly an arm's length, balanced perfectly on his nose and chin in the dew-soaked grass before coming to a stop. The fiery pain of the wicked Elvish shaft drove him mad with agony, but the image of the Goblin armada sailing gently into a massacre still fresh in his mind forced him to keep his senses. Stretching, he reached back but his stubby, fat fingers couldn't find purchase. Gritting his teeth, his eyes glinting red, he stumbled to his feet. Huffing with each step reached a top speed of a lumbering trot, gaining protection from the never-ending rain of arrows in the shadow of the tree line.

Bark-Bite defied his lead-heavy limbs as he ran, his breath gasping from his punctured lung. Low branches raked his face, shin-high rocks rose before him. Stumbling with reckless abandon, he emerged from the forest. Down the loamy hill, Bark-Bite could see the transport ships still offshore, trapped on a carefully engineered underwater sand bar. The lighter boats of the advance team had sailed unsuspectedly over them, but the deep draft landers were stuck fast.

Bark-Bite squinted, trying to clear the blur of his vision, searching for the banner of the command ship. He couldn't find it. He couldn't identify anything. He touched a shaky hand to his temple.

His glasses were gone. He had skived the previous owner to get them after stalking him for three months. The sound of the ocean's incoming tide was drowned out by the horrendous labor of his working lung as he looked around on the fuzzy beach. He realized that, at this moment, he would be hard-pressed to find anyone as blind as him.

The rim of the sun, red and angry, edged higher, lighting the black Goblin sails.

Sizzling balls of purple Elven magic arched over head and plunged into the water, sending plumes into the air. Bark-Bite watched as the landers opened their ramps and thugs, motivated by their sergeants, charged out into the water. Their newly-issued iron armor was ballast and Bark-Bite could see the tops of their caps and turtle shells cresting the waves. They marched determinedly on the ocean bottom, most of them in the right direction.

Unable to scream a warning, Bark-Bite charged out into the surf. He chugged as best he could, letting his feet grope for the sand bar to keep his head above water. He plucked a thug or two passing by, trying to turn them around, but they only ignored him. Their orders were to 'Go that way and kill things that are not thugs' and where Bark-Bite was pointing wasn't 'that way.'

Bark-Bite waded where he could, then dog paddled, looking for a ship that could sound retreat. More Elvish magic fell from the sky with the sound of tearing linen. Ships instantly exploded into flaming splinters, ripping thugs apart in the radius. Catapults flung heated shot, gouging holes into the landers and setting them afire.

Bark-Bite ignored everything around him, the angry spank of the exploding magic against his face, the cold water that bubbled around the hole in his lung, even the Milking Fish that found its way into his shorts. Bark-Bite unfurled the battle map in his head, calculated where the lead ship should be, and paddled towards it.

It was riddled with holes, thugs scooping out water with their caps and dumping it out as quickly as it filled. On the prow, glaring majestically into the new sun, Fleet Commander, Captain Mysor Ripnail the Fifth stood unflinchingly as rocks, magic and ballista bolts whizzed past him, snatching at the bleached peacock feathers in his hat.

Bark-Bite climbed the side of the ship, using the punched holes as a ladder, wheezing desperately at the Commander. "It's... an ambush!" Bark-Bite swallowed down the foaming blood rising from his lungs. "Sound the... retreat!"

Captain Ripnail turned his head, as if sniffing a particularly rank stench. "Retreat?" He peered down, the permanent furrows of his frown were sharp in the brightening sun. "What makes you think we're losing?"

Bark-Bite gripped the top gunnel and paused. He looked back towards the beach and could only see the orange glow of the burning ships and more flashes of Elvish magic rising up from the tree line, like glowing fingers reaching over and raking into the black waters. He could see far enough to know that there were no Goblin formations on the beach, no banners, but even if there were, they would have to march up the slope into blistering magic, hell-storms of arrows and Human and Dwarven shield-walls beyond.

Bark-Bite felt his one good lung sprain itself. "It's a trap!" he snorked. "They're waiting... over the ridge... knew we were..."

Ripnail's frown deepened. "Is that an arrow in your back?"

Bark-Bite wanted to say, No, it's bloody hands free fishing, you twit! I'm angling for bass right now! but could only wheeze.

"There is only one way to get an arrow in the back," Ripnail said dangerously.

First-mate Moto peered over the gunnels. "You could back up into it."

"How about..." Pilot Wayne Hornack spoke up from his post at the tiller, "a hideous physical deformity that looks like an arrow growin' out of your back?"

Bark-Bite desperately tried to pull himself up, but Ripnail stepped on his hand, crushing it into the gunnel. "No," he sighed patiently. "It's cowardice!"

The First shrugged. "I donno, I think if you was walkin' backwards, right..."

Ripnail rolled his eyes. "Would you two shut the fuck up?" He let out a calming breath. "Now where was I?"

"Cowardice," the First whispered quickly.

Bark-Bite desperately struggled to free his fingers from beneath the captain's boot as Captain Ripnail's frown turned into a sneer. "And there is only one way to deal with cowards." His fingers wrapped around the hilt of his talwar.

"Pull him onboard..." Bark-Bite rasped quickly. "Treat his... wounds... Offer him... cookies?"

"NO!" Ripnail bellowed, slowly drawing his heavy, bladed sword from its scabbard. "You kill him where he stands."

Bark-Bite kicked his feet, showing that he was dangling. "I'm... not standing."

"He's got you there," the First said quietly.

Ripnail lifted his sword up over his head, its sharp edge burning gold in the morning light. "Close enough," he mumbled.

A ball of purple light zoomed by, hissing like nails on a chalkboard and showering the ship with sparks. Ripnail stood, his arm frozen, his head neatly sheered off at the shoulders.

Bark-Bite wriggled his fingers from beneath the captain's boot. He grabbed a better hold and heaved himself up. "Sound... retreat!"

First-mate Moto glared wide-eyed, pointing at the captain's still standing body. "What say, Captain?"

The captain's body swayed with the ship.

Bark-Bite turned on the pilot. "Turn the... ship around!" he ordered.

"Seems to me," the Pilot pointed at Bark-Bite, "that he's standing now."

The First-mate nodded. "Captain's orders." He pried the tulwar from the captain's hand. "Kill cowards who are standing."

Lil' Elfie flashed and plunged into the First's chest, stopping him just as he raised the captain's sword. Leaving Lil' Elfie to feast, Bark-Bite's head swiveled at the pilot, his eyes glowing red. "Sound retreat... and turn the ship!"

The Pilot sagged on himself. "But only the captain can order..."

Bark-Bite ripped the captain's baldric from his headless shoulders and put it on. He then nudged the captain and let him tip overboard. He wrenched Lil' Elfie free of the First and let him drop to the deck. Bark-Bite turned, eyes enraged, his breath a tortured rasp, a silhouette, his back to the burning sun, Lil' Elfie pulsing blue as each bomb of Elven magic flashed by. Black Goblin blood dripped fresh from its blade quickly congealed, then faded to nothing as the magic sword drank its fill.

The Pilot whistled to the signalman who then put a horn to his lips and began to blow a mournful cry of retreat.

"And that is how we lost everybody," Bark-Bite said sadly.

Shard had shoved a stick down his pants for a good scratch. "I thought you said that you sounded retreat?"

Bark-Bite nodded. "Oh, we did. However, the admiral was afraid someone would accidentally sound retreat so he made sure not to teach any of the thugs what to listen for." Bark-Bite shifted on the rock he was sitting on. "You know, I saw your lieutenant with an Obese Gnome Nad Scratcher wedged in his nose. Why don't you use that?"

Shard had broke the stick off in his pants and was trying to fish the other end out. "'Cause it's frigging stuck. He thought it was a Dwarven Nasal Nugget Extractor."

Bark-Bite jerked his head in surprise. "That looks more like a corkscrew with fingers. What made him think he had a Dwarven Nasal Nugget in need of extraction lodged in his nose?"

Shard pulled out the broken end of his stick. "Fuck do I know?" He gave it a sniff. "I guess it's the most likely spot to find a Dwarven Nasal Nugget." Shard tossed the stick into the woods. "He's been all whiny lately. 'Oh, I'm dying and I have a Nad Scratcher stuck in my nose.' I'd fucking gack him and get it over with, but he's the only one who can translate the supply log." Shard sat up on his rock. "So is there a plan?"

Bark-Bite smiled, showing off his perfect white teeth. "It's so rare to hear a thug ask that question. Yes, there is a plan. Leopolis the Hungry has built a fortress on the very same knoll that I blew up ten years ago. It's mostly wood with the main structure built from rock quarried from a pit in the lowland area. Why he didn't build the whole thing out of stone is anyone's guess. Around the hill itself is a wooden palisade about two thugs high. There are two gates, northeast and southeast. In the southwest, in the quarry area, there is a water gate where an underground river surfaces, channeling through the quarry to a river. That gate is used for a sewer."

Shard stared at him, unblinking.

Bark-Bite shifted off the rock and dropped to his haunches. Taking a stick, he drew a map. "Fort, palisade, gate one, gate two, terrain feature, terrain feature, sewer."

Shard blinked as he nodded. "Okay, I was getting stuck on the placement of the gates." He pointed to a terrain feature. "What's that?"

"That's Momoo."

Shard's mono-brow arched. "And what's that he's hold-ing... Ugh, forget I asked and I don't want to know what the other terrain feature is."

Bark-Bite shrugged. "Actually it's a cave where a big..."

"Don't want know," Shard cut him off. "And we are go-ing to attack via the sewer."

"Exactly!" Bark-Bite clapped a hands. "Right before moon-rise, we sneak under the gate, kill some guards, send some of my engineers to blow the fort itself and everyone else to plunder, rape and lastly burn the village." Bark-Bite rubbed his hands together. "Oh, and if I know Leopolis, there'll be cattle and pigs ready for slaughter. We'll eat til we're stupid!"

"That won't take much," Shard said. "What about the loot? You made it sound like Leo's got scratch." Shard gave his crotch another scratch.

Bark-Bite leaned close and whispered. "It's right under his nose." He turned and spat, cuffing his chin. "You see, twenty years ago, the very spot where he parked his castle, we parked ours. We dug a deep cellar to hide the loot we had amassed. When the Humans rallied and forced us off the continent, we couldn't grab everything so we sealed the cellar off and hid the entrance."

"What makes you think he hasn't found it yet?"

"Because he'd have a much nicer castle." Bark-Bite's eyes loomed large behind his glasses. "This is more than a bar tab, Shard. It's enough to buy both yours and Momoo's butts out of the fire."

Shard nodded wistfully. "How much for just my butt?"

Bark-Bite frowned. "For someone whose just been told he's not going to die horribly, you're a little glum. When I say die horribly, I mean stripped naked, every bone in your body dislocated, dumped like a rag doll on a sun-baked rock and left to slither into the shade." Bark-Bite turned his head and spat. "I would not at all be embarrassed if you said, 'Thank you, Major. Thank you for looking out for this lowly thug. I'm sure you have better things to do than cover my dumb, burn-before-you-plunder, ungrateful goblin butt.'" He shook his head. "Nope, not embarrassed at all if you said that. Here, go ahead and try it. See if I get embarrassed."

Shard regarded the Major. "Yeah, well you see, I'm not used to someone giving a smashed rat's asshole over whether or not I die horribly."

Bark-Bite clamped him on the shoulder and, using him as a crutch, rose. "You're quite welcome, Shard. Quite welcome."

Shard rose from his haunches and put his fists into his back and leaned back, popping vertebrae in his spine. "Yeah, uh, thanks." Shard sighed as he pulled open the flap of his kit and rummaged out a canteen. He worked the cork out with his teeth and took a sip, wincing from the burn of the Dwarven rum. He handed the canteen to Bark-Bite.

"Cheers." The Major took a gulp, then gasped for air.

Shard smiled weakly. "Cheers." His mono-brow sagged. "It's just that I'm thinking."

Bark-Bite paused in mid-tilt, his black eyes glistening in the star light.

Shard searched the ground, distractedly. "I'm surprised that you're bailing us out like this."

Bark-Bite tilted his head back and took another swallow. He cuffed his chin as he handed the canteen back.

Shard took back the canteen and took another hit. "I mean, I know the Colonel sent you to help us get to the shore, but this is a bit out of the way." Shard plugged the cork back. "A lot of work just to save a couple captain's."

Bark-Bite's eyes, huge behind his spectacles, narrowed. Shard suddenly realized that Bark-Bite might be far more dangerous than he let on as he wondered who the Major murdered for those glasses.

Shard coughed nervously, then curled his bottom lip and matched Bark-Bite's glare. "What I'm asking is... is this just for Momoo and I, or is this a mission of revenge?"

Bark-Bite's face was stoic, unreadable. He shuffled closer. "We're in a bad way, Shard. We, meaning our entire civilization. For as long as anyone remembers, since the time when the Humans first came down from the stars and forced the Goblins to Bratanich, we have come down from the frozen lands, warred, raided, pillaged and farmed enough supplies so in a few years when the Humans and their allies get around to kicking us off, we can survive a couple years in the barren wastes before coming back to do it again. We've done it like that for a millennium. However, in the last twenty years, the Humans have outsmarted us at every turn. We can't farm and we can't raid. They beat us at the shore. When we try to outflank them, they maneuver around, countering instantly.

Faster than they should be able to. Thugs are dying wholesale. Even now, only months into this campaign, we are already in defeat. Our western front is cut off, left behind as fodder while we sneak the Princess away. Once again, we all leave empty-handed while at home everyone starves."

Bark-Bite turned and spat. Then he took the canteen from Shard's hand. "You can't grow crops on an ice flow." He yanked the cork and took a swig. "Oh, we've tried." He gasped as the rum burned the back of his throat. "There were those Blister Reeds that popped into a lovely crisp treat when fried. Tasteless, and not one scrap of nutrition, but filling if you ate a peck of them and when you dusted them with salt they go well with beer, but you can't feed a nation of thugs on fried crisps." He jiggled the canteen, gauging how much was left, then took another swig. "Mmmm, I am feeling that." He looked up at Shard. "We need a ray of hope. A victory that stings the Humans, makes them back up and rethink their plans. We need a few thugs with half a brain to lead the attack. The Colonel thinks you might have a part in that attack. Perhaps Momoo, too." Bark-Bite stoppered the canteen. "No, not Momoo. Why he forbade you not to kill him is a wisdom beyond me." He shrugged. "Treasure will buy us more supplies and buy your pimply ass out of the Emperor's dungeons." He handed Shard the canteen.

Shard nodded, trying not to smile in spite of himself. "So, it's not about revenge."

Bark-Bite punched him in the head. "Of course it's about revenge! You git! Haven't you been listening? Those bloody bastards shot me in the back! Do you know what a pain in the ass it is to explain over and over how you got shot in the back?"

Shard's mono-brow gave a half hearted shrug as he shook off the blow. "Tell 'em you backed into it."

"Backed into it?" Bark-Bite roared. "Backed into it?" Bark-Bite caught his breath as his eyes fell distant. He turned and looked at a passing Goblin. "Hello there!"

The thug turned and saluted sharply. "Sir!"

Bark-Bite beamed a smile of all straight teeth. "I was out here during the campaign of Lickity Tonsil the fourteenth. Took a nasty wound though. Backed up into an Elvish arrow."

The Goblin winced with phantom pain. "Ooh, that must've smarted, sir. Bastard Elves."

Bark-Bite nodded numbly. "Yes, bastards. Carry on." He nodded as the Goblin walked away. "Fuck," Bark-Bite whispered to himself, then looked up at Shard. "Sort of kills the mood, doesn't it?" He spat. "No, it doesn't. We're going to knock those bastards off that fucking hill!"

Shard's Revenge

Acrid, wet and heavy air clung to the back of Shard's mouth. He could taste the foul stench of the man made marsh the Humans used as an open sewer. He lay on his stomach, watching the dark walls of the palisade. The guards along the walls wandered back and forth, but avoided the sewer gate, repelled by their own waste, and effectively leaving their back door open.

The Boil Flies were beginning to swarm, hunting for the tender skin behind Shard's ears. He had to get his thugs on the move soon, before the incessant buzzing roused the guards in the otherwise still night. Eventually, even the most insipid guard would notice over three hundred thugs hiding in the tall grass just down the hill.

Shard looked to either side. Most of his thugs were going to ram the gates, but he was taking his Chosen Thugs over the wall in an escalade. He had started with a hundred and twelve Chosen Thugs. Minus Smiley and three others who were wounded and nineteen others who were killed, by his calculation left a hundred and fifteen extremely psychotic killing machines. The Chosen Thugs, who wore a fleck of black dragon scale on their baldrics, had spent the longest time in steel armor and all had man-swords, grinded short to fit them better. They were motivated by their Captain, Wiggletooth Shard; a most dangerous thug. Despite not really knowing what a hundred and fifteen really looked like, Shard knew he'd lost more thugs than that, and other thugs were stealing Chosen Thugs baldrics and filling ranks, but if they fought with fury and listened to orders, Shard didn't care.

Shard was grinning from ear to ear, unable to calm his delight. He was surrounded by good thugs, armed with good steel and backed by a good plan. Even his rift with Momoo hadn't dampened his spirits.

"Ah, here you all are!" he had announced, making his way into the clearing. "Bloody incompetent messenger failed to tell me there was a staff meeting." He was wearing his padded purple tunic with a steel breast plate and paulderons tied clumsily in place. Everything was too big for him and the breast plate was already wearing out the armpits of his tunic. Behind him was his banner carrier, bearing the colors of the *Other* Black Dragon Company un-cased so its faded purple standard hung sadly, yet free. Behind this proud thug was the flutist who continually stared at the ground.

Shard glanced hotly at Ribsplitter-Jones to see who blabbed, but the Sergeant Major only shrugged with a twitch of his cheek. Shard sighed. "Yeah, well, give your armor to that thug by the fire. He'll black it up for you." Shard pointed with his chin at a thug by a small smoky fire. He had dropped in black balls of resin that burned with a sticky black smoke. Holding a weapon or armor bit in its thick, tarry smoke quickly turned it black. It took a little effort to get it off, but it made for great night-operations camouflage.

Momoo winced. "We're officers, Shard. We should be seen." He said impertinently, then caved. "I'll soot up before we head out." He nodded to himself as he looked at the Officers and NCO's gathered, nodding to the Sergeant Major and the First Sergeant. He smiled warmly when he noticed Smiley was up and about. "Still have that Nad Scratcher, eh?"

All of the staff looked at Shard with the expression of 'What's he doing here?' Shard tightened his lips and glanced over at Bark-Bite, but noticed that the Major had become very still, his eyes averted and looking down at the map scratching in the dirt. Shard blinked and squinted as the Major began to fade slightly, as if the spot where he squatted had suddenly dropped into shadow. Shard looked around and no one else seemed to notice.

"Ahem," Momoo said, as if it were a word and not a sound made by politely coughing to get someone's attention. "Ah, yes," he began. "I realize that I have not been as helpful as I could have been during this mission." His gaze shifted, never quite meeting with the eyes of his audience. "And while I realize that you will surely pull this off without my assistance, sitting out of a fight isn't the Momoo way."

The staff all shifted on their haunches. First Sergeant Shiro quickly bit her hand to stop from laughing, while Gunny Glenkar farted to cover up his snork.

"The point is..." Momoo went on quickly, "that I have decided to commit the full resources of the *Other* Black Dragon Company and place them under your direct command, Shard." He beamed proudly at the notion, then tilted his head toward where the two thugs were standing behind him.

Gunny Glenkar fell over giggling. First Sergeant Shiro punched him to shut him up.

Shard's mono-brow was arched and he rose to his feet. He looked behind Momoo half expecting more thugs to come marching out of the woods. When they didn't show, he looked at Momoo who was still smiling proudly. Shard glanced over his shoulder at the null space where Bark-Bite should have been. The Major was nearly gone save for a slight shift of his hand, open palm to the ground. A calming gesture. "What company is that, Momoo?" Shard turned back, his face struggling to remain stoic and sincere.

"The *Other* Black Dragon Company." Momoo drew a sharp breath through is nostrils, lifting his nose a tad. "I'm sure you recall, formerly *The* Black Dragon Company?"

Shard then looked at the two Goblins standing behind Momoo. The Bearer of the Standard was a brute of a thug with a brick square jaw and thin slits for eyes. His massive arms gripped the banner tightly, the veins pulsing like vipers beneath his skin. Shard could hear him clicking as his teeth ground together. It was the banner carrier's job to make sure the colors never fell. They were to carry the glaring target unflinchingly into blistering barrages of Elven magic and arrows, to stand fast as waves of Human shield-walls charged and, if all was lost, to defend the colors with the wicked sharp pike at the top and be the last Goblin standing. To take Goblin colors was to pay an unimaginable price.

This thug had watched Momoo send his brethren, wave after wave, into Dwarf lines to be obliterated with glory and honor, but when it came time for him to lead the final wave, Momoo held back and he watched the last of his company fall to Dwarven steel without so much as blooding one Dwarf. Now, disgraced, mocked with open stares and verbal jeers, this proud thug stood staunchly obedient, carrying his colors with pride beyond measure.

While anger broiled within him.

Shard blinked, finding his eyes drying out as they subconsciously engaged in a staring match with the unblinking thug. Shard could use this thug. He'd be hard pressed to keep him from breaking ranks and charging forward with abandon, but the Bearer of the Standard for the *Other* Black Dragon Company would be a living storm in battle, indiscriminately killing in its path.

The other thug, the flutist, was standing slightly behind the banner carrier. He was gangly, defeated, with his head down, shoulders hunched forward and his eyes forever searching the ground as if looking for something.

Shard forced himself to nod. "Yeah, Momoo." He looked at the thug holding the colors. "We can use this thug. The first thing the Humans will see is the banner of the *Other* Black Dragon Company coming over the wall."

The granite chiseled face of the thug cracked ever so slightly into a smile of pride.

"Oh, come now, Shard," Momoo scoffed. "Don't be silly. We can't endanger the colors."

Suddenly, a grisly, skin crawling noise grated to a quick, nasty pop as one of the teeth of the color bearer split asunder as he swallowed another indignity.

Momoo glanced at him curiously, then looked back at Shard. "The colors of the Black Dragon... of the former Black Dragon Company, have been in the family for more than twenty campaigns. It has received distinguished ribbons in six campaigns, one awarded by the Senior Chief Executive Deputy to the Junior Assistant Under-Secretary of the Army." Momoo folded his arms proudly across his chest, then unfolded them as the steel breast plate pinched his arm pits savagely. "These colors must never be sullied!"

Shard sighed desperately. "By Andraxia's double pussy whore, what troops are you giving me? The sedan bearers?"

"You've already annexed them," Momoo shot back quickly. "And I'll expect compensation for them!" He waved a finger at Shard, then pulled his hand back suddenly afraid of getting bit. "Despite all of your cheeky behavior to a senior officer, I've still decided to entrust the jewel of the *Other* Black Dragon Company to your command."

Shard paused trying to figure out what senior officer Momoo was talking about, then tried to figure out what jewel he was talking about. "Rampaging Oyster Fuck, Momoo! What the fuck are you talking about?"

Momoo smiled, smugly. "The one thing your company lacks."

Shard didn't say, "A cowardly assbag such as yourself?" Instead he put his hands to his head to keep them from chicken choking Momoo. "Fucking speed this up," he spat through his teeth. "Who? For Horic's sake?"

Momoo tilted his head towards the flutist. "A band!"

Shard could hear the harsh barking laugh of Ribsplitter-Jones. The NCO's had fallen off their haunches and were rolling, laughing and farting in the dirt. Shard didn't look back, but only took Momoo's arm, turning him away, but before he could say anything, Momoo spoke up.

"There is nothing better to fire the troops into a furor than a skilled musician."

Shard's mono-brow was arched. "Momoo? That," he pointed as the gangly thug tried to hide behind the standard bearer, "is not a musician. He's a fuck useless thug. Give me the standard bearer and I'll get you another ribbon for your flag."

Momoo breathed hotly. "You miserable thug," he swore. "My mother bought that flutist from the Longenth School for Accomplished Arts. Just because your untrained ear can't hear the subtle nuances..."

Suddenly Shard's eyes narrowed, burning red as blood quickly boiled. "My untrained...? My ears are..." Shard felt his needler slip into his palm before he realized what he was doing. Shard sucked wind through his teeth with a loud hiss and battled to calm himself. He stared at Momoo, his left eye twitching, unsure why Momoo's lame jibe twisted his bowels so violently. "My ears are just fine." Shard whispered dangerously as he pushed his shank back up his sleeve. "Okay, Momoo. Let's see if he's good enough for *The* Black Dragon Company."

"How dare you?" Momoo shouted as Shard turned away. "He is from the Longenth School! Beyond the question from a blockhead like you!" Momoo growled, then quieted as he realized everyone was listening. "We paid prime coin for him."

"Excellent," Shard said, feeling more control of himself. "Then he won't mind a little audition." He looked at the thug who was still searching the ground. "Would you?" he asked the thug.

The thug trembled and looked up at Shard, matching his gaze then looking down quickly.

Momoo stepped forward. "You have my assurances of his superior talent, Shard. That should suffice."

Shard smiled. "And it does, Captain Momoo." Shard's voice was level. "Then a little entertainment perhaps, for the senior staff." Shard leaned close to the thug. "Orgrax Lullaby. Play that for us."

The thug shivered.

Momoo stepped forward but Gunny Glenkar stood up, followed by the rest of the NCO's. Momoo glanced nervously at them, then to Shard. "Come now, Shard, you've made him nervous."

"Come on," Shard coaxed. "Four notes, you know it. Every thug knows it. Dah, dah, dee, day, dah, dum," Shard sang gently. "A good thug can play in the middle of an all out charge at a full run." Shard shook his head. "He can't be afraid of me." Shard leaned close, his voice low and angry. "Play for me."

The thug fumbled for his flute, pulling it out of the bag that hung from his belt. His fingers shook as he brought it to his lips. His first note was soundless.

The NCO's chuckled but Shard silenced them with a hand. "He's warming up." He nodded at the thug. "Go ahead."

The thug only hung his head. His fingers limply holding his flute.

Shard snatched the flute from his hand and held it up, squinting. He stepped over to Momoo. "There's cracks along the blow hole. You'll never get a decent note out of this." Shard held it up for his inspection.

Momoo sighed relief. "There you have it. He can't play!"

Shard put the flute to his lips.

The four notes of Orgrax were methodical, repetitive and boring as all hell and guaranteed to put any young, hypervelocity Goblin to sleep after only a few rounds. When Shard played with perfect pentameter and inflection, it was spell-binding, drudging up memories of momma rocking them to sleep; warm, fed, content and happy.

Shard stopped in mid refrain, leaving his audience lurching on the edge of rapt attention. "I'm sure you can hear that, Momoo. The way it grinds in your ear." Shard played another magical note. "Argh! Disgusting." Shard suddenly raised his knee and broke the flute much to everyone's horror. "Unplayable." Everyone's eyes followed the broken flute as Shard dropped it to the ground, almost hoping it could somehow be fixed, be played again, for the wonderful melody to continue. Shard stepped on it, ignoring someone's gasp as he walked up to the flutist. "Has it been cracked all this time?"

The thug nodded feebly.

"Speak when an officer asks you a question, thug!" First Sergeant Shiro had slipped behind the flutist. "We can't hear what's rattling in your noggin."

"Yes, sir," he squeaked. "It's been cracked since the battle of Tel-fang."

"And where's the new one?" Shard demanded.

The thug looked up, straightening slightly. "The new one, sir?"

Shard nodded impatiently. "Yes, the new one. Surely a flutist of your caliber would have carved a new one, or should be carving a new one." Shard glared at him. "You mean you've had a busted flute all this time and haven't started carving a new one? Tel-Fang? Isn't that when you took on the Dwarves? You haven't found a bone, or stick since then?"

"Perhaps he's picky?" Momoo spoke up.

Shard's angry eyes swiveled towards Momoo. "A true flutist can make a flute out of a long turd." He looked back at the thug who was searching the ground again. "At least a thug from Longenth School."

Shiro barked at the thug again. "Stand at attention, thug!" The thug sprang stiff.

Shard came closer, glaring at the thug. "You're not a flutist, are you?"

From behind him, Shiro bellowed. "Answer the Captain!"

"No, sir," he squeaked.

Shard tilted his head. "You're just a thug, aren't you?"

Shiro smacked him in the back of the head and he answered. "Yes, sir."

Shard's nostrils flared. "You watched the first platoon get ground into lunchmeat, so when no one was looking, you gacked the flutist and took his flute." Shard surmised. "You stabbed him in mid-note. His teeth clamped down and cracked the mouth piece." Shard shrugged. "Something like that?"

"Yes, sir." His voice was a breathless whisper, but Shiro only took half a step back, slowly, silently, drawing her sword.

"So, you're just a murdering coward?" Shard took a half step back.

As the thug opened his mouth, a sharp pike edge, flashing in the starlight like a bolt of lightning, plunged into his ribs, twisted, cracking and spreading his cage wide, then withdrew, dragging a torrent of Goblin blood with it.

The thug crumpled to the ground.

All the NCO's looked up, startled, then at the Bearer of the Standard for the *Other* Black Dragon Colors, who had not only expertly gacked the last of his company, but didn't get a drop of blood on the flag.

Shard smiled, impressed as he side-stepped the freshly formed stream of blood. "Tell you what, Momoo, I'll still take the color bearer." Shard looked up.

Momoo was gone.

Now, in the shadow of the fort, Momoo was still nowhere to be found. To Shard's right, Ozny, the Bearer of the Standard for the *Other* Black Dragon Company lay on his belly, the colors cased so that they would not touch the ground. He was going to follow the ladder crew. Shard had several ladders made, wide and sturdy, just high enough to clear the wall. As they threw the ladders against the palisade, Ozny was going to uncase the colors and charge up, leap over the top and start the killing.

All they needed now was a boom.

Bark-Bite was taking his engineers up the sewer passage, into the quarry, then up the slope to the wall of the inner fort. After it exploded, Shard would take his thugs over the wooden wall into the quarry, then into the inner fort. It would have been impossible to sneak all hundred under the palisade and, if they tried to charge, they'd quickly become mired in the bog. However, if they stormed over the wall and ran, they could enter the inner fort with speed and force.

Shard checked the horizon; the moon was moments from rising. Once it rose, the watchtower of the palisade would see them in the grass. The element of surprise would be blown.

He couldn't wait any longer. Shard grit his teeth, then nodded to Ozny.

Ozny rolled to his side, put his hands to his lips and blew an owl hoot.

Owls hooted back as dark shadows suddenly sprang from the tall grasses and moved without battle cry towards the walls. Shard watched Ozny, stripping the case as he ran and flinging it to the ground. The colors of the *Other* Black Dragon Company unfurled and raised up, its ribbons streaming in glorious wake, the pale, dawning moonlight glinting off its un-blackened pike head, sharpened to razor's edge.

Trolls rose from their position, lubberly making their comical run, their arms hanging loosely across their backs, building speed before stopping and violently whipping their rocks up into the watchtower.

Shard could feel the thunder of his thugs on the run, drowning out the beat of his heart. He lunged to his feet, following the charge. Up ahead, the first ladder crew, only a half step ahead of Ozny, threw the ladder against the palisade but before they could chock it firm, Ozny leapt the wide rungs and vaulted straight up, both hands still gripping the banner, cleared the pickets and charged down the catwalk, his pike leveled.

Shard watched two human guards, casually chatting and sharing the warmth from the torch light suddenly sense their imminent danger. Perhaps it was the sudden silence of the crickets or the clunk of the ladder hitting the wall. A ricocheted rock glanced off a helm into the warning bell of the watchtower with an off-note clank put them on full alert. One guard turned and looked out into the night, trying to peer past the blinding shimmer of torchlight. The other looked up into the watchtower, wondering if those Elves were diddling each other again.

Ozny plunged into both of them. His feet skidded as he desperately tried to stop, but only crashed into them, his pike piercing them both.

Shard watched as his thugs climbed up the ladder unabated. As he neared the ladder, he looked west, towards the sewer.

Still no sign of Bark-Bite.

Still no boom.

Shard climbed the ladder quickly, then clambered over the edge of the catwalk ledge and dropped down inside the palisade. It was quiet. No one should be moving about at this hour, but it was exceptionally quiet. No dogs were barking. No drunks wandering.

Nothing.

And the moon crested the horizon, its gentle light to a Goblin's eyes was as bright as day with shafts of brilliant white casting jagged shadows across the grounds, across the buildings.

Still nothing moved.

Shard barked and thugs fell in line. Gunny Glenkar drove them to quick march, keeping them in formation and also kept them from wandering off to begin the looting, or worse, the burning. They moved as quietly as possible. Their heavy foot-falls and clinking armor were the only thing to betray their movement.

From the rear, Shard looked around. No baying sheep, no lowing cows.

No boom.

Shard looked to the western walls of the inner fort loom-ing above him. The moon was rising! Where in Algrax's rubbery snatch was Bark-Bite?

A horrendous roar suddenly ripped through the night air. Shard felt it like a punch to the gut. A boom finally popped off, but it was too faint for the massive detonation of six Tech Lieutenants. Another roar sounded, more angry this time. It drew air like a heavy-toothed saw on hard lumber, then bel-lowed again.

Gunny Glenkar kept the thugs in line, kept them run-ning. Shard could hear the battering rams working on the gates on the east side, the thugs there chanting, the Sergeant Major shouting above it all.

Still the village was quiet.

A Human guard stepped out from an alley tying up his fly. His face open in complete surprise as four blades hacked at him simultaneously. As his head rolled back into the alley, his expression was unchanged.

Shard nodded to himself as he mentally confirmed his fears.

They were trapped like rats.

Shard cursed as Gunny Glenkar turned the column of thugs west, toward the sewer, toward the roar, toward the trap. The town had been evacuated, probably moved behind the inner fort. A skeleton crew of guards had been sacrificed to maintain appearances. It was brilliant.

Shard tightened his lips and his mono-brow hung low over his eyes. He still had the escalade ladders and wagons of Black Dirt That Blows Stuff up. He also had his Chosen Thugs. Whatever the Humans had in store for him, Shard was going to show them the error of their ways. He snarled out loud as he came to the clearing. His snarl stopped abruptly as he slid to a halt.

Black tendrils grew suddenly from the ground, rising out of the quarry. Tech Lieutenants laid strewn across the ground, their kegs broken open. Shard could hear the beast drag itself, like stone on stone from out of the quarry.

More tendrils rose. White horn nubs embedded in the pseudopod's underside flashed as it reared back and swept forward, slashing at the thugs charging in. Two shields flittered up into the air like confetti as thugs rolled ass over head into the pit. Thugs swarmed the pit, hacking at the rubbery flailing arms to no avail as more thugs were swept into the pit.

Shard tightened his lips as he drew his man-sword. He ran full force at a sweeping tendril, bearing down with both hands. His sword bounced back with more force, nailing Shard in the helm. A heartbeat later the tendril slammed into him, knocking him end over end across the grass. Shard spread his arms out, controlling his fall and stopping just on the lip of the pit. Quickly scrambling up, he peered down.

Into a cave of fangs.

Shard caught his breath and his balance as he gazed into the bowing, oh-ing, ring of teeth, dashing armor and Goblins into scraps of metal and meat. Anger filled Shard's vision as he turned away, hoisting his sword up and lunging at a flailing tentacle, hacking brutally at the scaly thing. Black speckles formed, followed by thin ribbons as Shard found a chink in its hide. Shard swung with fury, screaming incoherently, feeling its tendons fray as its blood began to spurt from a gash, its thrashing flinging it everywhere.

As Shard's sword reared back he felt a dark shadow pass across his neck from behind as another tentacle swept in behind him.

Something slammed into his side, knocking him under the sweeping path of the spiky pseudopod and dangerously toward the pit. Shard swung down to strike whatever hit him with the pommel of his sword, but hesitated when he saw the worn, purple tunic.

Momoo had taken off his steel armor, and the broken remnants of his turtle shell helm were tangled in his hair. His face was a mix of terror, fear and ecstasy.

"It's a Humongous!" he screamed desperately. "You can't win!"

Shard's angry eyes suddenrifically flashed with confusion as the realization hit him, that Momoo had just saved his life and was suggesting that a foe could not be defeated by simply sending thugs at it.

"It's a hellish beast!" Momoo shrilled. "You'll be killed! We need another plan!"

Shard ground his teeth. He didn't like Momoo telling him what to do, but he also needed another plan. Laying flat, under the sweep of the tentacles, Shard looked around desperately. Two dead Tech Lieutenants lay nearby, their kegs of Black Dirt that Blows Stuff Up unbroken on their backs.

Thugs were still charging it, hacking frantically at the looming tentacles, getting swept into the pit.

Shard struggled to his knees. "We get the fuck out of here," he shouted to Momoo. "Get the thugs to fall back and on your way out, see that keg there, roll it into the pit!"

Momoo nodded. "I have nothing to light it with!"

"Just fucking knock it in, fuckwit!" Shard leapt to his feet. "Fucking go!" Shard staggered like a drunkard over the uneven ground, by luck ducking the sweep of the Humongous, to the Tech Lieutenant's side. He hacked at the ropes of the keg on his back and kicked it rolling into the pit.

Shard turned on his heel, screaming the retreat. Behind him, he could hear the monster shift as it began to heave itself up out of its cave. Shard stopped just out of the creature's reach and fumbled in his pouch for flint and steel, his mind racing for an idea.

"Need a light?" Bark-Bite held up his brass Gnomish lighter and sparked it to a lantern he had scavenged from inside one of the abandoned houses. He squinted from its blooming light, sloshing its dark oil around in its decanter. "Give this a toss, will you?"

Shard took the lantern, noting the bleeding gash on Bark-Bite's head in the shifting light. Shard felt his stomach churn as he turned, holding the lantern aloft and waited several heartbeats for his thugs to clear before heaving the lantern. Its glowing flame arched and vanished beneath the ledge.

The Humongous gave a final heave and lifted itself out of the pit, its open mouth glowing from the burning oil of the shattered lantern.

"Oh fuckshit!" Shard exclaimed as he turned. Bark-Bite was already gone and Shard sprinted behind the cover of a building.

Two booms, one after the other, shook Shard hard. Dust rained from the rotting planks of the shack he leaned against. Two kegs filled with broken glass, rusty nails and the Black Dirt that Blows Stuff Up in its mouth should be enough to turn any creature's tiny brain into scrambled goo. Shard breathed a sigh of relief. He had to regroup quickly and have the wagon of Black Dirt That Blows Stuff Up brought up. He could charge the walls, throw up ladders and climb over. While the humans dealt with that, Bark-Bite blows the wall and the remaining two hundred thugs would drop in to say 'Hi' to Leopolis.

Stone ground on stone as the Humongous moved.

Shard held his breath. It was a death throw, a spasm. Nothing more.

It moved again, intently, purposefully.

"Fuck me!" Shard hissed. "No, really, fuck me up the ass with a Passion Mango!"

"Isn't a Passion Mango on the small side, Shard?" Momoo said peering around the corner. "Perhaps a Knobbly Nut?"

"Do you have one?" Shard asked.

Momoo looked back at him. "No."

Shard kicked him the butt. "Then shut the fuck up." He then motioned with his chin. "Can you see it?"

Momoo risked another glance. "Yes, it's burping up smoke and retreating back into the pit." Momoo pulled his head back. "All its tentacles wriggling." He wriggled his fingers to demonstrate.

"Not dead at all?"

"Not like any dead thing I know."

Shard grated his teeth painfully. "Fuck me up the ass with a..." He shook his head, then looked up, his black eyes steady. "Thanks,"

Momoo matched his eyes for a breath. "Forget it." He then quickly added: "Unless you decide sometime in the future that you're going to kill me or bugger me with a Knobbly Nut. Then I want you to remember this day, this moment." He grinned.

Shard frowned, glancing about for Bark-Bite. Not seeing him, he looked back at Momoo. "Fine, one stay of execution or Knobbly Nut buggering." Shard glanced over, checking to see his First Sergeant was rounding up thugs, then back to Momoo. "Just what the fuck are you doing here?"

He rose hauntingly. "Well, since you've commandeered my banner carrier, and gacked my flutist, I had little choice,

did I? So long as there is a living Momoo, there will be a Black
Dragon Company, I mean, *Other* Black Dragon Company, and
as long as there is fighting, the Black Dragon, uh, *Other* Black
Dragon Company will be in the midst of it!" He swelled with
pride, holding up a broken iron sword. "And look! I stabbed
someone! In the guts!" He smiled like a girl on Meat Day. "I
think I'm the third Momoo to kill someone."

Shard blinked, his mono-brow arched in surprise. "I'm
sorry, do I know you?"

"And it was a Human! Or at least a non-thug. He was
wearing armor!" He held up the remains of the blade. "Look,
red blood! And he wasn't already dead because he ran off after
I stabbed him."

"Oh, okay, it is you, Momoo." Shard nodded.

"That makes me the second Momoo to kill one of the
enemy." He beamed.

"He ran off. That means he's not like any dead thing that
I know." Shard wiped the blood from his sword.

"Don't poop on this moment, Shard," Momoo shot back.

Shard sheathed his sword. "Momoo, if I did not think
you were a sickening, perverted, useless piece of butt crust,
I'd be proud of you."

Momoo smiled as if he'd just been promoted. "I'll take
that."

Shard shouted at the First Sergeant to get him a butcher's list. He then ordered a runner to find Sergeant Major
Ribsplitter-Jones and bring him over. He looked around for

Bark-Bite but there was no sign of the enigmatic major. Only Momoo, grinning like an idiot.

"What the fuck's in that pit?" Shard finally asked.

"A Humongous. My second grand uncle attacked a full grown one with an entire division. Even sent the cooks to their death." Momoo's eyes sparkled in the moon light. "He got four wives and six mistresses the night he retold that story."

Shard peered up at the walls of the inner fort. He could see the silhouettes of the guards peering down at him. He could swear they were laughing.

"Tragically, it turned out," Momoo went on. "one of the mistresses was the wife of one of the lieutenants that was killed. So the day after their baby was born and he declared it was a Momoo, she strung up Grand Uncle with Mooserat-gut and eviscerated him. Ha, ha, ha, ha!"

Shard eyed the stone wall and the steep slope leading up to it. *Bastards! That's why the didn't finish the wall! They had a un-killable monster to guard the flank.*

"She then ground up his organs and baked them into a pie and served it to his other wives!" Momoo exploded into laugher. "For breakfast!" he squeaked.

Shard growled. "Momoo, you don't want to use up your stay of execution so soon, do you?" Momoo quieted. "Tell me about the Humongous."

Momoo shrugged. "It can't be killed." He sniffed. "That's what I went out to tell you. When I saw you fighting it, I thought..."

Shard glanced back at him quickly. "You what?"

"I thought," he began again.

"Okay, who are you?"

Momoo puffed up. "I'm just as good, if not better than you, Shard, at being an officer," Momoo said hotly.

"You bloodied one human," Shard growled. "That doesn't make you squat."

Momoo shoved the broken, bloody sword into its scabbard. "Then how's this: I've got a plan!"

"Won't work," Shard said curtly.

"You haven't heard it!"

Shard motioned with his chin. "If we charge up that steep hill, three hobbits armed with a sharp stick can hold us off for months."

Momoo looked like Shard had punched him in the stomach. "Alright then, I've a back up plan."

"Is it to tear down these huts for good timber and have the Major build us a siege tower to get us over the slope and over the wall fast?"

"Maybe," Momoo answered tentatively.

Shard frowned. "Won't work."

Momoo slapped his thighs in exasperation. "Why bloody not!"

Shard eyed the walls. He wasn't sure. The Humongous obviously never strayed too far from its pit. Feed it a couple pigs and it's the perfect rear guard. The slope was treacherous, but not unscalable. It would take time to build a siege tower.

"Time..." Shard whispered as the idea rolled in his head. "They're stalling. They've played us but good," he growled.

"Right you are!" Bark-Bite shouted.

Momoo and Shard looked up at Bark-Bite who was hunkered down in a watchtower, peering through a far-seer.

"By Othiffer's cavernous bung hole, how does he do that?" Shard swore as he trotted towards the tower. He peered up the rickety ladder to the tiny hatch in the floor of the tower, then eyed the inner fort and its bobbing shadowy heads peering over the chiseled picket wall. Shard scrambled quickly up, and a few half-hearted shafts launched from short bows whizzed by. He crawled to the gunnel of the tower where Bark-Bite sat, just enough of his head exposed to peer over.

He leaned back, adjusting his spectacles and handing the far-seer to Shard. "I was wondering that very same thing." Bark-Bite sighed, picking up the conversation in thought. "No resistance at the wall? That was the place to put troops. The inner walls are a last ditch, but they let us right to it." He turned and spat down the hatch.

"Hey!" Momoo shouted from below. "Is it raining? It smells like... Ugh!"

"Sorry," Bark-Bite mumbled, cuffing his chin. "Anyway, Shard, they wouldn't lead us here without reason."

Shard scrambled to his knees and lifted the far-seer over the gunnel.

The sky was a pure, dark blue disk across the world. The moon had fully cleared the horizon and the bushy trees sparkled silver as they gently shivered in the light wind. In the darkness, Shard could make out the still ocean in the distance, the lights of the ships in the harbor glowed dimly. "Lemme guess, Human ships?"

"Mmmhmmm." Bark Bite nodded. "Chasing away our ships and preventing us from getting the Princess back home." He nudged the far-seer. "Look that way," he instructed.

Shard squinted, then could just make out a thin, rumbling stream of dust rising messily in the night air off in the distance.

"They're marching at night," Bark-Bite said somberly. "They are the hammer."

Shard slumped down, peering at the darkened form of Bark-Bite. "And we're sitting on the anvil." Shard's monobrow lowered, a straight line over his eyes. "How the fuck did they know? How the fuck could they have guessed we'd come here?"

Bark-Bite sighed tiredly. "Fuck knows?" He motioned his hand for a drink and as Shard fished out his flask, Bark-Bite spat his chaw down the hatch.

"Eeew!" Momoo exclaimed. "Will you please stop that?" The tower shuddered. "What was that?" Momoo cried. "Am I being shot at?"

"Climb down, Momoo," Shard said as he handed the flask to Bark-Bite.

The tower shook again. "If there's an officer's meeting up there…"

Shard growled. "Then dodge the arrows and get up here."

The tower shook again. "Dodge the arrows?" Momoo whined. "How am I supposed... Oops!" The tower stilled as Momoo fell off the ladder. He landed on his butt with a curse.

Bark-Bite took a swig and handed the flask back. "Did I ever tell you what my goal in life was, Shard?"

Shard stoppered the flask without taking a swig. "No, sir."

"It's to become an alcoholic. Do you know how to become an alcoholic?"

"No, sir."

"Drink alone."

Shard un-stoppered his flask and took a swallow.

"Damn you, Shard." The Major smiled.

Shard felt this throat burn as the Dwarven rum slipped down. "Am I so dumb that I can't outsmart one Human?"

"Yes, you're that fucking dumb." Bark-Bite smiled, his straight teeth like old ivory. "They know our every move. I don't know how. They snuck up on us. If we run flat out like stupid sons-of-bitches they'll snipe at us with Elves and wear us down." He shrugged. "We're stuck."

Shard took a breath, feeling the rum burn his sinuses. "They know the moves of the whole fucking thug army." Shard thought carefully. "But we took Old Gourd Head? They didn't think we'd climb that fucking hill." Shard nodded at his own logic. "So they can be fooled. They can be outsmarted." Shard's eyes glazed to a flat black. "So that's what we do. How much time do I have?"

Bark-Bite fumbled in pocket. "Rough roads, soft Human troops, two fast companies..." He took out his Chronodisk, opened it up and checked the moon rise, then nodded to himself. "They will be in attack range before noon."

Shard pushed out his jaw as he thought. "Remember that map you sketched in the dirt? The one with the terrain features?"

"The one with Momoo and the sheep?"

Shard nodded. "What was that other terrain feature?"

Shard's Fortress

THE WARMING BLUSH of dawn painted the quickening blue sky with watercolors of pink and orange as Shard shifted lower on the grassy glen. He glanced over his shoulder, back at the dark shadow of the fort, then hunkered down further, beneath the possible gaze of a far-seer.

He listened for a moment. He could hear a chirpy bug fucking around near by. Ribsplitter-Jones would probably know its name and what it was actually up to but Shard couldn't give a Jerk Chicken's crinkly ass what the bug's name was, or what it was up to. However, Shard knew if it was chirping, it probably meant he was alone.

And Shard didn't need witnesses.

Lower on the glen was a ring of boulders surrounding a depression that funneled into a hole.

Keeping an eye on the hole, Shard unshouldered his pack. He unstrapped his bedroll, then quietly pulled out his spare skivvies and laid them out beside him. He gently laid his mess gear on top of them. His whetstone, wrapped in an black oily cloth, and his tin of healing salve came out next.

He pulled out a serrated brass bladed claw that he used to hack off the nastier bits of foot calluses. He gave that a sniff, then thumbed the blade. He set that aside. The last of his Dwarven rum, his coffee mug, his coffee pot and his grinder went beside that. He found some hardtack that he'd forgotten about. He brushed off the dusty mold, picked out a dead grub and gave it a funeral flick off into the grass, then set the tack beside his skivvies. He had two bags of coffee. One that he had brought from Bratanich and hoarded miserly. The beans were furry with fungus, but that only mellowed the taste. The other he had taken from a Human commander along with a deck of marked cards. He had two shiny brass doorknobs from Ol' Gourd Head. Ornately carved, expensive and proof that he had taken the fort that could not be taken. Beneath that was part of a black dragon scale that he had rummaged from the smoldering barn. He had been shaving pieces of it to give to his Chosen Thugs to wear. It made them proud and proud thugs fought like sons of bitches.

Below that was a leather valise the Colonel had given him. His orders. Below that was the bottom.

Shard looked around. The grass was still dark with night, the stupid bug was still happily singing to itself and a soft morning wind was in his face. Only him and the hole in the ground beneath the carefully arranged circle of boulders.

Shard picked at the stitches at the bottom of his pack. Invisible stitches that to the eye of a carpet weaver were gross and hastily done. Beneath the flap were three little bags, packed flat and stitched tightly. Shard palmed each one, checking its weight, thumbing the coins to count them through the cloth, to make sure all his gold, silver and pennies were there.

He stashed them under his skivvies to hide them again.

A sliver of gold crested the horizon as the sun finally began its climb. Shard had to hurry. He felt safe in the cold shadow of the tall, squared boulders that had been stood up around the hole in the ground, around Bark-Bite's other terrain feature.

But the little bug sang its song. Its solo. It was the only bug as far as Shard could hear.

Must be jerking off, Shard thought as he peered into the bottom of his very empty kit.

And Wiggletooth Shard picked at the tight, tight stitches on the bottom of his pack to reveal its hidden, hidden compartment.

Dry, padded with soft Shark-rabbit fur was a pouch three thug hands long. Shard looked around again. Only him, the masturbating insect and the tall, chiseled hunks of rocks paraded in a circle around the big smelly hole.

Shard took out his secret pouch, along with his cold memories of abandonment, loneliness and warm, simmering hate.

Like a thousand, thousand times before, he opened it.

Goblinwood is a hard, pain in the ass wood to work with. It is nearly indestructible, growing only on the treacherously high snow-covered peaks of the craggy mountain range of Gah with tortured, deformed boughs, tiny poisonous leaves, and sneaky razor-sharp thorns. It doesn't burn well and stinks butt-awful when it does. It is hard to carve, instantly blunting any chisel with its boiling mass of knots. Lastly, it was most unforgiving to the blade. One false cut and it would shatter like glass, destroying years of hard work.

Worst of all, Goblinwood is ugly. Shaved monkey balls ugly. Ribbons of okra green flow through its dark, red wood, prompting the Elves to name it *'Towa a o'wall gnit'* the Tree of Bloody Snot.

Goblinwood has one, and only one, usable quality.

Resonance.

Lyre, harp, drum. Add its shaving to a horn as a reed for sounds never heard before. An angel's voice, a baby's cry, a lover's moan. It was the perfect wood to use in any instrument, but it was far too ugly for the Elves to think of touching it, let alone have the patience to try carving one. Hobbits have the skill and the patience, but are far too enamored with Elves to acknowledge the existence of the wood. The Dwarves have the skill, patience and couldn't care less for fashion, but are all born tone deaf. Humans are far too lazy to work the craggy, unmerciful wood.

Only Goblins ever bothered, but their iron chisels were no match for the irritable wood. To say the least, an instrument of any kind made from Goblinwood was a rare artifact indeed.

Polished into wet, rippling glass, his fingers sliding gently across its perfect holes, its beautiful rune carvings, Shard awakened the hate, the evil of the monstrosity in his hands.

He couldn't read the Goblin words delicately carved in beautiful, flowing Elvish font, but he knew what they said.

And it pissed him off.

Shard's flute was perfectly straight, perfectly toned and carved so the natural flowing stripes of vomit green accented the engraved, bubbling, bloody swath so that the light played happily within, causing it to pulse, to ooze, like an infected seeping wound. A magical Goblin thing of beauty.

Shard wanted to smash it.

He wanted to smash it all those years ago. He wanted to build a massive pyre and burn it. He wanted to find the bitch who made it and drive it into her head so its fickle gooey green flowed into her brain, and then play it directly into her grey matter.

He had written a song when he was six years old for just the occasion. It was so awful and filled with brash, flat notes that it gave Shard a four-day migraine from the first six bars. The middle refrain gave him a nose bleed. He passed out from the searing pain across both eyes one night as he practiced. One day, he'd play a final performance. She would close her eyes, her delicate brow furrowed with pain, and she would weep, then die horribly.

Shard set it aside, then re-packed his pack and shouldered it.

Then he picked up the magic Goblin flute and drew breath to play.

Shard took the flute from his lips and breathed out the hate. He wouldn't be able to play what was needed with the foul mood rising within him. He calmed himself and looked up at the newly birthed sun and the pink-filled sky. He breathed in the cool, shadowy air. He metered out a beat, taping his foot to the dancing chirp of the masturbating bug and played something chipper, something pretty...

Something Elvish.

White gossamer ghost birds sailed into the warming sky that blossomed into magic, glittering rainbows that rained joyful dark chocolate frogs with gold buttery eyes that cast beams of funny moonlight guiding charm moths that sang tales in choral harmony of old forest green and laugh-out-loud purple kittens play fighting over swirling beds of Bio-luminescent sherbet blue yarn spun from the finest new fallen wintery frost.

Shard wanted to puke, but he played on. Beads of sweat steamed on his brow as his tune carried itself. His eyes were closed tightly as he tried to keep the happy, happy mood of the Elves in his head. He didn't actually know any Elven tunes, their musical theory far too complicated for him, but he could play something Elf-esque, and hopefully that would do the trick.

And the hole grunted, then grumbled.

Shard played.

The hole snorted, then grumbled again, then farted wet and nasty.

And Shard played on, eyes tearing from the rising stench.

"Wz't?" Deep from the hole, something stirred. "Hah? Wazat?"

Shard played, his eyes open and carefully watching the hole.

"Whodat?" The hole farted again and something began to move, sniffing towards the hole, toward the light.

Shard stashed the flute quickly. "Elves! You Elves get away from here!" Shard shouted. "You shouldn't be here!"

"El's!" Something from the hole barked. "Frin som a ate fugly ELVES!" Its malformed head poked from the hole, one big tusk leading the way from its jutting jaw. "Fugly el's!" Its massive head swiveled around and spotted Shard, its dark eyes narrowed. "Hew El's?"

Shard was offended. "No! A whole fuck load of Elves just ran that way!" Shard pointed at the fortress. "They pissed on your rock garden here and..."

Suddenly the beast howled in pain. "Ais 'ate fugliels!" It lunged from its hole. Rising to its full height and hoisting its long, massive, bowed arms to the sky, it screamed again. Its lumpy, boney head sat directly on its hunched back shoulders. A mane of black, spiky hair spewed back from its head like the wind was always blowing in its face. Ritual scars, keloid and fat as a thug's small finger ran the length of its heavy arms like the rungs of a ladder. Its vast stomach sloshed back and forth, chaffing itself as it rubbed across the tops of its furry thighs.

It heaved itself forward on massive, tree-trunk legs and charged; its cock, an offensive member, whacked side to side with a painful slap.

It was circumcised.

Shard took off after the monster, the Ogre he had summoned. It was one of the few creatures with a hatred of Elves comparable to his own. "There!" Shard pointed at the fortress. "I think I saw them! You see them?"

The Ogre stopped, panting, then looked down at itself. Shard had woken it from a dead sleep and slowly its brain was kicking in. It shook its head sadly, then turned and lumbered towards its hole.

"Where the fuck are ya going?" Shard asked bewildered. "They fucking pissed on your rocks! Are you gonna let them get away with that?"

"Ahs come!" It shouted back. "Hols yers, I get ma dress!" The Ogre slipped back into its hole.

Shard waited the long pause as the Ogre found his clothes.

The Ogre burst from its hole, still naked, but now brandishing a club, as long as two thugs tall and a Nagril's horn as thick as Shard's arm, hammered through the business end. The Ogre bellowed furiously and charged after the non-existent Elves.

Shard ran faster, passing the heaving Ogre and cresting the hill. He pointed and shouted at the Elves that weren't there and the Ogre followed suit. "I saw them!" Shard shouted. "That way!" Shard ran through the broken front gates and ducked behind a house. Panting, he chirped out a few notes on his flute and then kept it out of sight. "This way!" Shard shouted as he ran through the houses, making his way to the low area of the fortress. "I can smell their perfume!" Shard ran on, leading the way, trying not to laugh with trilling fear that he had just awoken a furious, brain-dead monster that could turn Shard into a chunky, bloody smear with a single swipe of its club.

Shard leaped over a broken barrel and weaved between two buildings, panting, fighting to keep the lead, scream ob-scenities at the Elves, and not laugh out loud. He paused and whistled a quick Elvish staccato and ran on, towards the southwest gate, toward the quarry where the other monster lived.

Shard burst into the clearing and leapt down into the quarry, trying to whistle some notes with a short breath. With each harsh breath, Shard could taste the rotting stench from the Humongous' hovel. The creature had vomited out the indigestible steel armor and it glistened in the new morning sun, strewn across the dried black blood and mud that lined the monster's hole. Shard felt his anger brewing. "I got a little present for you," he whispered.

A shadow flashed across Shard as the Ogre leapt over-head into the pit, its massive Johnson trailing behind him like a fleshy tail. Shard struggled to his feet. "There!" he shouted. "In that cave! The Elves ran in there!"

The Ogre heaved his club over his shoulder, gripped in both hands, and bellowed ugly as it charged without hesita-tion into the Humongous' lair.

Shard felt a sudden pang of guilt, but dispelled it with a snort as he looked back at the houses. "Now!" he shouted.

Shard could feel his heart pounding out the long seconds as he waited. His mono-brow bunched up on itself. "I said now! Fuck bag!"

Momoo poked his head out from behind a building. "Now, what?"

Shard reeled back, trying not to howl. "By Grinfoul's odorous ass rash!" He howled anyway. "The plan!"

Momoo looked cross, surprised that Shard had forgotten his own plan. "You said to wait for the signal."

"The signal is 'Now!' You twit!" Shard screamed, wanting to choke Momoo.

Momoo made a small 'Oh' and looked back. "Alright you thugs! Get to it. Look sharp."

Twenty thugs marched out from behind a building carrying doors and tables in front of them and over their heads. "Double time!" Gample shouted from within the Goblin *testudo* and the thugs broke into a trot. Shard watched as they ran past his position, mentally counting the seconds.

Now! He thought and the Trolls broke position on cue from behind the buildings and ran forward, gaining momentum with their rocks ready to fling. Arrows were raining on the wooden formation as it trudged into range, some picking targets in the unshielded sides, but the formation moved steadily on. As the faster moving Trolls reached arrow range, archers changed targets but found the darting Trolls a challenge to hit. Once at long range, the Trolls let their ungainly missiles fly. They had no chance of hitting anything at that long distance, but their job was to harass and drive the archers from the walls for only a few crucial seconds.

Seconds for the little wooden tank formation to deploy the Bug Heads.

Newly appointed by her Highness, six thugs were promoted to the rank of Tech Lieutenant. Wearing the Black Dirt that Blows Stuff Up that was taken from Ol' Gourd Head strapped to their backs, the new Tech Lieutenants didn't have the shinny armor, but they did have the Princess' favor– her panties– awarded to them by her delicate hand herself, which they wore on their heads, giving them a bug eyed appearance.

The wooden tank smartly parted, opening ranks to allow the Bug Heads a clear shot at the rampart walls. They charged as fast as they could with the massive kegs strapped to their backs, smoke pouring from the bungholes, hunched over from the unbalanced load, the rope digging painfully into their shoulders, rubbing flesh bloody raw, black stains tarring the straps, but they ran happy, proud and determined to deliver her Highness' message.

Up the steep palisade, on hands and knees they crawled. Archers above leaned far over trying to find an angle to shoot down, their arrows thudding into the barrels, the thugs obeying their Sergeant Major's last instructions. "Keep yer heads down and run straight at 'em."

And they did run.

From the cover of the wooden tank, Trolls continued to harry the archers above with impunity as the archers focused desperately on the impeding threat from below. Crawling, grunting with effort they climbed, slowing as the ground steepened, but their goal in sight, they climbed with ever more determination.

The wooden testudo was pulling back, the Trolls threw their last rocks.

The archers were retreating from the wall.

The Tech Lieutenants climbed.

Shard ducked below the lip of the crater.

At the wooden wall, the only weakness in Leopolis' defense, the Tech Lieutenants lined up, pulling each other up to the thin ledge where they could stand. Clinging to the log fort they chanted in Human tongue: "A present from her High..."

They vanished in a shattering clap of thunder.

Shard clambered over the lip. A playful wind pulled aside the curtain of grey smoke to show the entire wooden portion of the fort was gone along with several feet of stoneworks. Shard sneered as he thought, *Leopolis didn't see it coming.* He didn't reinforce the wall with a berm or a second wall. He thought his monster would be enough to protect his fat ass.

Thugs erupted out of hiding at the charge, escalade ladders in the front. Shard leapt from his position and lead the way, bellowing the new battle cry: "No burning! No fucking burning, you fuck bags!"

Up the slope, Shard let the faster thugs with the ladders take the lead while he joined up with Ozny, the *Other* Black

Dragon Company's standard bearer who ran closely behind the ladders. The ladder crews climbed as high as they could run, then jammed their ladders into the ground, and with mallet and spikes, secured them. Ozny didn't wait that long. He vaulted up the ladders, up the soft, freshly blown up dirt and over the broken, jagged teeth of the wall.

Shard followed as closely as he could, running up the rungs, but bogging down on the soft earth beyond the ladders. More thugs ran up and Shard grabbed and pulled at them to heave himself higher, ordering his thugs onward. Shard felt a hand on his butt and looked to see Ribsplitter-Jones pushing him along. The Sergeant Major then reached down, grabbed Private Stalycks and, with a grunt, flung her up over the broken wall. In flight, she drew her short swords, one in each hand, and joined the growing fray.

Shard clambered over the shattered logs and drew his man-sword as more of this thugs scrambled around him, chanting: "We're counter-attacking! We're counter-attacking!"

The Humans, dazed from the explosion, ear drums shattered, loosely formed a shield wall, their pikes leveled. Shard charged into them, batting the pikes aside and lunging forward, slamming into the shields and voraciously hacking with abandon. The Human ranks broke as the on-rushing tide of thugs poured in. Shard stepped forward, driving his man-sword with both hands furiously, grunting with almost every blow: "Who's laughing now, asshat?"

Shard chopped down with a quick, shallow stroke, cracking a Human helm as well as the skull beneath. He swatted attacks aside and riposted with lethal cuts, stomping on the fallen, still screaming at the Humans, and charging on.

At a run, the Humans in full rout, Shard ordered his thugs to root them out. "Kill any human with a weapon or any male taller than yourself!" And the thugs cheered and flowed in. The entire Black Dragon Company at the run, their sergeants falling behind their voracious enthusiasm and bellowing to keep ranks and burn nothing. Shard ran toward the center of the fort and thugs fell in behind him. He was chasing the last of the Humans, running panic-swept with open and empty hands, their eyes wide and desperate, toward the quickly closing doors of Leopolis' manor.

The doors slammed shut in their faces with the echo of a tomb.

The Humans pounded on the unyielding doors but could only hear the heavy locking bar slide into place. They turned, startled at how close the thugs were, and threw themselves to their knees to beg for mercy. Shard stopped, hearing their cries, and raised his sword. They had laughed as his thugs were ground into bits by their monster. Shard wanted to hear them laugh again.

The Black Dragon Company fell on them angrily.

Shard was a little miffed that he didn't get to swing, but he turned to his artist, pointing. "You got that, right? The cowering, me holding the sword? Tell me you saw that!"

The artist who spoke not a word of Goblin, just kept sketching.

Shard shrugged with his mono-brow and looked at someone to bark orders at. "Hey, numb fuck!" Seven thugs stopped dead and saluted. "All of you go find something to break this door down." They nodded, then looked around the ground quickly and seeing nothing there, seized the smallest thug and hoisted him up. Shard put up his hands. "Stop!" He ordered. "Get a log or something heavy!" Shard watched them scramble, picking up cobblestones, bottle caps and piles of manure. "Go back to the wooden palisade, find a log as thick as a thug and as long or longer than this many thugs standing on each other," Shard held up three fingers, "then bring it here." The thugs nodded, saluted and ran off. Shard then bellowed for his First Sergeant. "I want a hundred thugs at the ready to storm this place." She nodded and started barking orders.

Suddenly a Goblin ran by with tendrils of orange fire streaming from his burning body. "I said no burning!" Shard shouted. "You thugs! Find that thug, extinguish him, and gack him!" Four thugs ran off to comply and Shard shook his head. "No burning," Shard mumbled to himself. "How hard is that?" He quickly looked to the artist. "Don't draw that! Just rip that up!"

The artist kept drawing.

Shard decided to go through his sketchbook later as the thugs brought up the log. Shard nodded, climbing up on a hay bale and checking how many thugs he had. It certainly looked like a hundred with more on the way. Ribsplitter-Jones was wading through, his flat head, even through his polished turtle helm, could be seen. Shard waved him over. "We're taking these hundred thugs into the manor to clear it out."

Ribsplitter-Jones looked around. "Yer gots twenty-fives heres."

Shard nodded. "We're going in waves." He recovered quickly. "I need more thugs."

Ribsplitter-Jones looked at the manor walls. "I'll say."

Shard punched him lightly in the arm. "Well go frigging find some! You'll lead the second wave."

"E'rats, begging the Captain's pardon in all," Ribsplitter-Jones said, "Ares you thinkings of leadin' the first wave?"

"Why not?"

"Aahs well, there is a bit of danger with that, there is. Don't know what's behind that door. E'rats be a trap."

"And who do you suggest lead them?" Shard's monobrow was level across his eyes.

Ribsplitter-Jones looked around, then pointed. "Hey! Gunny Glenkar! Take these thugs on a suicide charge through this door. Kill all the male humans taller than you and don't set fire to the place."

Glenkar nodded. "And what do I do with humans shorter than me?"

"Punch 'em in the guts and keep going."

He smiled and then bellowed to the crowd amassing around him. "Suicide squad, fall in!" All the thugs saluted, then at Glenkar's direction, formed up into column. They parted as the heavy battering ram that Shard had ordered arrived.

The doors withstood the first blow, trembled with the second, shuddered with the third and exploded with the forth. The battering ram crew led the charge. Shard lead the second wave.

There was little left.

Bodies of humans lay still as they had in their final seconds of life, in daring defense of their lord's home. Shard walked through the only blood-free trail he could find, and deep into the hall. The walls were a warm, dark wood paneling, highlighted with faded red drapes and sober family portraits. As Bark-Bite had promised, Leopolis lived miserly, more evidence that he had not found the treasure that Bark-Bite had squirreled away so many years ago. Shard felt his frown deepen. It was sparse, obviously the bare minimal stuff for the spot the Goblins raided first every few years. Shard looked around, where he needed to go was down.

But first things first.

"Has anyone found Leopolis?" Shard shouted over the din of Goblins chasing women and children.

Glenkar looked up, a human female kicking and screaming over his shoulder. "What's he look like?"

Shard had no idea. "Well dressed fellow, taller than a thug, a little aged, balding, blue eyes and surrounded by the most guards." Shard pointed to the grand portrait on the wall. "Looks like that guy."

Glenkar's face faded to a blank as he ran images through his mind. Shard moved on. "Never mind. Get all the Human women and take them out to the wall for the next part of the plan."

Suddenly the thugs all stopped as they remembered the next phase of the plan and smiled.

Shard pushed through, waving Ribsplitter-Jones over and the ten thugs that were with him. Shard had noticed a thug peering into a door beneath the stairs and Shard could feel the cold breeze wafting from it.

The basement.

Shard pulled him out of the way and, brandishing his man-sword, took a look for himself.

Glowing torch light flickered, throwing shadows across the stairway. Shard could see heads bobbing up and down, looking uncertain. These would be the elite guards; the disciplined, well-armored, trained killers. Their chosen battleground was cramped and narrow where thugs could not overwhelm them. This is where they would feast on Goblin blood. This was where they would make their final stand and clog up the tunnel with Goblin dead. They would die, but at an expensive price.

Shard ground his teeth as he thought. He waved his thugs back, out of the doorway and looked around the hall. He looked to his closet thug. "Bring me oil."

He looked confused. "But you said no burning..."

Shard punched him in the face and looked at the thug standing next to him. "Bring me oil."

The thug nodded and quickly ran off. Shard grabbed the thug he had punched and pointed where the second thug ran off. "Go help him."

As the thug, still holding his nose, ran off, Shard turned and looked at the portrait on the wall. He reached up and gently lifted it down, then turned and smashed its frame. He picked up its pieces and torn canvas in his arms. His black eyes sweeping over his confused thugs. "Smash those chairs. We need wood. For burn." The thugs scrambled, falling over themselves for things to burn.

Shard flung the portrait down the stairs, listening to its heavy frame clattering all the way to the bottom. He reached back and grabbed the broken chair that had been carved from a thousand-year-old camphor tree and hurled it down. He stepped back as his thugs tossed down a credenza that had been carried on the back of a slave from the across the world. They tossed down a porcelain sink kilned in the mountains of Havak Haugh and heard it shatter into a shower of tiny bits.

He could hear the men below moving uneasily, confused. Shard smiled as he hefted two crystal lanterns, sloshing full with oil and flung them one after the other down the stairs.

Panic clashed down below as Shard ordered his thugs to back up and form a half circle around the door. More thugs ambled over, drawn by curiosity, and Shard forced them into the formation.

Then he drew his man-sword.

And waited.

A thug stepped forward with a fiery brand and Shard grabbed his arm. "I said no burn!" He whispered harshly at the confused thug. Shard took the brand and snuffed it out in a potted plant. He had a better plan to deal with the enemy.

They were noble knights and were not going to die burned to death in a basement, their swords unbloodied, their women unavenged.

Shard only had to wait.

Their heavy, armored feet thundered on wooden steps in single file. In a desperate charge, they assaulted the narrow, winding stairs, the first with his shield lifted high, guarding his head like a battering ram in a blind run. He fell to Ribsplitter-Jones's heavy axe swing to the back of his neck. More knights squeezed through, tripping over the fallen body and thugs hacked furiously. One paused in the doorway, his eyes wide from the horror and the bristling ring of Goblin steel. Shard reached over and grabbed his arm and pulled him into the masticating machine of death.

Shard sneered as he watched them die, just as they had watched thugs die at their walls or drown off their shore.

Shard nodded and two columns of thugs charged down the stairs to clear out anyone left behind. There was only one knight left and he had taken his sword and somehow beheaded himself. The thugs respected this immeasurably and left his body unmolested.

Shard made his way down, pushing thugs out of his way, past the headless knight, doomed to haunt the land of Glambin-Sur, and further in, towards the final door. The thugs seemed unwilling to go further, peeking nervously around the bend, but Shard paid little mind and pushed on.

As he turned the corner, he stopped, his breath still in his lungs.

Leopolis, or the guy in the portrait, floated before him, hovering in the air, his mouth agape in mild surprise, a line of darkening red blood across his face and Lil' Elfie sticking out of his forehead, nailing him to the door.

Shard caught his breath and regained his composure. With a angry growl, he seized Lil' Elfie and yanked it from the door, dropping Leopolis to the ground in a crumpled heap. He looked at its magic blade, quickly flickering a mystical blue hue, signaling Elves in the area. Shard sneered, glancing around. Probably some elf trinket or some such lying around. Shard simply plunged it back into the body of Leopolis.

He then knocked on the door.

"'Bout time you arrived," Bark-Bite mumbled through the door.

"I had to hack my way through," Shard growled irritably. "Have you found the treasure?"

Suddenly the door opened and Bark-Bite poked his head through, his eyes a little distracted. "Treasure?" He blink-ed. "Of course I found it! Now make sure your thugs aren't burning everything!" With a sharp bang, he slammed the door. He then opened the door, reached through and yanked Lil' Elfie free with a torrent of blood and slammed the door again.

Shard shook his head, a little surprised that the Major was taking his cut first and not trusting Shard to make sure he got his percentage.

Shard stomped back around to where his thugs waited. "Top side! Let's move it!" he barked.

They nodded and turned, banging their shins as they slipped in the oil. Shard watched them go, then turned to the headless knight, his sword still clenched in his gauntleted hand. Shard set his face as he pried the fingers apart and pulled the sword free. It felt good in his hands, balanced. He squinted at the edge. It had been sharpened, nicked, re-smithed, nicked again and sharpened again. It wasn't a dress sword. Many thugs had fallen to this wicked weapon.

Shard took the gauntlets and the helm, liking their fit, then headed upstairs, careful not to bust his ass on the oil-slick steps. His thugs had made quick work of the bodies and what they had carried and everything else that wasn't nailed down. Shard quickly ran outside where Ribsplitter-Jones had ordered all the loot to be piled up. "I want a helm, and one of those swords ear-marked for her Highness."

"Heya, good stuff?" Ribsplitter-Jones noted.

Shard showed him the gauntlets. "Nice, eh?" He looked up to the Sergeant Major. "Snag yourself a pair. And get a new helm, that one there should fit your flat head. You don't have to wear this stupid turtle shell anymore." Shard reached up and yanked it off the Sergeant Major's head. "I don't know why you still wear this."

"E'rats a good home for the turtle."

Shard's mono-brow twisted. "What?"

And Ribsplitter-Jones' helm bit Shard in the soft web between this thumb and finger.

"Fuck shit!" Shard yanked the turtle free. "By Aagvar's extra leaky tit!" Shard sucked on his hand. "Why the fuck is the turtle still in there?"

"E'rats I was supposed to do wit 'im?" Ribsplitter-Jones snatched the helm back before Shard had a chance to hurl his beloved helm somewhere. "Can't havs a nekkid turtle runnin' around. Pathetic lookin' that is."

Shard looked at his hand to survey the damage. "The little bastard!" Shard looked up at Ribsplitter-Jones. "How come he doesn't bite you?"

"E'rats, Skippy gets a little nippy around strangers."

Shard could see the clumps in Ribsplitter-Jones' hair where Skippy had gotten nippy. "Get a box to keep Skippy in and get yourself a real helm. Meet me by the wall when you're done." Shard pushed him out of the way and stormed off, winding his way through the narrow alleys. At the wall, First Sergeant Shiro and several thugs had taken several crossbeams from one of the houses and propped them up on saw horses and lashed the whole thing solid. Gunny Glenkar and his crew were busy dragging the women forward. Each one they strapped belly down across the post, then lashed wrists to ankles, enjoying their squeals of protests.

Shard nodded and turned towards the lookout tower. "Well, Momoo?"

Momoo took his eye from the far-seer. "The Human army is advancing. Humans on horseback just galloped into view and galloped back."

"Get out of the tower and get back behind the wall." Shard then paused. "Good job!" he shouted.

Momoo's head appeared above the gunnel. "What?"

"Get your lame ass over here!" Shard snapped. He turned and climbed the rampart, peered over the wall down below to the front gates where thugs busied themselves dumping trash and debris and spreading it around. "Alright you thugs! That's good enough. Get behind the wall." Shard looked to the tree line. He could see humans on horseback, their far-seers open, their lenses trained on him.

Shard smiled and waved, then called down below. "Gimme this many thugs!" Five thugs lumbered up the ladder and presented themselves. "Up on the wall!" Shard ordered. "Watch the spikes. Careful, get your balance." Shard helped them up, teetering on the awkward edge. "Alright! Preeee-sent, Arses!" He ordered and with a brief look of confusion, the thugs untied their trousers, ringed them around their ankles and presented their derriere to the enemy. Shard then waved at the enemy along with a big, toothy grin.

"What? No commence fart?" Momoo said.

Shard waved them off the wall and all five fell forward to the rampart tangled in their trousers. "There'll be a nice, big, nasty fart in a few minutes. Get to the main manor and get yourself a good sword and helm. We whacked a dozen knights. They have the nice shit."

"What good will it do?" Momoo whined. "They're going to siege us. That's all they have to do: surround us and let us starve. Shard's Siege. Brilliant bloody plan, Shard."

Shard turned back to the wall, just peering through the gaps as humans on foot were using hooked spears to poke at the garbage and pull the makeshift blockade apart, waiting for the Goblin attack. Two Elves with arrows knocked, cowered behind the shattered doors. Shard doubted their arrows could reach him at the wall from there, but he took no chances.

"You've got five minutes before our guests arrive." Shard looked back to Momoo. "Make yourself presentable."

Momoo drew his broken iron sword, still sticky with human blood. "My blade has acquired a taste for blood. I think I'll keep it."

Shard suddenly and viciously grabbed Momoo's wrist, then yanked free the sword. With a casual toss, sent it over the wall. "Next I'll kick you in the balls, fuck nut. Now get suited up."

Momoo mewed as his sword spun out of sight, already missing it. "They're going to siege us, Shard," Momoo answered flatly, anger starting to rise. "There won't be any killing. And I wanted to save that sword as a souvenir. I'm the third Momoo in history..." He winced and doubled over as Shard kicked him in the crotch. "Ooof. I see your point, I think," he squeaked. "I have to admit, the Princess has a better kick. Hurk!" he chirped as Shard kicked him harder. "Oh, yeah, that's what I'm talking about," Momoo wheezed.

Shard peered down from the rampart to see if there was anything soft to land on. There wasn't. He nudged Momoo off the rampart and flinched when the Captain landed with a thud. He then turned and peered at the enemy.

The light cavalry pranced at the tree line. Their pickets had reported they could take the outer wall without resistance and now they were going to make a show of it, a show of power. With streamers dancing from their shiny lances, their horses at a parade canter, they made their way in column formation toward the broken front gates to show the nasty Goblins their place.

Shard looked below the wall and skipped his fist against his open palm.

The thug nodded and quickly sparked a light to his fuse.

Shard watched the processional of the light cavalry make its way through the gates. First the pickets, hoisting heavy shields over their heads to protect them from the Troll's stones. Then came the officers with their pretty lances and tall shakos with a blue plume springing from the crown, riding their light, fast horses at a trot, followed by their footmen running like little sons of bitches to keep up.

Shard sighed. Absolutely no imagination at all.

The trash and debris left by the gate had been smeared with snot to discourage the Humans from touching it more than they had too. If they had looked closely, they would have found the two kegs of Black Dirt that Blows Stuff up before it found them.

Shard watched the pickets and horsemen as they moved safely past. They were not the targets.

Four ranks of footmen in columns of three vanished in the blast of smoke and fury. Three more ranks were knocked flat and not getting up. Another two writhed in agony and screamed. The remaining footmen scattered in confusion as the horsemen fought to rein in their rearing mounts.

Shard only smiled and waved.

They were pissed now.

Pissed and stupid.

The horsemen galloped through the town toward the quarry and Shard ran to greet them. The thugs had piled up a quick fascine where they had blown through in the initial attack and now were crouched down behind the debris of the fort walls, keeping out of sight. Shard dashed over and crouched beside them, leery of Elven arrows. The Human commander's weren't stupid enough to try the treacherous slope to the heavy, iron-reinforced front gates where Trolls could unmercifully rain stones on them and the fools hadn't the forethought to cut a tree for a battering ram.

Without a key, they weren't getting in that way.

Leaving only the back door.

Rolls reversed, now it was Shard at the wall, watching the invaders below.

Footmen scrambled about the pit of the Humongous. Not hearing anything, they tried teasing the beast to come out, but with shrugging shoulders reported to their commanders.

An Elven arrow let loose, its pluck like a tuned guitar string and with a white flash of its white feather, arched unerringly up and into the buttock of a Goblin who had stood up on the barricade and mooned the enemy. The thug howled and yelped, hopping back and forth. Suddenly a rapid fusillade of white feather shafts hissed by, trying to hit the thug. The other thugs couldn't help but laugh and Shard let it go on, letting the Human commander think him distracted.

The Elves were putting up cover fire.

Two horsemen at full gallop charged from the cover of the houses reaching up halfway before bogging down in the newly churned soil. The thugs became alarmed, poking their heads up to see, but Shard barked and they settled. Someone reached up and grabbed the yelping thug by his member and, with a startled squeak, yanked him from the barricade.

Shard eyed the horsemen. With perfect conditions, they might have made it right up over the barricade and into the fort followed by the rest of the light company and the thugs would have had a hellish battle on their hands, but they were slowing in the soft, black dirt, their horses struggling, heaving and snorting, their riders driving spurs into their flanks. Well-trained and strong with proper feed, the horses dug in. Brave, determined riders, if they made it, all they had to do was stay alive for the rest of the company to follow their example.

They might have made it.

Shard signaled and four big thugs hoisted a boulder up and over the barricade.

It landed with a low thud and slid down the slope, then tripped, flipped and began to roll.

One horse reared, throwing her rider, then it too fell rolling over itself, legs akimbo, snapping like twigs. The second pranced carefully around and the rider, struggling to keep balance, turned his mount sideways. Unable to make it up the hill, he tried to bring his horse back down, but the horse, panicking now, skipped sideways and fell, rolling and crushing its rider still in the saddle.

Two lame horses, one rider trying to comfort his prize beast while the other rider lay sprawled at the bottom of the hill and unmoving. Footmen dashed out and grabbed the arms and legs of the dead rider and dragged him away. Officers unhorsed and led the living rider away as an Elf stepped forward and with a swipe of his tulwar silenced the horses cries.

Shard poked his head up. "Tell Dru," He shouted in Human, "Wiggletooth Shard sends her another empty-handed soul!" He ducked as an arrow flashed overhead. He giggled to himself as he peered through a crack in the barricade and watched as the surviving unhorsed rider drew his saber, bellowing with rage and ordered the charge. His superiors said nothing as they watched with grim approval as the footmen amassed for the assault. Shard knew what they were thinking. *There's a smart assed little villain up there in need of a little discipline.*

"All right ya gamey bastards," Shard barked at his thugs. "This is what we've been waiting for!" Shard gripped his new man-sword. "Wait for them to come to us!"

And they came.

With a bellowing cry, the men assaulted the hill. Charging with fury, without plan or shield, and only four Elven archers providing cover, they climbed the hill, swords in scabbards to leave their hands free to climb, they came up the stiffening slope and Shard smiled.

He struck his fist into his palm.

Tech Lieutenant O'rawk of her Highness' Special Bug Head Guard, wearing a lacey pink panty on his head, leapt over the barricade with a tail of sparking, angry smoke spewing from his keg, and charged at the enemy with arms outstretched wide. He stumbled as an Elf arrow found its mark, cutting though his breast plate and into his right lung, but he quickly found his footing. Building up speed on the slope, his tongue flapping past his ear, he skipped long strides towards the round, white, fear-filled eyes of his enemy.

The lead Human, a man-at-arms who just that morning, for the first time in his life, had to shave his face whiskers to pass inspection, changed his eyes of fear to eyes of determination. He didn't understand war, or fully swallowed the rants of his sergeant. He didn't know the Bug Heads and couldn't understand the fire spilling from his back, but it all suddenly looked familiar to him. He'd played this game as a child. The opposing team had the ball and all they had to do was break through he and his mates.

And no bleeding sod ever broke through him.

He crossed his arms in front of his face and ducked his head.

He smashed into the Bug Head with a grunt and felt his feet sink into the soft earth, but he held his ground, kept his balance and knocked the stupid thug on his ass.

And he evoked the Falcon's war cry, the totem of his team as he glared down at his defeated opponent.

Who smiled back.

Stupid thug! Moron! You're down! Play over! You've lost! The Human shouted obscenities.

And the thug laughed.

The Human grabbed the thug, hoisting him up and shaking him and the thug paid him little mind, only watching the other Humans move past, climbing in the soft earth on their hands and knees.

And Tech Lieutenant O'rawk stopped laughing.

His fuse coughed, spat and died.

And the Human cried in triumph like a Falcon again, a smile across his face from ear to ear.

Tech Lieutenant O'rawk had woke up yesterday morning as Private sub-class O'rawk, trained in the arts of latrine digging and setting off trip-wires to see what they do. While filling in a latrine, his sergeant strode over and told him that the beautiful Princess Hiroki, the maiden whose captivating image was so beautiful that thugs would see a picture of her and spoon out their eyes so the last thought in their heads were of her, was giving thugs the honor of sniffing her laundry.

O'rawk gacked the thug in line before him just so he could see The Princess that much sooner.

He knelt before her averting his eyes, knowing full well that should he look upon such beauty he would go mad, and breathed in her delicate perfume. He shook, he sweated, he prayed that Dru, goddess of Death, to take him then and there, when the Princess took her delicate finger and touched under his chin and tilted his head up.

And he saw her rapturous rising like the dawn over her mountainous bosom.

"I need Tech Lieutenants." He heard angels sing. "Would you strap on this big ass bomb and wear my favor?" Her lips, so soft, so full, blew clouds of rainbow butterflies at him. "Thanks so much." Crystal bells chimed.

As they strapped a keg of Black Dirt that Blows Stuff Up, Princess Hiroki hooked her thumbs into the waist band of her lacy, pink panties and slowly, slowly, slid them down her callipygian hips.

When he came to, he found himself lying face down on his mat. A dream? He thought as he stirred, but the bomb on his back and the panty on his head confirmed that he had volunteered to blow up her Highness' enemies.

And Tech Lieutenant O'rawk was delighted to do so.

And he had failed. The fuse was a dud, Humans were assaulting the hill and he had just been captured by a peach-fuzzed school kid.

Tech Lieutenant O'rawk's eyes of despair turned into eyes of anger. He reared back and drove his forehead into the Human's nose, smashing it flat and causing blood to squirt from both nostrils.

The Human reeled back, his eyes blurring from flooding tears. He grit his teeth and drove his head forward into O'rawk's.

A cascade of stars rained across O'rawk's vision and the ground heaved around him like a rough sea, but the Human was still holding him and that point of reference was what he needed as he slammed his head into the Human, busting out the boy's front teeth and staining the Princess' panty with blood.

The Human cried like a falcon as he drove his forehead into O'rawk's mass of teeth, tearing open his forehead and busting the Goblin's lip.

O'rawk bellowed his war cry, "We're counterattacking!" and drove his head forward.

And exploded.

A full radius blast of rusty chain, glass and rock gouged a crater into the soft ground, leaving a red bloody smear in its radius. The few humans who reached the top were blown over from the force directly into the killing blades of the waiting Goblins. Others scrambled over the top, holding shields above their heads to protect them from the hail of rocks, hurled themselves over desperately, dragging their swords from their scabbards only to fall beneath the press of Goblins. Not enough humans had made it over and those that did were horribly overwhelmed and hacked to death.

Shard took a human head and tossed it at the retreating humans. He then picked something from his nose and flicked it at them before ducking away from an arrow shot. "Alright assbags!" he ordered his thugs. "Get ready for the next wave. Gather more rocks! Keep your heads down!" Shard peered over the edge of the wall, watching the humans scramble. They weren't going to try a rush again. They had bigger units coming. All they had to do was sit tight and wait and Shard would be very fucked. Shard watched as his thugs took up a huge wooden beam and drove it into a wall until it smashed into suitable rocks. They quickly piled them up behind the palisade.

Shard re-gripped his sword and turned. "Gunny! Stand by!"

Gunnery Sergeant Glenkar and six thugs had taken all the women of the fort and tied them across sawhorses. At the command, he lifted their skirts exposing their creamy skin, untanned from the sun. Gunny Glenkar stood behind them, affectionately giving one a pat, admiring the firmness.

Shard checked the line of thugs and nodded. "Gunny! Begin!"

Gunny Glenkar and his six thugs heaved broad bats and began paddling.

It wasn't so much the pain, but the debasement, as the wives of knights and lords were cruelly and brutally spanked. They let out a shrilling howl that filled the fort, rising over the din of the thugs and down the hill where the Humans were, filling them with rage, blind killing rage.

Without command, they charged the hill again.

Shard waited. He watched them clambering up, shields over their heads against the rain of rocks, slogging in the bloody mud, heads down with knuckled determination. Inching their way ever higher, closer to rescuing their women from the defiling Goblins. What terror they must be inflicting? Befouling!

Shard eyed his men, then nodded.

Twenty thugs stepped back and heaved over a massive log, formerly the crossbeam to the town hall ceiling, and tossed it rolling down the hill. The Humans skipped and tripped and fumbled over it, turning ankles and spraining knees. A few swords and shields broke as the Humans fell. Some were flattened into the muddy ground but were otherwise unhurt. It was a slowing tactic, breaking up their mass and forcing them to look up.

Rocks suddenly took their toll as the Humans tilted their shields down to watch for another log. Brained, the rocks caved in their helms and knocked them senseless. They tilted their shields up and Shard sent down another log. Not as fat or heavy as the first, but enough to get them to look up into the rain of rocks. Desperate and very brave Humans made it over the top, only to have thugs grab them and drag them over the wall and out of the way where they were quickly beheaded and their noggins tossed back.

The second wave retreated from the shore, their anger abated.

Shard peered over the wall. There were not enough dead humans sprawled across the hill to risk a counterattack. He had to lure them up again.

"Gunny!" Shard bellowed. "Spank harder!" The horrible wail rose to a shrilling pitch and Shard winced from the dreadful sound. He risked a quick glance over the fort. The Humans were going nuts, trying desperately to rouse themselves for another charge up the hill but the commanders barked orders to stand fast. Shard watched two footmen strip their armor and begin the furious Berserker dance, driving themselves into frenzy and froth. Their strength would be unparalleled; their bodies would withstand tremendous damage and their attacks would be deadly.

But they weren't coming.

Shard grunted and turned from the wall, slamming into the Princess. He bounced back with a stumble.

"So you see my problem!" She bellowed.

Shard blinked. She had found a gleaming, chainmail hauberk that draped from her shoulders to her ankles. She had taken a knight's white belt and cinched it around her narrow waist. It showed off her most handsome curves. "Problem? Your Highness?" Shard spoke only to stop himself from staring.

"Look at me!" She pointed at her breasts. "This flattens me out! You should have been knocked on your ass!" Four thugs nearby suddenly flung themselves onto their backs. "You're all late," she yelled at them, then looked back to Shard. "This just won't do."

Shard shook his head clear then looked at her. "I'll have the hammersmith make you a new under support. You'll have to model for him."

She smiled. "Excellent. Have his eyes gouged out when he's done." She then looked at the all the thugs looking at her. "Your thugs aren't looking at me, are they?"

"And risk having their eyes gouged out?" Shard shouted at his thugs and they quickly averted their eyes. "No, not a one. Did you find a new sword?" he said, trying to change the subject.

She drew it from the scabbard on her hip, its polished mirror finish catching the midday sun. "It's a little long for me, but the balance is perfect!" She quickly performed a kata, slicing the razor-sharp blade through the air.

"My ear!" A thug shouted, clamping his hand to stop the black blood pouring from the side of his head.

"Did that thug say something?" Hiroki asked.

"No," Shard said and again changed the subject. "I was just about to drive the humans nuts." He said taking her arm and pulling her from the front lines and glancing about. "Where is that artist?"

The Princess shouted something in Human and the artist came out from his hiding spot. "He's been drawing me trying on new armor."

"He's got a new mission." Shard stepped over to where Gunny Glenkar was beating the women. Sweat was pouring from the Goblin's brow and he grunted with each stroke. "At ease!" Shard bellowed and the thugs stopped their paddling. "Out-fucking-standing! Well done." Shard congratulated the panting Goblins. "The Humans are getting smart. Too smart. They are going to wait until reinforcements arrive, then overwhelm us. I need more of them to die before the counterattack." Shard found a log and kicked it over as the thugs all around began to whisper, *'Counterattack'*. Shard walked up to the first woman, a young comely baroness with a blazing red derriere and set his log. "We have to convince the Humans to attack and attack now." Shard stood up on his log, pulling off his helmet. He thrust his hips to her butt and held his helmet aloft. "If you would, your Highness, tell the artist to start sketching."

She narrowed her eyes. "You're raping a Human while I'm standing right here?" she asked with a threatening grate.

"Not with his pants still drawn," Momoo said clanking over. "Come now, Shard, even I know the fundamentals of raping." He laughed soundlessly. "Wearing pants!" He looked at the Princess, but she wasn't laughing.

273

"Are you breathing my air?" Her voice hissed like a sword being drawn from a scabbard. "Certainly you are talking with air you brought from somewhere else?" Her sharp, stunning eyes cut into Momoo.

Momoo froze, daring not to inhale. He smiled and bowed and tried to back up.

"I don't recall dismissing you!" she said quickly.

Momoo stood stock still, his eyes bulging, searching for a way out, fixing on Sergeant Major Ribsplitter-Jones.

"E'rats a first," he said ambling over. "We've entered the rape phase of an operation and somebody has to tell a Ribsplitter." He grimaced, then shook his head sadly. "I had hope in you boy. E'rats I did." He then looked at the Princess. "Boy's still got his pants on." He grimaced and then punched himself in the head for a salute. "Morning, your Highness. Hey now, are you a little, uh, flatter? Hey!" He suddenly turned and punched Momoo in the head. "E'rats smellin' my arse!"

"He's breathing your air," Princess Hiroki informed him.

"E'rats fug bugly!" Ribsplitter-Jones swiped at Momoo again. " 'at where I draw the line!"

"Captain Momoo!" Shard's order cut in. "Get to the main line and keep the thugs from attacking. They are to prepare to repulse the Human line!"

Momoo nodded and quickly stepped off.

"I don't recall saying he could leave," Hiroki yelled at Shard. "And for the Love of the Demon Goddess of Hate, Shard, take off your damn pants! Must I show you how to rape some one?"

"I figured 'e knew," Ribsplitter-Jones confided, then grimaced.

"Oh, he knew this morning," the Princess whispered back.

"E'rats! I hear nothing! Oi, Oi, Oi!" Ribsplitter-Jones put his hands to his ears.

She smiled, her dimples showing. "Say it!"

The Sergeant Major looked down, abashed. "My little Princess Twillter Buggy Boo!"

She squealed. "It's times like this that I really love being a Princess." She looked back at Shard. "Shard, I'm going to have your nuts ripped off and fed to you for banging someone while I'm standing right here, so you might as well enjoy it!" She shielded her eyes. "Sergeant Major, will you help him out, please."

"Your Highness," Shard said simply. "I am not raping anyone." He turned back and looked at her. "Yet." He smiled as she blushed. "I am merely posing." He stepped off his log and walked over to the artist and smiled at his sketch. The Princess and Sergeant Major peered over as the artist finished the last lines.

The baroness' face was turned to the audience, her horrible shame in free-flowing tears was obvious. Shard's broad, toothy smile, his pants around his ankles, one hand holding his helmet aloft, the other grabbing her hair for purchase was the rest of the picture. In relief were the rest of the women, their faces turned in shame and thugs lining up for their turn.

Shard tore the sheet from the artist's book. "Stand by for a fight!" he said grinning.

Shard folded the paper neatly, then signaled Squiff's attention. The Troll leader saddled over and Shard handed him the paper.

He nodded, and with gangly fingers, tied it to a rock.

He peered over the wall, then scuttled back, fanning thugs out of his way. He nodded to himself, grunted and ran at the fort with his arm bent over his back. He skidded to a stop at the fascia and jerked forward, flinging his arm and hurling his rock into the air.

Shard watched it arch high, towards the Human houses, then down at the cluster of commanders arguing their next move. One looked up, a warning shout from the troops, and watched the missile miss by a wide margin before returning to his meeting.

It was an elf, his arrow knocked and searching for any thug up on the wall stupid enough to give a target, who noticed something about the rock, about its arc. His whisper-thin brow rose with curiosity as his eyes followed it to the ground. He retrieved it, unfolding its note and gasped in horror at the pornography it contained.

"Stand by!" Shard bellowed at his thugs.

The Princess nodded slowly. "I think I get it." She then shook her head. "I'm still vague on why you just didn't rape her and draw a picture of that. All this *posing*. Silly." She sighed. "But now I have no reason to have his nuts ripped off." She snorked. "Like I need a reason." She then looked at Ribsplitter-Jones. "So, you agree? I am flatter?"

"Eyah, s'a bit." Ribsplitter-Jones pinched his fingers.

The Princess threw up her hands. "Argh! I hate this damned armor!" She slapped her thighs with a clash of metal.

"Eyah, well look." Ribsplitter-Jones pointed to his new helmet. "He's made me find a new brain bucket."

"You retired Skippy?" Princess cried.

"He's nearby," he confided.

Shard looked over. "If he's in your shorts, he's going to suffocate."

"Ooh, look o's knows all about pants!" he said with a grimace.

Shard watched the Elf run to his commanders and show the sketch. A junior lieutenant took the parchment and his eyes bulged in horror. Without conference, he shouted for an attack that he would personally lead. Broken and defeated men were slow to assume formation until the little piece of artwork began to circulate. Quickly, anger spread like wildfire and the Humans were suddenly howling to charge, the berserkers in front screaming revenge.

"Here they come!" Shard shouted. "Wait for it!"

And the Human lieutenant, his mare in the lead, drew his sword and pointed. He was going to ride up and over and lay waste to the impertinent Goblins, free the women and restore their honor, even with his dying breath.

Shard smiled.

The Human shouted his family's name and drove back his spurs.

He balked at a shout from his captain, his horse skipping to an obedient stop.

His head swiveled with anger and confusion as the berserkers ran past, their blood lust unabated.

The Captain looked up tiredly, bothered, the parchment in his hands. He ripped it in half slowly, then quarters, then wadded it up and tossed it in the mud.

His horse then stepped on it.

And the men stood down.

The lieutenant, unsure of what to do, sheathed his sword, muttering a curse.

The two berserkers reached the top of the hill, leapt over the wall and were hacked to bloody pieces very quickly, their remains tossed back.

The Humans, forlorn, watched the pieces of their comrades roll down the hill, then sadly, slowly drifted from formation. They pulled off their helms and sat in the mud and waited.

Shard frowned.

"Fuck me to tears," he mumbled.

Momoo rose up next to him. "Alright, Shard. Help me out here. I'm really vague on this plan. How is this to work?"

"Shut the fuck up," Shard hissed.

"Oooo! I understand now," Momoo grinned. "This plan failed. We're back to the Humans waiting us out, are we?" He smiled and clamped a hand on Shard's shoulder. "Well, it's time for a proper fight. Over the wall and have at them!" He smiled as excitement filled him. "Every able thug in full charge. Those Humans won't stand. They'll fold like starched laundry."

Shard pursed his lips as he thought. "Two flaws in your plan. One, there are too many cavalry. They'll mount and flee by time we hit the bottom of the hill, then regroup and take us out on the open ground. Two and most importantly, her Highness is a stickler when it comes to you breathing her air."

Momoo's face drained as the idea crept over him. "Did she walk up behind me?"

Shard nodded.

"Ah, bugger," he moaned.

Cool, delicate fingers slipped beneath Momoo's new chain-mail shirt and expertly found his fundoshi and grabbed it.

Momoo made a most unusual noise as Princess Hiroki hoisted him off his feet by his underwear. She held him there for several seconds, until her arm began to shake from the strain, then handed him off to one of the line sergeants. "Don't let his feet touch the ground until the Human's begin their charge!" she ordered.

The sergeant nodded, trying to conceal his amazement at the strength in the Princess' sword arm.

Princess Hiroki forgot about Momoo and turned to the artist. She spoke Human to him and he nodded, his charcoal moving like a blur.

She drew her sword, checking its razor edge. "Get ready." She smiled at Shard.

Shard glanced back at the artist who ripped the page from his book and handed it to the Troll and before Shard could stop him, watched as it sailed over the wall.

It was the same Elf who picked it up.

Shard watched the Elf's sharp ears drive back and blush fill his alabaster cheeks.

Princess Hiroki found her way to the middle of the formation, practicing with her new sword, enjoying its balance. "First Human over the wall is mine," she announced. "Any thug lays a hand on that guy shall be suffocated in his own ass!" She took her stance, giving her long braid of hair a toss with a shake of her head so it curled obediently around her shoulders. "You can have the rest."

Shard looked back over the wall, at the new buzz in the command circle as the artist's page was being passed quickly to the Captain who snatched it angrily, his hands ready to rip it to shreds.

Shard opened the sections of Momoo's far-seer and focused it.

The Captain's face turned to blood and fury.

The Human signalman sounded his bugle and the Humans clambered to their feet. Faces of bewilderment changed to faces of outrage and indignity as they pulled on their helmets and pushed their arms into shield straps. The Captain drew his sword.

"Uh, your Highness?" Shard looked up from the far-seer. "What was in that drawing?"

The Human bugler sounded the charge as the Captain drove back his spurs.

And the charge began.

The massive black stallion cost a year's salary from a trader from the north who wouldn't part with the beast for a penny less. The horse had no lineage, no family and the breeder was obscure, but the trader was obstinate and haggling was useless. Most officers turned away disinterested and the trader let them go, showing them other horses more reasonably priced, but the Captain stayed, his saddle over his shoulder, matching the fiery glare from the horse that would be his.

The trader took a banknote.

The black Percheron was power and fury. He had no interest in races or competition. His eyes of fire were only for battle. He bit stable boys, other horses, anyone who came too close. He only stood still for the donning of armor, his face shield with twisted unicorn spike and hauberk of chain. His hooves were shod with good steel and he knew how to use them.

He galloped effortlessly up the hill, dancing over the log the Goblins sent rolling down. He side-stepped both keg-bearing Bug Head Goblins, leaning so the Captain could slash them both, one left, one right, sending them headless down the hill, ignoring their final blast into troops behind. He ran unhindered to the top, leaping over the wall as the Goblins scattered in fear.

The Princess shrilled a war cry and lunged forward, the horse reared, flashing both hooves at her, driving her back. He hopped and swung, then plunged down, driving his horn forward. Princess Hiroki stumbled back, tripping over the long chainmail skirt and landing hard on her back.

The Human Captain nudged his horse forward and the great stallion reared, his hooves of steel flashing, preparing to drive down on the Princess.

Shard stepped over the Princess and, with a brutal swing, sliced off the horse's rearing fetlocks.

The big beast screamed in horror, hopping for balance and the Captain, not knowing what had happened, drove him forward to finish the supine Goblin.

The big beast fell with a tremendous crash of metal.

Kicking and bucking, streaming blood and in pain, the big horse thrashed wildly in fear and panic, the Captain pinned beneath the muscular body only raised his shield to fend off the wave of triumphant Goblins.

"Back off you thugs!" Hiroki screamed. "Don't you fucking touch him!" Shard took her elbow as she clambered to her feet. "Leave him alone!" She jerked back her arm back from Shard, then elbowed him in the face, driving his nose guard into his nose. "I fucking said he was mine!"

Shard blinked the blurring tears away. "You said Human, your Highness. I took out his horse."

"Fucking lawyer!" She punched him again but he turned his head and took it on the side of his helm. "Remind me to kick you really hard in the nuts later." She turned back to the Captain only to find the thugs were on him again, his horse still trying to fend them off, kicking with its mutilated fetlocks and biting. "Get the fuck away, you ass hats!" Hiroki lunged forward, stabbing a Goblin in the chest. She wretched her sword free and backhanded another, slicing open his throat.

Shard moved forward, desperate to stop her from killing any more thugs. "To the wall, you fuck bags!" He kicked one, shoving him into another. "Kill the other Humans!" Shard grabbed another thug and dragged him along as he went to the wall to face the Humans clambering over. Shard slashed violently, hacking at the exposed hands that gripped the wall for purchase and legs that heaved over. A berserker leapt over and Shard swung, sparking off of the Human's dual axes, knocking him out of his reverie in amazement that he blocked Shard's powerful blow. He was still staring in amazement as Shard thrust fast into his stomach, piercing him through.

The Princess stood over the Human Captain. She saluted with her sword and spoke to him in his tongue. He nodded, uncertainly, then wriggled himself out from beneath his horse. He rose, standing over the panting animal. He placed one hand over its eye, then plunged his sword into its heart. It grunted, gave a final kick, then died. The Captain faced the Princess and saluted, ignoring the anarchy all around him. She stepped back to allow him room to fight and he asked to change from his melee sword to his tournament sword. Hiroki nodded.

He turned to his saddle only to find it was gone and all that remained of his horse was bones and a Goblin gnawing on a back leg.

Princess Hiroki bellowed for the sword to be returned and quickly it made its way through the ocean of chaos to her. She sheathed her sword and grabbed the hilt of the Captain's sword and un-scabbarded it. She liked its balance and weight. She flicked it, expertly castrating the thug who brought it to her, wiped it off on his tunic, then re-scabbarded it. She took the sword as the hunched over thug hobbled away. She turned and tossed it to the Captain.

They both saluted, then charged.

Hiroki leapt forward, then slid right, using the Captain's shield to her advantage, forcing him to swing wide to get around to her, but he extended into a wrist lead, whipping the blade from the hinge of his wrist and sparking off her helm as her sword struck his exposed vambrace, cutting deep and scoring blood.

He flung open his shield, bashing her, forcing her to stumble back into her chainmail tails, tripping her. He threw a furious barrage of sword strikes, keeping Hiroki off-balanced, then slammed her again with his shield, knocking her down. He quickly thrust down, bringing his weight to bear, aiming his perfectly honed sword for her heart.

Sparks exploded as Shard struck the sword off course. The Captain took several steps forward to gain his balance and Shard stepped out his way, shoving thugs clear as he did. The Captain threw a flurry at Shard who, with teeth clenched in desperation, barely fended them off.

"Fucking, Shard!" the Princess screamed. "I'll have your nuts! I'll have them cut off with a rusty knife, sewn back on, then cut off again!" She seethed. "This is my fucking fight!"

Shard didn't take his eyes from the Captain who abated his attack. "He owed you a let up." Shard growled. "You let him up, he owed you one."

"Interfere again, Shard, and I'll kill you for days!" she hissed, then called to the Captain to resume their fight. He nodded at Shard, his eyes promising to kill the thug when he was done with the Princess.

"Your Highness?" Shard said. "After he kills you, he's going to kill me and therefore pre-empt you from killing me."

Hiroki took her stance. "I'm going to assume that makes sense and take offense to it." She screamed her war cry and charged at the Captain, sliding right and swiping at his sword arm again. The Captain didn't give up the target but instead swiped at her upper arm, ripping her chain sleeve. Princess Hiroki pulled away, backpedaling quickly and the Captain charged forward, trying to force her back on her mail tails. When she stumbled, he drove his shield forward for a bash but instantly recovered from her faint trip and stepped left, driving her point forward into his breast plate, letting his forward motion slide it home.

Princess Hiroki took his sword from his numbing fingers, then stepped out of the way as he fell. "I like this sword," she mused, smiling at the dying Captain and kissing the air. With a lightning swipe she took off his head. She carried it with her as she walked away from the battle raging around her. Her personal guard attacked the Captain's britches, collecting his nuts for her Highness' collection.

Shard thanked the gods as he turned back to the battle. Ribsplitter-Jones had pulled the thugs back into a half circle, a killing pocket, letting small squads of Humans in and then hacking at them from all angles. As more Humans poured in, they pressed each other, crammed into the tight space and could only defend themselves poorly. As they raised shields to protect their heads, thugs stabbed from below. When they lowered their shields, thugs hacked from above.

And more poured over the wall. Ribsplitter-Jones swung furiously with his Dwarven axe, slicing through hardened leather like paper. The Human dead were piling up, forcing them to climb over the grisly, clumsy wall, making themselves targets for Goblin steel. They propped up their shields, building a ramshackle bastion in order to catch their breath and form a plan, but Ribsplitter-Jones chopped furiously into the center shield, carving into the wood and the arm that held it. When he fell back, Shard lunged forward, wielding his sword with one hand and stabbing quickly. Shard pulled back as the Humans closed ranks. More were spilling over the wall, soon they would have enough to break through.

"Spears!" Shard shouted. "Spears to the front! Work them! Get them in there!" Spears lunged through cracks, stabbing quickly. Some had sharp, metal points, some had bent nails, and others were only chiseled wood, but they worked their toll, breaking up the shields as Shard ordered his forward thugs to drag away the Human wall and get it out of the way.

The Human column pressed their attack trying to break out and the Goblins swung furiously, giggling with merriment and delight. Shard guided the spears, pushing thugs out of the way and picking targets. "Kill that fat fuck!" he shouted, and four spears focused on the one Human. Only able to block one, he fell quickly and Shard pressed the attack, swinging with his sword, hacking at the enemy blades and anyone trying to break through. Sweat stung his eyes and blurred his vision as his breath dragged on sore lungs.

And still the Humans came. They charged, trying to push their way through and gained several yards, but Shard bellowed for his thugs to push back and push back they did. Few swords swung. It was now only the press of bodies and the Goblins had more bodies. Standing the Humans up, Ribsplitter-Jones swung recklessly, cleaving heads in a row.

Goblins seethed and slammed into the Human shield wall, knocking them down, stumbling on the uneven carpet of bloody corpses and hacking them where they lay. Spear points dulled with each thrust, Troll rocks crashed and scored on a flat trajectory, and Shard swung and swung, feeling his arms fill with lead. His thugs were stepping back, unable to keep their blood lust they grew sloppy, reckless, tired.

And more Humans came. They would not break. They ignored their losses, the cries of the fallen. They only pressed their attack with blind rage.

The Goblins were spent. Run ragged for days with little sleep or rations without respite, they now defended against an enraged enemy that was stronger and more skilled. They were stepping back from their lines, letting the Humans move forward onto better ground, giving them more space to fight.

"Now!" Shard found his wind gone, his lungs unable to fill to shout his orders. "Counterattack!"

And the Goblins, on the brink of exhaustion, went wild as their eyes filled with blood, burning an unmerciful red. With a shrilling howl, they shrugged off their weariness and charged forward, smashing into the Humans, knocking them down and stomping their heads as they trampled, up to the wall and over, the banner carrier of the *Other* Black Dragon Company was in the lead followed by the banner of The Black Dragon Company.

Shard caught two full breaths then shouted for Momoo. "Kill the fallen!"

And Captain Wiggletooth Shard went over the wall.

The Humans had pulled away most of the wall so Shard only had to step over a couple blood-soaked logs. He stumbled down the steep incline, eroded away by the Human charge. Shard stabbed a fallen Human as he rose, then lumbered forward. His lungs were a torrid flame as he tried to breathe. Giving orders and fighting winded him quickly, but he had to press the attack.

At the bottom of the hill the Humans made a stand, but when they looked at the tide of thugs flowing from the fort, their eyes grew wide as plates, their knees became weak and their hands were numb. Dropping their weapons, they either ran or fell cowardly to the ground. The Goblins showed no mercy. Overwhelmed and surprised, only a handful of Humans made it to their mounts, but were pulled from the saddles before they could ride. One horse bucked and kicked as several thugs leapt on and chomped down on the horse's flanks with their tusks.

Shard was looking for the Elves. Fleet and fast, they could harass the Goblins if left alone, scoring horrible casualties. There had been four of them and Shard watched one swoon and crumple from a Troll rock striking him in the temple. One turned and fled down an alley. Unfamiliar with the city, he mistakenly chose a dead end. He launched shaft after shaft into the approaching mass of Goblins who crept forward with shields raised.

The shrilling, panicked cry of the Elf chilled even Goblin blood.

The last two turned down the main street toward the gate, picking up speed.

Shard ran after them, cursing, swearing, unable to breathe, slowing as his limbs stiffened with exhaustion. He called for his thugs, but he only had wind enough for a whisper.

Shard gritted his teeth, his mono-brow low over his eyes, and ran.

And his limbs drained of weariness and his lungs filled with breath and Shard ran.

Shard looked around as streets streaked by in a blur. He was out of the gate, moving like the wind. Ahead, the Elves slowed, thinking they were beyond Goblin threat and one turned back, hearing the light, fast pad of Shard's feet, thinking it was another surviving Elf.

His eyes grew as wide as a rabbit's and he ran.

His partner, unsure of what was going on, looked back.

Shard's long sword, light and fast in his hands, sliced through him, flesh and bones without resistance, like a hand through a cascade of water, parting the Elf and his face of horror and surprise in two.

The last Elf ran faster, dropping his ancestor's bow.

Shard raised his sword, growling like a beast, his ears filled with the song of the dead. The Elf was increasing his lead, widening the gap, but Shard couldn't stop, wouldn't stop. He would not let this Elf go. His vision tunneled as it focused on him and his breath filled with the perfume of Jasmine.

On her.

Her long robes with sleeves that trailed on the ground and her hair of spilling tar; her hands trailing sparkles of lavender and she looked back at Shard, her silvery eyes smiling with mirth.

And Shard's fury exploded.

He gained on her quickly as she turned, still smiling, a little surprised, her hand elegantly covering her mouth.

"Oh," she said.

And Shard recognized her gentle voice of falling bells.

Shard drove his sword down with a banner of angry fire, carving into the archer, the Elf, from shoulder to hip, parting him in two, his blood spraying in a delicate, warm mist. The world was still a blur and the Elf was floating, slowly drifting apart in two, even pieces. Shard swung again, hacking off a spiraling arm, then a jerking leg, then the other in a circling pass. Shard leapt forward, rearing his blade back as he went after the half of the Elf that still had a head. The Elf's face of terror had changed to horror as he watched his body float away in so many directions. The world suddenly rolled and bounced as the Earth rose up and hit him.

Shard stood over the head as the song of the dead faded from his ears. The first sound he could hear was the wheeze of his lungs, then the pounding of his heart.

His limbs suddenly flooded with weight and it jerked him to the ground. Shard lay in the grass, unable to move, unable to breathe. He felt the world spiral away and he clung to it to stop it from leaving him, pushing back the darkness.

It wasn't her, he thought.

Shard struggled to his feet, feeling the pain shooting through his limbs in protest. He staggered, then leaned forward and stumbled towards the fortress of Leopolis the Hungry. His eyes dragging, fell on the Elvish bow. Using it as an excuse for him to stop, he picked it up and carried it, resuming his trudge back to the fort. The bow was amazingly light, as if it were carved from a cloud, but to Shard's weary limbs, it was heavy and cumbersome. He carried it anyway. He made the effort to look up and was amazed at how far away the fortress was.

Shard marched slowly back.

While his thugs ran riot.

He could hear Ribsplitter-Jones bellow over the mob as he made his way through the streets. The thugs were grabbing everything from iron hinges to broken butter churns and piling them up at the bottom of the hill in three piles, under the direction of Smiley.

"Oh, for the love of Dru's grace!" Smiley shouted, shaking his head. "What is it with these two-legged stools? No more two-legged stools!" He picked one up and looked at it. "Where in Lonna's cavity-filled false teeth are they getting two-legged stools?"

Ribsplitter-Jones looked at it, sniffing. "E'rats fresh!" He looked around. "One of the thugs must be breaking one of the legs off."

Smiley looked up at the Sergeant Major. "Why would he do that?"

Ribsplitter-Jones cocked his head and made a face. "Fug would I know?" He then looked over at Shard stumbling closer. "Hey, E'rats the boss."

Smiley smiled brightly and saluted, taking a side step from the effort. "Captain! There you are!"

Shard leaned against the side of a shack and eased himself down onto a stool, crashing to the floor. "What the fuck?" he shouted.

Ribsplitter-Jones reached down and gave him a hand up. "E'rats we was wondering. Hey now, israt one of them damned Elven toys?"

Shard nodded.

Ribsplitter-Jones smiled, showing all of his cracked and darkened teeth. "You ran the flighty bastard down! E'rats fugging unbelievable!"

Smiley nodded approvingly and handed a passing thug the two-legged stool. "Put that on the burn pile, please."

"Did someone say burn?" A thug who had been yanking nails with his teeth looked up expectantly.

"No!" Smiley shouted. "No burn!"

Four other thugs looked up hopefully. "Burn?"

"No! You dumb fucks!" He shrilled, panting for breath. "Keep looting!" He moaned and placed a hand on his festering wound, then shrugged it off. "Last time I use the B-word, that I do."

Shard clamped his lieutenant on the shoulder. "You're looking much better."

Smiley shook his head, his smile faltering. "I'm just cocked off my ass, sir, that I am." He hoisted a jug from the ground by his feet and took a swig, then offered it to Shard. "Major Bark-Bite found that. I think it's amazingly old Scotch, that I do. Delightful stuff. I think, sir, that if I survive, I'll be an alcoholic and a drug addict. Bark-Bite says that's if I'm lucky. So, did you have a good run? Meet anyone nice?"

Shard took a swig from the jug and was amazed at how sweet and smooth it was. "Killed two Elves."

"How delightful!" He chirped and then called over his shoulder. "Private First Class Fisher! You owe me dinner, that you do!" Smiley ducked his head, leaning towards Shard. "He didn't think you'd do it."

Shard smiled. "Thanks for the confidence."

"Hmm? Oh, no. I was smashed off my ass when I made the wager, sir. I would have agreed to anything."

Shard nodded. "Uh, huh. Fisher!" He shouted. "Get over here." He watched as the PFC trotted up. His face was dripping from fishing in the small stream. Shard cocked a finger at him and when he was close enough, kicked him in the nuts, doubling him over. "That's for betting against me." He then kicked him in the shin, making him hop. "That's for Smiley. I can't kick him till he's better. Now go shove your face in that stream and get me dinner as well. And a big one for her Highness." The thug saluted, and waddled off, blowing down his shorts to cool them. Shard turned back to Smiley. "So you've seen Bark-Bite?"

"Oh, yes sir! That I have! He has a wagon with a big pile of loot covered by a tarp. He commandeered ten thugs to guard it and has taken off down the road. He wants us to catch up after we burn the place."

Someone piped up: "Burn?"

Smiley bellowed. "No!"

"Go?"

"NO!"

"Oh."

Shard reached down and picked up a stick. He walked to a clearing and stabbed it into the ground. He took a second stick and stuck it several inches from the first. "Alright you thugs! Listen up! We are now in the rape phase." He pointed to his stick. "When this shadow reaches the second stick, the rape phase is over so you better get yours now!"

"And then we burn?" a thug asked.

Shard mustered a half charge and drove his head into the thug's nose, breaking it with a shower of blood. "I said rape! Now, did anyone hear anything else? No? Good. Get to fucking work!"

Shard watched as his thugs climbed back up the hill to the citadel and Shard felt the weariness in his bones. He had never before felt this level of exhaustion. The thought of sitting out a rape phase seemed like a good idea to him.

He squinted as Momoo made his way down the hill. "Ah, Shard! There you are! I got laid!"

Shard felt yet another level of tired. "It's rape; Momoo, not laid." He looked at his shadow clock. It hadn't moved. "Wasn't that a little fast?"

"Bag one princess and suddenly you're the authority on rape," he shot back hotly.

Shard nodded. "Yeah, actually, that's how it works."

"Well, I've been at it all this time. After you ran off chasing Elves, I gacked many Humans then went back and scarfed one of Gunny Glenkar's brides. Think of it, Shard! I'm the first Momoo on this continent to lay pipe."

"More like thread needle," Ribsplitter-Jones mumbled.

"What was that?" Momoo barked, his chin rising with authority.

"Ares said," Ribsplitter-Jones growled loudly. "More like thread needle. E'rats meaning you have a small dick, sah. Thread like in nature, sah."

Momoo cringed. "Ah, thank you for clearing that up." He turned back to Shard. "Anyway, Shard, I think she rather liked it."

Shared jerked his head in surprise. "Come again?"

"No thanks," Momoo scoffed. "I think the one is sufficient."

"Moronic fuck bag, what makes you think she enjoyed it?"

"Oh, the way she was grabbing me and trying to pull me back into bed and wrapping her legs around me."

Shard looked skeptical. "I think you weren't quite done."

Momoo looked indigent. "Oh, no. I was quite done."

"E'rats." Ribsplitter-Jones tossed a broken stool onto the burn pile. "I'll head up thar and finish 'er off."

Momoo looked offended. "And what do you mean by that, Sergeant."

Ribsplitter-Jones set his jaw and growled. "Meaning yer a fuck waste whose can'ts even rapes right 'cause you're a fuck dick and ifs ya ever fugging talk to me again, I'll smoother you in me arse!" He snorted, then turned towards the hill, then turned back. "Sah!" He gave a feeble salute and turned away.

Momoo sniffed. "Glad we got that sorted." He looked back at Shard who was looking into the cave of the Humongous. "And what are you thinking?"

"About how fucked we all are."

Momoo shook his head. "Oh, no Shard. While you were off busy chasing Elves, some of us were getting fucked."

A horrendous growl echoed harshly from the cave. Momoo looked about for Shard and Smiley only to find they had already retreated beyond the row of shacks. Momoo quickly joined them.

They could hear it scrape from the cave, kicking scraps of armor out of its way.

"Frum shitckle pus shum!" It shouted.

Shard crept towards the edge of the pit and peered down. The Ogre stood there, wavering on unsure feet, dragging its broken club behind it. "Fees lipperum! Lipperum!" It nodded, then slowly, like the felling of a tree, dropped onto its face and didn't move.

Shard cocked his mono-brow. "Smiley?" He called. "Get our shaman to bind its wounds. Then get two carts, tie them together in tandem and put him on it. He's coming with us."

Smiley peered down into the pit. "Uh, um, yes, sir. But what do we do when he wakes up?"

Shard frowned. "Fuck do you care? You'll probably be dead by then."

Smiley nodded at the logic. "Quite right." He looked at Shard. "Uh."

Shard looked annoyed. "Uh, what?"

"Aren't you going to be participating in the rape phase?"

Shard shook his head slowly, then looked at his lieutenant. "Fuck are you asking for?"

Smiley shrugged. "Oh, nothing, sir." He then added. "I just saw the Princess and it just struck me, sir, that it did."

"The Princess?" Shard whispered and slowly turned around.

Then looked up.

She was glowing in the afternoon sun as the playful wind tugged at her mail tails, her breath-taking breasts casting a dark shadow across her wasp-pinched waist. Her dark, sharp eyes were scanning the streets below, fixing on Shard.

"Shard!" she screamed. "The thugs are up here, fucking their brains out!" Her breasts heaved as she drew breath. "There's a little bastard up here fucking a crack in the wall! You've got a thug up here banging a milkmaid. A girl thug, Shard! Banging a milkmaid and she's going at it like a pro! Now you get your fucking ass up here, tie me to a saw horse, paddle me right good, then *Drop Your Frigging Pants,* and bang my ass! Right fucking now!"

She turned from the wall and was gone.

Shard looked at the steep hill made steeper from the mad climb, first by the thugs then the Humans, and sighed, feeling his body turn to mud.

Momoo clamped a hand on Shard's shoulder. "Duty calls, my friend. Duty calls."

Shard wanted to turn and bust Momoo in the teeth, but saved his energy and began to climb instead.

And the tug of the playful wind flittered a sheet of parchment rolling, tumbling upon itself across Shard's path. Weary, looking for distraction, Shard stepped on it, trapping it with his foot. He bent down and picked it up.

It was a drawing.

Shard blinked his vision clear. It was the second drawing, the one the Princess commissioned. The one that drove the Humans wild with unquenchable blood lust and furor. The one that drove them up a wicked slope into the barred gates of death. The one that won the day.

It was the exact same drawing that Shard had commissioned.

His shit-eating grin and smiling eyes were the same, one hand balled in the baroness' hair, the other holding his helm. His pants were ringed around his ankles. It was the same drawing.

Except for the Baroness. Her face, still turned to the audience, was not in humiliation, but of ecstasy. Her eyes, closed in rapture, her lips slightly parted in a passionate, satisfying moan. There were no bonds holding her to the beam. She was there of her own free will. Her hand pushing against the bar, forcing herself against Shard's body, driving him deeper into her.

Shard shrugged with his mono-brow, folded the page, and tucked it into his breast plate. He drew a breath and again began to climb the hill to where the Princess waited.

Shard's Sire

THE SPICE THAT floated majestically in the air was Jasmine.

Fragrant, clean and beguiling, Shard filled his senses with it, felt comfort with it. Spoonfuls of brown sugar in his porridge with goat's milk warmed him. Shard was giggling, giggling hysterically. Her smiles rained stars on him and her laughter, falling bells. Her porcelain skin, so fair. Flawless as a sculpture.

"Tell me about your father, Shard."

Shard lunged from his sleeping mat, his needler hissing from its scabbard as his blurry eyes flared to red, searching for a target. The last of the firelight danced with black shadows against the trees and the forest growled with snoring thugs. Shard had forced them to march in the day, leading horse-drawn carriages filled with freshly slaughtered pork from Leopolis' private stock. He would have looted grain from the surrounding farm lands but there wasn't time. Humans were on his trail. Humans who somehow knew his every move. He had to keep moving. He ran his thugs to exhaustion, then a little further, kicking and threatening them until the sun poised to set behind the black ridge of mountains where he found them a place to camp in the gloom of a wetland.

"Who's the fucking cunt?"

Shard whipped his head around until he could see the flash of Bark-Bite's blue uniform caught in a playful flare of firelight. "What?" Shard felt his voice drag against a dry throat.

The Major adjusted his spectacles. "You were saying something about a fucking cunt."

Shard blinked his vision clear. He had overdone it with Smiley's pilfered rum which had dated back before the reign of Leopolis the Abstinent. Shard shook the mist of sleep from his head. "I don't know what you're talking about," he lied.

Bark-Bite let it go as he settled beside Shard. He reached over and grabbed the jug of rum, sloshing the dregs around. "Ooooh, you put a hurting on this." He uncorked it and took a swig. "Now that's mighty fine."

Shard slipped his needler back up his vambrace. "You didn't have to wake me to pinch some booze."

Bark-Bite handed him the jug. "Good thing I did. You'd have gacked me with that shiv had I reached over you."

Shard took a sip, letting the aged rum linger on his lips. "You know what they say about sleeping thugs?"

Bark-Bite nodded. "Wake them from a distance. I've done this officer thing for a few years, Shard. Haven't been gacked yet." He took the jug back. "Came close a few times. Had a conversation with a Horcule Basum who, to my surprise, sleeps with his eyes open. Thought he was hanging on to my every word until he started to snore. Made the mistake of reaching over to close his lids before his eyes dried out. Tell me about your father."

Shard blinked. "What?"

Bark-Bite looked at him. "Your father, Shard. What did you know about him?"

Shard jerked his head back in surprise. "Fuck do I know? I never met him."

Bark-Bite peered at him. "They never told you about him? Anything?"

Shard sat up a little more, rubbing his back. "Fuck do you care?"

Bark-Bite took a swig. "I realize that I do have a bit of a jovial and fraternal manner, but please remember that I am a major in His Majesty's service which means when I ask a fucking question of a junior officer, that junior officer will answer it as quickly and to the best of his reckoning as he can, regardless of whether or not I bloody give a used dog's shriveled nut bag."

Shard straightened. "Yes, sir. Sorry, sir."

Bark-Bite shook his head. "Call me sir one more time, Shard, and I will hang you by your tongue." His bottom lip pursed as he thought. "That would be the third captain that I've strung up that way. The other two were for excessive butt-kissing. I can only stand my butt to be sniffed so many times." He sighed. "I have yet, however, to ask the same question of a thug, any thug, three times. Make me ask again and I'll will not be happy." He hooked his finger into the jug and hoisted it to his lips.

"They told me he was a hero," Shard said quickly. "They hung that over my head. That I had to be good 'cause my dad was a hero."

Bark-Bite cuffed a drip from his chin, then licked the precious liquor from the back of his hand. "They tell you why he was a hero?"

Shard shook his head. "For killing Elves. That's all I know."

Bark-Bite snorted, thinking to himself. "Did they give you any of his things? His kit? Sword?"

Shard snorted. "They told me he got a medal posthumously. That I was supposed to get it. I never did."

Bark-Bite leaned in close, his eyes narrowing. "Think, Shard. Anything at all?"

Shard leaned away. "No."

Bark-Bite pressed him. "By the hallowed breath of Dru, goddess of Death?"

"By the heavy-breasted whore of T'chal Oroak," Shard shot back. "I have nothing of his save his name. He was dead before I was born."

Bark-Bite didn't relent. "But you share his hatred for Elves."

Shard looked insulted. "Every thug with a nut sack hates Elves. I'm thinking even Elves are creeped out by themselves."

Bark-Bite softened his glare. "Ah, that is true. I'd rather lick a fly's ass than talk to an Elf."

Shard winced. "A fly's ass?"

"You'd be surprised," Bark-Bite sat back. "A fly's ass has very little real taste."

Shard's lips curved to a small 'O'. "Can I go back to sleep now?"

Bark-Bite shook his head. "Did you know his name?"

"Longbrow," Shard said. "Longbrow Shard."

Bark-Bite sighed looking tired. "Longbrow was a hero, Shard." The Major shifted and pulled a pebble from beneath his seat and pitched it into the darkness. "Longbrow Shard was a bully which made him a great sergeant. He was stupid and unimaginative and therefore extremely good at following orders, which is why everyone was most surprised when, in the middle of battle, he broke ranks and charged the Human lines. He ignored the arrows ripping through him and slammed into them, carving them into pieces. His sword at his third kill broke, so he took a Human sword and went on. His helmet shattered, his shield trailing behind him by a broken strap, and Humans hacking at him unmercifully and yet, he went on." Bark-Bite looked up. The firelight faded to angry, red coals leaving him in a mask of darkness except for his eyes reflecting the glow, watching Shard flinch as he spoke. "They cut him. Hacked off an arm in a single swipe. They tried to tackle him and wrestle him to the ground, but there was nothing that could stop him. He shrugged them away, killing and killing with his sword, wailing with one hand until he broke through the Human lines.

"Elvish magic bounced off him. Bounced! It landed on the Humans chasing him, setting them on fire. The Elves lined up and let him have a volley of arrows. Not one missed. Not one! He didn't break stride. He tore into the Elvish line, wrecking havoc as the Elves scattered. The Humans, still chasing him, struck him again and again leaving a bloody black swath. He ignored them."

Shard was startled by the hiss in his throat. He was gasping.

Bark-Bite patted his pockets. "Your father made a pact with Dru, goddess of Death." The Major found his chaw and fished it out. "And she lived up to her end of the deal. She would stay her hand for just a little while and he would bring her the souls of Elven mages." He clamped the chaw with his back teeth and heaved, squinting his eyes until a chunk broke off. "He endured such pain, Shard. Such horrible pain." He mumbled around the lump of chaw in his cheek. "He was alone and mortally wounded, but yet he didn't stop until he reached the line of mages." The Major cuffed his chin, wiping away the black drool. "Now I've seen thugs promise to Dru before. We all do it. I've seen an entire battalion cut themselves open when they kissed their swords and swore to bring Dru as many souls as there were to reap, but never, Shard, never have I heard about so many being killed. Elves always exaggerate, but never about a thug gacking them wholesale." The Major turned and spat into the fire, then cuffed his chin. "As Longbrow broke into the line of mages, a most curious thing happened." Bark-Bite took in Shard with magnified eyes. "The mages, the most cowardly of the Elvish forces, suddenly attacked. Physically! Wielding their staves and wands like swords and clubs. Your father made short work of them. He hacked his way forward until they gave way and finally fled from his rampage, leaving one Elf before him." Bark-Bite spat into the embers getting a soft, popping hiss. "It was there a second most curious thing happened. The seemingly unstoppable Longbrow Shard stopped. Perhaps it was exhaustion. Perhaps his wounds had finally caught up with him. Perhaps Dru was satisfied with his blood lust." Bark-Bite looked at the fire sadly. "But as Longbrow Shard raised his sword to kill another mage, he stayed his hand. He hesitated. Only for an instant. A Dwarf that had been chasing him finally caught up with him and cut him down at the knees with a quick, sharp chop. Both legs, one blow!" Shard flinched as if he'd been cut. "The end came quickly and brutally after that." Bark-Bite sighed and spat. "And you were never told any of this?"

Shard blinked not realizing that it had been a while since he had done that last. He blinked again for good measure. "No," he whispered. "I always thought him a drunk bastard."

Bark-Bite snorted. "Oh, well he probably was. Don't let me take that from you."

Shard rubbed his head. "Why didn't anyone tell me this?"

Bark-Bite shrugged. "Perhaps because you were born after he died. Perhaps the story never made it so far. Perhaps they didn't know." He spat. "Who was your mother?"

Shard looked up startled. "My mother?"

"Yes, Shard. That cunt you dropped out of was attached to a woman, did it have a name?"

Shard blinked again. "The cunt?"

Bark-Bite rolled his eyes. "No! The woman attached to it!" He glared. "Don't get stupid on me now."

Shard opened his mouth to speak, but didn't. He took up the jug of rum and took a big swig. "You keep changing the subject. No, I didn't know my mother." He breathed.

"Hmm," the Major mused. "That would explain the whole 'orphan' thing."

Shard tilted the jug all the way back, letting the last drops burn his tongue, hoping to ease the dryness of his throat. It didn't. He heaved the jug into the darkness with disgust. He didn't hear it break. "I never knew her," he whispered.

Bark-Bite spat into the drying embers. "I'm not surprised." He picked up a stick and stirred up the coals, sending plumes of sparks into the air.

Shard watched him. "They should have told me. The slavers at the orphanage. All they said was that he was hero."

Bark-Bite frowned at the fire. "I'm sure they would have told you if they knew. I'm willing to bet they pawned the medal."

Shard suddenly looked up sharply. "How do you know about my father? Begging the Major's pardon, but..." Shard paused.

"But why would a major of His Majesty's army give a Troll's pimply foreskin about a crazed sergeant that died twenty years ago?" Bark-Bite spat into the fire pit, flickering to life. "I don't."

Shard jerked his head back. "Then what's with all the fucking questions?"

Bark-bite let out a long, sad breath. "I've done a bad thing, Shard. It wasn't bad when I started, but now that I have gotten a chance to know you, I see that it was a bad thing." He looked at Shard, his face lighting up from the struggling fire. "You're a thug, Shard. Let's be honest about it. Thugs are expendable." Bark-Bite tossed his stick into the tiny fire. "You are expendable. Just as I am."

Shard glared at him, cocking his head. "The loot?"

Bark-Bite nodded. "Ah, now there's the Shard I've come to know. Clever as always, Shard. Your life would go much easier for you if you weren't so fucking clever."

"There wasn't any?" Shard's face filled with pain. "And you knew?" Shard's eyes fell, searching the ground. "I lost," he paused as he thought, "a bunch of thugs." He looked up. "We went out of our way... put the Princess in danger..." Shard put his hands to his head.

"You can't figure this out, Shard," the Major cooed. "Don't hurt yourself."

Shard looked up, his eyes red. "There was something there. Something important. Something worth losing us all for."

Bark-Bite twinged as if he'd been stung. "Well, perhaps you will figure it out."

Shard shook his head quickly. "No! I won't!" He snapped then shrank back, remembering who he was talking to. "What was in Leopolis' basement that was so bloody valuable?"

"I'm not quite sure," Bark-Bite said softly, his face lighting up from the fire flaring as his stick caught. "I don't know what it is." He spat and cuffed his chin. "We're rightly fucked, Shard. As a people, as a nation, we are, as the kids say, 'Screwed with a Knobbly Cock.'"

Shard put up his hand. "Is this the speech about us trying to live off of Blister Crisps? We went over this."

Bark-Bite's eyebrows rose. "Oh, we did? Do I have to go over it again?"

"No."

"Excellent!" He mused. "Uh, we're fucked, every thug one of us. The Humans are guessing our every move and kicking our asses..." He looked up at Shard. "What part are we up to?"

Shard sighed silently. "What was in Leopolis' basement?"

Bark-Bite's eyes were large as he glared at Shard. "It's a scrying pool."

Shard tilted his head. "A crying pool?"

"Scrying, Shard. A big basin that when you look into it, you can see something far away." Bark-Bite cupped his hands. "It's filled with water and you peer into it and it shows you things."

Shard looked into Bark-Bites hands. "Uh, okay."

Bark-Bite sighed. "It's magic, Shard. Don't try to figure it out." Bark-Bite un-cupped his hands. "What we know about scrying pools is that they are short range and can only see things that the viewer knows about. Very specific things."

Shard leaned back. "If they know about it, why do they have to watch it?"

Bark-Bite tightened his lips. "And the brain light fades back to normal...." He cupped his hands again. "Let's say I send you on an errand. I can look into my pool and see how you're doing."

Shard looked into the Major's hands. He saw nothing. "Does it show, everything?"

Bark-Bite nodded slowly. "I would imagine."

Shard looked up. "Everything?"

Bark-Bite paused, then sighed. "Yes, Shard. If you were jerking off, it would know!" He put his hands down. "We, the Colonel and I, believe that they have a scrying pool that can see great distances and the entire thug army."

Shard reeled. "Ugh."

Bark-Bite spat and cuffed his chin. "No, Shard, not the entire army twanging their puds, but unit placements, formations, tactics, and logistics! They can see what we are doing!"

Shard's mono-brow arched. "Oh. So why not call it a Spying Pool?"

Bark-Bite sighed tiredly. "Because it's an Elvish invention and Elves have to, by contract, over-complicate things." Bark-Bite looked at him expectedly. "But do you see the big picture?"

Shard nodded. "That's how they figured out the Black Dirt That Blows Stuff Up."

"Excuse me?"

"They looked into their little pool and watched us make it." Shard scratched his crotch.

Bark-Bite paused. "Yes, I guess they did."

"Fuck," Shard hissed, then looked up. "But we got their toy, right? They're blind."

Bark-Bite looked defeated. "We have one, Shard. There are others. Our only hope is that now we have it, we can figure a way to counter them. Block the spell."

"But there is no loot," Shard said. "Like, shiny loot."

Bark-Bite shook his head.

"And when His Majesty finds out there is no loot, he's going to gack the officer who tells him."

"Hmm, something like that."

"Regardless of the fact that I was instrumental in saving our collective butts."

"The Emperor can be a little too linear in his thinking at times." Bark-Bite spat.

Shard scratched his crotch. "So, why the fuck did you ask me about my father?"

"I was hoping you could tell me that."

Shard paused, his mono-brow pinching his face. "Wait, you want me to tell you why you asked me about my father?"

Bark-Bite smiled, showing his straight teeth. "Precisely."

Shard's mono-brow sagged tiredly. "Last month I drew private's pay. Do you know how much a private gets paid?"

"A kick to the head from their sergeant," the Major answered knowingly.

Shard nodded in agreement. "But I got two kicks for doing a good job. I'm sure I don't want to know what a captain gets paid. I just don't. But what I want to get across is that I'm not up on this backwards/forwards thinking pattern on so little sleep, so with due respect, Major, you are going to have to spell this out for me." Shard drew a breath to form an official pause. "And in short sentences with small words." Shard pinched his fingers to show how small.

Bark-Bite pulled a leather-bound book from his coat pocket. "While looking for the instructions for the pool, I came across the story of your father." Bark-Bite flipped through it, then handed the open book for Shard to look at.

Shard shied away, putting his hands behind his back. "I'll take your word for it."

Bark-Bite shrugged and put it away. "I realize it must be disturbing to find out the Elves had some interest in your father..."

"I'll say."

"But don't let it get to you," Bark-Bite dismissed. "I had only hoped to shed a little light on it."

Shard winced. "Perhaps he gacked the Elf who made the pool." He pursed his lips as he thought. "Maybe that part was, a history of the pool. The 'making of' portion."

Bark-Bite nodded. "Perhaps."

Shard looked at the flickering fire, watching the flames die. "It's all moot anyway."

Bark-Bite peered at him. "How so?"

Shard looked up, surprised the Major didn't know. "They know where we're headed. They know our mission. They've probably dropped their army on the shore to wait for us.

They sent some troops to harass us, keep us moving. To make sure we don't backtrack."

The Major smiled. "I'm ahead of you, Shard. I've sent word to the Colonel to send us two more companies to smash through anything the Humans have put up before us. We are still in control of this area, Shard. Whatever the Humans sneak behind our lines will be nothing to what we can muster."

"But they want us to fail," Shard said, his voice cutting.

Bark-Bite hiccupped and gagged on his chaw. He coughed and spat into the fire. "Oh, we went over that?"

"No, I figured it out."

The Major nodded. "Did we cover the part about the Colonel wanting you to succeed?"

"Figured that out, too," Shard answered.

"Ah!" Bark-Bite smiled.

"Ah! Are these guys loyal to the Colonel?" Shard's frustration was coming through.

Bark-Bite dismissed the notion with a wave. "Who cares? Their mission is to escort the scrying pool back to Royal Command." He smiled, his perfect teeth showing. "I'll order them to put it on the same boat as Her Highness."

Shard leaned forward. "And what about replacement troops?"

Bark-Bite looked confused. "For what? Shard you have thrice the amount of thugs as you should and come payroll time you're either going to have to give them to Momoo or get them killed."

Shard scoffed. "Most are privates. They only get kicked in the head."

"Shard..." Bark-Bite said softly. "You don't really get kicked in the head, your sergeant was just stealing your pay and kicking you in the head if you complained."

Shard's mono-brow dropped over his eyes. "Fuck!"

"And your captain got a cut of it." Bark-Bite scrambled to his feet. "Alright then. Think no more about it. Now I have to get out of here before Momoo shows up." He turned and slipped into the shadows.

Shard looked up and the Major was gone. He sneered and plopped himself back onto this bedroll, gritting his teeth from the flash of pain from a root stabbing him in the kidney.

And he swore.

He closed his eyes and felt exhaustion swirl over him.

Jasmine.

"Ah, there you are, Shard," Momoo said sadly. "Your quarters are ready."

Shard's eyes sprang open. He had only just slipped off to sleep and yet the perfume of Jasmine still filled the air.

Shard felt his eyes burn from lack of sleep. "What quarters?"

Momoo sighed tiredly. "Shard, when all this is over, you will look back fondly at all that I have to teach you."

Shard rolled over and closed his eyes. "What, about being a fucking idiot?" Shard held up his hand, his fingers splayed. "You have this many heartbeats to get lost or I'm going to string you up by your nut sack." He started counting down.

"Captain Shard is such a kidder. He is one of the most brilliant strategists I have ever had the fortune to mentor."

Shard opened his eyes when he realized that Momoo was talking to someone else. Someone who didn't know that Momoo was a complete idiot. Shard rolled over and looked up into two darkened mountains hovering over him.

"Lieutenant Aules Gnar Gnar Gnar, reporting as ordered, sir!" Her voice squeaked with enthusiasm and Shard winced in pain as he sat up. He could only see her heaving breasts straining against her Rhino-Rat leather cuirass.

Shard stumbled to his feet, blinking sleep from his eyes and trying to see over the horizon of breasts. "Where the fuck did you come from?"

Her black eyes sparkled with stars, almost hidden by her happy apple cheeks and coal-mine-deep dimples. Her curvy, puffy lips were smiling with glee. "Your Major sent me as a replacement for Lieutenant Gralfange who was killed in battle."

Momoo laid a fatherly hand on the girl's shoulder. "I tried to tell her there is no Gralfange here, but I am thinking of taking on a new lieutenant."

"Shut up, shit brain!" Shard growled. "Take your meat hooks off of her! You're not allowed to have any more thugs." He then looked at the girl, almost squinting from her brightness. "You mean Smiley?"

"And Smiley is not dead, no he's not," Smiley mumbled.

Everyone looked over at a large pile of trash made after going through all the loot taken from Leopolis' that ultimately wasn't loot, like used toilet rags and socks without matches.

Shard's mono-brow raised in surprise. "Lieutenant Gnar? Would you uncover Lieutenant Smiley, please."

With a flash her curved dagger, short, cruel, and sharp was in her hand, her face lit up from its reflection. "And finish him off?"

Shard flinched not even seeing her draw. "Let's get this straight, no one is allowed to gack thugs but me."

She looked hurt and put away her dagger. "Yes, sir. Of course, sir." She looked up, her nose crinkling as she smiled. "No gacking!" She saluted smartly and began to gently and expertly move trash off of Smiley.

Momoo smiled. "See, I'm not such an idiot."

Shard looked at him in amazement. "Yes you are."

"I knew you were going to hog her to yourself." Momoo smiled knowingly. "I knew you weren't going to let me use your tent for an hour to bed her."

"What tent?"

"Oh, come on, Shard," Momoo whined. "Share for once! You're banging the Princess! Let me have this."

Shard's mono-brow arched. "Momoo, you're pushing your luck. You've lost a company of thugs, bloodied a Human and plowed some hapless Human's field. You've accomplished so much!" Shard looked over his shoulder. "What tent?"

"It was in with the loot, I fished it out and set it up." He pointed with a nod of his head. "I didn't want to do this, but you owe me."

Shard blinked and sighed resignation. "Fuck her perky little brains out. I don't care." Shard bent down, shouldered his steel cuirass and gathered up his bedroll. "But I'm dead fucking tired and I have to get some sleep!"

"So you'll let me have the tent?"

"No!" Shard hissed. "I don't want to be disturbed for this many hours!" He held up four fingers.

Momoo sniffed. "And where do you want me to bed her when there's no bed?"

Shard pointed to the ground. "Nice fire, clear night. Remember what Ribsplitter-Jones said about foreplay? The romancing phase?"

Momoo's eyes fluttered with instant boredom. "I must have dozed during that silliness. Refresh my memory."

"Figure it out," Shard growled.

"But Smiley's right over there!" Momoo pointed.

Shard looked over to where Gnar was brushing used coffee grounds away from Smiley's face. "Until I say so, you will not hear or see anything that happens over here, got that, Smiley?"

Smiley nodded weakly. "See nothing, hear nothing. Is there any more rum left?"

"Gnar, find hooch!" Shard barked, stepping around Momoo. Having Gnar seemed to have its benefits.

Shard made his way carefully along the path from where Momoo had come and, in the darkness, his Goblin sight easily found the square officer's tent. It was lopsided, the fly was missing and the guy lines were all slack, but it was a spot where hopefully no one would bother him.

There was a thug sleeping in front of it.

Shard didn't bother to kick the guard in the head for sleeping on duty. He side-stepped him, ducking into the flap.

The thug reached up and grabbed Shard's arm. "Hold it. No one's allowed in this tent by order of Captain Momoo." The thug's eyes were still closed.

Shard turned, slipping his breast plate from his shoulder and heaving it against the thug's head with a clang. Shard then kicked him in the nuts. "You take orders again from that limp dick and you'll be skinned, tanned and used as a welcome mat. Now make sure I am undisturbed. Got that?"

The thug scrambled to his feet, punching himself in salute and mumbled something of an apology, but Shard was already inside. It reeked of mold and Shard could see the myriad patterns and colors of layered mildew, but he didn't care. It had a cot and a stool. He dropped his breast plate on the stool, his kit on the floor and his roll on the cot. He then plopped face down on the cot.

And instantly fell fast asleep.

Her thin-slit eyes almost closed when she smiled, a sliver of silver peeking out from her long black lashes. Her hair of jet shaded her face when she turned, but with a casual flip of her long, delicate fingers, she brushed it aside and Shard could see her skin, smooth and pale, like cream pouring over porcelain.

Laugher. Laughter like crystal bells.

And Jasmine.

Hands rubbed abrasively on his back, trying to reach him through the chainmail. Shard felt grit all over his body and the sharp stench of moldy canvas, her voice purring like a soft growl. "I want you," she whispered.

Shard felt her weight on his back and he shrugged to get her off as he tried to shake off his dream. "Princess," he mumbled, turning around, his face brushing into her boob.

Shard knew in an instant that it wasn't the Princess.

Shard sat up and blinked his vision clear. The tent was glowing from the light of a small candle and its glinting, flickering light danced across her bosom. A bosom that was blocking out the rest of his view.

He grabbed her arms and held her at a distance so he could see her face. Lt. Gnar's eyes looked back at him in wanton pain. She was naked, her hands rubbing herself. "Oooh!" She squealed. "My nipples are bursting! Pinch them! Pinch them hard!" She took Shard's dumbfounded hands and tried to get him to twist her oversized teats.

Shard shook his head to awake. "Gnar? What happened to Momoo?"

She looked aghast at the mention of his name. "Who cares? I came here for you, sir! I want you so bad. Take me, take me now!" She pushed Shard back down on the cot and straddled him, her hands pulling the leather cords that held his chainmail. "I want your big cock in me now!" She grabbed the hem of his mail and tried to pull it up over his head.

Shard blinked to make sure he hadn't switched to a different dream. "Wait... Wha..." His stuttering was cut short when she grabbed the back of his head and planted his face into her left tit.

"I volunteered to come here," she explained. "When the news reached headquarters of what you'd done, I had to come. I want to have your baby! Right fucking now!"

There, buried in tit flesh, Shard succumbed. He allowed himself to be dragged to his feet and his mail yanked off him. She took his hands and put them on her breasts to keep them out of her way as she attacked his pants, dragging them down to his ankles.

Shard had not bathed in weeks. He was covered in layers of waste, sweat and blood, all percolated within the air tight seal of his steel armor and the offending stench made even his eyes tear.

"By the divine holy goddess of Light!" She squealed when she saw him in his glory, her beautiful eyes filling with sparkles. "May I taste it?"

And something ground harshly on the back of Shard's brain.

"It's so big!" She squealed.

Her voice was a pin into the backs of his eyes.

"I need both hands just to hold it."

The smell of Jasmine filled his senses, burning the fine hairs of his nose. "Stop," he mumbled.

"I can't wait! Fill me up!" She reached for him, but Shard pulled back.

"Stop," he commanded. "Just stop." He reached for his pants.

Her eyes were gigantic in confusion. "What? What's the matter? Please! Let me please you!" She grabbed Shard's pants, trying to pull them down as he pulled them up. "Please! Fuck me! I'll pay you!"

Shard growled, struggling with his pants. "Stop! Okay, just stop!" Shard wrested his pants from her. "Keep off my pants!"

She pulled back, hurt. "What's wrong? Aren't my breasts big enough?" She held them up, offering them to him.

Shard squinted from her breastly glow. "They're great, really." Shard tied off his pants, unable to figure out why he was stopping. "I'm very tired tonight. We can do this some other time." He lied. He wasn't *that* tired and he didn't want her later. He wanted her to be gone. "Go. Bugger off. You're very pretty and you have great breasts. Now get the fuck out."

Tears, gigantic dollops splashed on her round cheeks. "Ok," she whispered. She thrust her chest up into his face. "Here, feel my breasts!" she screamed. "Swear on my breasts you don't want to come in my mouth and I'll leave!"

Shard recoiled as if he'd been stung. He couldn't. "It's not that I don't want to fuck you... A fuck lot. It's just, not this very moment."

"Oh," she conceded. "How about now?"

"No."

"Now?"

"No."

"Now?"

"No, not for sometime." Shard nodded to the tent door. "Now, bugger off. I'll call you when I can't stand to be away from you anymore."

She rose to her feet, sniffling, pouting. "Okay." She headed to the door, then turned. "Not!" Her dagger flashed in her hand and Shard leapt back but she had already cut the strings to his pants. "Awooogah!" She screamed and jumped into the air, wrapping her legs around Shard's arms and riding him to the floor with a crash. She planted one boob into Shard's face to keep him docile while she rummaged around. "I'm gonna need a little lard to grease the rails." She looked down at him. "There, see! You wanted me! I knew it!"

Shard couldn't breathe, but buried in the pillow of her breast, he didn't care, ignoring the gray dots dancing in the dark of his vision. He felt everything swirling into an even darker darkness.

Suddenly the weight of her breast lifted and Shard blinked at the searing light flooding his senses. He rubbed his eyes clear.

The Princess stood towering over Gnar with a handful of the Lieutenant's hair balled into her fist. "What the fuck do you think you're doing?"

Pain was etched on Gnar's face. "Uh, I'm not sure how to answer that." She squeaked from pain as the Princess jerked her back. Gnar suddenly rose, driving herself back into the Princess' grip. Gnar reached back and grabbed the Princess' wrist and took hold. She rose to her feet quickly, pulling the

Princess off balance, then twisting the Princess' arm around and driving her into an armlock, and keeping her bent over with a painful wrist twist.

"Ow!" the Princess exclaimed in surprise. "You're hurting me! How dare you!" She winced again as Gnar twisted hard, driving the Princess down.

Shard shook the butterflies from his brain and leapt to his feet, his eyes locked on Gnar's face, a sudden mask of sadistic glee. Twice before, Shard had seen her wrist flick, the blade instantly appearing in her hand, its blazing, horrific speed and even faster, lethal strike.

Shard caught her wrist and drove the blade down, curving it back in and letting Gnar's own strength drive it home.

Gnar gasped, looking down at the knife plunged into her belly. "Ow," she whispered.

Shard grabbed her arm and lifting up, carved deeper into her. Gnar screamed from the terrible pain of being disemboweled, then whimpered. "Nice cut, sir." Shard dragged the weapon free, its back hooks ripping her open and spilling her guts all over the dirt floor. "Oops." Her voice was a tiny whine. "I'll get that." She let the Princess go and dropped roughly to her knees. She quickly began scooping up her entrails and stuffing them back in.

Shard grabbed her hair, brandishing the knife. "Who are you? Who sent you?"

She looked up, her eyes gentle and longing. She kissed the air softly and collapsed into her own pool of blood and offal.

The Princess rubbed her pained wrist. "Shard, I want that thug tried and executed immediately!"

Shard knelt down, looking at the curvaceous body. "She's dead, your Highness."

The Princess tightened her lips. "Then you better hurry."

Shard sat back on his haunches. "She could have killed me at anytime. But she didn't. What kind of assassin was she?"

The Princess scoffed. "She's a dead stupid thug, Shard." She sniffed in disgust. "I'm not going to testify at her trial, but I'll give a deposition you can read at the arraignment."

Shard shook his head, bringing the candle closer. "She's not a thug."

The Princess gasped in horror as the gentle light sparkled off of the light red blood, the color of a winter's sunrise. "Eew!"

"This isn't thug's blood." Shard sniffed it. "I'd almost swear it was..." Shard forced himself to say it. "Elven."

The Princess snorted. "Absurd!" She then shouted over her shoulder. "Bark-Bite!"

The Major was in her left boob. "Hmm?"

She slapped him, sending his glasses off his face and bouncing them off the tent wall. "How long have you been standing there?"

Bark-Bite picked up his glasses. "Not nearly long enough."

Shard pointed at the body on the floor. "She said you sent her."

Bark-Bite put on his glasses, then looked at the Princess' boob. "Who said?"

Princess Hiroki grabbed Bark-Bite's head and pointed it toward the girl bleeding out on the floor. "Her!"

Bark-Bite peered down. "Her breasts could be bigger."

Shard sighed. "She said you sent her to replace Smiley."

Bark-Bite looked up. "What? Did Smiley die or something?"

"No," Shard answered.

"Hmmm." The Major bristled, then pulled out his tobacco pouch. "That's Elf blood," he said knowingly and with a flash drew Lil' Elfie. It glowed a frosty blue. "There you have it. Lil' Elfie says she's an Elf."

"She doesn't look like an Elf," Princess Hiroki said.

"Oh, Lil' Elfie is never wrong." He held it against Gnar's body and it flickered blue. "See. Elf." Then he held it up to Shard and it flickered brighter. "See, not Elf." The Major suddenly looked confused. "What?"

Shard felt the breath in his lungs freeze solid. He then held up his hand, dripping with Elf blood. "It's reacting to this."

"Oh," Bark-Bite said, then held Lil' Elfie towards the Princess and it dimmed. "See, not Elf."

Shard pressed him. "But she said you sent her!"

"What's that?" The Major sheathed his sword. "I did no such thing."

Shard's mono-brow hung limply. "What the fuck?" He then looked up. "Momoo! I left them together! She must have gacked him!"

"Hurrah." The Princess cheered disingenuously.

Shard shook his head. "But if she was an assassin, why didn't she gack me in my sleep?"

Bark-Bite pulled out a wad of tobacco from his pouch. "I thought I heard she wanted to fuck you."

The Princess glared at Shard. "Yes, I heard her screaming that she wanted you."

The Major packed tobacco into his lip, wiping the loose flakes on his coat. "And you said something like, 'No, bugger off.'"

The Princess glared at Shard. "Yes, I heard that too! Why didn't you fuck her? First you keep your pants on during a rape and now this!" She crossed her arms. "Frankly Shard, if it wasn't for the fact that you've done an adequate job saving me from the fangs of boredom and that which is Momoo, I'd wonder about you."

Shard stammered. He didn't know why he didn't just turn the girl on her head, drive her like a tent spike into the ground and be done with her. "Uh, because her beauty and boobs were lacking to yours, your Highness." He looked at them both. "Uh, how long where you two standing outside my tent?"

"I showed up at the part of, 'Can I taste it?'" the Princess said.

Shard looked at Bark-Bite. The Major bristled. "I got here about the same time."

Princess Hiroki looked at him. "How come I didn't see you?'

"You have a blind spot," he said, matter of factly.

Princess Hiroki looked indigent. "I do not! Where?"

Bark-Bite stepped to her left side and sneaking under her arm, planted his face into the side of her left boob. "Here," he muffled.

Princess Hiroki cranked her head down, but could barely see the Major back there. "Fuck," she whispered, then slapped him upside the head. "Get away from there!"

"Hmm?" Bark-Bite looked up. "What did you say?"

She slapped him again, sending his glasses atilt on his face.

"Oh, right." He adjusted his spectacles, then looked at Shard, kneeling over the body of Gnar. "What do you have there, Shard?"

Shard picked up Gnar's knife and wiped it clean. "This isn't Elven."

Bark-Bite eyed it expertly. "No, I think it's Ork."

"Ork!" the Princess roared. "That son of a flea, Prince Gorontech! I'll kick his nuts up into his throat when I see him next!"

Shard shook his head. "It was a set up."

Bark-Bite nodded. "An Elven assassin plants an Orkish blade to drive a rift between the Orks and the Goblins." He spat. "Clever."

Princess Hiroki grunted. "I'm kicking Prince Gorontech in the nuts next time I see him just in case."

Shard picked up his kit. "Well, whatever." He shouldered his chest plate. "This is beyond me. I've just gotta get some sleep."

Bark-Bite put a hand on his shoulder. "Shard, the Elves have sent an assassin to have sex with you. There is something wrong!"

Shard glared bleary-eyed back at the Major. "Perhaps she wanted to gack me looking stupid. Seduce me and whack off my dick." Shard nodded. "Fate worse than death." He pushed past the Major and the Princess.

"Where's he going?" Princess Hiroki demanded.

"Shard!" Bark-Bite put on an officerly growl. "I did not dismiss you!"

"I gotta check on the guard I posted out here," Shard said, trying to ignore them.

"What?" Both Bark-Bite and the Princess said.

Shard stopped and stared blankly at the thug by the door. He was still sitting on his stool, still sitting with his sword across his lap. His neck had been slashed open and his tongue dragged through the slot so that it hung across his chest. "She was good," he admired, then turned and walked back to where he left Momoo.

Princess Hiroki followed. "Actually, Shard, I came to your tent to, you know, get you to fuck my brains out." She skipped up to him. "And seeing you disembowel that thug made me, well, want you to fuck me more."

Shard plodded on.

"I'm not going to drop any further hints!" She called after him. "I think I was clear enough!"

Shard stopped in his tracks, looking down the trail. "Fuck me..." he moaned.

Princess Hiroki stopped behind him. "Oh, well, that would be a change of line up." She nodded, feeling a flash of embarrassment. "Um, how exactly do I do that?"

Shard only pointed, numbly.

Momoo lay beside the fire pit, the tiniest of glowing coals shown bright in Shard's Goblin sight. Captain Momoo, of the Momoo family clan, commander of The *Other* Black Dragon company, was on his belly, his hands bound behind his back and lashed tightly to his knees and his feet brought up behind him, tied securely to his elbows and the rope then looped around his neck. If he moved his feet in the slightest, he would choke himself.

"She didn't gack him," Shard said remorsefully. "Not even a little."

The Princess looked at him for a moment. "But did she fuck him?"

Shard made his way into the clearing, crouching down at Momoo's side, peering at him. He was gagged with his own britches. Shard then stood, looking over to where Smiley lay. "Are you alive, Smiley?"

"Yes, sir," he said sadly. "Gnar brought me some nice rum, that she did."

She was a good officer, Shard thought. "What happened over here?"

"I don't know, sir," Smiley answered. "You told me not to know what goes on over there, that you did."

Shard nodded. "That I did." He thought about untying Momoo, then decided against it. He draped his roll over

Momoo's head, keeping him in the dark, then dropped his kit and armor beside him. Shard then lay down, looking back at the Princess. "Your Highness, forgive me; I've neglected you."

She strode over. "Damn straight!" She settled beside him in the grass, glancing over at Smiley.

Shard shook his head. "Don't worry about him, he's been ordered not to watch."

She scoffed. "I want him to watch! I want him to know what he's missing!"

Shard plopped onto his back, spreading his arms wide. "Take me, your Highness! Take me, now!"

She clambered over him, straddling him. "Oh, I'll take you, Shard!" She grabbed his pants and pulled them down. "I'll make you scream like my bitch!" She glanced over at Smiley. "Are you watching, thug?"

"I've been ordered not to, hear or see anything over there, your Highness," Smiley said, tilting his jug of rum into his lips. Golden rivulets tricked out of the corners of his mouth.

Princess Hiroki growled. "Shard! Tell this thug to watch! I want him to know how it's done!"

But Shard was fast asleep.

Shard's Hero

Shard marched.

He marched with unwavering strength and a gait with perfect meter and cadence. He frowned with anger, and his thugs, sensing it, marched silently, fearfully onward, slogging through the mud churned up by their calloused feet. They struggled with the wagons that sank quickly into the soft earth. They slid staves underneath and, with twenty thugs surrounding each wagon, hauled them around like a strange bug.

The armorers on the wagons worked feverishly on the swaying, moving platforms, like a rough ship at sea. They ground down swords to fit a thug's hand, reworked breastplates and re-wove chainmail to fit their bodies.

Shard's thugs marched.

They could smell the sea, still yet miles away, but looming large in their minds. Their bellies were full of pork and beer and their hearts were full of victory. They marched in silence, but smiles were carved into their faces. Smiles of pride.

Shard didn't smile.

His frown was laid deep in his face as he led the way with a pouting bottom lip.

Shard was troubled.

Certain death lay ahead. The Humans knew their every move and Shard rattled his brains to frayed ends without a new plan to trick them. Despite the reinforcements that Bark-Bite promised, the Humans would not be so easily overrun. The Humans knew they were coming, knew their numbers and weapons and even the shantiest, hastily thrown up fortifications would be more than enough to stop his thugs in their tracks. If the charge stalled, they would die wholesale to arrows, magic and Dwarves.

Oddly, that didn't bother Shard all that much.

Princess Hiroki wasn't talking to him. She was furious that Shard fell asleep in mid fuck and vowed to harvest his nuts only after they were cooked well and juicy over a slow-roasting fire.

Shard didn't seem too worried about that.

An Elven assassin, disguised as a Goblin, tried to trick him into having sex with her, which would somehow start some sort of civil rift between the tenuous Ork and Goblin alliance.

He'd almost forgotten about that.

He had a half-dead Ogre hauled along in a tandem wagon that would lay waste to them all when he awoke.

Didn't bother him in the least.

It was the dream.

The world was so big and tall. He was in a warm, dry, three-bedroom, two-bath, hollow tree. She was there. Her robes of sea foam green and sandy yellow, rose petal pink and eggplant purple pooled around her like a pond as she sat on the floor beside him. He sat on the tails of her robes, nibbling on the end of the flute she'd just given him.

Her hair was night, her eyes sharpened-edge blue, and her laugh was a cascade of magic chimes.

Her perfume was *Jasmine*.

"Don't you want to learn to play, Whig?" she asked, her voice like sweetened cough syrup.

"Nup," Shard continued chewing on it.

She laid a cold hand on his head, then braced herself as she wretched the flute from his mouth with the other. "Well, you mustn't eat it. I think Goblinwood is toxic."

"Tok sic?" That sounded awful to Shard. He put out his hands. "Gimme!"

She sighed, the first winter's gust of snow. "No," she said and put the flute to her lips.

Shard's face lifted as he glared at her in wonder. He looked at the end of the flute to see where the heavenly music came from. Not seeing anything, he only glared up at her, and her beauty. She had aquiline features, and a sharp, hawk-like nose a smidgen too long. Her long lashes swept like fans across her alabaster cheeks.

Shard laid his head in her lap and listened.

Her little song ended and she asked him again. "Do you want to learn to play?"

Shard looked up and smiled showing a face of sharp, sharp teeth. "Yup."

Shard marched onward, grunting with each step, pulling away from the thugs who struggled to keep up.

The dream bothered him. Like a mouthful of canker sores, it kept pulling his attention back to it. Shard squinted as he tried to think, but he could not tell if it was a memory recalled or some overtired fantasy.

The dream bothered him.

That, and someone had untied Momoo.

"'Old up!" Ribsplitter-Jones bellowed and Shard stopped on his planted heel, pivoting quickly.

"Why?" Shard's mono-brow was a flat line, low across his eyes.

Ribsplitter-Jones trudged after him, his breath heavy in his lungs. "E'rats yer losing yer thugs, 'at's why!"

Shard drew a deep breath and his nostrils flared. "We don't have time to fuck around, Sergeant Major," Shard growled. "Every second we sit around twiddling our puds, every shit-wit Human their pansy king can scrounge is ass piling right in front of us. We gotta fuck them thug style and fuck then fast, cheap and dirty before they can prepare." Shard peered back down the trail and watched the thugs struggle with the wagons. He wrestled with the idea of scraping them. They carried the last of the Black Dirt that Blows Stuff Up, beer, pork and the Ogre. "What's with the Ogre?" He asked Ribsplitter-Jones.

Ribsplitter-Jones smiled. "Ah brewed him a little Kick-a-Poo Joy juice, I did." He winked. "E'rats I's found some

Wikikit Beatles and puts 'em in a little tea fors 'im. He drank it all up, then downed two kegs of beer and ate a pig befores 'e passed out again. I's bound his wounds and put Camphor Moss in 'em." Ribsplitter-Jones turned and pointed back to the one cart the thugs preferred to pull as opposed to carrying. Shard noticed that the Sergeant Major had found a brass-bird cage in the pile of loot and put Skippy, his pet turtle in it, then strapped it onto the back of his kit. The Sergeant Major turned back. "E'rat whats we're gonna do with 'im is whats I wanna know."

Shard didn't know. "Just keep him happy for now." Shard put his finger in his mouth and swirled it around, then pulled it out and put it in the air. "Bark-Bite thinks as long as the wind keeps the Human ships bottled up north, our ships might be able to put ashore further down the coast." Shard wiped his finger off. "If the wind shifts, we're fucked a lot." He ground his teeth, watching his thugs struggle, hauling up the wagons. "Fifteen minutes for water. Not a half second more." Shard turned and started marching again. He could hear Ribsplitter-Jones barking at the thugs, telling them they had ten minutes.

Shard crested the hill and made his way through the scrub trees. As he broke the tree line, he stopped and took a swig from his canteen. He then unfurled his map and studied the pictures it had for the eighty-seventh time, turning his whole body to orient himself. He had chosen a horrible route. He wound his thugs deep into the craggy hills, away from any roads and flat ground. He backed-tracked and wandered about in hopes of confounding the Humans on his trail while he made his way to the shore.

He knew they were still following him, watching him with their Scrying pool, confirming the location of the Black Dragon Company. The Humans would make no mistake this time around. They were going to crush Shard with every-thing they had.

Shard was out of options.

He scanned the landscape, then went back to the map. He could see the shore in his mind, smell the high tide. He knew that long boats would be there, waiting to pick up her Highness and carry her away with Shard and Momoo safely in the brig, carted back to explain to his Majesty why the only loot was a pile of two-legged stools and cheap tourist souvenirs.

Shard sighed, rolling up his map. If he only knew where the Human army was he could avoid them; or even better, attack them at their weakest point. He looked out over the valley, almost hoping to see them tucked away in the green scrub below.

Shard blinked as he noticed the domed roof of a gamey, reed thatched cottage, camouflaged in the foliage. He squint-ed, trying to make it out in the dense brush. It looked to be of Goblin design.

Shard ambled down the hill, getting a closer look. He found a trail, well-beaten yet covered from view from any-one peering into the valley. Shard knelt at the trail pounded out from the heavy footfalls of a Goblin. Shard moved down further, past a farm of small tiers of Rustle Sprigs paddies dug out of the hillside, to a clearing of seven huts. All of them had the round, grassy roofs of Goblin style, and they were dotted with mushrooms and mildew. A hoe, rusted and lashed together with thread and straw, leaned against the wall. Shard noted the hoe's blade was a broken thug's sword.

Smoke wafted from the chimney of one of the huts. All seemed quiet.

Shard ducked under the overhang of the roof and reached for the ratted cloth that served as a door.

A bucket of water crashed on the hard-packed earth behind Shard and he spun quickly. A Goblin stood there, her cavity-filled jaw hanging open. She wore a green tunic that didn't start out green. She wore a mildewy leather cap on her nappy head and her eyes, round with surprise, peered from beneath the brim.

The thug's knees shook.

"Don't tell me, Addiko, " someone bellowed from within the hut, "that you fucking dropped the bucket." Heavy feet shuffled to the door and Shard stepped out of the way. "By Lanna's haunted beard, girl!" A heavy, malformed hand yanked the curtain aside. "How do you expect me to have my mid-afternoon coffee break without water to boil the fucking coffee." A fat Goblin waddled out of the hut. He was stripped to the waist and his body glistened with sweat and rank stink. He was bent over from a crippling hump on his shoulder. He had a tusk, pushing crudely from his lower lip that made him forever drool. He wiped the spittle from his lip, then raised his heavy hand to strike. "How many times a day must I smack you around?"

Addiko paid him little mind, only pointing at Shard with a trembling finger. "It's the Emperor! Look, Rottie!"

Shard turned around to see what she was pointing at, then realized she was pointing at him.

Rottie was having nothing of it, rearing back to strike Addiko. "Right. And I'm the fucking Pope."

"Hello, Pope," Shard said menacingly.

Rottie froze as his face slowly drained of emotion. He looked at Addiko who was on her knees, her forehead in the dirt. He slowly lowered his hand, then slowly turned, keeping his eyes downcast and averted. He could see Shard's metal shod feet, caked with mud and blood, the glint of shiny metal winking through.

Rottie threw himself to the ground. "Oh, your great Majesty!" He cried with joy. "For whom the sun awaits your official nod before rising each day, for whose crown is adorned with the stars of the sky and must go walking around at night to give the astronomers something to look at..."

Shard sneered. "Shut the fuck up. I'm not the bloody Emperor. I'm Captain of the Black Dragon Company. Who are you? What is this place?"

Rottie kept his face in the dirt. "A mere humble servant, your great Captain Emperor, sir!"

Shard barked. "Fuck brain! I'm not the fucking Emperor!"

Rottie looked up surprised. "Oh, a thousand pardons, Captain sir. I saw your fine armor and felt the regal air about you. That strong, handsome, emperorly chin of yours."

Shard reared back and kicked Rottie in the head, sending him rolling over. "Get the fuck up, both of you. Now I asked you a fucking question!"

Addiko scrambled to her feet quickly, then grabbed Rottie's arm to help him up. "We are farmers," she said, still bowing her head.

Rottie found his feet then wrenched his arm free, threatening to smack her as he did. "I'm talking to the Captain, bitch!"

Shard slapped him in the back of the head. "And I'm waiting for fucking answers." Shard pointed at the tiers of Rustle Sprigs. "Is that all you're growing?"

Rottie shook his head. "We have many tiers dotting the hillside." He grinned with pride, showing his gums and the one savage tusk rising from his lower jaw. "See, Rustle Sprigs is the main element in making hard tack for thugs to eat and this shady valley is the perfect environment in which to grow it. Grows a stronger stock than back home."

Shard's mono-brow arched. "And what exactly is the other ingredient to hard tack?"

Rottie seemed surprised that Shard didn't know. "Sand. Now, sir, captain of the Black Drag Queen company, how much hard tack will you be ordering?"

Shard's lips tightened. "That's Black Dragon Company, shit bag. I don't need any fucking tack. What I need is someone to guide us through these hills and you're it." He pointed to the other huts. "Where are the other farmers? How many of them are you?" He looked at Rottie. "I need you to tell me where the Human emplacements are and how to get around them. I'm on a mission of dire importance for the Emperor himself, so I suggest you stop fucking around." He looked at Addiko. "You, go gather the other Goblins and get them here, right fucking now."

"Hold up, Addiko," Rottie said stiffly, looking at Shard. "Begging your high and mighty captain of the Black Dragged Goon Company, but I'm not one of your thugs that you can go ordering about. I'm a citizen of His Majesty and you can't stroll in here with your fancy armor and start barking orders, not buying my good hard tack, and not showing a warrant of some sort. I know my rights!" he said defiantly. "Now, perhaps if you were to place a moderate order to feed your hungry Baa, Baa, Black Ram company, we can discuss..."

Rottie choked and bent over as Shard punched him in the stomach. Shard then took a step back and kicked Rottie solidly in the balls, lifting the Goblin off his feet. "Fuck-for-brain-citizen, my inflamed asshole." Shard reached back and grabbed the hoe from the wall and broke it over Rottie's hump. "You're a fucking thug. A deserter. A real farmer would have real farming tools, or at least hammer the metal into something useful and not tie his broken sword on a stick." Shard grabbed his sword hilt. "I should fucking gack you where you stand."

Rottie gasped, still bent over and hands on his knees. "Please, it's not like that!" He wheezed. "I was wounded and left for dead. When I recovered, the Goblins had been beaten. I tried to find them, but they sailed away." Rottie hiked up his butt check, then the other.

"What are you doing?" Shard asked.

Rottie shook his head and grunted. "Trying to get my nut back into the sack."

Shard kicked him in the remaining nut, sending that up into Rottie's nether region. "You fucking old fuck! How many campaigns rolled through here? Couldn't find any of them? Fucking coward!" Shard glanced at Addiko. "She's not that old." Shard grabbed Rottie by his stringy hair and hoisted him up. "Fuck she come from? She's not from your unit."

"She was born here, sir," Rottie whimpered. "She's the daughter of Odishu and Oddiki." He looked over to one of the other huts showing where they lived. "Addiko is my woman."

Shard sneered. "And they're out working the paddies while you sit on your fat ass?"

Rottie looked up. "Well, I'm the mayor."

Shard kicked him in the nuts again, nailing both just as they had distended. "Now you're a fucking private again." Shard grabbed him by the hair and hoisted him painfully up. "You've got work to do before I string your cowardly ass up."

"Holy fucking crap!" He wheezed painfully through his teeth. "Oh, by Framin's fake metal ass! Longbrow!"

Shard froze, his lip trembling. "What did you say?"

Rottie looked up, his eyes filling with tears. "Longbrow! I'd never forget a kick to the balls like that. It's me! Rothschild! Rothschild Hurlbutt. Don't you remember me?"

Shard sneered. "You fuckingly stupid assbag!" Shard fished a nugget from his nose. "I don't know what game you're playing, but it won't work." Shard shoved his booger-covered finger into Rottie's ear and swirled it around. "You're back in his Majesty's army, thug!"

Rottie made a face of disgust. "Oh, I hate it when you do that, Longbrow." Rottie tried to dig it out with his finger, but his fat finger only stuffed it in further.

Shard grabbed hold on Rottie's tusk and yanked him around. "You shut the fuck up about Longbrow!" Shard let go of the slimy tusk and wiped his hand on Rottie, only to get more slime on his hand. He looked for somewhere to wipe his hand and Addiko shuffled over, offering her tunic. Shard wiped his hand on her back.

Rottie looked down, his face saddened. "No. No, you're not Longbrow." He shook his head. "Longbrow's gone the long walk of Fo." He looked up at Shard. "Ah, but you're the spitting image of him. I'd swear you're his rugrat if I didn't know he never squired."

Shard squinted at him, expecting another trick or sales pitch. "How do you know Longbrow?"

Rottie smiled, showing his grey cracked gums. "He was my Sergeant! Kicked me in the nads on a daily basis." Rottie looked sad suddenly. "Which may explain why I can't have kids or a puffy." He brightened. "We was side by side from boot camp until his last campaign. I was there when he got promoted to sergeant and I was the first thug he kicked in the nuts. He'd been kicking me in the nuts up to that point, but I was his first as a Non-Commissioned Officer." He beamed proudly.

Shard was unmoved. "What makes you think Longbrow didn't have any kids?"

Rottie seemed surprised Shard didn't know. "'Cause of his deformity."

From the echo of the hills, Ribsplitter-Jones called. "Hey! Shard! E'rats the fuck are ya?"

Shard turned and shouted back. "Down here! I'm interrogating some locals. Be up in a second."

Rottie's jaw worked up and down in amazement. "You, you're a Shard?"

Shard looked at him. "Wiggletooth Shard."

Rottie hissed a laugh. "What a fuck stupid name is that?"

Shard belted him in the eye, making him rock back on his heels. "My name, fuck for brains. What deformity did my father have?"

Rottie stumbled from the blow, then peered at Shard through his swelling eye. "You're Longbrow's."

Shard raised his fist and Rottie shrank back. "Answer the fucking question!"

Rottie nodded quickly. "I'll show ya!" He turned and shuffled into his hut. "I saved it!" Shard could hear Rottie ransacking his hut. There was silence, then Rottie came out, grabbed the broken hoe/sword, then ran back in. Shard could hear him attacking the floor boards. "I kept it safe all these years!" Rottie was panting for breath. "Here it is!" Rottie stumbled out of the hut holding a long, narrow, rotting wooden box. Shard thought it was a sword case. Rottie turned it, then flipped its catch. He smiled as he opened it up.

Shard peered in.

At first he thought it was a snake.

"That," Rottie said, "was your Dad's."

As Shard looked closer, a cool shadow passed over and the air filled with the gentle sent of Chesterwood blossoms. "I see someone has a growth spurt coming," Princess Hiroki said musingly. "But I do see the family resemblance."

Rottie looked up at Princess Hiroki. "Wow, now you're a hottie." He smiled, his tusk flashing. "How'd you like to ride Rottie's big tooth?"

Hiroki didn't look up. "Shard? Is this thug talking to me? Have his nuts ripped off. I'm paying good coin for a de-nutting crew who are just sitting on their asses."

"Eeep!" Rottie squeaked.

"'Bout time," Addiko mumbled.

"Shard?" Hiroki asked. "Is this other thug talking in my presence? Have her nuts ripped off." She waved her hand dismissively, then blinked. "No wait, that won't work." She pointed at Rottie. "Rip his nuts off, sew them onto her, then rip them off her."

Shard gently took the box from Rottie, his mono-brow bent in bewilderment. "What the fuck is this?"

Hiroki peered over his shoulder. "It's a cock, Shard," she lectured. "I'm sure you've seen one before. Just an amazingly, frighteningly, yet titillating, monstrous cock."

Shard's face flashed with anger. "This isn't my father's!"

"Not anymore it's not," Hiroki said sadly.

"My father died twenty fucking years ago! This thing looks..." Shard made a face of disgust.

Rottie nodded. "I know! Like he ripped it off yesterday! It hasn't aged or anything for twenty years!" Rottie nodded, his jowls quaking. "It's a holy relic!"

"I'll say," Hiroki mumbled dryly.

Shard's mono-brow was flat across his eyes. "Ripped it off?" he said quietly.

Rottie's eyes were wide with excitement, the memory flashing across his vision. "Yes! Right before we attacked the Elves! He dropped his trousers, grabbed it with both hands and ripped it off!"

Hiroki sat down. "Oh, this I got to hear!"

Addiko dove and slid under the Princess just in time to be a chair.

Rottie swallowed nervously. "It was right before we attacked the enemy lines. Longbrow was missing that night– wandered off somewheres. We couldn't believe that he would miss a fight, but right on time he showed up. He was a little dazed and quiet and didn't kick anyone in the nuts. He kinda just grunted orders. Then the Field Marshall came by and gave everyone a pep talk. He told us there were Elves on the hill, magic throwers. Well, that old glint came right back to Longbrow and then some. He started seething, then foaming. He was cussing Elves something fierce, using words we never heard before, like Fubulishtilicitus and Cunfukzbaloboic. He worked himself into a berserker rage. As we made ready to attack, he ripped open his pants, grabbed his Longbrow and ripped it right off! He swung it around his head and charged, right into the Human shield wall, smacking them left and right with his cock. He wasn't movin' too fast cause his pants was round his ankles. When he kicked them off, things really got goin'."

The Princess giggled. "Another Shard having trouble with his pants."

"While it freaked the Humans out pretty good," Rottie went on, "it didn't hurt them much, so he tossed his cock and grabbed a sword from a grossed out Human, and started the blood-letting. We had been running after him, he was our sergeant after all, and I got smacked right in the face with it." Rottie nodded. "Knocked me right off my feet."

Shard realized that his mouth was hanging open and closed it. "You're saying my father could not be my father because he ripped his dick off?"

Rottie scoffed. "No! It's 'cause when he laid pipe, there wasn't much left, if you know what I'm saying." He laughed. "Not much left at all."

Princess Hiroki leaned forward and peered into the box. She sniffed contemptuously. "I could take him."

Shard closed the box, a sneer on his lips. "I don't know what shit you're pulling, Rottie, but rest assured I'm gonna gack you slow for it!"

Rottie put his hands up to ward off a blow. "I swear! That's Longbrow's. Why do you think we called him Longbrow?"

Shard's head jerked back. "His name wasn't Longbrow?"

"Naw! We called him that on account when he was at attention, he came up to here." Rottie put his hand up by his temple.

Princess Hiroki frowned. "And he only made Sergeant?" She tsked. "Find his commander and have his nuts ripped off."

Rottie bowed. "Begging your pardon, Ma'am. Colonel Hatchetfist was killed in the war."

The Princess rolled her eyes. "Then dig him up and rip his nuts off! Must I think of everything myself?"

Shard ran his hand gently across the surface of the chest, picking up an angry splinter as he did. "What was his name?"

"Colonel Hatchetfist." Rottie gave a half bow. "That was his name."

"My father!" Shard roared.

"Oh, Harsh. Harsh Shard Jr."

Shard looked down at the chest in his arms.

Hiroki peered up at him. "Hey, for a thug who's just discovered his Da is someone to look up to, you're not happy."

Shard dismissed the notion with a twist of his head. "It answers nothing. I still don't know who my mother was and why the Elves..." Shard held back his thought. He decided Bark-Bite wouldn't want him babbling about the Elves' interest in his father. "It answers nothing."

Hiroki rose. "Oh, it answers what I'll be doing on the voyage home." She matched Shard's look of hurt. "Come now, Shard! Your father is up for sainthood with that perfectly preserved cock. You can't deny your father the chance of immortality? Or fucking a Princess?"

"I'll be on the boat, too," Shard said.

Her eyebrows rose. "Oh, so you will. I'll schedule you in."

Shard sighed, tucking the box under his arm. "I don't believe I'm competing with my dad's disembodied dick."

Hiroki laughed breathlessly. "Unless you've been holding back, I don't see any competition."

Rottie giggled and Shard kicked him in the nuts. "Oof!" He doubled over. "You're Longbrow's son all right."

Shard glared at Rottie, hissing. "I still need to know where the Human lines are and a cheap, fast way to the shore."

Rottie rose to his full, hunched-over height with a moan. "I don't know where they are. This is the first time I've heard of them."

Shard kicked him in the nuts again and he collapsed onto the ground. "Well I'm gonna keep fucking kicking you in the nads until you figure it out!"

Addiko spoke up. "I know where they are," she said in a little voice, climbing to her feet. "And there's a way to the shore. It's through some caves, but it's tricky. It's very narrow and I have to show you. I can sneak a dozen through. Any more than that and they'll get lost and drown." She motioned to Rottie. "Don't stop kicking on my account."

Shard snorted hotly. "I'm letting the swelling go down."

Curled up in a fetal position in the dirt, Rottie moaned. "Addiko, you fucking bitch. I'll kick your ass for this."

Shard kicked him in the kidneys to get him to open up, then kicked him in the nuts with a back flick of his heel. "You'll be lucky if you can fucking walk after this. You should have given my father's cock a proper burial." Shard looked at Addiko. "I want a map of this area. Troops, both Human and thug, terrain features, the works, and I want it now."

Addiko tightened her lips. "Take me with you."

Shard's eyes narrowed as his mono-brow lowered. He wasn't in the mood for bullshit. "You'll fucking do as I say or I'll gack you, pry your fucking brain box open, roll some parchment over your squash and get an imprint of a map that way."

"Okay." Addiko nodded nervously, her breath quickening, her eyes matching Shard's. "Do it." Breaking under Shard's building anger, she averted her gaze, glancing down at Rottie. "Do anything you want, I don't fucking care. As long as I don't have to live with this shit." She spat on Rottie.

Rottie looked up, blinking tears of pain from his vision. "Addiko?"

She turned on him, fury unleashed. "Shut the fuck up!" She shrilled.

Hiroki took a step back. "Careful, Shard. You don't want any of this to get on you."

Addiko ignored the Princess as she charged at Rottie and kicked him, hitting in the thigh. "You shut the fuck up!"

Hiroki coached. "Roll your shoulders back, a little hip twist, then follow through." She gave a light, demonstration kick in the air.

Addiko just kept kicking. "You fucking coward! You told me you were a hero! You said you were discharged. 'Above Honorable'! Turns out you were simply defeated by a mutant penis to the face!"

Rottie blocked her kicks. "Stop that!" He squirmed to get to his knees so he could get up, but Shard tripped him back onto his face. "Hey now, no helping her!" He shouted at Shard, then turned toward Addiko, blocking his head. "You're my wife! You must obey me!" he reminded her.

The Princess looked pensive. "And when was that rule passed?"

Rottie reached over and grabbed Addiko's kicking foot. "I paid good coin for you!"

Addiko hopped to keep her balance. "No you didn't! You bullied my Da! You cheated him!" She retched her foot free. "You're nothing but a fucking bastard!"

Shard reached over and nudged Addiko, knocking her off balance. She stumbled backwards and Princess Hiroki caught her instinctively, then realized it and dropped her on her butt. Shard looked at Rottie. "I think you've got your money's worth." Rottie clambered to his feet, but Shard tripped him again. "I didn't say you can get up."

Rottie looked up. "She's mine. I paid for her!"

Shard shrugged and stepped out of the way. Addiko, back on her feet, ran over and commenced kicking him again. "I'm sick of making your stupid sand cakes that no one buys! I'm sick of giving you sponge baths! I'm sick of your fucking insults! I'm sick of you!"

"Follow through! Follow through!" Hiroki shouted. She shook her head and grabbed Addiko by the shoulders and pulled her away. "Stop kicking him in the arms. Watch this." She kicked Rottie brutally in the gut, taking the air out of him, then in the nose, smashing it flat into his face with a splat of blood. "See? Gut, head, gut, head. He can't block both. Mix it up."

Shard drew his sword catching everyone's attention. He glared at Addiko. "You really want to be a thug?" He asked her.

Addiko turned, almost surprised that Shard was still there, catching her breath as she thought. "Yeah,"

"You're gonna be kicked in the head by sergeants who know how to kick, insulted daily if you need it or not, and your life thrown away attacking an enemy you have no hope of defeating."

She paused, wiping the sweat from her upper lip. "Anything's better than riding Rottie's big tooth."

"Eeeew!" Hiroki shivered.

"Hey!" Rottie squeaked, still trying to catch his breath from when Hiroki kicked him. "You said you liked to ride my big tooth."

Addiko turned, her lip in a sneer. "I faked it."

"Bitch," Rottie mumbled.

Shard set his jaw, raising himself up officially. "Kneel," he commanded. When she did, he went on. "Repeat after me: I, state your name..."

"I state your name," she repeated.

Shard sighed and went on. "Do solemnly swear to obey my Emperor and those appointed to carry out his will or suffer the eternal wrath of Dru, goddess of Death, who will think of horrible doomy things for me to suffer eternally, so help me Grimlick, god of all thugs."

She nodded enthusiastically. "Yeah, all that stuff you said."

Shard held out the sword. "Kiss the sword, don't cut yourself."

She leaned forward and kissed the blade. "Ow! My tongue!"

"Fucking thug!" Shard barked. "Fucking kiss it, no tongue!" Shard wiped the blade off on her tunic and sheathed it. "Now, thug, draw me a map. Show me where every fucking asshole is in this valley." Shard knelt and unrolled a map, laying it out for her. He fumbled for his pencil stub. "Fill in the blanks."

"I can show you!" she said.

Shard punched her in the head, making her stagger. "I can show you, sir." Shard instructed her.

Addiko blinked, shaking off the blow. She looked at Rottie still curled up on the floor. "You hit like a girl." She whispered at her estranged husband, then turned to Shard. "I can show you, sir."

Shard shook his head. "Nope. You're gonna sneak Princess Hiroki and her guard to the shore."

Hiroki spoke up. "I don't think so!"

Shard rose and turned to the Princess. "Your Highness, I can't risk the Humans capturing you. They will use you as a barging tool against your father and he will sacrifice all to save you. It's been twenty years since the Goblins have held any captured lands here. If we don't win this campaign, we will all starve."

She planted her fists into her hips. "Yeah, so? I just got this armor tailored and I'll be damned if I miss out on a fight!"

Shard pursed his lips as he thought. "And the Humans will capture you and lock you up all alone in a tall, dank tower," he said. "alone." He emphasized. Hiroki went to speak but Shard answered her unasked question. "Without Longbrow's longbrow."

Hiroki's lip bent down, pouting. "That's not civilized!"

Shard nodded. "Humans have never been known to be a civilized species."

Hiroki tightened her lips defiantly. "And what of my Nut Ripper? And the loot? Your Dwarven banner?" The last part sounded more like a plea.

Shard looked her in the eye. "We'll bring it around the long way."

"Why can't I go the long way?" she demanded.

"Because the Humans will throw everything they've got to stop me."

"How do you know this?"

"Because that's what I would do," Shard said simply. "If the Humans see me charging the shore, they will think you're with me. You'll be able to sneak on by."

The idea suddenly struck her as Shard's plan loomed before her. "And what of you, Shard?" She asked gently.

"We'll be killed. Every last thug of us."

She shrugged. "Well, in that case." She looked at Addiko. "You said there was a cave, right?"

She nodded. "Yes." Then corrected herself. "Yes, sir!"

Hiroki made a face. "It's not dirty, is it?"

Addiko shook her head. "No, but parts are underwater. You'll have to duck your head a few feet. Other parts are narrow. You'll have to, uh, go sideways, sir." Addiko gestured around her breasts. "You'll get a little, uh..." She patted her small breasts. "You'll have to get, uh..."

Hiroki looked at the Goblin curiously. "Get what? Thugs to widen the cave?"

Addiko blinked. "Ah, no, sir. You'll just get a little squished is all. On account of your, uh, royal boobies."

Hiroki looked skyward. "Oh, no." She looked at Shard. "No fucking way."

Shard sighed. "My dad will be with you."

Hiroki looked back at Addiko. "And how long will the royal boobies be inconvenienced?"

Addiko shrugged. "A couple feet, sir."

Hiroki rolled her eyes. "Alright, Shard. This better fucking work, or I'm so going to rip your nuts off."

Shard nodded grimly, then looked up as he heard Sergeant Major Ribsplitter-Jones yell for him. "We're coming!" he shouted. Shard looked around the little farm, curling his lip in disgust. "Let's get out of here." He grunted and turned away.

"And what of me?" Rottie's voice was a tiny plea. He had gotten to his feet, but was looking none to steady, hunched over more than usual.

Shard looked at him, surprised he was still there. "Tell me, Private Rottie, if you were a corporal, and there was a thug in your unit that was a coward, a bully, a lying, lazy fuck, and a twenty year deserter, what would you do?"

Rottie gave an evil smile. "I'd fucking gack him!"

Shard nodded. "Congratulations, you are hereby promoted. Corporal, gack yourself," he ordered simply. "Now."

Rottie's face filled with fear as he realized what had just happened. He looked at Shard, but realized the captain wasn't kidding. He then looked for something sharp, but there wasn't any. "Um, how?"

The Princess stepped forward. "Okay, I'm feeling generous for some reason," she said, bending over and touching her toes in a stretch, demonstrating great flexibility. "I'll give you a freebee." She leaned back, her arms upraised, until she heard a gentle clicking in her back. She then rolled her head side to side, rolling her shoulders. She nodded, feeling loose. She glanced at Addiko. "Pay attention, this little trick might come in handy one day."

Princess Hiroki took a few steps back, then leapt into the air, spinning in flight. She landed on one foot, her toes pointed, and spun around quickly, her arms drawing huge circles in the air. She leapt a second time and landing gracefully she turned and sprang again, kicking out violently with her foot sailing over her head with such force that it lifted her higher into the air, then over and back down again.

She landed solidly, her breasts heaving from the force. She smiled brilliantly, triumphantly. "So how's that?"

Addiko and Shard looked back at her confusedly.

Rottie squeaked.

All heads turned as Rothschild "Rottie" Hurlbutt dropped to his knees, clutching his crotch. His eyes were bulging, turning red. He wasn't breathing. Bits of bloody foam drooled from where his big tusk pulled at his lip. Slowly he pulled his hands away and looked down at his crotch. There was a crater sucking his pants into a puckered ring where his fly used to be. He slowly reached up and gently, tentatively, touched his temple. A rivulet of blood trickled from his ears.

A small whine escaped his lips as his body began to shudder. His hands became claws and his face etched torridly. Agony swept through him as his muscles tightened and his bowels let loose. He fell over, twitching, air trying to escape his lungs to scream.

They watched him for a moment, jerking and spasming, then Shard looked up. "What did you do?"

Hiroki smiled proudly. "The Terrondom Death Kick. I've launched his balls up into his brain."

Addiko turned, dropping to her knees before the Princess. "Oh, Princess, Sir! You are truly magnificent!"

Hiroki nodded. "You got that right." She looked at Shard. "What is her rank?"

"Private, your Highness," Shard said quickly, respectfully, still watching Rottie die slowly and seemingly very painfully.

Hiroki waved her hand regally. "Promote her to..." She hummed as she thought. "Something, non-private."

Shard bowed. "As you wish, your Highness." He then looked over at Rottie who was now bleeding out his entrails from his ass. Shard forced down a revolted shutter, then looked back up the hill. "Let's get out of here now," he commanded and, without looking back, began the long walk up the hill.

Shard's Charge

THE VALLEY OF deep, green grass lay before them with a river of perfumed purple blossoms lazily running through its center. Broken, rotted spars rose from the tall grass, blackened, caked with mud and blood, sunbaked to a hard, crusty finish like an un-dead skeletal hand pushing up from the ground. Great machines made to topple kingdoms lay about themselves in sad distress, burned and broken, like the spirit of the Goblins who made them. Spearheads of rusted iron crumbled to dust, leaving imprints in the soft, black soil, fed rich and green on Goblin blood.

Twenty years ago, the Goblins swept across the valley like a black tide. Bristling Human defenders stood on the hill, side by side with Dwarves, Elves and Hobbits, bravely standing their ground. They were legendary divisions of vast armies stacked a hundred rows deep and they disintegrated beneath the massive Goblin onslaught which overwhelmed them.

The Goblins seemed unstoppable. Magic burned them, arrows pierced them, swords cut them down like grain and still more Goblins came on a highway paved with their own dead. The earth up-heaved and the trees buckled and broke to the horrible and seemingly unending supply of thugs.

First came the elite thug division with their matching polished leather cuirasses and shining studs. They wore smoke-lensed goggles making their eyes large and fierce. They rode triumphantly into battle astride massive Banwolves. The gleaming quill coats made them difficult to ride and even worse, they were half staved from the long sail over and mad for blood. In the frenzy of the attack, a fifth of them turned on their riders before reaching the Human lines.

There they sated their hunger on tastier flesh.

They had a preference for Hobbits.

Behind the elite Banwolf riders came the thug regiments.

And more thug regiments.

And even more thug regiments.

Massive storm drums pounded a evil cadence that drove the thugs wild. Charging into arrow barrages that darkened the sky, their eyes seared by blistering magic, they ran into the heart of the enemy lines. Only the Tech Lieutenants, with their heavy kegs of Black Dirt That Blows Stuff Up, ran faster. Their enraged minds filled with their grim task, keg fuses burning away. They even ran faster than the Banwolves. With arrows bouncing off their shiny, steel armor, magic unable to track their furious run, they leapt at the enemy, scattering their neat, disciplined ranks, opening them up for the Banwolf riders, and then wave after wave of Goblins.

The Dwarves in formation were indestructible, but un-movable. The Goblins gave them a wide birth. The Elves fled screaming before first contact. The Hobbits were stead-fast, but crumbled as the voracious Banwolves leapt into their ranks.

It was the Humans who fought.

And they laid waste to the Goblins.

Flashing swords raised and fell with precision, cracking into turtle helms with ease, carving open cuir bouilli armor, splitting shields. They hacked and hacked and hacked, build-ing mounds of Goblin dead.

And the day settled on the horizon, casting the valley into night.

And more Goblins came, their eyes, blood-raged in the Human torchlight.

The Humans kept killing until their swords blunted and their arms grew weary and they could no longer land a killing blow.

And then it was the Goblin's turn.

They clambered over the piles of dead, swinging iron swords and cut until their swords then dulled, then bludgeon-ing their way through, crushing the Human lines with the sheer weight of their bodies.

It was here, Shard imagined, his father died.

There were many beachheads where the Goblins landed their ships and many valleys where they clashed with the en-emy, but Shard could almost sense it in the air. He could see the thugs slogging through the soft ground, bogged in mud and dying in wholesale fashion to the rain of Elven arrows, their white, goose feather fletchings streaking through the air, while more Goblins poured into the valley, crushing the thugs below and making a highway of their fallen dead.

Twenty years ago, the Goblins had pushed the Humans all the way to the river of Quim and held them off for two years. It took three more years for the Humans to push the Goblins off the continent and back to the frozen wastelands.

Five years.

They needed to keep the Humans at bay for that long. Long enough to farm and raid and to build supplies to last them until it came time to do it again.

Shard shouted over his shoulder. "Gunny! Take apart the wagons!" He ordered. "We're building scootums. We'll need them to protect us from the Elven archers." He looked around. "Hey, Corporal!" Shard held up three fingers. "Take this many thugs and head down through the valley. I want to know how muddy the ground is. See if you can find a firm spot for us to make our charge." Shard heard him call for three thugs. Four ran over. "Oh, and most important!" Shard called after them. "Keep your frigging heads down. I don't want any fucking Elves picking you off just yet. Now hurry up, I'll need that reconnaissance."

"You won't be needing that." A thug said, making his way over to Shard.

Shard turned, his mono-brow low over his eyes. "I'm sorry, did you say, 'Please, Captain, kick me really fucking hard in the nut sack'?"

Shard watched the thug, an officer by baldric, pick his way through the scrub that Momoo directed him through. Momoo proved to be an awful guide as he led them through a large clump of Cowitch. Shard held his breath as he noticed the baldric the thug wore was of a major's rank.

Shard hated him, instantly.

"Here he is, Major Ogfeet," Momoo said, in his best suck up voice. "My protégé, Captain Shard."

The Major stopped and looked up, his face frowning in disapproval. "He looks like a bag of smashed assholes." He had a peculiar, high voice, seemingly delicate.

Shard growled, but before he could say something offensive, Momoo spoke up. "Ah, well, he might be a little rough around the edges, but he was the primary on the assault on Old Gourd Head." Momoo smiled. "He's the finest strategist I've ever had the pleasure to take under my wing." Momoo nodded.

The Major sneered.

Shard set his jaw, glaring at the Major. "Ya fucking ass bag..."

"And our two companies," Momoo spoke quickly, louder than Shard, "took a Dwarven banner." The Major's head swiveled around to look at Momoo, his interest piqued. "I led the charge on that myself," Momoo added offhandedly.

The Major sniffed. "Got everyone wiped out, I imagine, Momoo?" His voice squeaked. "The only thing you Momoos are good for is getting thugs killed." He looked at Shard.

"And this?" The Major belched. "Your personal ass scratch buddy, I imagine."

Shard's tusks flashed as he barked. "I'll show you a buddy, ya gamey ass bag."

Momoo placed himself between the Major and Shard. "Actually, sir, with Shard's company and mine we number over three hundred."

Ogfeet squinted. "And you took Ol' Gourd Head?"

"And a Dwarven banner," Momoo said proudly. "We also took down Leopolis and raided his cash vault just for laughs." Momoo turned back to Shard. "Isn't that right, Shard?"

Shard tightened his face, pointing at the Major. "Fuck him!"

"A little side trip, but we thought, what the hey?" Momoo said chirpingly happy to the Major, then whispered over his shoulder to Shard. "Shard, this is Major Ogfeet, a real officer and an up-and-coming commander. Next in line for colonel."

Shard's mono-brow rose mockingly. "Oh, well then. Fuck you, sir!" Shard saluted.

The Major looked skeptical. "And you two idiots have three hundred thugs left?"

Momoo pursed his lips as he thought. "We had about three hundred to start with, not counting the Trolls. We've picked up a few stragglers along the way, but we've kept our losses low."

Ogfeet cocked his head back, then held up two fingers. "How many fingers am I holding up?"

"Two, sir," Momoo answered.

The Major held up four fingers. "How about now?"

"Four, sir," Momoo said, a little tiredly. "Sir, I did graduate from Grinkshooks Academy. I can count."

The Major was unimpressed. "And you're a Momoo. You would think nothing of wasting a battalion on the walls of Ol' Gourd Head if you thought it would get you laid." And he glanced over at Shard. "And I don't know what to think of... this... thing." He sniffed Shard and made a disgusting face. "You're not a proper officer, are you?"

Shard laughed breathlessly, "Every time I think I like you, you fuck it up." Shard frowned. "You're as useless as this fuck Momoo. I got to move this along." He turned his back and called for Ribsplitter-Jones. "Sergeant Major! Get the Tech Lieutenants! They will be in front. Is my reconnaissance team back yet?"

Ogfeet swelled with anger. "How dare you turn your back on me!"

Shard turned hotly. "Like this!" Shard drove his foot furiously into the Major's crotch, bottoming out on the Major's pelvic bone.

The Major didn't blink.

Shard's face drained of all expression with surprise. "What the fuck?"

Momoo coughed into his hand. "I think the Major has met her Highness."

The Major's high-pitched voice squealed as he looked around panicky. "She's here?" he gasped. "She doesn't have that accursed machine with her?"

Momoo looked around. "I have not seen her all day." He looked at Shard. "Shard has been her personal liaison, if you know what I mean."

Ogfeet looked at Shard with hesitation. "Captain, I must warn you, she has a machine that... that..."

Momoo laughed. "We know that machine well," he said with relief. "A close one for us!"

The Major looked surprised. "And you still have your nuts? Impossible."

Shard sighed. "I gotta speed this the fuck up." He kicked Momoo and the Captain squeaked and bent over.

"Ohhhh, fuck," Momoo whispered. "The left one, again."

Shard glared at the Major. "Alright ya nutless wonder, I don't have all fucking day. I gotta screw over this hill and fuck anyone on the other side and I gotta do it fucking today." Shard gritted his teeth, getting up in the Major's face. "I got one mission in life and that is to get to the shore. You are either with me, or so help me I'll strap you into her Highness' nut ripper and go for seconds!"

Momoo looked up, wiping tears of pain from his eyes. "He'll do it!" he warned the Major.

Shard was already yelling at his thugs. "Sergeants! Dress those lines! Gunny Glenkar, how are those shields coming? Sergeant Arn, is that Ogre awake yet?"

Sergeant Arn peered up the hill. "He's drinking all the beer!"

Shard nodded. "Let him."

He shrugged. "We couldn't stop him if we wanted to."

"Bivouac everything here," Shard said. "Camouflage it all. We're going in fast and mean."

Momoo straightened up, shaking his leg to encourage his plum back into the sack. "Shard is a brilliant tactician," he explained to the major. "He has the most complicated plans that all work." He smiled at Shard. "Come, Shard, dazzle the Major with your hyper-complicated plan." He looked back at the Major. "It'll take about ten minutes to explain it. He has ruses within ruses. Fakes and feints and then lures the enemy right into our traps!" Momoo laughed and turned to Shard. "Shard! Explain your clever plan to the Major."

Shard looked over gruffly. "We attack in column."

Momoo laughed, looking back at the Major. "Amazing, isn't he? Who would have thought of..." Momoo shot a look at Shard. "Did you say attack in column?"

Shard was ordering thugs around and looked back botheredly at Momoo. "Yes. Tell the Major that his troops will take the left flank and try to keep up." Shard glanced at the Major, then moved toward the top of the hill and pointed north. "Major, your thugs will go right down there, into the valley and up again. At the top, bear right and keep going until you see the shore. Straight line from there the whole way."

Momoo blinked.

Major Ogfeet folded his arms across his chest. "Attack in column. I don't think anyone has ever come up with that one before," he said sarcastically.

Momoo stepped over and grabbed Shard's arm. "That's not the whole plan," he said desperately, then hissed into Shard's ear. "The only reason the Major hasn't gacked you for being the rude, insubordinate thug that you are is because I told him you were a genius."

The Major spoke up. "I haven't overlooked the fact that you kicked me in the... Uh, assaulted me."

Momoo nodded. "Yes, Shard. Abusing me is one thing, but the Major is another. Now you better amaze him with your brilliance."

Shard let out an angry breath. "You want brilliance?" Shard kneed him in the balls. "See the light?"

Momoo whined as he bent over. "Ha!" He said in a horse whisper. "You missed the left one that time." He fell to the ground and cried.

Shard glared at Major Ogfeet. He stomped back down the hill towards him, snapping a dead stick from a tree. The Major flinched, but Shard only dropped to his knees. "While you two were up here beating off, I was gathering intelligence. They sent fast companies to stop us. Companies that consist mostly of Elves." Shard sketched in the dirt. "The Elves won't stand. They'll give us hell, then retreat. The Humans might stand, but that doesn't matter. The Tech Lieutenants will clear out any fortifications they might have built, then we run up and start the killing. Just up and over, clearing out a path to haul the booty to the beach. It's steep, but manageable."

The Major snorted and stood up. "There are three hundred enemy troops over there." The Major brushed the dirt from his trousers. "Our combined forces are not enough to crush them."

Shard rose, his mono-brow flat across his eyes. "We can take them."

The Major laughed. "You and what army?" He pointed down the hill at Shard's thugs. "All you have is a bunch of prettily dressed thugs!"

Shard tightened his lips. "Your orders, Major, are to get us to the shore!"

Ogfeet put his face against Shard's. "Don't you dare tell me my orders, Captain! I'm here as a favor to Bark-Bite, not you."

Momoo scrambled to his feet and put his hands up apprehensively. "I would not do that, Major. Shard bites."

Shard matched the Major's glare. "Fine, ya nutless coward. I'll take Momoo over your flappy scrotum sack any day."

Momoo plucked at Shard's elbow. "Uh, Shard, mind your manners."

Major Ogfeet bristled. "I'll hang your hide in my ancestor's feast hall!"

Shard flared his nostrils. "You can hang it next to your balls!"

"Did I mention," Momoo shouted, "everyone gets a cut of the loot?"

Shard and Ogfeet turned on Momoo, noticing him there for the first time.

"The cash vault?" Momoo went on quickly. "The one we swiped from Leopolis? We all get a cut from it when we shuffle it to the shore." He laughed weakly. "You remember the loot? The reason we're all here?"

Shard looked at Momoo curiously while Ogfeet pointed a wagging finger. "And I get a Major's cut!" He demanded.

Momoo nodded emphatically. "Of course!"

Ogfeet nodded. "Fine! I'll let your pet monkey take primary, Momoo. The Black Poison Scorpion Company and the Black Burnt Toast Company will be on the left flank." He pointed his finger at Momoo, his voice in a high pitched shrill. "You just make sure I get my cut!"

Shard put up his hands. "Hold it! Who the fuck said we need him?"

"Done and done!" Momoo announced, louder than Shard. "Say what you want about a Momoo, Major, but we will deliver the goods." Momoo smiled.

Shard tried to push Momoo out of the way. "Fuck him!"

The Major pointed a finger at Shard, then pulled it back in fear of getting it bit off. "You idiots need me. You don't know what you're up against."

Shard looked at him dismissively. "And you do?"

The Major pushed past them and climbed to the top of the hill. He pointed across the valley. "There!"

Shard and Momoo followed. Momoo pulled out his farseer and Shard snatched it from his hands, lining up where the Major pointed.

Sparkling armor of silver and gold cast magic shafts of sunlight throughout the woods. Blades sharper than sight were held unsheathed and at the ready. Statues, scarcely breathing, unmoving, disciplined.

Waiting.

Shard thought them too small for Humans. He thought it was a unit of Human females, but they seemed all too flat-chested. He blinked and re-focused the far-seer.

His mouth suddenly went dry as his jaw slackened. "No," he whispered.

The Major nodded. "Yes!"

Shard felt his eyes tearing for staring too long. "It can't be!"

"It can, Captain," the Major said. "Your story of taking a Dwarven banner and Ol' Gourd Head explains their presence." The Major looked across the valley. "The Humans are pulling out all stops. They want you dead."

Momoo squinted. "Who?"

The Major signed grimly. "The Horretika."

Momoo looked back at the Major. "Huh?"

Shard handed Momoo the far-seer. "They're Elves," he said in quiet amazement. "In armor."

The Major smirked. "Not that they need it. Horretika, so I'm told, is Elven for 'Six Bloody Steps.' Their blades are so fast and keen that they can slice into a thug a dozen times in a blink of an eye. Cuts so clean, a thug can walk six steps before he realizes he's been cut and simply falls to pieces."

Shard blinked. "Elves that stand and fight?"

"Worse than Dwarves." The Major went on. "They can move, or so I'm told."

Momoo gulped nervously. "I've never heard of them."

The Major glanced at him. "I'm surprised there is a method to throw away a bunch of thugs that you don't know about. No thug ever survives an encounter with them. No one has ever lived to see them fight."

"Elves," Shard repeated, "that fight?"

"Yes, Shard," the Major pressed. "And they are your worst nightmare. Why do you think I've been sitting on this damned hill? Why do you think I haven't attacked?"

Shard blinked. "'Cause you're gutless?"

He pointed a finger at Shard's chest. "You charge that center, Shard, and you'll kill all of your thugs." He motioned at Momoo. "You'll make your mentor proud."

Momoo nodded. "That's sure to get you laid."

The Major shook his head. "The Horretika will run your thugs down. No survivors."

Momoo looked at the Major. "And why are you agreeing to this suicide mission, Major?"

"You said I'd get a Major's cut, right?"

Momoo nodded. "Yes, sir."

"You can have my cut," Shard said distantly.

Ogfeet and Momoo looked at Shard. The Major scoffed. "Surely, Shard, you'll be nowhere near the bloodshed."

Shard looked at him. "I'll be in front."

Momoo waved his hand in front of Shard's face to break his stare. "Shard, you do realize that you have to survive the battle in order to get laid, right?"

Shard sneered. "Oh, I'll survive." He looked at them both, his eyes flashing red. "'Cause they are Elves, and they are going to stand and fucking fight!" Shard turned, grinning. "Sergeant Major! Get the scootums! We're going in!"

"E'rats!" Ribsplitter-Jones said looking up. "What's wrong wit yer face? S'all stretchy."

Shard spread his arms and shouted for all his troops, a smile on his lips. "Listen to me, my thugs! Listen! Dru, goddess of Death has laid before us a wonderful prize! A reward for serving her so well! She has presented us with a unit of Elves who will stand and fight! Now, line up in formations, in column. Stand by for full attack!"

The thugs cheered, drawing their swords.

The Major shook his head. "You're still going to attack the center in column? Attack the Horretika?" He looked at Momoo. "I could have come up with that. You said he was a genius."

Momoo shrugged. "He's not explaining everything, I'm sure." Momoo turned to Shard. "Shard? The Major wishes for you to explain the entire plan."

Shard looked up. "We attack in column!"

Momoo sighed impatiently. "Shard, the whole plan."

Shard ran up to them, almost giddy. "They're Elves! That fight!"

"We got that part, Shard."

"And why haven't they run over here and gacked us faster than we can blink?"

Worry flashed Momoo's face. "Perhaps they already have!"

Shard smiled knowingly. "They know that we know that they are over there waiting for us, right? And we know that they know that we know that they are over there waiting for us. But they don't know that I know why they are waiting for us."

Momoo turned to the Major. "Complicated enough?"

Major Ogfeet folded his arms across his chest, looking down at Shard. "Why are they waiting for us?"

Shard's eyes were glowing red with excitement. "Reinforcements. Super killing Elf squads aren't going to stand around fucking each other all day for no reason. They know we took Gourd Head and they know we took Leopolis, and they know we took a Dwarven banner. A real super killing squad wouldn't wait and risk us somehow escaping. But they're an *Elf* super killing squad and like all Elves they're fucking cowards, so they're waiting for reinforcements. But they don't know that I know that they know they have reinforcements coming. And they don't know that I'm going to run over there and blow them the fuck off that hill!"

The Major seemed unmoved. "It's suicide, Shard. Certain death."

"So?"

He shrugged. "Just so you know." He looked at Momoo. "A Major's cut of the loot and Shard's if he doesn't make it." He pushed past Momoo and started barking orders to his officers to make ready.

Sergeant Ozny, Momoo's banner carrier and last living member of the *Other* Black Dragon Company, and Sergeant Carrugg, banner carrier for the Black Dragon Company, ran over and saluted sharply. "Permission to lead the charge, sir?" they said simultaneously.

Momoo looked up at his last remaining thug. "Denied, you stand here with me." He waved a hand at Carrugg. "You're not my thug, but if you were, I'd have you in the rear with me as well. You bear the colors, and the colors must not fall. You two must stay safe and away from harm."

Ozny and Carrugg saluted again. "Thank you, sir!" They chirped brightly, then ran over to the front of Shard's amassing line.

Momoo sighed, then waited for Shard to pause in shouting at his troops. "I thought you were not going to throw your thugs away?"

Shard looked back at him. "This isn't throwing them away."

Momoo pointed across to the other hill. "Those are still Horretika over there. They are going to hack you all into steaks." Momoo squinted as he watched the two banner carriers nudge each other back and forth in a less than subtle game to be in the center. "And what kind of banner is that? It's just a black flag!"

Shard looked at his company's new banner. "It's a sinister rampaging black dragon eating a sable in a field, or something."

"Oh," Momoo conceded. "So it is." He faced Shard. "It'll look good when they slice you into tiny bits."

Shard stepped closer to Momoo, lowering his voice. "All that was bullshit for the Major. We have to attack. We have to launch a big enough distraction to allow the Princess to escape to the shore. An attack so big and so reckless that not only will those Elves have a fucking fight on their hands, but any reserve unit on the beach will get called up to help. The Princess will have a clear path and the Admiral can put boats ashore to pick her up."

"And we all die?"

Shard looked at him, his mono-brow bent sadly. "Yes!" he whispered urgently. "What else do we have to live for?"

"Our cut of the loot?"

Shard blinked in amazement. "Momoo, the only loot we have is a pile of two legged stools and some nicked bric-a-brac. You know that. The most expensive thing we've got is currently wedged in Smiley's nostril. I thought you told Ogfeet there was loot to get his cooperation."

Momoo nodded. "I did, but I was so convincing that I believed it myself."

"So, you're coming?"

Momoo looked offended. "Into certain death? Shard, if I don't survive to get laid, then the *Other* Black Dragon Company died in vain."

Shard conceded. "But, imagine the story you'll have! I bet Duchess Renrow will bed you."

"Renrow?" Momoo seemed lost in revere. "Her boobs are so big she has to haul them around on a trolley!"

Shard nodded. "And all you have to do is die horribly."

Momoo nodded. "I'm your thug!"

Shard nodded. "You're taking the right flank. First Sergeant Shiro will take the lead. Just stand behind her and look like you know what you're doing. Every once in a while, say 'Carry on, First Sergeant.'

"Carry on, First Sergeant," Momoo repeated. "I like the sound of that!" Momoo nodded and stepped off. "Carry on, First Sergeant!"

Shard grabbed his arm and turned him around. "That way."

"Right!" He troddled off.

Shard turned as Ribsplitter-Jones climbed up the hill. "E'rats a bit of trouble with yer Ogre."

"What's his fucking problem?"

"E' ain'ts wanna go."

Shard sighed and scrambled down the hill. The Ogre was propped against a pile of empty beer kegs, his manhood lying like a dead snake across his leg. Shard noticed that Longbrow Shard could give him a run for his money.

The Ogre belched as Shard approached. "Izzin wan go!"

Shard pointed to the top of the hill. "On the other side of this hill is an army of Elves."

The Ogre waved a massive hand. "Git goin ya!"

Shard turned his head and spat. "Fuck you then. I'm gonna go kill all the Elves myself."

The Ogre squinted. "Youse? Kill Elks?"

"Yeah."

The Ogre clambered to his feet, picking up his club. "Arliks! Wan kill Elks. Wore arday?"

"Follow me," Shard said and turned to walk back up the hill, almost knocking Smiley over. "What the fuck?"

"Reporting for duty, sir." Smiley moaned, his permanent smile gone.

Shard made a face as he reeled from the stench. Smiley was grey, his eyes lackluster. His neck was puffy and bulged in the tight clamp of his gorget. "Are you still fucking alive? I thought you were trying to drink yourself to death?"

Smiley sniffed, wincing. "I fucked up, that I did. Now all I have is this splitting headache."

Shard shook his head. "What the fuck do you want?"

"Momoo said we were going on a suicidal charge."

"Yeah?"

Smiley straightened. "I'm here. I volunteer to be a Tech Lieutenant, that I do."

Shard shrugged. "Sure, but you know they explode loudly."

The Lieutenant put his hands to his head in pain. "Oh. Let's skip that."

"You take rear guard," Shard ordered. "In case anyone flanks us."

Smiley smiled and saluted, knocking himself out.

Shard stepped over his body.

And drew his sword.

He stepped to the top of the hill and peered down. The thug reconnaissance team had left trails of trampled grass where they had passed. The ground was solid enough.

He looked left and right. The Tech Lieutenants, Bug Heads brandishing burning punks, were at the ready. He glanced back. His Chosen Thugs were amassed in line, their polished black dragon-scales flashed iridescent, their smiles a grimy green. Sergeant Major Ribsplitter-Jones saddled up to his left. His turtle cage was strapped to his back. He had woven stiff bramble through the bars for camouflage. The Sergeant Major smiled and winked as he hefted his Dwarven axe.

Shard looked up. Through the spaces of the trees he could see the blue sky above. There wasn't much time before the sun set.

He silently thanked Dru, goddess of Death for this wonderful present.

Then he raised his big sword and charged down the hill into certain death.

Shard's Conquest

And he ran.

Shard was home.

Hundreds of thugs on his flanks poured out of the tree line and cascaded down the hill. The Tech Lieutenants lead the way with their giant kegs of Black Dirt that Blows Stuff Up, their fuses now burning furiously away. Shard followed them, ready to throw himself to the ground before their horrendous blast of rock, nails and glass. His thugs knew that when he dropped, they would drop. Shard cursed himself for not mentioning it to the Ogre, though.

Shard eyed the path on the way down. Shard felt the tall grass bogging him down, tripping him up. Thugs tripped and rolled uncontrollably to the bottom. Others thought that a fast way down and threw themselves ass over head. It was a great plan until they slammed into the wreckage left in the valley. The jagged, rusted metal of abandoned spears and lances proved to be just as lethal now as they were twenty years ago.

The grating bark of Ribsplitter-Jones kept them in line and discouraged others from trying the same stunt.

At the bottom of the valley, Shard slowed his pace, letting his thugs organize themselves. The Tech Lieutenants were already making their way up the slope. Shard scanned the top of the hill. There had been no response from the enemy. None at all.

White feathered arrows streaked from the tree line, two striking a Tech Lieutenant and standing up his charge. The thug leaned himself forward and plodded on, snapping the arrow in his leg and arm. Four more arrows appeared in his armor and he chugged on, ripping at the grass for purchase. Arrows appeared in the keg, his shoulder, his hand and under his gorget.

The thug rose and fell back, rolling back down the hill.

Shard bellowed and dove behind a wrecked siege engine. His thugs obediently dropped flat as the Tech Lieutenant rolled towards them.

The other Tech Lieutenants climbed on as the archers concentrated their firepower on them. The Bug Heads ducked, letting the kegs take the hits. Shard peered over the gunnels of the engine and watched their progress. He glanced up the hill. There seemed to be very few archers. They were ducking out from behind trees, shooting and ducking back. Shard eyed the dead Tech Lieutenant and gauged the remaining fuse, then signaled for the Trolls.

Shard glanced back at the Ogre tramping up but the archers seemed to ignore him, worrying more about the

Tech Lieutenants instead. The Trolls crept up seemingly unnoticed, darting from one spot to another, their natural camouflage changing their skin to a green with purple dots. They had to get closer to get into rock-throwing range.

Squiff ran forward, his arm bent over his back and let his rock fly. It arched up, then down, and beaned an Elf in the head. The Elf stumbled forward and rolled down the hill. At the bottom, thugs ran forward and dragged him, dazed and disoriented back to their lines. His screams of terror, as he realized what was happening, made Shard smile.

Alarmed, the remaining archers now took aim at the Trolls who flung their rocks and ran for cover. Shard watched as the first Tech Lieutenant neared the top of the hill. Then he eyed the dead Tech Lieutenant lying at the bottom of the hill, the last inches of his fuse burning away. He could hear the Ogre running up behind, his heavy footfalls pounding in Shard's chest. The Ogre was running straight at the fallen Tech Lieutenant and the keg of Black Dirt That Blows Stuff Up. Shard's Charge was bogging down already and he was a heartbeat away from losing his Ogre.

Tiny purple flowers gently waved in the breeze, casting their perfume at him.

Jasmine.

Shard snorted, blowing the scent from his nose, and drew the Ork dagger. He clenched his teeth and ran at the keg. He could hear the grinding, hot breath of the Ogre behind him.

Above, the first Tech Lieutenant exploded.

The shock slapped Shard's exposed cheeks. It could only mean that the others, lit one after the other, were seconds from exploding.

Shard closed his eyes and dropped on the keg. His fingers groped for the fuse, writhing like a angry snake. He grabbed it, feeling its furious heat through his gauntlets. He breathed relief as the Ork dagger sliced through it.

He felt his ribs flatten as the Ogre ran over him and up the hill.

Shard staggered to his feet, sucking air. He blinked as his thugs rose from the tall grass and charged, Ribsplitter-Jones egging them on. Shard turned, drawing and holding his sword like a banner and charged up the hill, trying desperately to breathe.

Ahead, the Ogre was silhouetted against the blue sky and blocked Shard's view.

A brilliant corona of purple fire erupted and the Ogre was blown off his feet, rolling back down the hill. Shard dove to the side, avoiding the smoking, smoldering giant body plummeting by. Shard screamed, stating what everyone now knew. There was a mage at the top of the hill.

The Trolls focused their rocks on the mage now he exposed himself, leaving the Elves free to fire at the Trolls.

More Tech Lieutenants detonated. Shard realized that it was the mage who blasted the first one to keep him from reaching the front lines. It meant that he had done no damage. Once the mage blasts the rest of the Tech Lieutenants, he would be free to lay havoc to the thugs scrambling up the hill.

Mage aiming at Techs, Trolls aiming at mage, archers aiming at Trolls.

No one was bothering with the thugs.

Shard gnashed his teeth and charged on, shouting his thugs to follow. More Tech Lieutenants exploded and the shrill of Elves filled the air, meaning at least one had made it. The sound drove the thugs onward and upward. Shard suddenly realized there were only a handful of archers and less wizards, possibly only one. He had a chance to face the Horretika in hand-to-hand combat and die with an Elf in his grasp!

Shard felt the ground level as he neared the top. He risked a glance behind him. The setting sun cast a final shaft of warm light into the valley. His thugs were a black and silver wave of fury flowing through the valley. Shard felt his throat thicken at the beautiful sight. He screamed, holding his big sword aloft to show them he had made it! It was time for the killing to begin!

With a breath, the sunlight snuffed out like a candle.

Suddenly everything went grey and dull and cold. Shard looked up as a massive stormcloud brewed directly overhead. Shard cursed the sudden change in weather. He had to get his thugs up the hill before the rain made it too slippery to run. "Come on, you fucks!" he bellowed. "By Cornusic's bi-truncated cock! Run!"

Shard could smell jasmine, coming from behind him.

Shard turned around just as a ball of sizzling violet magic screamed past his head. He could feel its intense heat through his plate armor. Shard aimed his sword like a lance and charged. He trampled through the scrub and brush, squinting as the trees and branches smacked him in the face, blinding him.

Jasmine filled his senses: long, black hair like hot tar cascading down her shoulders and pooling around her; Shard sitting on her silk robes, hyperventilating as he played the first squeaky notes on his flute. She carefully stroked his head, combing his spiky hair with her fingers and occasionally pulling a barb from her hand, ignoring the pinpricks of pain.

Shard shook his head, clearing the memory coming at a lousy time from his head. He could hear the Elven archers falling back, splashing through the bushes. Shard cut a path through.

The mage had also retreated, but now stood in a clearing, brandishing his staff.

Shard smiled.

Jasmine filled his senses.

His sword jammed into heavy lard, knocking it from his hands. Shard stumbled forward and slammed into thick air, bouncing off it and falling on his ass. His sword hovered before him, stuck fast in nothing. The mage only smiled.

Rocks arched over head and thumped into the mage's protective barrier. Other thugs ran up, striking the barrier, their swords sticking to it. They kicked it, hacked at it, bit it, but nothing happened.

Shard struggled to his feet, but the smell of jasmine took his strength away and he fell back clumsily.

More thugs surrounded the mage, including Ozny, the *Other* Black Dragon Company's Banner Carrier, his flag staff buried deep in the mage's magic shield. He grunted as he tried to jerk it free.

And the mage laughed.

It was suddenly obvious to Shard what was about to happen. He forced air into his lungs and bellowed. "Get down, you fucks! Down!"

The mage suddenly began to glow.

Shard still couldn't move. "Ah, you numb fucks!" Shard screamed. "Drop and give me twenty!" They looked back at him, bewildered. "You, fuck fucking fucks! I said drop and give me fucking twenty!"

Light exploded from the mage, peeling into a disk that fanned out like a ripple in a pond, cutting Ozny in half just as he wretched his banner from the magic field. It sailed over the circle of thugs grunting as they did their push-ups.

Shard climbed to his feet just as Major Bark-Bite strode past him, Lil' Elfie glowing a brilliant blue in his hand. "Allow me, Shard." He mumbled as he struck at the invisible shield. Shard winced as he heard it tear asunder. Bark-Bite snarled as he slashed down again. The mage, in surprised panic, raised his staff and countered. The two weapons screeched on contact, spewing blue and purple sparks. It looked as if the mage and Major struggled, each one trying to force the other down, but then Shard realized that they were trying to pull their weapons apart.

Shard stepped up to the mage, drawing his Ork dagger and with a quick slice, carved him open, spilling his entrails all over his curly-toed shoes. "Tell Dru that Wiggletooth Shard sends her another empty-handed soul." He growled in Elvish.

The mage's staff turned to ash and crumbled in his hands. He looked aghast at his blackened hands, at the bloody intestines snaking out of his body. He looked up at Shard and his face filled with a new horror. He said something, a single word, then Bark-Bite buried Lil' Elfie in his head.

The Major left the heavy blade there for a moment, letting it drink deep on Elven blood before wrenching it out and letting the mage fall. "Strange last word," the Major said, sheathing his weapon.

Shard was bellowing for his thugs to regroup. He could hear Ribsplitter-Jones still climbing the hill. He checked his flanks. Major Ogfeet was taking his dear, sweet time. Momoo, however, was faring much better as the right flank crested the hill. Shard turned towards the thick woods. The Horretika had pulled back and were scattered in the trees. Shard ground his teeth. Fucking Elves, even their advanced super kill squad consisted of useless twits. It also meant he would lose sight of his thugs in the heavy scrub and lose his command and, most importantly, his control. It would not be the first time that battle-frenzied thugs lost in the woods fell on each other.

Bark-Bite was down on one knee, rifling through the mage's robes. "Why did he say that?"

Shard picked up the fallen banner. "What?"

"Right before he died." The Major snorted, finding nothing of interest. "I thought he was going to cast a spell, but instead he said, *'Ahhorant'.*"

Shard looked at his thugs still doing push-ups. "Get the fuck up! Gimme a line! Right here." Shard handed one of them the banner. "Who the fuck cares?" He called back to Bark-Bite. "Fucking cocky bastard thought he could take on my whole company."

"A strange thing." Bark-Bite pulled a chaw out of his pocket. "He looked at you and said, *Ahhorant.* That's twice now you've been called that."

"Maybe he said 'Ah've been bored by an ant!'" Shard said impatiently. "He'd just had his guts ripped out. I can't imagine he had time to be eloquent and witty." Shard picked up his sword. "In these woods are Elves reputed to stand and fight. You want a piece of that?"

Bark-Bate ripped off a piece of chaw and smiled with the black plug wadded in his cheek. "Who wouldn't?"

Shard turned, holding his sword aloft. "Charge!"

Ribsplitter-Jones reached the top of the hill and moaned. "Wot? I just fuggin got heres!"

Thunder exploded across the valley.

Shard looked around, alarmed. "What the fuck?"

Bark-Bite shook his head. "That wasn't the Black Dirt That Blows Stuff Up."

Shard's nose crinkled. "Smells like it."

A tremendous clap resounded and thugs suddenly turned into flying balls of smoking meat. Oily, black smoke filled the woods as more thunder resounded. Tongues of fire lashed in the smoke and thugs were torn into ragged shreds.

"Magic!" Ribsplitter-Jones shouted.

"No," Bark-Bite countered. "I've never seen this!"

"Fucking Fuck Shits!" Shard screamed above the din. "Go!"

And Shard's thugs ran.

Smoke choked Shard's lungs, burning them. More explosions rocked the woods and giant rings of smoke gently sailed at them. Shard could make out the lanky form of Elves hiding in the woods. They were holding burning punks in their hands. Shard tried to blink his vision clear, not believing what he was seeing: Elven Tech Lieutenants? They were standing beside giant pipes, the shadowy end pointed at the thug's rampant charge.

The Elf touched the punk to the pipe.

And the world exploded.

A thug, the thug behind him, and the thug behind him, disintegrated into bloody mist. Shard felt hot bone chips splash on his cheeks. Up ahead, the Elves were hooking pipes to horse trains and dragging them away. Shard bellowed his thugs on through the scrub, but the Elves, giggling, tittering, only unlimbered their pipes and pointed them at the oncoming thugs. Shard watched them load, stuffing in silken sacks then pouring in small, round rocks.

They stood back, holding a long burning stick, smiling.

Shard charged on, right at them.

The long sticks lowered, touching the backs of the pipes.

And it began to rain.

Fat, heavy drops dumped from the grey sky, splashing, splattering, turning the ground instantly to mud, weighing the thugs down. Shard cursed his luck as he squinted against the rain and sallied on.

The Elves, however, were not smiling. Their hair was flat against their heads as they fluttered about the pipes like frightened birds, banging them, stuffing the extinguished punks on them, snapping their fingers and throwing magical sparks at them.

Nothing.

And the rain stopped as quickly as it began.

Water still dripping from the trees above, Shard watched as the Elves looked up, surprised at how close the thugs had come and sprang to their horses, trying to hook the pipes to their limber, but their panicked fingers fumbled, tangling the block and tackle.

Shard dug his foot into the soft earth for purchase, his toenails digging deep. He leapt up and swung down with his sword, slicing into the Elf's back.

Shard blinked in amazement. Flighty bastards had spines after all!

The Elves ran, their screams shrilling against Shard's back teeth. The thugs howled in furor and gave chase, throwing parting shots at the exploding pipes. Shard glanced to the left; still no sign of Major Ogfeet. He glanced right, but had lost sight of his flank. He had wanted all the units to hit simultaneously, but that wasn't going to happen.

Shard followed the Elves and was surprised to see the trees thinning. He could see shafts of burning sun falling from the canopy. Bark-Bite was shouting something but all Shard could hear was the clatter of his armor and the pounding of his heart.

Shard broke the tree line, squinting in the horrid light. The sun was a giant burning ember settling into the dark, deep sea. All traces of the micro-downpour were gone. The sky was blood, cooling into purple and shadowy blue. The silhouette of Elves in straight, tight ranks loomed tall, the sun sparkling off their golden helmets. As Shard blinked the sweat from his blurring eyes, the Elves took on a holy glow, their two-handed scimitars dazzling like melting ice.

At a silent command, the Elves shifted, raising their weapons to strike.

The Horretika were precision, they were discipline, they were the pulchritude of military excellence. They had fallen back to this open ground, a killing ground of *their* choice. They had lured Shard to his death. They were going to carve the Black Dragon Company into dog food. There would be nothing left, not even songs to be sung in Goblin halls.

Shard was driving his thugs on, sending them into their certain fate just as Momoo had sent his thugs to the Dwarves.

Sweat dropped into Shard's eye, blinding him. Forcing him to blink.

Jasmine.

Cold.

Everything was so big back then. Shard was so small. He turned as he heard the boat scrape against the rock, sailing away without him. She forgot him! She was standing in the boat, looking away, her long black hair like a cloak. "Nana!" Shard screamed, tears welling in his eyes as fear and panic gripped his heart. "Nana!" If she turned, she would see him, she would come back for him. She could never leave him in this dark, horrible place of rock and dirty ice. "Nana! Turn around!"

Shard blinked again and was startled to see the bloody, fiery sun hanging fat before him.

Shard broke from the lines in a reckless charge, a ludicrous smile on his face.

Shard saw the Elf twitch, his sword a horrible blur that Shard could not even react to if he had wanted. Shard didn't. He only drove his sword, his Human sword of good, Dwarven steel, with a grunt at the space where the Elf's neck met his shoulder.

Their blades slammed against each other like the sharp ring of a cathedral bell.

Sword blows, equal and opposite, one driven by skill, the other anger.

And steel shattered like glass.

Shard's charge was arrested, standing him up with the sheer force of the blow, his hands ringing from the shock. Shard blinked. Across from him, Shard saw the Elf and his starlit, sparkling eyes. The Elf was looking at his great scimitar, broken, only a jagged hand's breath left.

Shard looked at his man sword, taken from the dead hand of Leopolis' knight.

There was a small, almost un-noticeable nick in the blade, about half way down.

The Elf looked at Shard and said, "Oh."

Even the Elves super killing unit believed heartily in form over function.

And Shard swung furiously, cranking his hips and heaving his shoulders for maximum power. Shard felt the metal of the Elf's armor fold, then render, splitting open like ripe fruit. Elven blood, cold and soupy, hit Shard across the eyes.

Shard felt the itchy, calloused hand of the witch grab his and pull him from leaping into the black water. He swung with his tiny fists at her, and, that failing, tried to bite her, but she only scooped him up and carried him away. Shard looked back at the boat sailing away, so small now, Nana standing there, still looking away.

"Nana!"

And the thugs went wild.

Shard growled and swung blindly, furiously. The Elves were forced to try to block, but their pretty swords folded at first contact. Their impressive armor shredded easily. Shard no longer gave commands as his ears filled with the song of the dead. The Elves opened their mouths to scream, but Shard heard no sound above the roar of anger in his head. He thrust forward, slipping his blade beneath the gorget of an

Elf and shoving until he struck spine. Shard dragged it free and let the Elf choke to death on his own blood.

Shard sneered as the last of the Elves disengaged and fell back.

And a cold shadow fell across him.

Shard looked up and watched as the rest of the Horretika moved forward. The main Elf forces had arrived. They had tried to second-guess Shard. They sent their mage and their exploding pipes and a small guard to tempt Shard to reveal his plan. They kept their main forces in reserve, not willing to risk them all. Now, realizing that Shard didn't have a plan, they were going to commit everyone.

And have numbers to their advantage.

"Stand fast!" Shard gasped for breath. "Hold the line! Form up!" Shard's thugs had run their last, their blood lust, waning. They were wheezing, coughing, gulping for air. Their faces shone with sweat, gold in the setting sun. Their swords were dull and blunted. Their shields weighed hundreds of pounds, dragging heavy on weary arms.

They were tired.

And the Elves were coming.

A fuck load of them.

Brave fuckers.

"They wanna fight?" Shard mumbled, trying to catch wind. "Elves that fucking fight?" Shard shouted quickly. "See them... you fucks?" Shard felt fire broiling in his arm. "They aren't going to run!" Shard raised his sword, his arm trembling. "They are going to fight!" Shard bellowed. "You fucking bastards, you beautiful, fucking bastards! I promised to send you miserable, undeserving thugs into the house of Dru with an Elf in each hand!" Shard pointed to the beach with his sword. "There they are!"

From the corner of his eye, Shard caught a flicker of darkness. Suddenly, Major Ogfeet's thugs broke into the open. Shard turned right as the rest of the Black Dragon Company came out into the light. Shard could hear Momoo's voice call out. "Carry on, First Sergeant!"

"E'rats! Dress these lines!" Ribsplitter-Jones shouted over the din. "Shields to the front! Stand by! S'not the time to get cocky!"

More thugs were coming out of the tree line as they found their way out of the woods. They looked confusedly for a place to stand in the massing formation. They were trembling with blood lust, growling and drooling, their sergeants slapping them in the heads to get them into line.

They looked like a mob, not a military unit. If they hit the main brunt of the Elves looking like rabble, the Elves would cut them to ribbons. The Elves had lousy weapons and useless armor, but they were still very skilled and, given half a chance, could hack at gaps in the armor; the elbows, the armpits, and score their kills that way.

The Elves had chosen their ground and were willing to wait. Shard eyed them and spat, but was willing to wait as well. Organized and disciplined, the Black Dragon Company would wipe them off the beach.

On the horizon, on the smooth as glass ocean, black ships sailed silently towards the shore.

The ships! They were pulling in for a landing which meant the Princess was somewhere on the shore, open and vulnerable. If any of the Elves looked back and noticed her, they would only have to send a squad and capture her.

Shard's mono-brow hung low. "We're out of time." He raised his sword. "Black Dragon Company!" Shard sucked wind, then screamed, his voice a torrid growl. "Counter-attack!"

The thugs howled as they charged.

The Elves raised their swords to strike.

Ribsplitter-Jones bellowed. "Knock 'um down! Stomps on their 'eads!"

The front line of thugs, with shields up to protect their heads, slammed home. The Elves flicked their weapons faster than sight, drawing blood before the thugs bashed them with shields. Shard shouldered his way forward and swung, but his target sidestepped out of the way and riposted, striking him in the neck.

Shard felt his gorget cave in. Had he been wearing thug armor, that would have been his head.

Shard ignored everything. He felt fire suddenly blaze in his shoulder as a blade pounded his pauldron, tearing it away, but Shard swung, feeling the cold mist of Elven blood on his face. They were swarming him and his attack was bogging down. Shard risked a glance to his left. Ogfeet's thugs were piling up on themselves, getting in their own way. The Elves stopped their charge dead.

Shard cursed.

Down the beach and across the tranquil, sun-drenched bay on the black Goblin ships, the Black Urchin Marine Company lined up on the quarterdeck watching the spectacle on shore. Their Captain, Hercule Rattyfuck paced back and forth, his shoulders hunched, his eyes cast down at the deck. He stopped abruptly and turned, looking hopefully at the Bridge.

Admiral A. W. Gor glared back at him. "I said, no!" Admiral Gor was not a man who repeated orders and his marine captain was seriously trying his patience. "I am not putting any boats ashore until the beach is secure!"

Captain Rattyfuck smiled unexpectedly. "Aye, aye, sir!" He pivoted on his heel and shouted. "Alright you demon dogs, you heard the boss. Secure the beach!"

And the Black Urchin Company all popped to attention, opened their mouths a cavernous wide and sucked air with a willowy moan. With bulging cheeks, they vaulted over the rail and splashed into the water.

And they sank like rocks.

In seconds, the bay was still again, erasing all traces of the Black Urchin Marine Company.

Admiral A. W. Gor ground his teeth as he hissed. "Fucking, Marines."

While on the beach, Shard heaved his sword. His arms were turning to lead, his sword moved as if it had been coated with glue and its edge dulled, breaking their fragile bones. Shard felt his strength leaving him and at best could only muster enough power to leave a nasty welt.

"Fugbugly Basterions!" Shard babbled. "Boogling nast-shit!" Shard drove his sword forward, plunging its dull point through the cheap Elven breast plate and into soft meat. The Elf collapsed, taking Shard's sword with him. Shard stumbled forward, pulled by his sword. As the Elf landed, Shard's full weight followed, shoving the length of his blade through the Elf and into the loamy soil beyond. Shard tried to draw it free as he climbed off the Elf's body, but it was stuck fast. Shard dare not risk wasting time digging it out, so he drew his Ork dagger and slashed at the next elf in line, its gutting hook catching and avulsing him open, spilling his viscera.

The Elf looked down, horrified that his armor had been stained with offal. Under normal conditions, he wouldn't be caught dead like that and he quickly bent and cleaned his guts off his shoes, an act that made perfect sense to him as he died.

Suddenly, the Elf line broke. With a piercing cry, they turned and fled in full rout. Shard blinked, trying to catch his breath. He was bleeding, but he didn't feel any of his injuries. He had lost his buckler. His right gauntlet was busted, leaving only his leather glove to protect his fingers. He had pulled off his broken gorget because its jagged edge was sawing into his shoulder. The Elves were on the run, their long hair streaming behind them. To their flanks, the pincers of Major Ogfeet and Captain Momoo where boxing in their escape. Before them, the expanse of the ocean, the tide rolling in. They were trapped.

Shard held up his hand, trying to signal his thugs to hold their formations. He had to regroup and attack as a unit to finish them off and minimize his casualties. He was going to storm down in column and push them into the ocean and let the fuckers drown.

On the beach below, tiny figures ran headlong into the Elven retreat, desperately trying to cut them off from the water.

Her breasts heaved with thunderous waves, threatening to smack her in the face.

Over the hill and far away, Shard could hear Dru, Goddess of Death, laughing her ass off.

Shard raised his dagger and, with gasping breath, shouted his thugs on.

The Black Dragon Company, the Black Poison Scorpion Company and the Black Burnt Toast Company merged as one gigantic cluster and charged headlong into the sand, screaming wildly.

The Elves reached the water's edge and turned, quickly forming ranks, their faces desperate but determined. Above, thugs poured like rain. Shard took the lead, screaming the loudest, trying to keep the Elves' attention on himself and not the Princess running in with her small entourage on the right flank. Shard glanced left and right. The thugs were scattered, their formation non-existent. The Elves were going to have their way with the weak Goblin attack.

Shard gritted his teeth and ran faster.

The Elves, their eyes of glacier ice blue, were hard and cutting, focused on the incoming maelstrom, unaware of the black shapes rising out of the water behind them.

The Marines had landed.

They had been trained to hold their breath and walk on the bottom of the bay to make their assault. Now as they crept up the beach, they drew their wicked sharp blades of obsidian and prepared to strike.

"Fuckers!" Shard screamed as he poured on the speed. No way the fucking Marines were going to have his Elves! The Elves were turning, confused as this new enemy silently took out their rear ranks with ease. Shard sprang forward, plunging his dagger in the heart of the first Elf, the Orkish barbs holding it fast. Shard slipped his needler into his palm and, as another Elf raised for his strike, Shard drove its lethal point into the Elf's armpit; a delicate, ancient forest green silk gambeson was his only armor there. To the needler, it was non-existent.

Shard ignored his own defense and stabbed as fast as he could, sometimes his strikes were shallow, missing any vital organs, but the Elves died anyway, more from embarrassment and fright than blood loss. All fell to Shard's needler, save one who turned and fled with Shard's blade still in him.

Shard shouldered his way through the crowd of Elves who were falling back onto themselves. The Elves were no longer fighting. They only fell to their knees and wept in dismay, begging for mercy, seemingly unaware that their angelic, pleas were driving the Goblins, who didn't understand a word they were whining, to blind rage.

Shard followed his needler. He saw the Elf suddenly stop at the water's edge, looking for somewhere to turn.

In desperation, he turned around.

Shard leaped at the Elf and grabbed him by the throat with both hands. Shard's momentum carried them down with him on top.

And Shard squeezed.

His heart pounded, threatening to bust from his chest. He felt his arms tremble as his fingers cramped. He felt cold, but shrugged it off focusing on the Elf in his grasp, squeezing with exhausted hands. Shard's ears filled with static, like the roar of the ocean. The world around him heaved unsteadily as he grunted. Shard's vision dimmed, fading to darkness. He realized that he must have lost too much blood. He wanted to succumb, he wanted to let death take him while he had his hands on the Elf's throat.

Shard blinked as a wave splashed over him.

"E'rats, 'ere 'e is!"

Shard looked up, startled. The beach was bright and cold with the moon's haughty stare, the ocean filled with stars. A wave rolled over him, splashing his face, burning his wounds with saltwater. Shard was waist deep in water, still straddling the Elf. Thugs were wading in the water, stripping the Elf bodies of armor and trinkets, then letting them float with the tide.

Sergeant Major Ribsplitter-Jones loomed over him. "Isart you're gonna skiv 'im, drown 'im or ring 'is scrawny neck, but makes up your fuggin mind and git on with it!"

Shard looked up, blinking in wonderment. He then scanned the beach noting that the long boats had been put ashore and thugs were loading them up. "Butcher's list, sergeant," Shard mumbled weakly.

Ribsplitter-Jones scratched his chin. "Ah, I figures we lost a hundred thugs between us and Ogfeet, mostly Ogfeet's." He jerked a thumb back up the hill. "S'a handful wandering around in the scrub lost. Figure they'll find their way once we start a cooking fire."

Shard nodded. "The Elves?"

"Alls of 'em, assumin' the Captain's done with that one." Ribsplitter-Jones pointed at the Elf Shard was sitting on.

Shard shook his head. "No, I'm not quite done, thank you."

"I thinks 'e's dead."

"So?" Shard said hotly.

"So..." Shard could smell Dwarven rum and chaw. He turned directly into the face of Major Bark-Bite. If Shard hadn't been exhausted he would had screamed.

"So, who's Nana?" The Major asked.

Shard's head jerked back as his mouth dried. "Wha?"

"Nana, Shard." Bark-Bite's eyes were unreal, his spectacles splattered with drying Elf blood. "You've been mumbling her name while throttling this Elf." Bark-Bite looked at the Elf. "Is that this Elf's name?"

Shard's mono-brow twisted upon itself. "No!" Bark-Bite looked up, startled at Shard's reaction. "No," Shard resigned. "I don't know this Elf's name. I, uh, thought 'Nana' meant 'Fuck you' in Elven."

Bark-Bite snorted. "No, it doesn't. 'Fshquart' is the closest thing the Elves have to a good cuss word." Bark-Bite looked up and motioned with a tilt of his head. "That idiot Momoo's found an idiot friend."

Shard looked to his right and noted the two officers making their way over. "I thought Ogfeet was a friend of yours, Major." Shard looked back and Bark-Bite was gone. Shard looked up at Ribsplitter-Jones. "Where did he go?"

"Where'd who go?" the Sergeant-Major replied.

"Shard!" Momoo called. "Are you still strangling that Elf?" Momoo looked up at Ribsplitter-Jones. "Sergeant, it would only be proper to salute the Major."

Ribsplitter-Jones glared at Momoo. "Hey, didn't I tell you to go suck shit from a fly's ass already?"

Ogfeet swelled with anger. "How dare you? Your Captain gave you an order!"

Ribsplitter-Jones slowly turned his angry glare to the Major. "Fshquart."

Ogfeet blinked. "I don't know what that means, but I'll have you gacked for that! What's your name, thug?"

"Sergeant Major Whoretwang Ribsplitter-Jones, the legitimized, despised and unloved bastard son of Field Marshal Ribsplitter."

Ogfeet nodded slowly. "I see," he said quietly and stepped to the other side of Momoo to address Shard. "You pulled it off, Shard. I'm impressed. More surprised than impressed, but still impressed." He surveyed the corpses floating back and forth with the tide. "I will see

to it the Colonel gives you a commendation of some sort."
He peered into the water. "What are you doing?"

Shard looked at the Elf he was sitting on. "Hmm? Well,
let's see. I've got my hands around an Elf's throat and I'm
squeezing with all my might. Would the Major care to guess?"

Momoo leaned forward. "Shard! The Major is paying
you a compliment! Be polite!"

Shard's mono-brow tilted. "You're getting a little ballsy
seeing my hands are otherwise occupied."

Momoo leaned in close and whispered into Shard's ear.
"Mark my words, Shard. Before the end of this night, you'll
thank me."

Shard barked a laugh. "You're going to gack yourself?"

Momoo shook his head sadly and turned to the Major.
"He's a bit grouchy about leaving the company."

Ogfeet sneered. "He seems to be a bit grouchy all the
time."

Momoo tittered a laugh. "Good one, sir." Momoo glanced
sadly at Shard, then back to the Major. "Shard is a fighter, not
much for the subtleties of office. I hope to give him a bit of
polish on the voyage home." Momoo turned back to Shard. "If
you like, Shard, we can load your friend on the boat and you can
strangle him all the way home."

Ogfeet's eyes narrowed. "You two chuckleheads are sailing for Bratanich?"

"Hmmm?" Momoo looked up. "Oh, yes and that reminds me, Major, if I may press upon you a favor? Look after
our companies for us. They are quite disciplined and should

not be a bother at all. I'll be sure to mention your role in this affair prominently." Momoo clapped his hands at Shard to get his attention. "Come, Shard! We must not keep the Emperor waiting."

Ogfeet snapped to attention. "The Emperor?"

Shard grumbled, shaking his head. "Yeah, I'll be there in a minute."

"You fuck-wits are going to see the Emperor?" Major Ogfeet asked, incredulous.

Momoo bowed, embarrassed. "We have been given the honor."

Shard snorted. "Honor? I don't think..."

"Yes, you are," Momoo cut him off with a wagging finger, "deserving of the honor, Shard." He finished.

"I wouldn't call it an honor, Momoo," Shard retorted.

Momoo turned back towards the Major. "He does have a humble side," Momoo explained. "But I think it's only proper that the captured Dwarven banner, all the loot we've gathered and now, the heads of the Horretika, be presented properly." Momoo beamed with pride. "But we will mention the Major's role prominently."

"A bunch of broken stools..." Shard began.

"And the Princess!" Momoo exclaimed. "He will be thrilled to have her safe at home."

Ogfeet shook his head. "As an officer of his Majesty's service, I cannot delegate such a task to a pair of feckless twits."

Shard jerked his head back. "Feckless?"

Ogfeet looked at Momoo. "You present this gamey thug to the Emperor and you'll be gacked instantly!" He pointed at Shard.

"Gamey?"

Momoo nodded sadly. "That is the task I must bear."

Ogfeet placed a hand on Momoo's shoulder. "While getting killed slowly might teach Shard a lesson, it would be improper to send two lowly Captains before the Emperor."

"Lowly!"

Momoo looked quizzically. "But someone should go and properly present the spoils."

"What spoils?"

Ogfeet sighed. "I will have to go."

Momoo's face filled with hurt. "Ah now, Major, that is unnecessary."

"I'll say," Shard added.

"You are a very important Goblin," Momoo went on. "Your thugs need you."

"They can do without me for the time being," Ogfeet said, nobly.

Shard laughed. "I wouldn't spend the extra coin on a round-trip ticket, sir."

Momoo ignored Shard. "Sir, I cannot ask this of you."

Ogfeet looked for his captain and signaled him over. "The decision is made. It would be irresponsible of me to present you two dweebs to His Majesty."

"Dweebs?" Shard grated his teeth. "Okay ya double-ring cock-sucker, let me explain to you why you are so fucking up right now."

Momoo turned on Shard hotly. "Shard! Your betters are talking!" Momoo gripped his sword and made sure it was lose in the scabbard. "You shall be silent!"

Shard blinked, his face stinging as if it had been slapped. "I'll be what?" His mono-brow lowered across his eyes in a straight line. "Oh, by Bosley's promiscuous girlfriend..." Shard shifted, climbing to his feet only to plop back down. "So help me as soon as I'm done choking this Elf I am gonna pull your stupid tongue out through your ass!"

Momoo caught his breath, screwing up his courage. "As soon as I am done speaking with the Major, you and I, thug, will have a long talk!"

Shard's mono-brow was arched with surprise. "I gotta hear how you're gonna do that with your tongue flapping out of your butt!"

Ogfeet sniffed contemptuously. "You will have your work cut out for you, Captain Momoo." Momoo turned back to the Major, prepared to plead his case, but Ogfeet shook his head. "I will entertain no further debate on the subject, Captain." He patted Momoo's shoulder. "I will detail your role in this affair to the Emperor, prominently."

Momoo nodded submissively. "Yes, sir. You're right of course."

"Ok, Major," Shard started. "Let me explain the big picture here..."

Momoo turned quickly at Shard. "Shard, just finish strangling your Elf. I want you to get your company together and ready to march within the hour!"

Shard blinked. "You want what? You want me to chicken choke you?" Shard caught the movement of breasts and chainmail out the corner of his eye. Four amazingly big thugs carried her Highness on a chaise lounge. "Alright, perhaps her Highness can spell it out for you."

Ogfeet sprang back, ducking behind Ribsplitter-Jones. The Sergeant Major growled and the Major stepped away, then jumped forward, startled. "Momoo! Are you sniffing my butt?"

"E'rat's, he's breathing your air." Ribsplitter-Jones answered for him. "That and he's a butt sniffer." He turned and nodded at the Princess, bowing his head. "Your Highness."

She smiled, her dimples deepening. "Say it..."

Ribsplitter-Jones blushed. "My little Princess Twillter Buggy-Boo."

Hiroki giggled to herself then turned to a large, brutish thug following her. "Admiral Gor? These are some thugs that have been following me." She waved at them. "I think one of them is in charge."

Admiral Gor glowered, as if he was smelling something bad. "Which one of you shits is in charge?"

"I am, sir." Ogfeet and Shard spoke up simultaneously then scowled at each other.

The Admiral looked them both over, his face unchanged. Noting the Major's baldric, he spoke to Ogfeet. "I hope you're ready to explain this clusterfuck to His Majesty, because I sure as shit won't."

Ogfeet smiled. "I'm your thug, Admiral."

Shard shook his head. "Major, there is something you should know,"

Momoo turned, violently kicking at Shard but stubbing his toe on the submerged Elf. Momoo began hoping around in a circle, howling.

Shard could only watch in amazement. "Did you just try to kick me in the nuts?" Shard laughed breathlessly at the stupidity, then looked back to Major.

He was gone.

Ogfeet and Gor were wading out into the surf while the Princess was being carried on her lounge. "But..." Shard mumbled.

"E'rats." the Sergeant Major said. "He's a smart Major, he'll figure it out."

Shard watched as his mission, his purpose of existence, was carried away from him. He felt suddenly cold, lost. He was certain that he'd either be killed or taken back to be killed and now found himself wallowing for purpose.

The Princess was leaning back on her chaise, the moon-light caught in the polish of her breast cups. Her long pony-tail draped over her shoulder and snaked down the back of her chair. She had one arm laid across the back of the chair as if she meant to turn around, to say goodbye.

She didn't.

If she turned around, she would see him there; she would come back for him.

Shard felt the eddy of loss draining him. The rising surf pounded him, roaring and hissing, each wave threatening to drown him. He wanted to get up, to go after her, but he couldn't move.

"Princess!" The waves crashed, filling the air with sound, drowning his voice.

She held up her hand, stopping her bearers.

Shard held his breath.

They turned and marched back.

She peered down, her face a little cross. "What?"

"He's an irrelevant thug, your Highness." Ogfeet spoke. "He shall be gacked for his impertinence."

The Princess looked up, wondering who spoke. She looked around acrimoniously before noticing Ogfeet. "I'm sorry, was I talking to you?"

Ogfeet held his breath and then whispered, "No."

"Uh huh, didn't think so. Admiral Gor? As soon as we're underway, remind me to rip his nuts off."

Ogfeet squeaked.

Princess Hiroki looked at him. "What was that?"

Ogfeet bowed repeatedly and humbly. "You already did that, your Highness."

Her face became expressionless as she thought. "Oh. A totally unremarkable experience." She shrugged. "I have no memory of the event." She waved offhandedly. "Fine, I'll have your nipples ripped off." She clapped her hands. "Now, everyone go away!" The sedan bearers turned and headed back towards the boat. "Except for you idiots!" She then looked down at Shard. "What are you doing?"

Shard was neck-deep in water now, peering up at Hiroki's moon-warmed face. She was so beautiful. Shard wanted her, wanted her more than ever. "Strangling an Elf," he whispered.

She nodded. "Well, have fun with that." She waved at her bearers and they turned away.

"Princess?" Shard called again.

She turned back, her eyes a little impatient. "What, Shard?" She sighed, her lips starting to smile sadly. "What did you expect, Shard?"

Shard nodded, sagging a little, then raising up again to keep his head above water. "I just wanted to say, goodbye."

"Goodbye. You were a fun fuck." She smiled. "I should have you killed—that way you're guaranteed to have spent the most happiest times of your life with me and you won't be blabbing about your conquest of a Goblin princess, but I think there's a good chance you'll just drown in a minute, so I won't bother. Perhaps if we meet again, which I sincerely doubt, but if we do, perhaps we'll fuck like bunnies again."

Shard smiled, feeling warm within the cold water. "I'd like that."

"You will." She waved and her sedan bearers turned her around and marched her out to the boat. They made it a few steps when she held up her hand and ordered them to stop. She turned around in her chair and cupped her hand to her mouth. "Sergeant Major!" She shouted. "Make sure the idiot doesn't drown!" She turned back in her chair.

Ribsplitter-Jones waded out. "S'rite, idiot. You 'eard her." He grumbled. "I've gacked my share of Elves so I knows when one of 'em's dead." He pointed. "'Eres one's dead."

Shard longingly watched as the Princess was loaded onto the long boat. "I know," he said, lifting his head to keep above water. "It's just that my hands have cramped up. I can't let go."

Ribsplitter-Jones threw his head back and laughed. "Fugging A Buggly Shit! E'rats a first!" He moved in front Shard and stepped on the submerged Elf. He grabbed Shard's shoulders and heaved, yanking him free. "'Ere ya go."

Shard stood up, stretching his back and flexing. He then bent back under the water and pulled his needler from the Elf's side. He rose, watching as the long boats raised oars and began to make their way out to the bay. Shard could see the Princess, still leaning on her lounge, looking out towards the boats. The Princess held up her hand and stopped them. She then pointed to Ogfeet. The Major looked nervously over the rail, then back to the Princess who was still pointing. Ogfeet then stepped over the side and into the water.

Ogfeet stood on the surface of the bay.

He seemed surprised and Shard could hear his high-pitched laugh. The Major looked a little confused as he started floating out into the bay, but then smiled as he realized he was standing on the head of a submerged Marine.

This worked very well for the Major, until the water became deeper and the Major sank beneath the waves.

Shard shook his head and waded towards the shore. He called to one of the thugs on the beach. "Sergeant? I want you to find Private First Class Addiko. I need her to find us a site to bivouac. We are too exposed on the beach." Shard turned and trudged towards where Bark-Bite and Momoo waited for him. Momoo was smiling. "Why the fuck does Momoo have a shit-eating grin on his face?"

Ribsplitter-Jones shrugged. "He got to sniff a Major's butt?"

Shard felt himself laugh as he made his way to the beach. He sloughed his way through the sand, leaning forward to let his armor drain of sea water. "Momoo? Let's get the fuck out of here."

Momoo only smiled.

Shard stopped, looking at the Captain cautiously. "What the fuck is your malfunction? Shard looked himself over. "Do I look like a sheep? Are you coming on to me?"

Momoo's smile didn't falter. "You have yet to thank me."

Shard blinked askance. "Uh, thank you, Momoo, for being the fuck up that you are and sending the Major to a certain death?"

Momoo's smile widened with pride. "You're welcome, Shard."

Shard's mono-brow tilted with confusion. "That wasn't a compliment, shit-head. You sent the Major to his death. The Emperor is never going to buy that we took a Dwarven

Banner, Ol' Gourd Head, and the Horretika and not one penny in loot. The Major will be fed to himself!"

Momoo brightened even more. "Yes!"

Shard was about to say some thing scathing, like; "Momoo, you cowardly sheep fucker! The Major was a prick and a nutless wonder and still ten times the officer you are, but you tricked him into going before the Emperor to present two-legged stools as booty and get gacked as only the Emperor can." But he only said: "F'wha?"

Momoo peered at Shard, bewildered. "Could it be, Shard? Could it be that you're a military genius and a master of slaughter and you don't know squat about the iniquitous beguiling world of his Majesty's court? Do you know nothing of skullduggery? The savagery of politics?" Momoo squinted as he studied Shard. "Or could it be that you're noble?" Momoo's face crossed with disgust at the notion, glancing at Major Bark-Bite. "He's noble!" Momoo leaned back and laughed. "Noble!" He turned back to Shard. "I have so much to teach you."

Shard's frown burned deep with building anger. "Noble this, ass sniffer!" Shard kicked him in the groin, but felt something hard. "What?"

Momoo laughed louder. "I'm wearing groin armor!"

Shard snarled and busted him in the face with a mailed fist.

Momoo stumbled back, then collapsed into the sand. "Blast it, Shard! What was that for?"

Shard's mono-brow hung low across his eyes. "You sent the Major to die!"

"Better him than us!" Momoo scrambled to his feet, keeping his distance. "You don't give a flaming crushed ass about the Major. You're just pissed that I figured a way out of a jam before you did! You were so set that we were going to die that you couldn't see opportunity drop into our laps. You believed your own hype! Clever, clever Captain Shard. If he can't figure it out, no one can. Well I did! Me! Captain Alluitious Momoo the Fourth!"

Shard blinked as all emotion drained from his face and his jaw slackened. He scratched his chin, then his crotch. He started to speak several times before he actually spoke. "Fuck, Momoo," he said softly, "you're right."

"You know I... What did you say?"

Shard wiped sand from his hair, realizing for the first time that his helmet was gone. "You're right, Momoo." Shard suddenly sagged, his feet sinking into the sand, as exhaustion overcame him. "I'm sorry I punched you." Shard looked at his feet. "You really came through." He looked up, his mono-brow sagging. "In front of the Major and the Sergeant Major, thank you."

Momoo looked askance at him, then nodded. "You're welcome."

Shard shrugged, then looked up. "With all these thugs running around, and Major Ogfeet gone, I bet you could round up the stragglers and impress them into the *Other* Black Dragon Company." Shard brushed sand out of his mono-brow, then looked up, his eyes sharp. "Just don't be trying to filch any of my company!"

Momoo pursed his lips has he weighed the idea. "A fine suggestion, Captain Shard." He looked up towards the tree line, noting the stragglers wandering out. "I'll do that," he said, looking back at Shard. "I'll catch up with you at the Officer's Mess."

Shard rolled his head from side to side. "Yeah, I'll get some thugs to set one up."

Momoo smiled. "You do that." He turned and strode up the hill.

"Fshquart," Shard mumbled, trying to melt the ball of ice in his stomach. "I think I'd rather face the Emperor." He looked to Bark-Bite. "Well, you got your fair fight with Elves."

Bark-Bite smiled sadly. "Yes, and my first boner in many years." His small smile faded. "The Horretika were fakes." He looked up, disappointed. "They used mages to lure thugs into the range of exploding pipes. The pipes were filled with small rocks and Black Dirt that Blows Stuff Up. The small rocks just lay waste to anything in their path."

"How come the small rocks don't blow up?" Shard asked.

The Major shrugged. "Don't know, Shard. Don't know. But we have scarce days to figure it out." He looked up, his magnified eyes saddened. "The Humans have pushed forward. It's a matter of time before they mass for the final assault." Bark-Bite motioned with his chin at the floating Elven bodies, drifting at the whim of the tide. "This is nothing. The Humans are gathering alliances to build a strike force that we cannot withstand." He fished his chaw from his pocket. "We've fallen back as far as we can, Shard. But

415

soon this beach will be filled with Goblin dead and there'll be no ships for us." He looked out across the bay at the ships waiting to sail away. "This was turning out to be a good war, Shard. We took some lumps, but I thought we could rally together and give those Humans what for. But now?" Bark-Bite ripped off a piece of chaw, then offered Shard a bite. He put it away when it was refused. "But now we're right, royally fucked." He rolled the chaw in his mouth. "Thank you, Shard." He looked up, his face still sad. "Thank you for letting Lil' Elfie drink deep of Elvish blood. Thank you for letting me gack some Elves before the long walk of Fo." He patted his belt then pulled out the Ork blade. "Oh, and I found this."

Shard scratched his crotch then took the blade. Shard wiped the sand and blood from it. "Why did they do that?"

"Who do what?"

Shard held up the blade. "The Elves sent a spy disguised as a thug to make us think there was an Ork assassin." Shard scratched again as he thought.

Bark-Bite scoffed. "In case she was caught, they could disavow her actions."

"Why would they give a flying fuck if we gave a flying fuck? We know the Elves are trying to kill us. Why make it look like the Orks hate us?"

Bark-Bite opened his mouth, then closed it again. He then spit. "Does seem like a lot of effort to do something, but they're Elves; that's what they do."

Shard nodded. "Let's get back to Battalion."

Shard's Nana

FAT, HEAVY RAIN splashed the windows, threatening to break in. The thundering pound of the incessant drops against the glass almost drowned out the chanting of the thugs marching up and down the parade field, Ribsplitter-Jones driving them on. They were not wearing their shiny armor. They were covered with mud. They had been crisscrossing through the building, muddy water, their hard, calloused feet churning the field into soupy, sucking mud.

They should have looked like a bunch of sad, cracked Gnome bungholes, but they marched with pride.

Shard sat in the company clerk's office listening to the rain outside. He listened to the thugs, his thugs. He listened to the rain inside dripping into a hundred buckets. He listened to the clerk shifting pages of vellum back and forth, occasionally scribbling something on one.

"The Colonel will see you now," The clerk announced without looking up from his papers.

Shard glanced around looking for the secret signal, but there was none. "How do you do that?"

The clerk only glanced hotly at Shard, peering through his ill fit glasses, then resumed his paperwork.

Shard sniffed, then pushed open the door to the Colonel's office.

The intense heat nearly blasted him on his ass. Shard stumbled back, shielding his eyes from the furnace. The Colonel sat in his chair before the crucible, immune to the horrendous heat. His head swiveled and his blood red eye fixed on Shard. His cloudy blue eye continued to watch the flames. "Shard!" the Colonel exclaimed happily. "I knew you'd make it! I knew you'd pull it off!" He slapped the arms of his chair. "I saw it in you! I knew that you had the two traits required in an officer: dedication, cleverness and boldness!" The Colonel clapped his hands. "A Dwarven Banner! Tell me! How did you manage that? Ol' Gourd Head! Secrets! Shard! Let me in on the secrets! I want details!" The Colonel shifted and his chair squeaked in protest. "Spill it, Shard! I want to know every moment of your adventure!"

Shard opened his mouth to speak just as the company clerk shouted from outside, "You can't go in there!"

Momoo burst into the room. "Once again, Shard, an officer's meeting that you failed to notify me of."

Suddenly the Colonel's sky blue eye rotated and locked onto Momoo. "Momoo!" The Colonel's red eye blinked unbelievingly. "Momoo?" He squeaked.

Momoo brandished a leather valise. "It's all here, Colonel. The details of our little jaunt." Momoo waved it at Shard.

"Details on how I broke the Dwarven formation and took their banner."

Shard roared. "You fucking bastard!"

Momoo glanced at him. "I know my father, Shard. Every good officer knows his father." Momoo looked back at the Colonel, patting his leather bound report. "Everything is here, Colonel, to include Shard repeatedly assaulting me." He looked back at Shard. "I want him up on charges."

Shard stood, jaw jacked. "You fucking asshole... "

The Colonel was stunned. "Assault? Those are serious charges... " His eyes looked around confusedly.

Shard was rasping. "Momoo! I saved your fucking life!"

Momoo looked surprised. "Did you?" He thumbed his report, letting the pages fan. "I don't see it here in the report." He looked at Shard. "Let's see your report and we can compare." Momoo looked Shard over. "Where is your report, Shard? Didn't you write one?"

Shard stood frozen as if he'd been slapped. "The Human artist," he began weakly.

Momoo couldn't conceal his wicked grin of victory. "No report, Shard? Why is that? Is it perhaps that you can't write? Every proper officer can read and write."

The Colonel fumbled, dropping his toasting fork. "Momoo? Would you hand me that, please?"

Momoo picked it up and handed it to the Colonel. "I demand this thug be disciplined, Colonel," Momoo said. "I want him demoted to sergeant, in my company, of course. He has some good qualities, but he'll need a bit of work.

The Colonel jabbed the end of the toasting fork into the hot embers of the fire. "Assault, did you say?" He rambled on. "Officer's assaulting officers? Improper! Improper!"

Shard grabbed Momoo's shoulder and spun him around. "You fucking useless ass scraper! Why are you doing this?"

Momoo seemed surprised Shard didn't know. "Partially for vengeance. You humiliated me, stole my company and kicked me repeatedly in the cods which endangers my noble heirs. I'm also doing it for power, Shard. It took me a while to figure it out, but I might get more than just laid out of this. A majority, Shard, and a better pick of women. Besides, Shard, I'm doing you a favor," he whispered. "You're not a proper officer. Plain and simple. While I'm willing to let that go, other officers are not so forgiving. You'll never be respected as one. You're a thug. Accept it. Learn your place." He held up the report. "And once this gets published, I will get laid like there is no tomorrow." He tapped Shard's shoulder with it. "I'll send my seconds your way." He smiled. "I'm not a total asshole."

Shard spat in his face. "Fshquart! I should have let the Princess rip your worthless nuts off!"

Momoo brushed the drool from his eye. "I'll see you in irons for that." Then he whispered, "I'd gack you, but I need that dedication, cleverness and boldness that you demonstrate so well." Momoo smiled. "Face it, Shard; you've finally lost. I know the Colonel has ordered that you mustn't kill me and unless you come up with a conflicting report, mine's the one of record. I doubt a Human's scribbles will reach the General's desk," Momoo mused. "Perhaps I can use them to illustrate my report? Hang on to them for me, Sergeant."

Shard's bottom lip curled, holding back the acidic fury building within him. "I've got Bark-Bite. He'll testify for me."

Momoo's smile faltered. "But he's not here, is he? No one ever knows where he is. I'll have command of your Chosen Thugs long before he shows up." His smile brightened. "You had a good run, Shard. You got to bang a Princess. Be content with that. Now it's time for you to return to your position in life... under my command." His smile broadened. "You can be my new flautist."

Shard gulped for air, fighting the rage within himself. "Fuck you, sheep fucker."

Momoo's tone grew serious. "You'll fall in line, Sergeant, or I'll have you gacked."

"Try it," Shard hissed.

Momoo's smile faltered. "And miss your chance to kill more Elves?" He opened his report. "Oh, how did I say it... ah!" He read: "Follow me and I'll see that you'll have an Elf in each hand to present to Dru." He chuckled quietly as he looked up. "I was in rare form when I said that." His eyes narrowed. "You'll fall in line, Shard. I'll have you gacked if you don't. Not even you can kill an Elf if you're dead." Momoo nodded. "You'll fall in line. You hate Elves more than you hate me."

Shard's mono-brow lowered across his eyes. "That's what you think."

"Momoo?" the Colonel called, stroking the fire with his toasting fork.

"Yes, sir!" Momoo chirped, brightly. He shot a glance at Shard, then turned to the Colonel.

The Colonel looked back, his fat hand reaching out. "Your report, bring it here that I may read it... over here where the light's better."

"Certainly, sir." Momoo gave Shard a last look, his face filled with smugness, then walked over to the Colonel. "You'll find everything in order, sir."

"Oh, I'm sure," the Colonel said botheredly, taking the report in his left hand. "Stand there a minute, would you?" The Colonel whipped the toasting fork out of the fire with his right hand, showering the room with scorching embers. With a grunt, he heaved his bulk against the confines of his chair and thrust with the fork, its tines white hot and smoking, and plunged it into Momoo's stomach.

Momoo howled violently, clutching the scathing fork and stumbling back, wrenching the fork from the Colonel's grip. Momoo yanked it free of his body, its points sizzling and smoking from his own fat. He wailed in pain and confusion, waving the fork around.

Shard blinked in surprise, but shook it off as his needler slipped into his palm. As Momoo backed up, screaming in agony, Shard grabbed him and shanked him, slipping the blade up into his ribs and into his lungs.

Momoo gasped.

Shard held him a moment longer, whispering in his ear. "Tell Dru, Wiggletooth Shard sends her another empty-handed soul." He gave his needler a sinister twist and drew it free.

Momoo took a step forward. "What the fuck?" He whispered, then crashed face first onto the hard, wooden floor, the toasting fork still in his hand.

Shard looked up at the Colonel who, with both eyes, was looking at the doorway. Shard turned to see the clerk standing in the doorway, his eyes round as plates.

"You, you saw it!" The Colonel accused him. "You saw Momoo try to kill me with my own toasting fork!" The clerk only blinked in confusion, but the Colonel went on. "Shard saved my life." The Colonel's blue eye looked down at Momoo, watching him. "Momoo became enraged when confronted with his failures as an officer. He tried to stab me with my own bloody toasting fork. Irony aside, Shard had no choice but to kill him. You saw, didn't you?"

The clerk, who obviously ran in when Momoo began screaming, shrugged.

The Colonel's red eye swung at Shard. "I'm in your debt, Shard." He snapped his giant fingers at the clerk. "My writing desk! Paper and ink!" His red eye looked back at Shard. "I'm in your debt, Shard! You've done me a good turn, Shard, now I'm going to do you a damned bad one." The clerk placed the writing desk over the arms of the Colonel's chair who snatched the quill and started scribbling. "A damned bad one." His hand flashed toward the ink pot. "I'm recommending your warrant to captain without reservation." Grabbing his stick of wax he held it in the fire with his bare hand. "I'm insisting on it." He dripped wax onto the page, then plunged his thumb into the puddle. He peered at it, checking the print, then held it out to his clerk. "Take this to regimental command immediately." He looked back with both eyes fixed on Shard. "You'll be a proper officer on paper, Shard. On paper." He shook his head. "The thugs will resent you and the officers will never see you as one of their own." He sighed. "A damn bad turn, I've done you." He pointed to Momoo. "Hand me my toasting fork, would you?" His blood eye looked back to his clerk. "Regimental Command! Go!"

The clerk vanished, his feet clunking on the stairs as he ran outside.

The Colonel sighed, reaching for his toasting fork. "Hand it here, Shard. Now come closer." Shard hesitated and the Colonel roared. "Come closer!" Shard, watching the fork, stepped forward nervously. The Colonel reached out suddenly, grabbing his baldric and dragging him over. "Just what the fuck did you bring him back for?"

Shard, in utter confusion only mewed. "What the fuck?"

Both of the Colonel's eyes focused on Shard. "By Lang-Ling's infested nut sack!" The Colonel swore. "How could you fuck this up? How could you bring Momoo back?"

Shard's mono-brow was twisted in confusion. "You told me to!"

The Colonel paused, his mouth agape. His sky blue eye rolled up into his head. "I told you no such thing!"

Shard glared back. "You did! You said not to kill him."

Slowly, the Colonel's blue eye rolled down, looked at Shard, then drifted off to the left. The Colonel moaned as if he were in pain. "By Nor'd Cee's leaky wart, Shard. I said don't *you* kill him. It's not proper for an officer to gack another officer. That didn't mean no one else could. You have Ribsplitter-Jones in your ranks, don't you? He's gacked more officers than the Elves have." The Colonel released Shard's baldric as he sighed. "Ah, the fact that you kept Ribsplitter-Jones at bay only reflects your skills as a leader." The Colonel held his toasting fork over the fire, glancing down at Momoo's body. "The Momoo family have been killing off good thugs for years. Seems they've got it in their heads that they can't get laid without getting their companies wiped out. While that may be so, we can't waste thugs this time, Shard. We're in a bad way." His face tightened as if he'd tasted something sour. "The humans have outsmarted us. We've fallen back to here and there is nowhere else to fall back to—unless we all learn to swim. It's going to take every thug one of us to keep them from overrunning us." He looked at Momoo's body with a sneer. "Get some thugs up here to dispose of the body."

Shard nodded submissively and headed to the window.

Momoo moaned.

"What was that?" The Colonel looked down with both eyes.

"I'm not dead," Momoo gasped.

Shard sneered, drawing his Ork blade. "Gimme a second, I'll finish you!"

The Colonel's massive hand blocked him. "Shard!" he shouted, then whispered; "Officer's must not kill officers. It's not proper."

Shard blinked confusedly. "But you...?" He shook his head. "Okay, I get it, I think." He turned and opened the window, squinting against the rain blasting in. "Sergeant Major!" He bellowed. "Send some thugs up here! Momoo has accused me of assaulting him..."

The Colonel coughed.

Shard nodded. "Momoo has allegedly accused me of allegedly assaulting him. Get some thugs up here to escort him to Regimental Command." Shard closed the window. He turned and looked down at Momoo. "You dying yet?"

"I, I think you missed my lung," Momoo gasped.

Shard pulled out his needler and looked at it. It was a broken schlager blade of decent steel, but Shard never bothered to have it re-tempered. He squinted at it.

It was an inch and a half shorter.

"By my father's mutant cock," he swore.

The Colonel tossed Momoo's report into the center of the fire. "What's that, Shard?"

"Hmm? My father's cock? Well..." Shard held his arms apart. "It's about this long and..."

The Colonel flushed. "I know what a cock is, Shard."

"Ah, yes, sir." He held up his needler. "My blade, sir. I hadn't realized that I broke it when we fought the Horretika Elves."

The Colonel put his fist to his head. "Ah, Shard—that reminds me—I want you to dispose of that Elf you brought in."

Shard blinked, then looked around the room. "What Elf is that, sir?"

"The one you bloody brought in, Shard, before you left on your mission. I believe you had Ribsplitter-Jones hanging off her."

Something in Shard's heart suddenly chilled as the scent of Jasmine filled the air. He found himself gasping. "She's still alive, sir?"

The Colonel waved at the writing desk on his lap and Shard took it away. "Yes, Shard. It would make for a most boring execution if she was already dead."

Shard suddenly found his mouth drying, his tongue clicking. "But, sir? She's a dangerous spellcaster."

The Colonel inspected his toasting fork, ensuring the tines were sterilized. "I highly doubt she can cast bugly shit at this moment." He set the toasting fork aside. "We gouged out her eyes, cut off her hands and ripped out her tongue." His red eye looked up at the door while his blue eye watched Shard. "Ah, Sergeant Major! Permission to enter, granted."

Ribsplitter-Jones, with water pooling at this feet, punched a sharp salute. "Prideful mornin', sah!"

The Colonel wiped a water droplet from his uniform. "You're wet, Sergeant."

"E'rats, suh. It's raining." He then bowed and saluted Momoo. "Mornin', Captain Momoo."

Momoo raised his arm to return the salute and a gout of blood spurted from his wound. "Ow."

Ribsplitter-Jones smiled, then turned slightly and saluted Shard. "E'rat's ya finally broke down and allegedly fugged up gacking 'im?"

Shard held up his needler. "It broke when we were fighting the Elves."

"Ah, suh," he said sadly. "E'rats my fault fer not noticin' when ya retrieved it from that Elf ya spent the better part of three hours gackin'."

Shard's mono-brow arched. "I think it broke in the one before him."

The Sergeant Major nodded, turning to the Colonel. "E'rats the captain eres spent his self three hours gacking an Elf," he explained.

"Really?" The Colonel mused. "I wouldn't think they would take that long to kill." He motioned at the fire. "Dry off at the fire, Sergeant Major, and recount the episode. Shard is a rotten story-teller."

"E'rats my pleasure, suh."

"Uh, I'm ready to go to Regimental now," Momoo whined.

"Ah, E'rats you are, suh." Ribsplitter-Jones gave a slight bow to the prone Captain, then looked towards the door at the two dripping wet thugs he had brought up with him. "Eres the Captain." The Sergeant Major snapped his fingers and two thugs scurried over and picked Momoo up by the armpits. Momoo mewed with pain. "E'rats yah gamey thugs, escort the Captain to Regimental Command." The Sergeant Major saluted to the Colonel. "Another time, suh!"

The Colonel waved tiredly. "Carry on."

"E'rats, suh. Carryin' on." The Sergeant Major took a step back, then about faced smartly. "Hey, be extra careful escorting the Captain down those traitorous stairs." He shouted at his thugs.

"Stairs?" Momoo asked in mild alarm. "Oh, wait—I just remembered I can walk!"

Shard winced at the hollow thudding of Momoo falling down the stairs.

Momoo screamed. "You incompetent imbeciles!"

"E'rats!" the Sergeant Major shouted. "You heard the Captain. Take him to see the Colonel so's he's can put you lowlife thugs on report."

"Uh, no wait. On second thought, it's okay, really." Momoo sobbed.

Shard blinked at the sound of Momoo banging up the stairs. It was the first time he had ever heard of anyone falling up a flight of stairs.

"It's alright," Momoo whimpered. "I'll just let you off with a warning."

"E'rats quite fairs of ya, sah. I'll see that these thugs gets disciplined rights whens we get back from Regimental."

Shard sighed as Momoo was thrown down the stairs again. He turned as the Colonel's cook stepped in with a covered tray.

The Colonel slapped his meaty hands together. "Finally! Dinner!" He squirmed excitedly as the tray was placed over the arms of his chair. "I'd dine with you, Shard, but this is just a snack to tide me over until supper." He stuffed a bedsheet into his collar. "Besides, you don't have the time."

"I don't, sir?"

The Colonel took up a fork in each hand. "No. The Elf has asked to see you before her execution."

Shard's cheeks suddenly heated. "She wants to see me?"

The Colonel stabbed a sausage. "Shard, please do not get into the habit of repeating every thing I say." He stuffed the piece into his mouth, the oil dribbling down his chin. "Yes, Shard. That's why we haven't killed her. Can't imagine what kind of chat you would have if she were dead."

Shard found himself gasping. "But, sir? What does she want with me?"

The Colonel slurped his wine. "Fuck do I know, Shard. Mysterious creatures, Elves. Unfathomable." Bits of sausage sprayed from his mouth.

Shard felt himself trembling and he had to force himself to stop. "But, sir, how is she supposed to see me if her eyes have been ripped out, or talk with her tongue cut out?"

The Colonel slammed his heavy fists on the tray. "Damn-it, Shard! I just told you I don't understand the inner working of Elves." He motioned to his food. "I'm eating! Deal with the damned Elf! Dismissed!"

Shard felt himself floundering. "But, she could have magicked..."

The Colonel cut him off with a hiss. "Shard, how is she going to magic anyone with no eyes, hands or tongue?"

"But..."

The Colonel motioned to his tray. "Eating!" He motioned to the door. "Get the fuck out!"

Shard took a step back and saluted. "Dismissed. Aye, aye, sir!"

Cold rain pounded Shard as he stepped outside. He side-stepped as Momoo rolled down the stairs behind him, cringing as he passed by and out the door. Shard watched him laying in a ball, bloody and muddy and crying pathetically.

"Please..." He sobbed. "I take it all back. Shard didn't try to kill me. It was all an accident. I don't want to go to Regiment. I want to go to a doctor."

The thugs stood around, scratching their heads. One looked up to Ribsplitter-Jones. "Isn't the doctor in this building?"

The Sergeant Major nodded. "E'rats 'e is. S'right! Take the Captain, to the doctor!"

Momoo squealed as they dragged him to his feet again. "No! I'm alright, really, fit as a fiddle." His right side was awash in blood. "'Tis just a scratch. It was all a mis-understanding. Tell them, Shard. It was a joke! Ha, ha!" Momoo craned his neck to look back at the stairs they were dragging him to. "Help me, Shard! They're going to kill me!"

"E'rats followin' the Captain's orders. To the doctor!"

Shard scratched his nose, then his crotch, as Momoo disappeared up the stairs. Shard blinked as the rain, cold and stinging, flung into his eyes. He should be rejoicing: Momoo was going to be out of his hair.

"Sergeant Major?" he called.

"E'rats, suh?"

"I don't think the doctor's in this building."

"Ah, thank you for that bits of information, suh." Ribsplitter-Jones turned and shouted up the stairs. "Eya, the doctor's nots in this building. Assist the Captain down. 'Careful, e'rats the steps are treacherous."

Shard sniffed as the gloom of a funeral embraced him.

He shielded his eyes from the rain and looked for the brig.

As he turned, he kicked up something in the mud.

Gold winked at him, like morning sun. Watery rivulets of blood streamed around it. He scooped it up, pulling it free of the mud with a slurp. Momoo's far-seer. There were symbols engraved on it. Shard couldn't tell what they were for. He'd never given a used, stale loogy about being able to read. He assumed he wouldn't live long enough to need it.

The rain washed away the last of the mud from the shiny, brass far-seer. He slipped it into his pouch and walked away just as Momoo crashed into the mud behind him.

"Please..." Momoo whimpered. "I'm sorry... Tell the Colonel, I'm sorry."

"E'rats! E' wants to see the Colonel. You heard 'im."

The brig was a lumpy stone building of rock and mortar behind the smoke house. It had been built as a prison by Goblins in wars past. They filled it with stories of unimaginable torture and painful deaths. The Humans used it as a potato cellar.

The two thugs outside the door popped to attention as Shard approached. He nodded to them weakly, his jaw slack.

"We'll be gackin' ourselves a little Elfy bitch in the morn, eh?" the guard commented as Shard trudged by.

Shard ignored him.

The heavy iron door squealed open leading to a long flight of crooked stairs down into darkness.

Shard took a step and stopped cold as the scent of jasmine hit his senses like a punch in the face.

The brig was filled with the reek of rancid potato and mildewy wet hay wafting up from the cold, cold tomb.

And the smell of jasmine.

Shard spat, then slowly descended the crumbling stairs. Behind him, the door squealed shut with a shrilling cry. Only a few, thin, grey lines of light slipped in beneath the ill-fitting door.

In the cold, damp darkness, rage began to build in Shard. Hot, boiling rage. His nostrils flared as they hissed with his breath, his hands were balled into fists, his knuckles clenched. All he could hear was the horrible grind of his teeth popping.

He ducked his head under the low overhang. There was no window, no pathway for light in the cramped, dank prison, yet Shard could see clearly.

She sat on the floor, her robes a pool of white snow around her. She was shimmering, like starlight, lighting up the room.

Shard couldn't breathe.

Her white robes were stained and bloody, the shoulder torn open where Ribsplitter-Jones had bit her. Her hair of jet, clotted and tangled, hung like a shroud, pooling on the shit-covered floor. Bruises, like shadowy smudges, criss-crossed her alabaster skin where she had been beaten. She sighed forlorn and Shard's heart went out to her. When they had found her covered in mud and blood, he didn't recognize her, but now, his memories awakened, her aura was as familiar as home.

Shard felt the heat building within him, smoldering rage in a crucible that he didn't understand. It was her. It was the fucking witch! Shard's lifelong hatred was suddenly sparked, but to his horror, it was dismay.

Dismay to see her like this.

And he was speechless.

She looked up slowly. Her hair draped over half of her face; her right eye, filled with twinkling stars, gazed upon him. Her lips, perfectly sculpted porcelain, smiled gently, proudly. "Hello, Whig." Her voice sang like crystal chimes. "It's been a long time."

Shard stepped back until he touched the far wall. He put his hand against the cold rock to confirm its solidity, to give him strength. He had planned this moment, this meeting, for so many years and now his words failed him. His breath ground against his throat. "You fucking miserable cock drip."

She nodded slowly, her smile undiminished. "And I see you're a captain. Congratulations."

Shard pushed off the wall, stepping closer, his mono-brow low over his eyes. "You shit stain in Momoo shorts. You colossal pile of maggot spit! You cunt shrimp!" Shard's eyes blazed red with blood. "You horrendous bulging bag of rancid goat cum! You heaping bowl of week-old eye crust in sour milk!" He roared.

"Breathe..." She coached him.

"You miserable," Shard had to suck air as the room began to swim, "collection of rat feces on a shit house floor that spells out Fshquart!"

Her smile faltered. "Now, that's a little out of line, Whig."

Shard's nostrils flared wide open as he hissed, trying to catch his breath. "All these years, all this time, you know what I've been planning?"

Her near invisible brows rose. "My horrible death?"

"Your traumatic, hell spawned, send the kids off to bed with bad dreams and mental scars legendary death that only drunken Dwarves will sing of when they re-tell ways that no one, not even Elves, should die!"

She nodded approvingly. "I'm happy to see you've kept busy."

"Stop looking at me like you're all proud and shit. Do you know what's wrong with my plan?"

"Not horrible enough?"

"It's not anywhere near horrible enough!"

"A suggestion?'

Shard stepped back, sneering. "I don't want your fucking help in horribly killing you!"

"In the middle of all that pain and suffering, have someone read Dwarven poetry."

Shard's face fell blank as the breath in his lungs went cold. Suddenly the spark within him roared to conflagration. "I hate you so fucking much!" he screamed.

"I know, sweetheart."

Shard charged the bars, his teeth bared. "I'm not your sweetheart, I'm not your puggy wampus and I'm not your Luddy Whiggy!"

"You are the bearer of my horrible death and Dwarven poetry."

"Don't you think I'm not going to do it. I'll find the one son of a bitch Dwarven poet. You'll be sorry."

"I already am."

Shard squinted. "And that's not going to work."

"I know it won't."

"And that won't work either."

"I know, Captain Wiggletooth Shard of The Black Dragon Company, hated enemy of Elves and all things chocolate."

Shard charged the bars, pointing his finger. "Ha! You don't know fucking everything, fuck brain! I happen to like chocolate!"

She sighed inaudibly. "And break out in hives."

Shard screamed, punching himself in the head. "I hate you so fucking much! I hate you so fucking much!" He began to sob.

"I know."

Shard howled. "And stop fucking saying 'I know'! I hate that!"

She looked mildly surprised. "I didn't know that."

Shard's mono-brow lowered over his red, gleaming eyes. "Oh, Dru, goddess of Death, grant me the power of resurrection so I can kill this fucking bitch twice!"

She smiled. "Then be sure not to gack the Dwarven Poet until after the second horrible death."

Shard's face brightened as an idea swept over him. "How's this?" Shard gripped the bars, snorting like a bull. "I'm gonna order my company, three hundred nasty thugs, into the chow hall and stuff themselves stupid. Then, right before sunrise, I'm gonna put you in a fucking hole and have my thugs shit in that hole until you fucking drown in a cesspool of Goblin turds!"

She winced, lines delicately etching in her perfect face. "And you say this is an impromptu idea?" She shrugged. "It sounds positively horrible. I would think that given a choice of drowning in Goblin shit, most Elves would chose not to." She smiled at her little joke. Shard glowered back at her. Her face suddenly drained and she bowed her head, hiding her face with her hand in shame. "Oh! What a horrible death! Woe is me! Captain, please, fling me off a cliff instead!"

Shard blinked, his mono-brow slack. "You horrible bitch," he said disbelievingly. "You're fucking mocking me."

She looked up, alarmed. "No! I..." Her eye suddenly filled with tears and she looked away. "I'm sorry, Whig. I'm so sorry. I'm sorry for everything I did to you."

Shard stepped back, his heart filling with needles. Out of all the scripts he plotted out for this meeting, her saying sorry never came into the picture.

She brushed her tears away with the sleeve of her robe, streaking mud against her cheek, then looked up, her gentle smile returned. "I know you've planned this moment for a while, don't let me spoil it for you."

Shard's face twisted, his frown carving deep. "You skanky, three day old smegma! You think I'm fucking with you? You think I'm not going to kill you until Dru, the goddess of Death steps in and says, 'Okay, Whig, she's had enough?'"

She squinted. "The goddess of Death calls you by your pet name?"

Shard drove his head into the bars with a horrible clang. "Ah, fuck! I hate you so much!" He whimpered.

She reached out, stroking his hair. "I know, Whig," She consoled.

Shard wiped his head back, out of her reach. "And for the love of Feral, the Master of Chaos, stop saying 'I know!'"

She bowed her head sadly. "Ah, Whig, I don't mean to be snide. I resigned my fate that day your thugs found me in the river with Ribsplitter-Jones. Out of how many billions of Goblins there are, I was delivered into your hands." She looked at her hand and the black quills from Shard's hair. "I knew then I was going to die and die unimaginably pain-fully." She plucked out a quill with her teeth, then spat it on the floor. "I wanted to present a better victim for you, but I'm just not a good actress."

Shard watched her plucking out the quills with her teeth. "Actress? You fucking fuck bitch! All you have to do is fucking wail in Elvish dismay, singing annoyingly long songs about how horrible it is to die by drowning in Goblin turds!"

She plucked out the last quill and spat it out. "I'm not familiar with that one, can you hum a few bars?"

"Argh! You fucking skank hole!"

She looked up, sighing tiredly. "I'm sorry, Whig. I know what you want me to do, but I just can't. I try, but I just can't bemoan my fate."

Shard seethed. "Why the fuck not?"

She gazed at him, her starfilled eye filling up with tears again. "I'm just so proud of you."

Shard felt his face sag. "You have no right," he whispered. "You don't have the fucking right to feel fermented piss! You abandoned me!"

Her mouth parted slightly in mild surprise. "Whig, that was the best thing I'd ever done for you."

Shard's eyes were wild. "You left me on that fucking frozen rock to fucking die!"

She lowered her gaze. "It was your home."

"No it wasn't!"

She leaned closer to the bars, her voice low. "What was I to do? What choice did I have?"

Shard found himself gasping, his heart pounding wildly. It was the question he'd been wanting to ask her for so many years. "Why didn't you bring me to my home? To my mother?"

She launched back as if she had been struck, her face filled with real fear, real pain. "By the ghosts of the north sky." Tears suddenly splashed on her polished cheeks, on her robe. She was laboring to breathe. "By the ghosts..." she whispered as she sagged lower to the filthy floor.

Shard blinked in amazement. He would have regaled in seeing her dismay if he hadn't been so surprised. He lowered his mono-brow, flared his nostrils and leaned in closer, until his cheeks wedged into the bars. "Why didn't you bring me home? Was my mother dead? Did you kill her, witch?" Shard tried to peer under the waterfall of hair that guarded her face. "I'll drag it out of you. I'll torture you to entertain my troops."

She looked up, her face filled with horror. "No, Whig, you mustn't do that! They must not know!" She suddenly bit her lip as if trying to hold back the words in her heart.

Shard fought not to smile in triumph as he snarled. "Must not know what?"

Her eye of stars blinked a stream of tears as she tried to speak, her lip quivering. "I thought you knew..." Her voice was tiny, almost inaudible. "I am your mother."

Shard's fists balled, his knuckles blanching. "Fucking cum licker!" He roared at the ceiling. "Stop fucking with me! I will skin you and roll you in snot!" He looked at her. "Now tell me the fucking truth, Nana!"

She was a puddle of mud-swept robes cast on the feces-covered cell floor. Her body heaved as she cried, wailing an ancient Elven song of lament.

Something stabbed at Shard's heart as the horrible noise tore through his ears. "Stop it, Nana!" He hissed. "Fucking knock it off!" He screamed over her horrible wail as tears brimmed from his red, blood-filled eyes. "Stop it now!"

She stopped in mid cry, rising slowly. She wiped her face on her sleeve before turning to face him. "I thought you knew," she said.

Shard rolled his eyes. "Knew what?"

She turned to face him, her face dower and defeated. "You are my son." She looked up, her right eye was dark, the stars gone. "There was no one to return you to. Your father was dead. I didn't know what clan he was from." Her gaze sank away.

Shard snorted. "What kind of bullshit is this?"

She looked up, her eyes filled with sorrow. Suddenly, she looked old. "I did a bad, bad thing, Whig." She sniffed. "I am not the villainess you always thought me to be. I am far worse."

Shard slowly shook his head. "This is a spell." He grunted. "You're trying to magic me. It's not going to work."

"I have no spell that will affect you, Whig." She sniffed and wiped her nose.

Shard looked as if he had tasted something foul. "This is bullshit. You can't be my mother! That's the most..."

Her hand flashed clamping over Shard's mouth. "Keep your voice down. They must not hear."

"Who hear what?" he said, pulling free of her hand.

"The guards, Whig." Lines creased on her brow. "No one must know. The Goblins would tear you apart."

Shard blinked. He would tear a half Elf half Goblin mutant freak inside out in a heartbeat. He shook his head.

"I'm not buying this bullshit for a second. No thug would dirty his dick and fuck you."

She sagged on herself, almost melting. "Listen, Whig, you must know this before I die. I'm the only one who will tell you. Twenty years ago, my clan, the Su-hor-talon, a group of dark Elves, in a vie for power, unlocked a most evil spell. A spell that my ancestors thought was too..." She paused as she fumbled for a word. "Gauche. So they locked it away. It was forgotten for a thousand years until we stumbled upon it. It was a weapon of sorts. We believed it was a weapon that would defeat the Goblins and spring us from an obscure, third-rate mage's guild into a ruling cartel. It was knowledge, Whig. A most potent scrying pool. We would know what the Goblins were going to do before they did it. The other clans would pay out their tight little rear ends for its use. We'd be rich; stupid rich."

Her face drained. "There was a horrible price to pay for the spell. There had to be an act of dark violence." She looked away. "The evil energy would bring forth the spell."

Shard closed his eyes and shook his head. "Dark evil, dark violence, dark Elves..." He looked at her with a sneer. "First of all, you ain't dark. You're fucking translucent! You've been sitting in shit for weeks and you're still fucking clean."

She looked at her mud-stained robe, then her snow-white hand. "Whig, we are dark Elves because we live in darkness. We are allergic to sunlight. Since we stay out of the light and hide in darkness, we are called dark Elves. That and we practice dark magic. Magic that is powerful, but requires a cruel price."

"Dark violence," Shard answered.

She nodded, still looking away. "Rape. But not just any plain old rape. A monstrous rape. I needed a Goblin to brutally rape me."

Shard snorted a laugh. "And what perverted sheep fucker would fuck you, let alone rape you?"

She looked up, her eye sharp and cutting. "None. We cast a spell, Whig."

Shard nodded, his mouth agape. "A dark spell?" he asked mockingly.

"Very dark. It drove your father mad. It pulled him from his campsite, across enemy lines and into my tent where he found me and did what he did best."

Shard was non-pulsed. "And his monster cock didn't rip you in half?"

She shifted uncomfortably, pulling her robes tighter. "Let's just say you won't have any brothers and sisters."

"And when he was done, he didn't just chicken choke the dark life out of you?"

She looked away. "When it was over and he realized what he had done, he ran screaming out of the tent and back to his company." She shifted, letting her hair shield her face. "I learned later that he was so horrified about what had happened, he ripped his own dick off."

Shard blinked as his mono-brow rose. His breath rasped in his lungs as the words of Rottie blared in his head. Forced to rape an Elf? Shard suddenly wanted to rip his own dick off just thinking about it. Shard felt the air grow thick around him as he gasped to breathe. He backed away from the bars. He slipped on the slick, cobblestone floor and landed with a painful thud. His eyes never left her.

She looked up, her eye soft and mournful. "And with that act, I gathered myself up and cast a spell on a cauldron, making a scrying pool. With it, we defeated the Goblins.

"Your father, however, was driven mad by what had happened. On the morning of the battle, the Su-hor-talon set up on the hill to watch the spectacle. Your father either saw or sensed me there and tore from the front line, carving a bloody swath to get to me. He slammed into me, knocking me down, but when he raised up to strike," she looked up, looking into the past, her hand raised, "I saw his eyes were not of rage, but of sympathy." She looked at Shard. "He wanted to kill me, but couldn't bring himself to do it." She shrugged. "I don't know why. P'raps he knew I was pregnant." She looked at Shard. "He couldn't kill his son."

Shard fought to breathe. He felt his cheek twitching. "A fucking half-Elf thug? You're telling me that my father wouldn't dump that abomination down the shitter?"

She smiled. "It's not as easy as you might think." Her smile faltered. "In that moment of hesitation," sadness flashed across her face, "the spears and arrows found him." She brightened. "He presented many Elves to Dru that day."

Shard fought the bile rising in him, trying not to vomit. "I, I am that abomination?"

She nodded. "You are the *Ahborant*."

"Huh?"

She sighed. "It's a name the Su-hor-talon came up with when they discovered I was with child. We all laughed about it." Tears welled up in her eye. "I laughed about it. They laughed at me for somehow getting pregnant." She cuffed away her tear. "We defeated the Goblins and all was right with the world. The Su-hor-talon were paid handsomely for our act which saved so many Human and Elf lives while I, the one who did all the work, was segregated–outcast." She swept the air with her hand. "Given menial and disparaging tasks. No one wanted to look at the Elf who carried the Ahborant. As I neared term, the market crashed on the spell when news of my pregnancy broke out. No Elf would dare try it again if the possibility of spawning an Ahborant existed. Our idea of spring-boarding into social prevalence backfired. We were a laughing stock. To try to save some face, it was suggested that I let the baby go to term. If some really diabolical dark spell could be cast with the blood of an Ahborant, we might be able to salvage our reputation." She cuffed her sleeve to her nose. "I secretly hoped for a stillbirth. We have potions that would have brought it about, but out of loyalty to the guild, and in hope that I could regain my status, I did not take them."

She sighed. "I gave birth to a baby Goblin." She looked at Shard. "You."

Shard sat on the wet, muddy floor, his face frozen in horror.

She went on. "I never thought it would happen. No one did. We all thought that at some point the gods would step in and evacuate my womb and end this abomination. Most Elf births end in stillbirths so there was no real chance that the would be born, and yet, you were.

"After the reality of it set in, it was too distasteful to keep the Ahborant alive. The Elves couldn't stand the notion of a half-breed and that outweighed any spell we could contrive from you. So, I was expected to leave you. That's what Elves do when they tire of something–walk away, move on to something prettier, more fashionable. Everyone thought it was a given. Myself included.

"Three days after you were born, I gathered you up and trudged out to the shadowy part of the forest and, in the moors of fog and mud, I left you to die. If you starved or were eaten by wolves was little concern to me. At that moment, it was as if you never existed. Save for the fact that I was sore and adorned with the ugliest stretch marks! I swear you came out sideways! That alone would prevent any Elf from thinking about giving birth, period. You were nothing to me. You didn't have a name, clan, or lineage. You were less than nothing! As I walked away, I gave you not a second thought.

"Until you cried. All thought went right out of my head as my heart rended. I ran back and scooped you up and held you, my ugly Goblin baby. I cried too–and I promised I would never leave you behind again. Isn't that funny? Me! I had cast spells that roasted ships full of Goblins. I delighted in architecting scripts that would turn Goblin bones into thorns and watch them writhe in agony! My clan, Whig, specialized in slow death and I worked hard to think of new ways to bring that about. I was the one they went to when a death wasn't chilling enough. I was the one who put the whore in horror. Me, running, tripping in a swamp to sooth the fears of an Ahborant.

"My Ahborant. My miserable Ahborant." She suddenly cried, but pulled back the tears with a sniffle.

"I couldn't go home to the guild. They would only kill you. Instead, I fled to the swamps where I found an ancient hollow tree and made my home. I forsake my clan, my life, to the powerful, sappy, charm of a mother's love. It was three weeks before I came up with a name. Wiggletooth. I discovered the hard way that Goblins were born with all their teeth. You had a strange habit of grinding your teeth while nursing." She rubbed her small breast in phantom pain. "You had this sick grin when you did it."

Perhaps I hated you then. Shard thought, paralyzed.

"So I named you Wiggletooth, a Goblin name. I wanted to name you Grindingteeth because that was all I saw when I tried to nurse you, but I couldn't get that to translate into Elven tongue. I had this fantasy that I could bring you to the Su-hor-talon and say—here is my son, conceived of evil—and they would welcome him. I mean, we are an evil clan, right?" She laughed at the thought. "What a fool." She bowed her head as her smile faded. "They would have killed you, p'raps me as well. So I stayed there with you, in the hollow tree. No fashion, no gossip, no culture, nothing that Elves do. But I was happy. I didn't think an Elf could be happy without the fawning adoration of others, but yet I was happy. P'raps it was the way you looked at me, that look of..."

She let the thought go with a shift of her head. "You were a growing boy and I could not keep you in that tree for long. As you fought to venture out, reality seeped in. Any Elf would kill you on the spot, as would any Human or Dwarf. I was a fool to think I could raise you." She shrugged. "Another crime added to the list."

"To make matters worse, the guild suspected I was experimenting with dark magic—what else could I be up to with an Ahborant? They were afraid of what I might come up with, so they sent an assassin to kill us. Not that they were afraid of my magic, but that I wouldn't let them in on their cut from the money I would make from the spells. Can't have that. I couldn't keep the tree protected forever. Eventually they would break through my spells of concealment. I was left with only one choice, Whig. I had to let you go.

"I spoke only Goblin tongue to you at that point, hoping you would forget Elven. As you neared the age of five, I sought out a slaver who would take care of you. It's not like I could look in the local registry for a prestigious, progressive Goblin orphanage. The slaver said she knew a nice one and I went with that. I paid, through the slaver, to care for you, to keep you safe and raise you well. Whether that happened or not, I had no control over. It tore me in half, Whig. That day, that stormy, grey day, when I left you and sailed away." A tear ran down her cheek and splashed in the mud. "If I had not been in that boat... If I could turn and walk back... I would have run back for you."

She shrugged, sniffling. "What would that have done? Only endangered you. The Su-hor-talon would have found out and hunted you down. They would not kill you right away, but save you, experiment on you. They'd hack you up for whatever fiendish spell they came up with."

Shard blinked. His eyes burned as if he had not blinked in a long time. "You are my mother?"

She nodded.

"You? You skanky whore, are my mother?"

Again, she nodded.

Shard felt his rage rise again. "How could you? How could you do such a thing?" He scrambled to his feet. "Is that why you brought me down here? To give me one last chunk of misery before you fucking die? One last cackling curse that I can't one up?"

She looked, her face drawn in pain. "No, Whig."

Shard stepped forward, grabbing the bars. "No? What did you think I would feel hearing the news that my mother is a fucking Elf? An evil bitch of an Elf? Is this your sick way of trying to make me feel better about myself?"

She was sobbing uncontrollably. "No, Whig, no."

Shard threw his hands up. "What then? Why the fuck did you bring me down here?"

She crumpled to the floor.

Shard leaned over her. "What did you say?"

She leaned back, her face downcast. "I didn't want you to go the rest of your life thinking that I didn't love you." She looked up, her lips trembling. "That no one loved you."

Shard reeled back and slammed against the wall. His feet skidded out from under him and he fell hard on the stone floor. "You bitch," he gasped.

Her eye looked up, blinking tears away. "I know your pain."

Shard frowned. "What the fuck do you know about my pain?"

"I know everything about you, Whig. I know about your crying at night, when you thought you were all alone."

Shard squinted. "What bullshit is this now?"

She looked down, almost ashamed. "The spell had an unexpected twist. It allowed me to see you wherever you were."

"What?" Shard clambered to his knees and crawled over to the bars. "You could see me? Like, when I'm taking a shit?"

She nodded. "Yes, Whig."

Shard shook his head in disbelief, then glared at her. "Even when I was..."

She cut him off with a wave of her hand. "There are sometimes when I chose not to look, Whig," she said quickly. "You're a growing boy... a man," she corrected, "with needs." She shook the image from her mind. "A healthy outlet for a lonely, virile young Goblin."

Shard arched his mono-brow. "I was talking about when I was banging the Princess into the headboard."

"Oh!" She let out a half smile. "No, I watched that. I was cheering you on." She snapped her fingers. "Which reminds me, before you kill me, take this." She handed him a biscuit. "Give that to Smiley and have him read it for you."

Shard looked at the biscuit. On its burnt bottom was tiny, brown scribbles. He looked at her curiously.

"That is the recipe for a potion that will cure your pox," she explained. "It will also cure Smiley's infection which is killing him, so make two doses."

Shard scratched at the mention of his flaming crotch. "You wrote it on hard tack?"

She looked at it in disgust. "They expected me to eat that. Can you imagine?"

"Where did you get the brown ink?" He sniffed at it.

She cocked her head, looking steady. "I am sitting in feces, Whig. I had to improvise."

Shard made a face. "Ugh, Elf shit!"

She scoffed. "I would never defecate under these conditions."

Shard winced. "So, you're saving it up?"

"I'd rather not discuss it."

Shard weighed the biscuit in his hand. "Is this supposed to convince me that you..." the word balled in his throat, "cared about me?"

She looked pained. "I have always cared, Whig." She shrugged helplessly. "I did what I could."

Shard gave a breathless laugh. "Did what you could?" His mono-brow rose. "When the fuck did you ever try to help me out?" His face lost all expression as an idea flashed in his mind. "When we were facing the Horretika..."

She nodded solemnly. "There was a storm sprite who owed me a favor. She rained on the cannons." She smiled knowingly. "The exploding pipes."

"And when I ran down those elves?"

"I sang a song of rage into your ears."

Shard felt suddenly sick. "And that lieutenant? Gnar?"

She looked relived. "I tried to warn you, Whig. That was the Su-hor-talon assassin."

"What?" Shard's mono-brow twisted upon itself. "But she wanted to fuck me. Are you telling me that you're the reason that I didn't fuck her?"

She nodded with a patient sigh. "Yes, Whig. I can only guess at his motives, but I am confident that 'Love you long time' wasn't his plan."

Shard pointed his finger at her. "Ha! Apparently your little spy pool was on the blink. That wasn't a he, okay? I was not about to burrow my way into a he. That was not the suc-culent melons of a he that I was groping."

She closed her eye tiredly. "That was a he, Whig. He cast a spell of transformation to make him a Goblin female."

Shard felt his mouth opening and closing. "What kind of sick fuck-plan is that?"

She rocked her head from side to side. "To make a guess, I would say that he picked a form to allow him to pass easily behind Goblin lines. I'm certain that with the offer of oral sex he could gain access anywhere."

Shard winced with horror and disgust. "Is there no fucking bottom to you Elves? No point where you'll say 'Okay, this is just a little sick, even for us.'"

She pursed her lips as she thought. "I was about to say 'Give birth to a Goblin', but I guess not."

Shard sighed. "So, why did this assassin, who had ample opportunity to kill me, want to fuck me instead?"

Her near invisible brow arched. "I can only guess that he wanted to get pregnant with your child."

Shard blinked. "Male Elves can get pregnant?"

She shrugged. "Transformed ones can."

Shard rolled his eyes. "Then kill me and have an Ahborant all for themselves. Fuck!" He looked at her. "There really is no bottom to how low you freaks will go, is there?"

She smiled. "That's what I would do."

Shard glared at her. "But first create a spell to take care of those stretch marks."

She suddenly clutched at her stomach. "They're not that noticeable, are they?"

Shard's mono-brow was level across his eyes. "A little sensitive, are we? One, you're fully clothed, and two, I think I'd go blind if I saw you naked."

She glared at him. "Your father didn't go blind."

Shard glared back. "You are not succeeding in endearing yourself to me in the slightest. You know that, right?"

"I'm not trying to." She said.

"Oh," Shard hesitated, then nodded, "so, you're just going to use your magic and blast your way out of here, then."

"No," she said quietly. "I can't." She flicked her finger against the iron bar. "Whig, do you think I would sit in feces if I had the choice?"

"I'm thinking you'd eat a stolen rancid doughnut from a bucket of stale vomit."

She squinted. "You really have no clue how Elves think, do you?"

Shard threw up his hands. "Every time I think I have a handle on it, some big-boobed, cross-dressing killer for hire wants to have my baby." He sniffed. "Yeah, I got the whole race pegged."

She took a deep breath, letting it out slowly. "When I was captured, I was too weak to cast any magic. They sent a Goblin to cut off my hands, gouge out my eyes and rip out my tongue."

"So I heard."

"Well, he came to do it, but they didn't send the most self-motivated Goblin." She shifted, rolling up her left sleeve. "I suggested that he could save time since Elves cast spells with their right hand so he only needed to cut off my right hand." She held up her left arm, bandaged at the stump where her hand should have been.

Shard smiled. "He knew that all Elves are left handed."

She nodded. "That's what I thought when he grabbed my left hand. So, after all the screaming on my part when he hacked off my left hand with a rather dull and un-sterilized blade, I told him that he need not poke out both my eyes. Since Elves cast spells with their left eye, he only had to poke that one." She pulled back her curtain of hair and exposed the massive hole where her left eye should have been.

Shard felt a pang of horror at the sight of her perfect beauty marred, but he suppressed it. "Why the fuck did you tell him which eye to poke out?"

"I assumed he thought I would lie and poke out the other eye."

Shard nodded. "But he knew that you cast spells with your left eye."

She draped her hair across her eye again. "Did you know what eye an Elf uses to cast spells?"

"Uh, no."

She nodded, pursing her lips. "I don't think he did either. After he gouged out my eye with this, gnarled prongy thing," she demonstrated with her long fingers, "I realized that he simply didn't know his left from his right."

Shard barked a laugh. "Well, good for him. So why didn't he rip out your tongue?"

She smiled, her eye sparkling. "After the screaming and thrashing on my part, I congratulated him on doing such a fine job on my left hand and my left eye. Then I told him I still had my tongue left. It was important to rip out the right one."

Shard's mono-brow arched, then lowered. "Ah crap. Since you had your tongue left, to rip out the right one he..." Shard made a pained face.

She sighed, pleased with herself.

Shard stood up, plucking bits of soggy straw from his trousers. "Well, aren't you clever. A Goblin ripped out his own tongue just so you and I could have this little chat."

A small laugh hiccupped from within her. "He looked so silly clamping his tongue and pulling and pulling." She mimicked the Goblin. "He howled and screamed and gagged and then it popped out! He smiled with a mouthful of blood, so proud of himself." She hid her gentle laugh with her hand. "He showed me his tongue and I congratulated him."

Shard's mono-brow hung low across his eyes. "Your evil side is showing."

She looked up surprised. "What other side have I shown?"

Shard sighed tiredly, grinding his foot into the mud. "It's not going to work."

Her eye searched confusedly, then looked up. "I suspect we're having two different conversations."

Shard hissed, throwing up his hands. "Whatever little game you're playing is going to fall short!" He waved an angry finger at her. "I still fucking hate you and you are going to die!"

She reached up, gently taking his finger. "Whig, I have to die."

Shard nodded. "Fuck right you have to duh, wait." He blinked.

She gasped, holding in a sob. "Whig, the Sur-hor-talon are not going to rescue me or they would have done it by now. If they find me alive then they'll assume I am in league with the Goblins and I will be turned over to the Humans for torture and execution. I can't stand torture. All they have to do is show me that eye gouger thing again and I'll give you up in a heart beat." She struggled to her feet. "Whig, I can't see you die."

Shard was frozen, her hand, cold on his. "Especially if they pop out that other eye," he mumbled weakly.

She looked down. "Whig, you ground my nipples till they bled." Her eye flashed sharply, taking his breath away. "I have stretch marks. Ugly stretch marks. All this misery that I've endured had better be for something."

Shard smiled. "I get it; it's all about you!"

"Who else, Whig?"

Shard pulled his hand away. "Well, just so you know, the Humans are going to kick our asses and I will be dead in the upcoming battle." He slapped his thighs. "So, your stretch marks are all for naught."

She looked down, the energy draining from within her. She shrugged. "P'raps."

Shard scoffed. "Perhaps? All of your efforts have been wasted!"

Her eye smiled as she looked up. "You banged a Princess until she screamed your name. You tangled with a dragon. You took a Dwarven banner and made yourself Elf Enemy Number One." She smiled as she mused. "Not bad for a days work?"

Shard looked down, his face dower. "Yeah."

She peered at him carefully. "You're not happy?"

He sniffed. "I expected more."

She nodded, a small smile on her lips. "P'raps in the next life."

"Perhaps."

She put her face up to the bars. "I will try to love you more in the next life."

Shard sighed. "I'll try not to grind your nipples so hard."

She sat back down in the mud, her good eye filling with a tear. "I would like to see the sunrise one last time." She cuffed her tear away. "What time will you kill me?"

Shard didn't look up. "Right before sunrise."

She smiled. "Excellent. I hate the sun. Bad for the skin."

Shard's eyes flared red. "You... You fucking bitch! I will kill you so much!" He stammered. "And, and I will grind the fuck out of your teats in the next life."

She threw her head back and laughed, her voice like crystal bells.

Shard grabbed the bars screaming over her laugher. "I will butt fuck you with a plow! You wretched stretch marked, scab-crusted sow! I will kill you so bad that my own thugs will vomit! And don't think I won't make you lick it up!" Shard squinted. "I know! After you're dead, I'll bury you in out of date fashion!"

She stopped laughing with a choke. "What?"

Shard smiled showing all his teeth. "You know I can do it. I know colors that would make an Ogre heave. You'll have more clashes per square inch than last call at a Dwarf's wake!"

She scowled, then a small smile crept upon her face. "Why that would be wonderful, Whig. I'd love that."

Shard beamed. "Hah! No you won't!" He mused, tapping his chin thoughtfully. "I think I'll have Bark-Bite translate a death certificate describing your death shroud of Avulsed Eye Lid Pink and Rancid Cheese Fuzz Green. I'll enclose a map where your body is interned."

She dropped to the floor and reached out of the bars to touch Shard's foot. "Please, Whig." She sobbed. "Not that."

Shard regaled. "I'm going to see what we have on hand. That and start a rumor that you and Captain Momoo were a love interest." Shard turned and made his way out, climbing up the crooked broken stairs. Her screams tore through him. She was wailing, reaching notes that could curdle milk. Shard found himself gasping for air, struggling to get to the top stair. Her wails turned to shrilling cries of pain, pain that scored deep into Shard.

At the top, Shard reached out as if he were drowning and grabbed the iron door and pushed it open, charging desperately out of the prison. He turned and shrugged his shoulder into the door, making sure it latched shut. He could feel her screams rattling his back teeth.

"You got her riled up sumfin' good!"

Shard looked back, startled at the grinning faces of the guards. He could feel the cool rain splash against his face, washing away his sweat and tears. "Keep this door locked," Shard said, shakily. "She's a tricky one. She'll string you up by your own entrails." Shard stumbled passed them. "Make sure that no one sees her. No food, no water."

Shard stumbled off, then stopped. He vomited. He dropped to one knee and vomited again, heaving brutally, trying to get his rear end higher than his head. He puked until only spit was coming out.

Slowly, all will voided from him, he climbed to his feet.

Shard trudged through the mud that sucked greedily at his feet. He shielded his eyes from the driving rain and made his way to the barn that bore his company's black banner.

He ducked under the doorway into more rain.

He peered up into the white sky framed by craggy, roofless walls, letting the rain wash his face.

Wash away his tears.

He sniffed and peered around the dim, muddy barn. The thugs had set up tents and tarps and were now sheltered beneath them. In the center of their little village, the smoke of a struggling fire of burning dung rose up a few feet and hung there, burning the eyes of anyone Shard's height. They were clustered on one side of the barn. On the other side, they set up Shard's moldy tent. In the corner opposite that was a tarp strung up between crates of rotten potatoes. The golden light of a flickering candle from within the shanty made it look downright welcoming.

Shard caught a whiff of week old puss that obliterated the stench of the rotting potatoes. Bleth, Shard decided. An infected wound. A nasty infected wound.

Shard sat down in the mud, peering into the shanty. Smiley lay within, writhing in a fitful sleep. The shanty was surprisingly dry, yet Smiley was soaked with sweat. His everpresent smile, his namesake, was faded and sad.

Shard gave his crotch a good scratch and leaned forward to get up and leave when Smiley started to moan piteously. Shard frowned, then nudged him. "Hey, Smiley! Wake up, you're having a nightmare."

His eyes snapped open and he gasped for air. He reached out and touched the potato crate beside him to confirm its solidity. His eyes roved around and finally fixed on Shard. "Oh, Captain," he squeaked. "Pardon my insubordination, sir. I can't snap to attention. I think the Elves hacked my legs off in the last battle, that they did."

Shard pointed to the toes poking through his blanket. "And whose are those?"

He peered confusedly down. "My word! They hacked off those leg's thug!"

Shard shook his head sadly. "You're losing it now."

Smiley smiled weakly. "I was just having the most wonderful dream, that I was."

"Didn't sound like it."

Smiley gazed distantly, his eyes dry and lackluster. "I dreamt I was dead."

"What was that like?" Shard asked, his interest piqued.

He shrugged. "I don't remember my dreams."

Shard held up the hard tack that Nana had given him, careful not to let the rain wash away its brown letters written in a beautiful font by a graceful hand. "Hey, uh, Smiley? I can't make out what this says. Can you give it a try?"

"Could you hand me my medicine?" he asked.

Shard looked around and spotted a jug of Goblin brandy. Shard fingered the ring and picked it up, wrenching the cork out with his teeth. The acrid perfume made Shard's eyes water. It was cheap Goblin brandy. "Here you go."

Smiley struggled to prop himself up on one elbow. "The thugs bought that for me, that they did. Wasn't that nice?"

"I think they're trying to embalm you."

"Now isn't that efficient?" He hooked the ring and hoisted it to his lips. It clanked loudly against the nad scratcher still imbedded in his nose. He set the jug down and reached up and fondled it. "Excuse me, sir? Is there a Gnome Nad Scratcher in my nose?"

"Yeah."

"Why?"

Shard angrily shoved the tack in front of his face. "Can you read this?"

Smiley squinted. "Yes, sir, that I can. Take three large dried leaves of a Camlick tree, grind it with a wolf's thigh bone..."

Shard cut him off. "Great." He craned his head back and shouted. "Addiko! Front and center!"

The private first class crawled out of the tarp village and stumbled over, splashing Shard as she skidded to a stop. "First class private... Private class first..." She sighed determinedly and started again. "First Addiko Class reporting..."

Shard sneered. "I know who the fuck you are, dumbshit."

She punched herself in the eye, missing her salute. "Ow, fuck!" She shook it off. "Private First Class Dumbshit reporting as ordered, sir!" She punched herself in the eye again, this time harder. "Ow! Fuck! That does start to hurt after a while."

Shard winced in sympathetic pain. "Just fucking stand there and listen. Lieutenant Gralfange has a shopping list. Get everything on it and then make two doses. Give him one and bring the other to my tent, got that?"

She nodded sharply. "Sir, yes, sir!" Her face suddenly lost confidence. "Uh, sir?"

Shard held his breath. "What?"

"Who's Lieutenant Gralfange?"

Shard's mono-brow bunched on itself. "Smiley! Ya fuck-wit!"

"Ah, right." She bowed. "Who's Smiley Yafuckwit?"

Shard growled. "Haven't you learned your company's officers yet?"

She nodded. "Yes, sir! There's Captain Shard and the idiot with the nad scratcher stuffed up his nose."

"That's Lieutenant Idiot to you!"

She bowed again. "Yes, sir! Where is Lieutenant Idiot now, sir?"

Shard thumbed under the tarp. "He's the one with the nad scratcher in his nose." Shard peered back at Smiley who had leaned the jug over his lips and was letting the brandy pour in. "Got that, Smiley? Read the list to Addiko and she'll get everything for you." Smiley nodded, gurgling as the cheap brandy went down. He swallowed hard and then looked at the jug, squinting blearily. "Your other hand," Shard coached.

Smiley looked at the hard tack in his hand. "Oh, I'm not hungry." He held it up. "You can have it."

Shard sighed and looked back at Addiko. "Can you read?"

Her face drained, looking lost. "Words?"

"Never mind." Shard scrambled to his feet. "Make sure he doesn't eat the hard tack and that he reads what's on it and you get everything he reads off it and you mix it up into two doses." Shard ambled towards his tent.

Addiko saluted, this time punching her head. "Yes, sir! Will do, sir!" Her face grew confused. "Uh, sir?"

Shard paused.

"How much is two?"

Shard continued his plod to his tent. "Ask Lieutenant Idiot."

She saluted. "Yes, sir!" She then stooped down and peered over Smiley. "Lieutenant Idiot? I'm Class First Addiko Private."

Smiley blinked, his eyes drowsing. "You're cute."

Shard stopped in front of his tent, and peering curiously at the puddle at his feet, watched the iridescent rainbow floating across the mirror surface before an errant drop shattered it. Shard sighed and pulled open the tent flap, ducking into darkness.

He paused, letting his eyes quickly adjust to the gloom. There was a crooked table, a broken two legged stool leaning against it, and a cot. Shard peered under the cot. Nothing but his kit. He fumbled around in his kit for a bit and pulled out a candle stub. He then stood there, holding the candle.

Suddenly he spun around to his blind side, brandishing his candle. "Do you have a light, Major?"

Bark-Bite feigned as if he'd been stung, his face wrapped in surprise. "How did you know?" He sparked the Gnomish device in his hand and lit the candle.

Shard tried to hide his pretentious smile. "You left a spit trail."

Bark-Bite bristled his moustache as he peered down at the black tobacco juice. "Huh. I must think to bring along my own spittoon from now on." He looked up at Shard. "Alright, two out of three. Close your eyes and give me a ten second count."

Shard held up his candle, lighting up the Major's primeval green, mud-stained cloak. "You've been out and about." Shard sat down on the cot.

The Major propped up the two-legged stool and sat, rocking slightly to get his balance. "I realize that my jovial manner lends itself to a relaxed air of familiarity, but there is a certain amount of respect due." His eyes loomed large behind his spectacles, glaring at Shard's bewildered face. "You have yet to offer me libation."

Shard shrugged. "I'm all out of Dwarven rum, sir."

Bark-Bite reached into his pouch and retrieved his flask, handing it to Shard.

Shard held out the flask. "Libation? Major?"

Bark-Bite's face lit up, taking the flask. "Oh, perhaps just a dram."

"How many Humans?"

"Hmmm, a staggering fuck load I'm afraid," Bark-Bite answered, making a face from the vicious bite of his liquor. "You see, we've been forced into a peninsula, our sides and back to the ocean. The Emperor isn't going to admit defeat this early in the campaign." He handed the flask to Shard. "So there won't be ships to carry us away."

Shard felt his eyes water as he took a sip, his face pinching. "That's not Dwarven rum."

Bark-Bite took off his glasses, cleaning them off with his shirt tail. "I made it myself out of furniture polish and dandruff." He put on his glasses, blinking now that he could see. "Aged it for an hour under my armpit."

Shard took another sip. "Alright, sir, I've learned my lesson. From now on I will have libation of some sort to offer the Major." He handed the Major the flask.

The Major took a sip and winced. "Ugh! Shard, are you trying to kill me with this crap? I realize that you've come up from the ranks and lack the inherent breeding to differentiate good hooch from furniture polish and dandruff, but as an officer you'll have to learn." He took another sip. "Offer this swill to me again and I'll have you strung up on the quarterdeck." He offered the flask back and Shard took it.

Shard nodded. "I'll remember that, sir."

"See that you do." He sighed sadly. "We don't know how to work the exploding pipes. I am inclined to think it's a Gnomish device and not magic." He shrugged. "It won't help anyway."

Shard took a sip.

The Major looked up, his eyes shifting in the playful candlelight. "We've only a few days, Shard. A few days to somehow turn this war."

Shard took another sip and smiled.

Bark-Bite reached over and took his flask. "Alright, exactly how much of this do I have to drink before I can smile like that?"

Shard let out a breath. "Who gives a fuck?"

Bark-Bite looked at his flask, impressed. "I think I may have something." He took another sip. "Perhaps not."

Shard shook his head. "Why didn't the Humans stop us from landing?"

Bark-Bite scoffed. "They tried their hardest."

"Did they?" He reached out for the flask. "How is it they are beating us now?"

Bark-Bite stammered, fighting for balance on his two-legged stool. "The same way they've beaten us for years. They rally together and ally under the Human banner."

Shard smiled, taking a sip from the flask. "Why not pile every swinging dick on the shore? Why not build palisades and stop the landing craft from coming ashore and blast us with their exploding pipes?" Shard leaned forward, his face tight. "They knew we were coming! Why wait until now to rally together?"

"Perhaps they're procrastinators. Are you going to hog that?" He took the flask back. "What are you getting at?"

Shard shrank back. "I don't know."

Bark-Bite coughed, then took a swig to quiet his cough. "Bloody hell, you got me all excited."

"What if they're not all united under one banner?" Shard asked.

Bark-Bite bristled his whiskers as he thought.

Shard scratched, then scratched again. "Fuck, I'm just blathering. It's too late for sneaky plans now. Too late to pull a victory out of our asses." Shard laughed breathlessly. "Who gives a shit? All we have to do is fight our hardest and Dru will welcome us all." Shard reached over and took the Major's flask. "I hope to see you on the long walk of Fo." He took a swig. "I've enjoyed our talks." He stoppered the flask. "But I'll bring the hooch next time."

"I'll expect you to." Bark-Bite said. "We do have one thing to look forward to." He brightened.

"What's that?"

Bark-Bite smiled, showing his perfectly straight teeth. "Tomorrow, you get to gack an Elf. A mage!"

Slowly, a smile made its way onto Shard's face.

Shard's Execution

THE SKY WAS a black woolen cloak. The endless rain had abated to a spitting mist that forced the fog to lay low on the cold, muddy ground like a ghostly quilt. In a grove of dead, pain-twisted trees, the Colonel sat in his chair, its legs sinking slowly into the mud, watching the whole affair. He was bundled up with three cloaks, two quilt blankets, a leather shawl and a hand-knitted, non-regulation hat. He harrumphed continuously, uncomfortably.

The company clerk stood up, his face in a frown and his tiny eyes tight as he held up the order. A thug beside him was holding a lantern and doing a little dance that comprised of crossing and uncrossing his legs. The clerk grabbed the thug's arm to hold the light steady to read the order of execution. "By His Majesty, God Emperor Spinecrack, grand imperial of the divine order of the universe, being sent by the gods to rule us unworthy and unwashed heathens, whose eyes glistening with starlight and his terrible sword of cruel and unmerciful fiery vengeance are proof of his awesomeness, brings tidings and joy to all those assembled as we carry out the just execution of the skanky, spooge licking, triple fuck hated, Elf mage, delivered into our undeserving hands by the grace of Grimlick, the ugly god of Goblins. The drinker of quim bitch Elf shall die by being buried alive in Goblin shit while wearing unflattering and out-of-date fashion!"

From the depths of darkness came a painful shrill followed by a whimpering mew.

The clerk nodded to the thug beside him. The thug dropped the lantern and ran over to join the line of thugs all prancing about, bent over from their cramping bowels, their hands squeezing their butt cheeks together.

The clerk picked up the lantern and blew it out. He then sat with a squish in the mud, crossing his ankles to watch the show by his colonel's side.

Out of the darkness and murky, eerie gloom, her white robes glowed, fluttering like a wounded bird on the ground. She slowly scrambled to her feet, but her guards tripped her again and she crashed to the ground, a wrinkled pile of silk. They prodded her and she crawled, slowly making her way to her feet. She staggered around blindly, tripping over her own chain.

One of the thugs dancing in the line shouted, "Get on wif it!"

The Colonel harrumphed, pulling his covers tighter. "Yes, bloody move this along!" He shivered. "Freezing!" He mumbled, wishing the clerk hadn't blown out the lantern. He sniffed and looked down at this clerk. He harrumphed again, but the clerk didn't notice and pay the Colonel due sympathies. That failing, he turned to his other side where Lt. Smiley sat.

Smiley's two-legged chair had long since sunk into the mud. He was draped in two thread-bare blankets that the Colonel eyed hungrily. Smiley paid him little mind, watching the spectacle as the guards now dragged the Elf towards the pit.

The Colonel harrumphed. "Lieutenant?"

Smiley sat, his gaze a little vacant, nodding to the beat of music that only he could hear.

"Lieutenant Gralfange?"

Smiley smiled, staring at the fog.

"Smiley?" The Colonel leaned forward slightly, his chair sinking deeper.

Smiley looked up. "Sir?"

"Your name is Gralfange, is it not?"

Smiley smiled and nodded. "Yes it is, sir! Thank you for checking."

The Colonel nodded slightly, while his blue eye watched the guards drag the Elf who now simply hung in their arms, his red eye studied Smiley. "Aren't you hot?"

Smiley looked up, trying to follow the Colonel's roving eyes. "No, sir. Begging the Colonel's pardon, but you have an eyeball that's wandered off."

The Colonel pressed. "So you're not on your death bed?"

Smiley brightened. "I'm a bit better, sir. Private First Class Addiko and Sergeant Major Ribsplitter-Jones whipped up a little kick-a-poo joy juice which seems to have done the trick." Smiley reached under his blanket and fished out a flask. "They think I'll live, as long as the booze holds out." He wrenched the stopper out with his teeth and spat it over his shoulder. He tipped it back to his lips.

"Lieutenant?" The Colonel interrupted him.

"Sir?"

Both of the Colonel's eyes were locked on the flask.

Smiley looked at it, then at him. "Would the Colonel like a bit?"

The Colonel's huge hand tunneled its way out from under the covers and grabbed the flask. "Need to warm the bones, boy," he mumbled taking a big swallow. His cloudy, blue eye rolled lazily up and out of sight. "Ugh!" He wheezed. "Bloody fuck! That's not bad a'tall."

Smiley nodded. "I suspect it's furniture polish and dandruff."

The Colonel took another nip, smacking his lips. "Perhaps it is, but in this miserable weather, it'll do." He handed it back and buried his arm from the cold. "Where is your captain?"

"Shard, sir? He's reconnoitering the battlefield, that he is." Smiley took a long pull from his bottle and coughed, fighting to keep it down. "I think you can really taste the dandruff as you near the bottom, that you can."

"Really?" The Colonel held out his hand for the bottle. "I'm surprised Shard isn't here for this."

Smiley placed the flask in the Colonel's hand. "I don't think he's fond of dandruff, 'less it's his own."

The Colonel snatched the bottle. "No, the Elf gacking."

Smiley gave a half shrug, watching the Colonel drink his hooch. "Shard took a dump into a bucket which will be poured into the pit. A real wet one!" He turned and noticed for the first time the Elf being dragged away.

"Ah." The Colonel handed back the flask. "Shit by proxy?" He harruphmed and pulled his covers tighter. "I should have thought of that." Both of the Colonel's eyes focused on the white form of the Elf being dragged to the pit.

Daphne wanted to vomit.

Her stomach churned like a cauldron. Her eye gleamed silver as she peered through the curtain of her hair at the looming hole. Shard was making good on his promise to kill her in the worst way. She was dressed in her own robes which were not only fashionable, but trend setting, but the Goblins didn't know that and all Shard had to do was start the rumor and eventually the Elves would find out. She would be effectively caught dead in Goblin fall colors in the spring. A bit of bile heaved up at the thought, but she didn't want the Goblins to know that Elves were capable of something as revolting as barfing.

She couldn't swallow it either.

And spitting never occurred to her.

I'm going to die, she thought, *by my own son's hand with my cheeks full of puke.*

She was disappointed the idea alone didn't kill her outright.

The hole loomed before her, getting closer. Even to her Elven sight, it was like a pool of oblivion, radiating with

473

stinging cold. She fought her instincts to try and run. She fought to ignore the suffering, the pain, the grit that was oozing into her panties–panties she had worn for weeks.

She screamed, bile spitting up on her creamy white chin, long strands trailing to the ground. Her caterwauling was piercing, like chewing on metal that forced the ears to cringe and the skin to crawl. The guards were now at double-time, trotting faster, struggling to hold onto the writhing Elf, hoping to silence her wails by throwing her in.

They didn't realize she was fighting to dive in, to hide her shame in the pit, her crypt of Goblin shit.

Daphne closed her eye and gritted her teeth, trying to stifle the horrible noise she was making. Puke was drooling down her chin. If the Elves had wanted to rescue her, it was too late. She would never let them rescue her alive with her chin sopping with gruel.

She jammed her feet down for traction and pushed off towards the hole, headfirst into her tomb of night. The Goblin guards couldn't hold on as she broke free, ducking her head and launching herself into the hole. Down into darkness, her robes fluttering slowly, gently, falling forever.

Light flashed across her eye when she hit bottom.

She thought the fall would kill her. She hoped the fall would kill her. She wanted the fall to kill her. Slowly she dragged herself to a sitting position. Her eye, glowing silver, pushed back the darkness as she peered around. Shrugging the shackle off her left stump, she peered up at the hole above and the feeble torch light corona. If she jumped, she could grab the lip and climb out. If she wanted to.

She watched as the hole was eclipsed by the twin cheeks of a Goblin ass.

She flattened reflexively against the wall as the stream of putrid excrement rained down, followed by a triumphant, trumpeting fart.

Above, the Goblins cheered.

Daphne crouched down, hugging her knees to her chest. Her eye scanned the hole for an indentation to crawl into and avoid the direct blast from the vengeful Goblins, and wait out the inevitable tide. Her mind flashed with the hope that Shard had left a knife for her to end it fast. To just cut her throat and be done with it.

Her eye froze as she realized she was not alone in the pit.

Light flooded from above as the first Goblin finished and roped up his pants. He was pushed out of the way before they were tied and the next bum took its place.

Daphne blinked in the darkness. Her Dark Elven sight allowed her to see in total darkness.

It was Momoo. Bound and gagged and cringing as shit splashed before him. He whimpered and the Goblin above grunted. "That one got her!"

The Goblins cheered. One shouted, "Get on wif it!"

Momoo's eyes were wide and trembling and Daphne fought hard not to laugh at him. She looked around for anyone else, but it appeared they were alone.

Then she noticed something.

She looked again. She squinted at it, blinked and squint-ed again.

In the darkness, she could make out an even greater dark-ness: a hole within a hole.

Daphne inched her way along the wall, blinking away tears from the stench of muddy waste that was quickly build-ing up. She ducked into the hole, hoping it was deep enough to hide in, to keep out of the direct torrent.

Long, winding, drilling its way into the earth, a soft breeze caressed her skin. She could smell a river and hear its soft, playful giggle.

Slithering on her belly, she crawled on her elbows and knees, shaking the crumbling dirt from her hair, spitting out sand and roots, and blinking the dirt out of her one good eye. Ahead, she could see the soft circle of light that meant the way out.

She didn't question the logic. Any stay of being shat on was more than welcome.

Ahead, a Goblin head poked in, then out. "She's coming!"

Daphne paused, catching her breath, trying to figure out what was going on. Behind her, she could hear a Goblin grunt as he heaved out a long python like peel that hit with a solid, heavy thud.

She started crawling again, this time in earnest.

Her lungs sucked fresh air as she emerged from the tun-nel, while hands roughly dragged her to her feet. She was on a ledge overlooking a babbling stream. Fog nested along the trail, sliding off the edge in rivulets. A Goblin stood before her, punching a sharp salute that made her cringe in sympathetic pain.

"Private First Class Addiko, sir!" The Goblin smiled.

Shard punched the Goblin in the back of the head so hard she had to take a half step to keep from falling. "Shut the fuck up and get the rock."

She stumbled, getting her wits. "Ugh, good one, sir." She shook it off. "Right, the rock." She bent down and started pushing a rock into the hole Daphne crawled from. Daphne watched the little Goblin vanish into the hole. She looked up slowly, noting the large silhouette of Ribsplitter-Jones lurking just off her blind side. She tilted her head at Shard. "You wanted to see me, Captain?"

Shard sneered. "You can shut the fuck up, too." His eyes burned red as he looked up at her. "I'll spell it out for you. Even the flightiest Elf could've figured out where you were, but they didn't take a hiatus from whipping each other with peacock feathers to come save you. They don't give a sweaty used fuck about you."

She risked a slight smile. "So glad to see you care."

Shard winced, trying to control his temper by grinding his back teeth. "Sergeant Major? If she so much as sniffles, bust her in the head."

"S'right," he grumbled, his voice, his breath, hot against her scalp. She could feel him behind her, smell the rum on his breath. He was a big Goblin, as tall as she was. Her shoulder tingled in phantom pain as the bloody memory of him biting her came to her mind.

She said nothing.

Shard peered up beneath her curtain of hair to catch a glimpse of her eye to make sure he had her attention. "The Elves abandoned you–and if they see you alive, they will suspect you crossed over to our side and kill you." Shard leaned to the side. "Sergeant Major? Do you know how Elves execute someone?"

Ribsplitter-Jones shrugged. "Beheading?"

Shard shook his head. "Nah, too bloody. They simply make you *invisible*." He looked at Daphne. "Isn't that right? They give you the ultimate silent treatment. They ignore you until you die of loneliness." Shard smiled.

Daphne swallowed nervously.

Shard nodded. "So you're in a bad way. The Humans would only turn you over to the Elves; the Dwarves would kick your ass and then hand you over. The Hobbits would take care of you, but what Hobbit can keep a secret? Sooner or later the Elves will hear you're alive and come for you. That leaves the Gnomes." Shard's mono-brow arched. "And I don't think Gnomes know what fashion means."

Ribsplitter-Jones laughed mockingly. She could feel it vibrate the back of her head, sending goose bumps down her back.

Shard went on. "So it's simple. You work for us."

She slowly raised her hand.

"What?"

She pointed to Ribsplitter-Jones.

Shard sighed and nodded to the Sergeant Major. "Don't punch her." He looked back to her. "What?"

"What will happen when the Goblins notice me in your ranks?" She whispered.

"You let me figure that out."

Something twisted in her stomach. She suddenly resisted her reflex to puke again. "You can't do this." Her voice was as tiny as a cricket's breath as a tear rimmed her eye. "Whig, you risk..."

"Sure as fuck I can do this." Shard's voice was loud and harsh, cutting her off. "In three days, maybe four, the Humans will push us off this rock and into the sea." His eyes narrowed. "I got nothing to lose but the chance to show the Humans what happens when Wiggletooth Shard's back is to the wall." Shard frowned, trying to look dignified. "So that's the deal. You work for us or you die horribly."

Her eyes roved confusedly. "What can I do? My magic is gone."

Shard was unmoved. "Think of something." His monobrow twitched.

Her breath froze in her lungs as a pain stabbed her heart. Shard was struggling, using any excuse not to kill her. To kill his mother. "Whig, the risk is too great..."

Shard seemed to swell with anger. "Captain Shard!" he hissed.

She closed her eye as life drained from her spirit. "Captain, you are risking..."

"Don't you tell me squat." Shard cut her off. "I know what I'm risking. In three days, I'll be trampled and left to breathe mud by the Human cavalry. By Jetum's cross-dressing mother, I'll not let that happen."

Daphne was startled by a sudden tear that ran her cheek. "But what can I do?"

Shard made up his face as if to spit. "Make me a Scrying pool."

She looked up, a little startled. "A Scrying pool?"

He nodded. "And stop them from Scrying us."

"Is that all?"

"Or so help me I'll throw you back to drown in shit with Momoo."

She reeled back as if she'd been slapped. She just escaped her last moments of looking up at Goblin poop-holes winking at her and had no wish to face that again.

She nodded.

Shard's War

In the hour before the dawn, the quickening sky fanned a distant berry blue, blotting out the stars from the sky, one at a time. A gentle breeze, like a soft wave, blew in from the sea. Shining armor, dulled with dew and tears, sat still and cold.

The armies of Hookfang Rottingtooth under the command of Field Marshal Ribsplitter, was on the high ground. Tech Lieutenants, in their polished, shiny armor, filed past one at a time before an old hag brandishing a burning candle. As they touch their oily punks to the candle, she quizzes them, asking for their pact with Dru. They don't answer; they don't speak. The pact with Dru, goddess of Death, is solemn and confidential. The hag asks only to make sure they have promised themselves to *her*. The hag's jaundiced eyes, crafty and sharp, watch for a pause, a stutter in their hearts, an indicator that they've not resigned their fate to the goddess of Death, that when the moment comes they'll hesitate to jam the smoldering punk into the bung hole of their keg of Black Dirt That Blows Stuff Up and blast the Emperor's enemies to itty, bitty bits.

Fast fingers, practiced and deft, unbuckled muzzles from the flashing maws of the Banwolves. The massive beasts whimpered, their quills fanning. Their riders rein them in sharply, lest the half-starved beasts turn and snack on them.

The heavy paws of the Sherrorrams leave gouges in the dry, hard-packed earth from non-retractable claws. The Goblin riders sit upright on their massive, six-legged steeds. On command, they don their dark, smoked glasses that not only protect their sight, but make their eyes big and fearsome.

Tickling flames flash quickly over the skins of the massive tornado drums, drying the heads and tightening the skins. The drummers, long deaf from the thunderous sound of their instruments, place their heads against the drums and tap them, feeling for the vibrations and testing the tones.

The sky fills with blush and Field Marshal Ribsplitter frowns.

Thousands of stragglers, cut off from their units, left for dead, lost or confused or over due, have made their way back. Sergeants quickly impress them, filling their ranks. The Black Nightmare battalion consists mostly of stragglers—the Black Dog and the Ebony Mace companies are completely so.

The Goblins of the Black Martyr Battalion shiver, their curved silver daggers in hand. At the moment of attack, as they prepare to engage, they will draw their blades deep into their bellies, a mortal wound. They will spend their last moments of life with reckless abandon, attacking with cruel, serrated axes, killing the enemy with an incomprehensible ferocity—unstoppable and fearless. The sight of their banner, a Silver Crescent sinister on sable, is a badge of honor for the fated Goblins, and an image striking terror into their enemies.

Ribsplitter turned his face to the sea. He closed his eyes and breathed deep the salty air, feeling the morning chill cool his burning heart.

His eyes opened, glowing red and angry. His lips sucked with a click as he drew the reins of his Sherrorram, turning his back to the dawn. His beast walked lazily to the front. The Black Fortress Battalion and the Obsidian Fortress Battalion, with their massive door shields of Goblinwood, shuffle apart to let him pass.

He growled, his teeth dragging against themselves.

Behind him, Brigadier General Lucius Ribsplitter the Sycophant, brandishing his barbed spear, watches the thugs like a hawk, ready to gack anyone who fails to show proper reverence to the Field Marshall. His eyes darted, searching for his half-brother, Whoretwang Ribsplitter-Jones. If there was anyone to count on disrespecting the Field Marshall, it would be him.

The Sergeant Major was nowhere to be seen.

Lucius sneered and drove his heels back to catch up to his father and inform him that Whoretwang was AWOL, but he paused and held his tongue.

His father was in the zone.

Field Marshal Ribsplitter turned his steed to the rising sun where all the Goblins could see him. His beast glowed with fire in the first touch of the new day.

Golden light cascaded across the black carapaces of Goblins, shining like the backs of beetles, seething like a swarm prepared to protect their hive. They were crushed together, packed like sardines to fit on the tiny field.

Streams of pale virgin daylight outlined the tight, disciplined formations that extended to the horizon. The silhouette of one million thugs on this field alone, a black seething mass of hate and desperation, glared back at him with tight, crimson eyes.

Field Marshal Ribsplitter struggled to keep his face from breaking out into a smile.

But he did indeed have a puffy.

He grabbed his talwar as he rose in the stirrups. Dragging it free, he hoisted it aloft and caught the first glow of the morning sun in his blade. His Goblins cheered as they marveled at his sword of flame!

"The Emperor is with us! The Emperor is with us!" They cheered.

Ribsplitter turned and pointed his sunfire sword into the shadowy fields below.

Slowly, slowly, the curtain of shadow drew back and Ribsplitter could see the Human forces and their allies.

The Crimson Saber Cavalry, armed with long, curved blades, honed to a fine razor's edge, had the honor of leading the forces. Their steeds, tall and willowy, were the fastest in the land. They were set to dash through the line of Tech Lieutenants being long out of blast range when the deadly casks exploded. They could out-maneuver the Banwolves and leap over the Goblin shield wall into the ranks where their blades would cut deep.

Directly north of the Crimson Saber was the Pooton Hobbit Support Battalion. Cooks, postal clerks, administrators and accountants, wearing copper pots for helmets, they were too cute and cuddly to even consider for combat use. The Humans were throwing them away, knowing the Banwolves would be unable to resist the tasty Hobbit flesh. The Banwolves would bog down eating and expose themselves to a rain of arrows, slaughtering the Banwolves and giving the Hobbits a merciful death.

What a horrific, brutal commander the Humans had!

Ribsplitter was warming up to him.

He squinted, waiting for the sun to rise a little higher.

Behind the Crimson Sabers was the Northern Mountain Dwarf Battalion. Known for their Dwarven rum, these Dwarves made fearless opponents. They were either numb from boozing, or hung over and pissed off. Either way, they made formidable foes.

Ribsplitter's mount snorted, raking the ground with its claws.

At the attack, he would hold back his wolves. He would command his first companies to run full out at the Hobbits. The Crimson Sabers would then turn north, into the Goblin's exposed flank. He would then commit the Sherrorrams into the Sabers' flank. The Dwarves would be forced to commit into the Sherrorram's flank; their formation breaking up as they ran to catch up with the galloping mounts.

The Tech Lieutenants would then plow into the Dwarven flank.

And one by one, each unit would commit, trying to exploit the chink in the armor of the other, until all the Human forces, even the reserves, were committed; leaving their flank exposed. Ribsplitter would then commit his remaining forces to turn that flank in on itself, trapping the Humans against themselves, cutting off their avenue of escape.

And there, in the winking eye of the whirlwind, the slaughter of the Human forces would begin as the adjoining fields of Goblins would arrive and bury the Human allies in uncountable numbers.

The Field Marshal nodded slowly, his lips racked back into a crooked smile. As the sun slowly crawled across the battlefield, Ribsplitter could count the Human forces and their allies.

They were coming up short.

Where Ribsplitter parked his army was a wide plateau with a narrow slope, easily rolling down to the vast plain below. To the flanks, rocks, jagged and pained, ripped from the earth like black fangs, forming intimidating, natural bastion walls. It meant the only way in or out was the ramp. For Command and Control of the thugs, it was very simple and necessary. Go that way and kill many, many things. But his units would have to be fast. No fucking around. His troops would be a massive ram, plowing into and through the Human defenses, but he had to load them into the slot and get them down to the plain before the Humans bottled them up.

Ribsplitter waited. He had to wait until the sun cleared more of the field. His thugs running from light to shadow would leave them blind and confused for only a few seconds, but that would be plenty for mass chaos. If he had a general he could trust to lead them, keep them focused, he could launch his attack immediately. He glanced back at Lucius, then looked away disgustedly. Better to wait.

"Whoretwang is absent without leave, Field Marshal," Lucius spoke up quickly.

Ribsplitter looked back, annoyed. "Who?"

Lucius stifled a sigh. "Your bastard son."

"You're all fucking bastards," he growled. "Which bastard?"

"The Sergeant Major," Lucius sniffed contemptuously.

Ribsplitter reared his Sherrorram around to face his son. "The one that fucking works for a living? The cock dribble that actually does shit?" Ribsplitter glanced back at his troops, hoping to see the tall Goblin standing out there. "If he's not here, then he's fucking dead. The insolent whelp. He wouldn't miss a fight like this unless Dru herself yanked him." He looked over to Lucius. "Unlike you, you fucking ruptured rubber. Try to stay out of the way today and stop being a fucking nark." He looked back at the troops. "What company was he in?"

"Last roster had him in the Black Dragon, father," Lucius said, looking down.

Ribsplitter reeled at him, flashing his talwar and cutting at him. "How many fucking times have I told you not to call me father! You should have been a fucking blow job!"

Lucius blocked his father's mad swings with the haft of his spear casually, the pattern memorized. Left, right, high, left. "Yes, Field Marshal."

Ribsplitter snorted, his face twisted as if he was going to spit. "Who's the asshat commanding the Black Dragon?"

Lucius pursed his lips as he thought. "I thought it was a Momoo."

Ribsplitter grimaced as if he sat on a tack. "Aw, fuck! Haven't we killed them all yet?" He scanned for the banner. "Where the fuck are they?"

"No sign of them, Field Marshall," Lucius said simply, filling with self-righteousness.

Ribsplitter sniffed. "Ah, the cum swab is dead then." He peered at Lucius. "Why can't you be more like him?"

"You mean, couldn't have been?"

"No." He grumbled and turned his Sherrorram back towards the enemy. More sun had filled the valley and Ribsplitter could see the center of the Human forces on a pimple of a hill; the Human command area. They sat calmly on their horses, squinting blindly; their white, enameled armor with gold piping was brilliant in the new sun. The Gross National Product of a large city went into the cost of building each set of their armor, and the funds from small towns had been dedicated to outfit their massive Percherons in full chain that draped and dragged behind them. Entire schools of mages dedicated at least a year into enchanting each set of armor, casting protective spells into the metal.

Wizards, mostly Elves, with wild eyes, groomed beards and disgustingly expensive robes, stood beside the Human commanders, staring unblinking into the sun, their faces twisted as if they'd collectively tasted something bad.

Ribsplitter felt his spirit rumble as he reached back and snapped his fingers for his far-seer. He focused its tubes, bringing their leader into clarity: Julian Jimenez, the Mad.

The Humans were pulling out all the stops. Julian Jimenez, when not leading armies into battle, resided in a quiet country asylum, bound securely in an 'I Love Myself' jacket. Julian knew nothing of losses, nothing of casualties or collateral damage. He was passingly aware of the concept of honor and chivalry. He knew only victory and how to achieve it; he was undefeated. During a drunken argument in a seedy bar, he once stabbed a man in the neck before admitting that he might be mistaken. He was once disciplined for assaulting a fallen soldier whose legs had just been brutally ripped off: "And what the fuck is wrong with your arms? Crawl, you bastard! Attack!"

Ribsplitter smiled. Julian's presence meant the Humans were desperate and afraid. They put up a good fight, but they were about to crumble. It was time to go and crush them but good.

Ribsplitter turned, raising his tulwar and signaling the attack.

The thugs let loose with a rousing cheer.

The Black Terror Company led the vanguard, followed by the beleaguered Black Martyr Battalion, slowing from blood loss. They ignored the Crimson Saber company, holding their shields above their heads to protect against the wicked sharp, but light, blade attacks.

Ribsplitter watched the brave but fucking stupid Hobbits marching in a tight, perfectly aligned, slow motion formation to meet the attackers. They were disciplined, unflinchingly marching towards the nastiest Goblin unit under Ribsplitter's command.

A Hobbit's bravery is unparalleled. They were steadfast to a fault. But they were useless as soldiers for they never showed up on time, giggled through drill and were constantly stopping for lunch breaks.

But this morning they marched, their nobbly boots crashing down as one.

Boots? Hobbits didn't wear boots.

Ribsplitter frowned, almost congratulating Julian on his brilliant and deadly plan as he lifted his far-seer to his eye.

Painted helms with handles welded on them to look like pots, bearded Hobbits marched with vicious smiles stretched across their faces.

Ribsplitter looked to his Banwolves. The beasts seemed to have no interest of the Hobbits they could easily smell.

General Julian Jimenez had somehow, impossibly, convinced Dwarves to dress up like Hobbits.

Dwarves in formation. Their wicked, wicked weapons moving ungainly, stiffly, that carved into shields, flesh and bone as if they were made of wet, moldy rice paper. Their armor and teamwork made them indestructible and horrible, and Ribsplitter had just thrown away his most frightening units into them. Into certain death.

No way to call them back. He was going to lose the frontal assault cold. Once his two units were ground into Goblin burgers, they would be stopped there; the Humans would bottle them up and whittle them away to nothing.

What Dwarf would ever dress up as a Hobbit? What words could Julian have used to convince the Dwarves to do such a thing? The promise of Goblin blood would not be enough. Dwarves have stories of waterfalls of Goblin blood cascading in their halls.

But there they were, grinning like idiots and marching slowly into the onslaught.

Ribsplitter saw the end. His entire frontal charge was stalled. Mages casting cheap spells into the horde pouring into the slope, the grass slick with Goblin blood. The Elves would move forward and rain white, fletched arrows into the pass. Not a single thug would hold back, not a single thug will fail to hear and heed the call of battle and not charge into the narrow gap, their Field Marshal's command of attack ringing in their ears.

And Dru would throw open the gates of Hel and laugh and laugh and laugh as the army of General Hookfang Rottingtooth under the command of Field Marshal Ribsplitter marched empty-handed down the long walk of Fo.

Field Marshal Ribsplitter rocked his jaw back and forth as he fingered the grip of his talwar and debated plunging it into Lucius' bastard heart just for the shits.

And the field exploded into fire.

Ribsplitter jerked his head and blinked at the dark, grey clouds hanging over the Dwarven/Hobbit company. They were stumbling, a gaping hole of charred black in their formation. More explosions ripped in their formation, flinging Dwarf bodies and parts across the field; the front line trying to stand, their eardrums shattered, their vision blurred.

The Black Terror Company, so fast, so brave, without thought, slammed into the Dwarven ranks, knocking them down like cards.

And the killing began.

Ribsplitter fought to catch his breath. The field had been mined! Some half wit had snuck out and planted kegs of Black Dirt that Blows Stuff Up on the field and timed it so that the Dwarves would walk across it. Ribsplitter snorted, suppressing a sneeze and glanced back at Lucius to see if, possibly, by some astronomical chance it was his son that had the brilliant stroke of strategy and forward planning.

Lucius fished a rather nasty booger from his left nostril and debated whether or not it might be good eating.

Ribsplitter turned back to the field.

Plumes of fire ached into the sky and, with a bloody tear, scored down at the Goblins. Ribsplitter scoffed, in his years of leading Goblins against the Humans he had never seen Elf magic with any kind of substance that could reach such distance.

Fireworks, he scoffed.

He watched as the torches of magic struck earth, way off from any target.

He began to laugh until he saw the angry, fizzing score of fuses.

Fuses that ran to the Black Dirt that Blows Stuff up. Two can play this game. The Humans had also mined the field and now it was Ribsplitter's turn to fear the shock of glass and nails and pointy things tainted with infectious bacteria ripping through his thugs.

Ribsplitter watched helplessly, fingering his talwar, wanting so much to ride forward and hack the accursed fuses dead in their tracks. But he knew they burned too fast, too furiously to stop.

They stopped.

Ribsplitter counted the seconds. In his mind, the torrid fuses burned their way into the heart of their kegs, heating up the Black Dirt That Blows Stuff Up to critical.

He winced, his teeth clenched, waiting for the kaboom, the earth shattering kaboom.

He opened his eyes, one at a time.

The Black Terror Company, riding their Sherrorrams unabated at full charge, galloped with the Black Scream Company and the Black Avulsion company whipping their Sherrorrams angrily to keep up.

No boom.

No cacophony of sound followed by shrilling screams and bodies turned to meat flung into the air at hundreds of feet per second.

He blinked, his fingers rapping against the pommel of his saddle. He had lost the ebb and flow of the battlefield in less than a minute. He glanced back to his son who had indeed found something nutritious in his nose. Ribsplitter snarled and lashed at Lucius who blocked his father's blows without looking up.

Ribsplitter turned back to the field. He had heard the possibility of the Humans gaining the secret of the Black Dirt That Blows Stuff Up, but he didn't think they had tactically utilized it as yet. Had they mined the field and the Dwarves set it off accidentally? Ribsplitter snorted. *Idiots. There's only one way to use the Black Dirt That Blows Stuff Up and that is to hand-deliver it.*

Standing up the in the stirrups, the Field Marshal watched with glee as his thugs tore deep into the Humans lines. Goblins poured onto the field like water, forcing Julian to commit more and more of his units. It was only a matter of time.

Ribsplitter lifted his far-seer to catch Julian's face of distress; that expression of growing fear as the finalizing idea of defeat dawned on his insane Human mind.

Julian was laughing.

Ribsplitter snorted a laugh himself. Julian was indeed mad.

He watched with squinted eye as Julian's aide-de-camp lifted a delicate cup of steaming tea and Julian accepted it with a smile. The Human general nibbled on cookies while chatting casually with his staff.

They were all insane. They should be running around like idiots, trying desperately to rally their troops into a psychotic froth, or counting and recounting, looking for a forgotten reserve unit, at a minimum making sure there was an avenue of retreat.

Ribsplitter growled. He watched the Black Creeping Horror Battalion commit to the field. The Black Cobra and the Black Infected Hangnail Battalion were loading into the chute. The Banwolves were getting fat on the fake beard-wearing Hobbit unit that pretended to be the Dwarves. The Elf archers behind them were in rout, their screams rattling the fillings in his back teeth. Julian had to have heard that sickening ululation and yet he only reached down to have his cup topped off.

"Asshole!" Ribsplitter screamed.

Julian wasn't insane at all.

Ribsplitter took the far-seer from his eye and blinked.

The sun's gentle light, soft and warm, peeled back the shadow of the field slowly, tantalizingly, bringing out the blue tint of the green grass. With a single command, whole armies shrugged off cloaks of concealing magic.

Complicated and frightening Gnomish machines of whirling blades were warming up, their flashing blades slowly making speed. Dwarves of the south, dark skinned and violent, began to sing sad, soulful songs of old. Their axes, whisper sharp, will all fall on the downbeat, in rhythm, hacking anything before them into steaks. The Elves of the west wore gowns of dyed feathers who, on command, will all lay on their backs, place their heavy bows on their feet and pull back the thick cables, to rain crimson fletched arrows from afar.

And there was row after row of Humans.

The Eastern Emerald Cavalry was moving into position, prancing their stallions in parade, colored streamers billowing from their lance heads. Northern Army Masters, wearing black and silver war paint and brandishing their great swords and glaives, followed at a trot. Guarding their flank were the Harion Hobbits with Gnome Fire Breathers at a full run. The Harion Hobbits, with their wide, round shields, could link into an impenetrable wall, while the Gnomes behind aimed their fire hoses through the gaps and pumped burning tar into silken fans of fury before them.

Slowly, slowly the sun slid back the night and Ribsplitter watched as more Humans threw back the cloaks that concealed them.

Ribsplitter looked back at his forces, his mind counting them again, hoping to find a regiment he overlooked. He scanned for another way off the plateau, another way to get more thugs onto the field. He then searched for an avenue of retreat.

He looked back to the field, a frown carving into his face and brandishing his tulwar. "Bite me, Julian!" he screamed.

Ribsplitter held his breath as the distant image of Julian looked up, his blue eyes sparkling in the new sun.

Julian smiled, his dimples like black dots on his cheeks.

Black bubbly smoke billowed from a western hill, behind the Human lines. Ribsplitter watched curiously as a playful wind snatched it away. He lifted his far-seer to his eye and watched as crews, so tiny in the distance, scrambled around their smoking brass pipes.

The sound of tearing linen reached Ribsplitter's ears, building in a desperate crescendo. Suddenly one of the black rocks that ringed the plateau exploded with a frightening crack, sending shards of rock cascading down the hill.

More rips through the air and Goblin blood spewed in a black, spotty mist. Ribsplitter felt his breath grow cold in his lungs as he watched the sudden swath appear through his massed armies like the sweep of invisible talons gouging through his thugs. Armor and broken turtle helms rained down in its path.

Paths gouged their way through Ribsplitter's thugs, leaving lines of bloody ichor carved neatly through, the sound of air screaming in its path. Ribsplitter hissed in confusion. *What magic is this and why aren't my shamans defending against it?* He looked over to their little corner where they prepared for the battle by summoning the spirits of the land by inducing near lethal doses of hallucinogenics. They were peering up curiously, and stumbling over to investigate, studying the chunks of meat and bits of armor that had once been a Goblin. One barfed.

Ribsplitter glanced angrily back at the field. The Eastern Emerald Cavalry was at a gallop, their horses charging into the flank of the Black Cobra Battalion. The Cobras would crumble and a bunch of Hobbits and Gnomes would finish them off.

And Julian Jimenez, with his blue eyes and deep cavernous dimples, was toasting him with a tea cup.

Ribsplitter screamed in anger.

Motion flickered on the field as more cloaks drew away. Ribsplitter felt his heart rend with fear as he waited to see what new horror the Humans had in store for him.

Goblins poured out! Running as if they were on fire, their captain brandishing a man-sword and screaming loud enough for Dru herself to notice. Ribsplitter blinked unbelieving as he watched them run across the wake of the Harion Hobbits and pell-mell into Southern Dwarf flank. He watched the Southern Dwarves turn, still singing, their deadly axes preparing to strike with the hiss of death.

The Goblins, on command, dropped flat.

Black smoke ripped across the field and the invisible demon's hand ripped his talons deep into the Southern Dwarf ranks, mixing dirt with Dwarven blood.

From under the cloak, Tech Lieutenants with smoking casks of Black Dirt That Blows Stuff Up on their backs and pink and blue frilly panties on their heads, ran past the prone Goblins into the bloody holes of the Dwarven formation.

Fire and rusty nails erupted in their ranks, bowling the Dwarves over. The Goblins sprang to their feet and charged into the bloody char, slamming into the stumbling Dwarves and hacking them with lust.

Ribsplitter was drooling. "By D'gril's zeppelin tits!" He turned to Lucius, snapping his fingers. "You! Shit for brains. Who's battalion is that?"

Lucius sighed, a little miffed that his father forgot his name again. He squinted down into the field. "Two companies," he reported. "The Queer Purple Fuckers Company," he squinted, "following the..." He strained his eyes, his hand shielding the sun's glare. "They're carrying a banner of a Black Dragon Rampant sinister on a sable field."

Ribsplitter growled. "Which means what, fuck-wad?"

"They're wearing steel armor... and some have a shiny black badge... fuck." Lucius slumped in his saddle. "It's the Black Dragon Company."

Ribsplitter snapped his head back and watched as their captain leapt at a Dwarf and hacked him in the neck, his steel sword chewing through the Dwarf's gorget and scoring deep. "That's Momoo?"

Lucius shook his head. "That, ain't Momoo."

Ribsplitter watched as Goblins poured into the Dwarven ranks, tearing them apart. He watched one Goblin, brandishing a massive, Dwarven double-edged war-axe, swing brutally, and a Dwarf head popped off and sailed into the already shaking formation of Elves beside them.

Ribsplitter pointed with one hand while handing off the far-seer with the other. "Who's that fuck ugly thug? The tall, freaky looking one with the axe?"

Lucius took up the far-seer, slowly focusing the eyepiece, hoping to prove himself wrong. He sighed. "It's Whoretwang."

Ribsplitter felt he'd heard the name before and as he watched Whoretwang leap into the air and swing his heavy axe down, cleaving a Dwarven helm in twain, it came to him. "My son," he whispered with brimming pride.

Shard felt himself slip on the slick Dwarf blood, but the driving bloodlust screamed in his ears, deaf to everything save Ribsplitter-Jones bellowing in his crashing voice, "Fifty-six one thousand, fifty-seven one thousand, fifty-eight one thousand, fifty-nine one thousand, sixty one thousand!" At the last count he shrilled and flung himself to the ground.

"Down!" Shard screamed, his order repeated by all of his thugs as they nose dived into the bloody dirt.

Cannons loaded with clay canisters, filled with jagged, volcanic rocks, vomited gouts of torrid fire. Massive shotgun blasts ripped into the Dwarves, followed by dark grey, choking clouds, robbing them of breath, of sight.

Bleary, blinking tears from their eyes, they saw too late the shadowy black figures charging at them with good steel weapons like hissing arctic wind.

Shard slashed low, cutting deep into a Dwarf's knee. Shard dropped his shoulder as he passed, knocking the one-legged Dwarf down, stomping on his head as he ran by. He coughed in the oily smoke that tightened the air as he bellowed for his thugs, driving them onward. The sun shone weakly through the gauze of smoke, but he could see the iridescent glint from flecks of dragon-scales, worn as badges of honor for his Chosen Thugs: Shard's Thugs.

Shard smiled.

"Attack, you fucks!" He gasped, coughing in the heavy smoke. "Don't you fucking chase them! Follow me to their command! Fucking follow me!" Shard turned and charged brandishing his sword as a lance. He stuffed another Dwarf in the throat as he ran by, dragging his sword free on the pass.

Shard charged at a Dwarf who had raised his heavy round shield to block. Shard swung wildly, chopping off the arm of the Dwarf to the right who was facing off against Lance Corporal Seven-Eights. The first Dwarf lowered his shield and took a swipe at Shard running by, but didn't see Ribsplitter-Jones running up on the left, heaving about his ungainly Dwarven axe.

"Fsquart!" The Sergeant Major cursed as he drove his axe deep. "I fuggin' lost count!"

Shard skidded to a stop, letting his thugs go by and looked back to his small row of brass cannons. The thugs were hauling them forward and re-aiming them, chocking the wheels. "Start the count now!"

Shard watched his thugs, their dragon-scale badges scintillating in the new sun as they swarmed through the Dwarf lines, their man-swords of good steel biting furiously. The Goblins bayed like wolves, their hearts filling with murderous lust. The Dwarves, with teeth clenched in grunting defiance, were helpless as the Goblins ran over them.

Shard was swept with euphoria. He turned back to his goal, the majestic Human banners made of billowing silk in Sunset Indigo and Stolen Gold. Their flag bearers strained against the gentle wind to keep the giant colors vertical. Shard was going to hit their command center and force the Humans to turn inward to protect their generals, thus causing them to implode into chaos.

And the Goblins would rule the day.

As Shard turned, following his thugs as they crashed through the last of the Dwarven lines and into the Elven lines, he couldn't help but smile like an idiot.

The Elves had all but fled, leaving a determined few on their backs, the heavy bows against the hollow of their feet and firing point blank range at the thugs. Their powerful arrows ripped through a thug, and the thug behind and then the thug behind him. Seven-Eights screamed, a thick Elven arrow in his belly, slick from the blood and entrails of the thugs in front of him. He stumbled, backing off of the arrow that was still stuck in the Goblin in front of him and scrambled to his feet, the thug next to him grabbing his arm and hoisting him up. Seven-Eights shrugged free and flung off his shield, its weight now bogging him down, and with fading strength, charged into the Elves, determined to take one with him down the Long Walk of Fo.

The Elves were scrambling, untangling their legs from their bows and taking flight. Seven-Eights was slipping on his own blood pouring from his wound, but he charged forward, swinging his man-sword, screaming for Dru to watch him. The Elf turned, and blocked with his heavy bow, lacquered chips flung like stinging shrapnel from the blow. The Elf kicked out, trying to stop the ferocious Goblin, but Seven-Eights only swung again with both hands, imbedding his sword into the Elf's shin.

Any Goblin within ten feet was paralyzed from the horrific scream of the Elf, but Seven-Eights' ears were filled with the song of the dead sung to him by Dru herself.

"What present you bring me?
Son of Go-rand.
A gift of a pretty soul
to stay my hand?"

And Seven-Eights, born Go-krand, son of Go-rand, heard nothing else.

He wrenched furiously to free his blade while the Elf hopped up and down on one foot. Twisting the blade and cracking the bone, Seven-Eights ripped his sword free and lunged forward, grabbing the Elf and dragging him down the Long Walk of Fo.

All around them, Goblins flowed like black, frothing water.

"Stand fast!" First Sergeant Shiro bellowed and the sergeants in the line repeated her order. Shard skidded to a stop. There was only a Human company of pikemen between him and the Human commanders. They lined themselves at the ready, a bristling wall of steel. They were wide-eyed and trembling, blinking sweat from their eyes. They had thought they had an easy duty, they thought they'd spend the day parading around while the rest of the army did all the work, until an ugly column of Goblins sprang out of nowhere and was charging at them like a smithy's hammer.

The Humans presented their pikes and hoped the Goblins would impale themselves on them.

They didn't. They were quickly reforming their lines, their formations. They were calling for their spearmen to the front line, promising to duke it out. The Humans watched with growing joy as almost a dozen spears were brought up.

The Human company was twenty men wide and lined three ranks deep. One kneeling, one crouching, one standing. Sixty pikes were presented, longer and sharper than any Goblin spear, against a measly scattering of Goblins wielding green saplings with whittled points.

The Humans were smiling now. They were going to bloody the enemy and still keep their easy duty.

Shard jumped up, glancing over the heads of his thugs. Field Marshall Ribsplitter's forces had overwhelmed any resistance in the pass and were now filling the battlefield with thugs. Shard jumped up again, glancing left. Cavaliers on light fast horses were at a canter, speeding to respond to the Goblin surprise, their frilly, royal blue plumes spewing from hand-polished helmets trailing behind them, their curved sabers leveled like lances.

Shard ignored them.

At the front line, Goblins were trading spear thrusts with the Human pikemen, giggling incessantly. The Goblin thrusts were woefully short while the Humans were just inches away. The Goblins laughed louder and the Humans, egged on, were breaking ranks, stepping forward and trying to bridge the gap.

"Back it up!" Shiro bellowed, her voice low and clear and the Goblins, winking at the Humans, shuffled back.

The Humans were breaking ranks and stepping out of line. One took a big step with his lead foot, thrusting his pike overhead and its point scored against a paulderon, punching through into the Goblin's shoulder. The Humans were incensed now, blood had been drawn. The Goblins were not going to riposte and they had free rein.

Ribsplitter-Jones' voice grew louder as he counted; "Fifty-eight one thousand, fifty-nine one thousand, sixty one thousand!" His voice thundered in crescendo.

"Down!"

Shard flung himself into the upheaved, blood soaked clods of earth and hugged the ground.

The brass cannons spoke in the tongue of a thunder clap, vomiting fire and hell. A grey, angry geyser erupted, spewing breath-stealing sulfur and oily smoke. The pikemen, garbed only in padded jackets and leather bands, were torn to shreds by the canister shot. The cavalier's mounts charging in from the flank were unaccustomed to such loud noises and panicked, rearing up and bucking their riders.

Shard scrambled forward, crawling up at a run, hoisting his man-sword over his head. He screamed at his thugs, choking on the smoke and blinking away the tears. Now was the time!

"Attack!"

Like black shadow ghosts in the mist, Goblins rose from the earth, their eyes an angry crimson, their steel blades glinting in the new sun.

The Humans were reeling, blinded by smoke and blood. In an instant, their world turned grey, the sun a hazy, white circle in the distance. The Goblins sprang forward, knocking the spear points down and away. Once inside the point, the Goblins hacked and slashed, filling the world of grey with red.

Shard could hear Ribsplitter-Jones counting. The Humans were trying to stand, but they fell too quickly to the Goblins. Once the pikemen were dispensed with, Shard could attack the Human command directly. He wanted to spray them with canister first, then begin the attack, but the pikemen were melting away and the Goblins were moving on.

Shard stumbled over the bodies of the first rank of pikemen. Unable to step back, they were merely fodder to the Goblin line. With hands raised for mercy, they died quickly. The second rank was in torrid confusion, stabbing out at anything that moved. Goblins were upon them, swinging low and hacking at their ankles. Once gimped, they too became easy prey.

The third rank, those not killed by canister fire, turned and fled.

Shard charged forward, screaming at this thugs to leave the wounded and keep moving, to press the attack. He pointed to the distant banners and pledged them all to Dru's care. He glanced back, his brass cannons so far behind, Human men-at-arms were making their way up the rise. The cannons were turning, slowly, like the hands of a ticking clock, each heave of the Goblin gunners slid their heavy cannons to face the desperate Humans running to silence them.

Shard had hoped for one last volley. He wanted the idiots to keep firing, not to waste time turning them to face an insignificant threat. Idiots. *Fuck them.* Shard turned back, his mono-brow hanging low over his eyes. He had to run his attack home. The main Human charge was already turning inward, their attack on the Goblins was faltering, allowing the Field Marshall to press *his* attack.

It was time for the final charge.

From the bank of angry smoke, where the pikemen had fled and faded, came the hollow clink and clop of horse's hooves casually stepping forward. Tall grey phantoms moved easily, calmly. Behind them, the sun, distant and white in the heavy smoke, cast fans of haunting, magic light, bathing them in a gentle aura.

A cool wind drew back the curtain of smoke.

Princes, lords, generals, four and twenty knights in full battle array moving unhurried towards the Goblin lines.

"Sergeant Major?" Shard called. "Send them in!"

Bug Heads sprang forth, six of them, with burning punks in their hands. Anxious for their moment of glory, they ran all out, hearts popping like blood blisters, tripping, stumbling, skipping to their feet and stuffing their punks into the bung holes, they out-ran the lines of Goblins and into the mulling crowd of knights.

And the rest of the Goblins dropped flat.

Six Bug Heads, wearing the silken panties of her Royal Highness, Princess Hiroki, flung themselves at the knights.

From the ground, Shard could feel the jarring blast of the Black Dirt That Blows Stuff Up. He could hear the glass and metal whizzing over his head and knew anything in its circle was being ripped to shreds.

It was time. Time to take it to them and destroy them. Time to finish it.

Shard scrambled to his feet coughing in the heavy smoke. His mouth was dry, his throat burning. "Get up, you fucks!" His voice dragged in a harsh growl. "Fight now!" Shard turned and heaved his man-sword one last time into the air and charged. "Counter-atta... Wha?"

He stopped.

In the swelling smoke, the phantoms stood. One ripped free his burning tabard and flung it to the ground. Beside him, a smoking black crater where a Bug Head once stood.

His horse pawed the steaming earth.

The wind stripped the smoke away and Shard could see them in color. Their pristine hauberks and coifs were blackened and stained and ruined. Their billowing banners had fallen, their bearers dead, but the knights were leaning over in the saddles, stretching to pick them up. The polish on their heavy bucket helms were scorched, but nothing more.

At Shard's command, his thugs, his Chosen Thugs, rose. His collection of thugs he recruited along his long journey, rose. His Trolls, rose. His ally, the only Goblin captain willing to go along with his half wit plan, Anton Malfist the VII, and his gallant Queer Purple Fuckers Company rose. Finally, the Black Poison Scorpion Company and the Black Burnt Toast Company, unknowingly stolen from Major Ogfeet, rose, their iron swords at the ready.

And, in a moment of lingering silence, waited.

Shard glanced around the field. The knights had waved off the responding companies and redirected them to the attack of Ribsplitter's forces. They were going to deal with

Shard and his upstart band of ragamuffins themselves. It would be good practice. A bit of sport.

Shard had failed. He was going to die a failure.

His thick fingers flexed along the grip of his mansword as he shifted his foot, grinding it down for traction. He was going to kill his thugs against the Human elite and kill them off faster than any Momoo had ever dreamed of killing thugs.

His face stretched into a macabre smile as he growled and broke into a blistering sprint. He was out of tricks. All that was left was to attack, and attack and attack.

And the Goblins screamed in sadistic glee, their tongues flapping from their mouths.

And with a sweep of Julian Jimenez's hand, the knights attacked.

The giant horses sprang, lashing with their deadly hooves and stomping on Goblins with disgust. The knights lashed left and right, their long, spiky maces sparking with magic, smashed into steel armor, knocking the Goblins flat, their bones crushed, to be stomped on by horses and other Goblins. The Goblins with spears stabbed, their points snapping on the knight's shields or the horse's chainmail tack. The Goblin weapons, good Human steel, only sparked and dulled against the knight's magic armor.

The Trolls lumbered forward, heaving their rocks with deadly accuracy, only to have them bounce off transparent shields of blossoming pink magic. The Human mages responded in kind, hurling flashes of cool, blue light. Shard watched as Squiff, the chief Troll stumbled back, the stump where his arm used to be spitting yellowy acidic Troll blood.

Shard made his attack, with a heaving swing he chopped into the prancing horse's fetlocks, amputating the horse's legs. The maimed animal screamed and fell back, toppling its rider. The Goblins leapt at the fallen knight, hacking and stabbing, their sheer weight holding him down but their weapons were useless. With anger and frustration, First Sergeant Shiro threw down her sword and picked up handfuls of green sod and mud and started packing it into the knight's breathing holes. She watched his eyes grow wide with horror as she plugged his eye slits.

Shard turned as a mounted knight charged at him, his mace already falling. Shard ducked and dove under the deadly swing. As the knight turned, Shard stayed close, stabbing with his great sword at the knight's head. Instinct made the knight flinch as Shard's sword sparked off his helm and Shard dove under the drape of the horse's chainmail. Shard switched his sword to his off hand, then slammed his mailed fist into the stallion's lowhangers.

The horse bucked with a shrilling scream, sending its rider to the ground. The knight quickly shrugged off the Goblins jumping on him as he climbed to his feet, but Shard leapt up onto his back, clinging on with one arm. "Tell Dru," Shard whispered into the knight's ear as he palmed his needler, "that Wiggletooth Shard sends her another empty-handed soul." And as if the knight's chainmail was not there, the needler slipped through the links. Shard stabbed again and again until the blood began to spurt in a brilliant, Murder Red.

As the knight staggered, stumbled, and fell, Shard rode him to the ground.

Shard could hear the clop of hooves trotting up behind him as he struggled to free his man-sword, trapped under the fallen knight. He let the sword go, turning to raise the buckler strapped to his arm to ward off the inevitable blow. As he did, he saw the unstained, white and gold tabard of Julian Jimenez before the world sank into sudden darkness.

There was no pain.

For about a second.

A demonic choir of gelded Goblins sang something evil, sanguine, into Shard's ear as he fought to regain consciousness.

Shard opened his eyes and all he could see was a blur of urine yellow as the choir in his head rose to a screaming crescendo that bored through his head like a rusty, iron spike. He put his hand to his head and felt the warm blood oozing beneath his fingers. His helmet was gone, crumpled flat. His needler was gone and his hands were empty. He turned and the world spun unexpectedly the wrong way and he stumbled like a drunken sailor. He blinked and forced his eyes to clear. Shapes moved out of the blur into sudden clarity and color. The knights were moving with impunity, their maces rising slowly, timed and dropping with whistling fury. The Goblins were falling quickly, their steel armor useless against the unyielding magic weapons, their bodies twisted and broken and bloody. Shard could see their shiny badges of dragon-scale winking through offal and churned, bloody mud.

Shard's heels kicked up as he tripped over the knight he had killed, slamming him to the ground. Shard scrambled over the man quickly. Heaving him over, Shard rolled the knight to one side and freed his man-sword.

He ignored it.

Shard grabbed the Human's mace as he turned to find Julian.

Suddenly, pain ripped up his arms with a grinding anger. Shard howled and his muscles tightened against his will, gripping the cursed magic weapon tighter. Shard drove the heavy head of the mace down and stomped on it until it ripped from his grasp. He wrenched his hands free, quickly blowing on them to still the stinging pain. His palms, smoking and charred, put up a stench that caused his eyes to tear. He flexed his fingers, making sure his hands still worked and the skin crackled and flaked away, the blood quickly seeping through.

Shard stuffed his hands up into his arm pits to stem the flow of blood as he heard the clod of hooves behind him.

Shard turned, his mono-brow hanging low across his eyes in anger.

Julian Jimenez, his deep dimples deepening, his blue eyes sparkling, his teeth a blinding white, smiled as he raised his mace. He had thought Shard was dead from the first blow. Now, he was going to finish the job.

Shard's eyes, tiny flicks of glowing red peering up from beneath his mono-brow, seethed as his mind raced for a plan.

There wasn't one.

Shard felt the cold shadow of the knight looming over him. He watched with stilled breath as the knight reached up and flipped down his helmet visor, obviously not wanting the splash of Shard's crushed head and mashed brains to get him in the face.

Shard ducked towards the horse. The beast instinctively reared up, lashing with its hooves. Its deadly steel-shod hooves drove at Shard's unprotected head as he tried to duck under the heaving curtain of chainmail. Quickly, Julian reined his stallion, turning it away and cutting off Shard's escape.

Shard ran towards Julian's shield side, out of the ripping arch of deadly mace's swing. Shard kept running, turning the knight full circle, ducking away from the knight's attacks and staying just out of the reach of the horse's chomping bite.

As they turned, Julian glanced up, checking his front lines, trying to keep up with the real battle. Field Marshal Ribsplitter was committing another company of Sherrorrams and his Shamans were casting rolling, flaming balls of bramble to clear the way for them. Julian looked to his mages, wanting to order them to counter that, but Shard suddenly sprang up at him, barking and lashing with this tusks. Julian lashed down with his mace, but Shard leapt back out of the way.

Shard watched as Julian's eyes turned from mirth to anger. Shard studied the knight, timing the next blow, circling towards the shield side again, using that extra time of the knight crossing over to hit him to get out of the way.

Julian suddenly reined his horse back towards his weapon side, turning into Shard's encroaching circle and cutting the annoying Goblin off. He had to mop this up and get back to crushing Ribsplitter here and now. He reared up in the saddle, standing up in the stirrups, and drove his mace down for a kill.

Shard skidded, trying to reverse direction, his heels sliding in the blood-slick ground. Shard ground his teeth in desperation as he felt his legs kicking out from under him. He watched Julian's crystal eyes peering through the narrow slits of his helmet visor turn to triumph.

And blink.

Shard slammed into the ground as the mace sailed over him.

Julian's horse reared up as Shard rolled out of the way. The horse was bucking and Julian was jerking the reins frantically. Shard was quickly looking for a sword amongst the dead when he spotted his man-sword sticking out of the mud.

As he lunged for it, his eyes filled with tears.

Shard suddenly hawked, choking, almost puking. He was blinking to clear his eyes and grab hold of the sword, but the stench that suddenly settled around him was overwhelming. His lungs filled with pepper, forcing him to cough and wheeze.

He could hear Ribsplitter-Jones shouting for the thugs to run. *Run where? Idiot, we're surrounded by the Human forces, there is nowhere to run.* Shard dove for the sword, blinking the stench from his eyes so he could see.

That horrible stench...

He felt a sudden sucking wind from behind, pulling the nauseating stink away.

Shard felt triumph as his hand slapped on the leather wrapped handle of his man-sword. He turned back, blinking the blur from his eyes as he brandished his weapon, ready to fight. Julian was controlling his horse by sheer will of command, driving the beast on as he raised his mace to strike.

Behind him was a waterfall of brimstone.

The gates of hell had been thrown open and a torrid, wave of fury rolled forth, incinerating everything in its path. Shard watched columns of Dwarves, in perfect, indestructible formation, flashed fried into instant ash. Elves ran, skittering like autumn leaves in the wind, but not fast enough to evade the crucible, the maelstrom of hate sweeping across the battlefield.

Coming right at Shard.

No mage, no spell, could have conjured this trick. The flashing streamers of gold and ivory curled themselves into fiery spheres of anger that devoured everything in its path.

Julian paused, a little disappointed. He was riding down a Goblin, an annoying Goblin who suddenly seemed unconcerned with the fate of getting his brain mashed out and more interested in what was going on behind him. Julian didn't dare look. It was the oldest trick in the book! Surely the Goblin didn't think that Julian would fall for such a thing. Julian set his teeth as he raised to strike again, but the Goblin only stared off in the distance.

Julian glanced back quickly, then again, a little longer.

His men were in full rout. The Goblins were in full rout. Everyone was running like idiots, throwing down their weapons and screaming like children.

Suddenly, the world turned white without shadows and Julian could feel the peppery heat flare a harsh line through his helmet visor. He cast his gaze down and noticed that the Goblin he was all set to kill was gone.

Instantly cool beneath the cloak of chainmail under Julian's horse, Shard's eyes adjusted to the dark just as the dim light filtering through the links flared to white light, brighter than the sun. Shard could feel the horse beginning to buck in panic; the Goblin captain reached out, grabbed a firm hold on the stallion's ripened nectars, and held on as the world around him turned into a dark, indigo tempest.

That horrible stench suddenly came back to his memory, exploding harshly. Shard held his breath as he clutched the horse's oysters, trying to keep the beast from moving, hoping the beast could provide some protection against the fire.

The dragon's fire.

The dragon had found him. Impossibly, it had somehow tracked him down.

The light dimmed and cooled and Shard blinked, trying to see. He felt the horse suddenly shift and collapse, its legs already stiffening with rigor mortis. Shard scrambled close to the horse's body, but the chainmail barding crumbled into streams of cascading rust.

Exposing him.

Shard looked out across the bleary landscape of scorched earth. Smoking black bones, like burning sticks, rose from the smoldering ground. The dragon's fire carved a brutal hundred yard long, fifty yard wide swath of total destruction. Shard could see the remaining Human forces running away out of fear and surprise. They were stumbling over themselves, trampling each other to get away. Shard sneered in disgust. He had to somehow rally the Goblins and press the attack, take advantage of their stroke of luck.

As Shard turned to signal the Field Marshal, the angry, warbling hiss of a mace made him flinch.

Pain ripped through his hands as the mace impact sparked off his man-sword. He had blocked the harrowing blow by instinct, but the vibration sawed through his already shredded hands, springing them open. Shard was vaguely aware of his man-sword falling from his stinging, numbed hands as he clenched them to stop the blood flowing anew.

He leapt back desperately, avoiding Julian's furious swing. The knight's armor was only mildly scorched, blackened here and there, his tabard singed along the edges. His eyes, arctic blue, were fixed with fury. He grunted as he stamped forward, swinging his mace for the kill. Shard jumped back and stumbled over a still burning corpse, slamming him into the mud. He could feel the mud cling to his steel armor, holding him fast as Julian eclipsed his vision, mace ready to strike.

Shard looked skyward, his mouth agape.

Julian spun on his heels and gazed up, searching for the dragon, but there was only blue, blue sky.

Grand Generalisimo of the Human and Ally Forces, victor of countless battles and campaigns, Duke Sir Julian Jimenez, had fallen for the oldest trick in the book.

His teeth ground against each other sounding like the ticking of a clock as he spun around and drove his mace down.

Shard was gone.

Shard was running, uncertain what to do next, his eyes furiously searching for a weapon. Man-swords, Dwarf axes, Elven bows and shafts, Hobbit cookware, all lay scattered across the field, but Shard dismissed them, knowing they were useless against Julian's armor.

Or the dragon's hide.

How did that fucker find me? Shard's brain burned as he tried to think. The dragon's fire dropped right on top of him. There were a million Goblins on the field and somehow that damned lizard found him.

And his Chosen Thugs.

Shard picked up his needler.

As he yanked his broken schlager blade free from the muck, he blinked as something sparkled in the blood soaked mud. Like a sliver chipped off a summer rainbow.

A tiny piece of dragon-scale.

Shard had handed them out to his thugs, his Chosen Thugs, his Black Dragon company. They wore them proudly on their baldrics. On his baldric.

Shard turned left, picking up pace as he ran. He glanced back to Julian, who was shouting orders to try and control his army. Frustrated, he turned, searching the ground for a signal banner, hoping to communicate with his lines. Behind him, his mage adorned in pristine robes of jet and crimson, searched the sky for the dragon's return.

Shard nodded to himself. It was the mage who saved Julian from the dragon's blast. The mage had cast a shield on himself and Julian, but couldn't spare enough magic to save Julian's horse. The mage was pointing skyward as he chanted. His bulging eyes bulged more as he deepened his stance, his fingers flashing, casting, preparing.

Shard palmed his needler.

He buried a war cry in his throat and swallowed his growl. His hand was throbbing. His needler felt loose in his bloody hand, foreign and insignificant to such a powerful foe. He sprang up, landing on a fallen shield and bouncing up higher as the shadow of the dragon fell across his back.

Julian turned, his flashing blue eyes looking back. Shard watched the tiny dots of Julian's frost eyes suddenly swell with oblivion. Shard could see himself in the mirror; his needler, as cold as winter, aiming for Julian's eye slit, his face stretched in triumphant glee.

Julian's mace swung out, its haft hitting Shard across the short ribs, knocking the wind from his lungs.

Shard struck.

Shard wrapped his feet around Julian's waist as he dragged his bloody needler free. He could hear Julian's muffled cry of agony as he stabbed again, aiming for the Generalisimo's other eye.

Julian thrashed desperately, flinging Shard off. He tried swinging his mace, only to find his arm was bound up, tangled. As he heaved and shrugged to free himself, Shard scrambled towards the mage.

Julian shook his shield free, and with his left hand drew his sword, hoping to cut himself free of whatever was snagging his arm.

Shard pounced on the mage, interrupting his chant by grabbing on to him, spinning him around, and pulling him down. Shard landed on the ground, the mage grunting as he landed on top. Shard pointed to the sky and the mage glanced over his shoulder.

And started his chant again.

Julian was nearly blinded with blood and pain as his one eye peered in confusion. He jerked free the baldric Shard had looped around his neck and arm. He blinked, trying to see what it was, as his shadow suddenly flung itself to the ground and ran like spilled Goblin blood.

Julian dropped his sword and dropped to the ground, scooping up his shield, his fingers wriggling through the straps.

Hellfire erupted with the roar of a territorial lion. Worms of morning glow writhed in hate and anger; Shard watched in amazement through the translucent pink shield of magic, until the worms bored their way through.

Fuck!

Shard felt the fire dig through the gaps of his armor like claws, rending his flesh. He pulled the mage closer, trying to bury himself in the heavy, magic, reinforced badger wool. Over the horrific sound, Shard could hear the mage chanting, pouring more magic into his collapsing shield.

With a slurp that sucked the last bit of air from Shard's lungs, the fire vanished into a puff of smoke. Coughing, choking, Shard gulped air only to hack it up again. The smoke was thick and oily, grating against the back of his throat. His eyes tearing, Shard looked up at the mage. His immaculate hair was a bushel of smoldering punks, his heavy waxed beard was mashed against his chin, and his moustache was burned to a crisp. His eyes crossed and uncrossed from the sudden, taxing drain of magic.

Shard kicked at the enfeebled mage to make him get off as he desperately tried to think of a way to kill the dragon. Julian was toast, he had to be. He was hit directly with a flaming dragon booger. Now with the general out of the way, Shard could contend with his old friend, once the befuddled mage got up.

Shard shoved the bewildered mage again, rousing him to get him off. As the mage stumbled to his feet, his head exploded like a rotted pumpkin and he slumped forward, back down on Shard. His blood, still pumping, spurted hot and steaming into Shard's stunned face, flooding into Shard's armor and pooling in his shorts.

Something shambled forward out of the wall of smoke. His shield was melted slag, his arm a cinder with crackling, burning twigs for fingers. His spiffy, shining, hero's armor was blasted black, pitted, corroded and ugly. He dragged his mace around, its head still glowing from the dragon's fire, the mage's blood sizzling from its flanges.

Shard blinked as the mage's spewing blood hit him across the eyes. Panicky, he pushed at the ungainly corpse. His hands crippled and slick with blood, he desperately sought purchase to pry it off him with little avail. Julian was laughing, coughing and wheezing as he stumbled a little closer. Shard could see Julian's one, good eye and felt its wintery kiss of death.

Shard pointed to the sky.

Julian ignored him and raised his glowing, angry mace, a growl on his lips.

Yellowy ivory claws wrapped around his body, lifting him into the air, crushing him. They punched through his plate armor like spears, anchoring him place. Julian flailed with his mace, trying to hit the dragon, but failed to find enough leverage to land a solid blow.

The dragon held him close, its golden eyes studying him, his wide nostrils flaring as it sniffed him.

"Oh, just take a fucking bite out of him!" Shard growled as he thrashed and kicked the dead mage off. Shard had to hurry. If the dragon figured out Julian wasn't the Goblin it was looking for, Shard was going to be warm, tasty, Goblin kibble in a fuckbeat. Shard lunged at the headless mage and with swollen, aching fingers yanked at the knot at the mage's sash, then attacked it with his tusks, prying it apart. Spinning the mage over and over, Shard brutally yanked the belt free. As he quickly wrapped his hands in yards of magic cloth, he searched the torrid battle field, ignoring Julian's horrific screams and curses.

Shard stubbed his sore toe.

The moment he thought he was beyond pain, it flashed wildfire up his leg and bent him over. Blinking the tears away and focusing past the pain, he glanced down and found Julian's fallen sword. It was bigger than Shard was accustomed to, a hand and a half. As he grabbed it, he could feel its wicked power surging through his wrapped hands, making him want to scream. He buried his agony in his throat, mewling like a child as he heaved up the ungainly weapon. He watched as the dragon first licked Julian, then lifted the knight up to his toothy maw.

Shard started his charge, his arm weighing, sagging, tearing in pain as he tried to keep the tip of the sword up. He had to time it; he had to kill the dragon after it killed Julian. He watched as the sinister teeth slowly closed on Julian's helmeted head and heard the crunch as they punched through the heavy metal.

Shard poured on the speed, trying to ignore the dragon's looming, growing size. It was perhaps eighteen feet tall sitting there, taller if it held its head up. Shard's heart filled with icy despair as his tiny, tiny sword shrank to the size of a needler compared to the dragon's gargantuan mass. Shard had to find a vital point, a weakness, but the dragon's armor was perfect; not a chink, not a space.

As the dragon snorted in disgust and tossed Julian's bloody body over its left wing, Shard noticed something.

Something rather important.

It was a boy dragon.

Its massive head turned, swinging down, its yellow eyes fixing on Shard as fire bubbled up in balls of azure from its throat. Spit drooled from its hanging tongue, snapping and popping like firecrackers, raining sparkles down its thick neck.

Shard ignored the weakness in his body, ignored the fire in his lungs, the coppery blood pooling beneath his tongue. He squinted as he felt the burst of heat slap his cheeks. His ears filled with a hollow, static din, growing, consuming.

A song of rage in his ears.

He could feel wind sucking around him as the dragon drew breath into its fiery heart.

Shard felt the blade plunge home, jarring into his tortured hands. He cried in pain as he ripped them free, his fingers cramping, the cloth soaked and caked black from his blood.

The dragon roared a squealing, warbling howl of anguish, its building fire snuffed with a pop and a puff of grey smoke. It looked down at the sword plunged into its lower belly, hissing and sizzling with angry magic. The dragon clawed at it, tried to bite it, rolled over and scratched at it. Flapping its wings furiously, it lifted off, climbing into the sky.

Shard watched as it grew smaller and smaller, until it was only a tiny dot on the horizon. He then realized it was only a speck in his eye, and he blinked it away. "Fshquart," he mumbled as he sank to his knees, then flat on his face.

Shard's Epilogue

SHARD WALKED SLOWLY, painfully, through the cold, damp night, trying to ignore the mewing sobs of his burned and wounded limbs. He wore the fog about his shoulders like a cloak as he made his way unwaveringly, feeling the unyielding cobblestone beneath his aching feet. He had never been here before. He had not a map, nor direction, yet he made his way as if he was going home.

He was.

He felt the darkness lift and could see glowing torches, endless torches, in a slow, sad parade, marching across the shadowy path, down the Long Walk of Fo. Shard shook off the chill gathering around him as he made his way down, his pace quickening, his pains lifting away. At the start of the path, he saw a gathering shuffling around, looking sullen. He saw Ho Sheck Yek Yak, Captain of the Black Raid company. He saw the Dwarf commander he slew. He saw many Elves, Archers and Horretika and, for the first time ever, they had nothing to say. He saw Humans by the handful.

They all looked at him expectantly.

Shard nodded. "You fuck losers are with me." He searched their defeated faces and sighed when he didn't see Julian. It was the dragon who killed him, Shard accepted, he would get no points for him.

Shard turned towards the Long Walk of Fo with his dead in tow and stepped off proudly, his journey before him.

And Dru, goddess of Death, waited for him at the foot of the path. She was dressed in long robes, the tails which draped and spread across the land like a dark ocean. Her hood hung over her face, casting a shadow of fear and emptiness, yet warmth filled the air. She was smiling, Shard could tell, even though he couldn't see her face.

Shard paused askance. He had always been taught that she would be at the end of the long walk, not the beginning. But he shook it off, and stepped forward.

She held up a hand and stopped him.

Her perfume was jasmine and she was humming a Goblin lullaby.

"The losers can go on ahead." Her voice was like crystal chimes, tumbling from her lips of autumn sunset. "But not you, Whig."

Shard's face stung as if he'd been slapped.

Her head turned toward him, looking up. Light flickered from a torch and splashed on her alabaster cheek. Her skin was polar white. Her eye was filled with mirth and stars in a sea of twilight.

And Shard knew her.

Her icy hand shot out and clamped over his mouth. "Shhh!" She hissed.

Shard blinked and light speared through his vision and into his brain with a hot brand. He tried to move, but the embers embedded in his limbs stirred to fire. Noise flooded his head. His senses suddenly aware and vengeful.

And the smell of jasmine twisted his stomach.

Dru hovered over him. Her face was hammered silver, bruised and tarnished. One giant, dark hole for her one eye; large, expressive and alluring. Tiny holes were punched like a frown for her mouth. On her right had was a glove of soft, baby troll leather, slowly scintillating with moving subdued color, matching whatever it was next too. She wore a cowl of soft wool, Sodden Log Green with Inflamed Liver Red trim with Jaundice Yellow highlights; the height of Goblin fashion.

She had her hand clamped over his mouth.

She leaned closer and Shard could feel death, a chilling air, grip him. "Whig," she whispered, "don't call me Nana."

Shard blinked. His head was throbbing unbearably. He tried to rub his eyes clear, only to find his hands had been wrapped into fat balls of muslin soaked with aloe and Spirit Root. "Where am I?" His voice rumbled through thirty yards of Agony Bramble.

Daphne turned to a small fire she had started and hung a small pot over it to boil. "A cluster of trees to the side of the battlefield. Smiley has re-grouped the thugs and sent them out to start scavenging the field before everyone else."

Shard turned his head and stars flashed against the backs of his eyes. He laid back down. "How long have I been out?"

"A couple hours," She said, fanning her fire.

Shard watched her tending the little pot. She was quietly humming her lullaby. Shard leaned forward and caught a glimpse of her eye, filled with joy.

"What," Shard growled.

She looked up, surprised. "Hmm?"

"What the fuck are you so fucking happy about?"

"Nothing."

"What?" Shard pressed.

She sighed patiently. "Nuh-thing."

Shard struggled to sit up and she pushed him back down with her stump. Shard made up his face. "Tell me what's so fucking funny!" His voice eeked out a harsh whisper.

Daphne put down her cooking spoon as she relented. "It's just... Well you..." She looked up. "Promise you won't get mad?"

"I promise I'll fucking string you up by your eyelashes." His mono-brow hung low over his eyes.

"You just look so cute when you're sleeping."

His mono-brow lowered, glowering. "I fucking hate you," he grumbled.

He could feel the smile beneath her mask. "I know."

"No, you fucking don't." He laid his head back, then looked up as the thought struck him. "And Smiley's in charge?"

"Hmmm. He ordered the thugs to look for booze. Sergeant Major suggested they also look for armor and weapons." She looked up. "Speaking of which..."

"E'rats!" Ribsplitter-Jones spat as he made his way. "Fug wit's alive!"

Shard felt himself curl like overcooked bacon. He held his bandaged hands to his ears. "At ease, Sergeant Major," Shard whispered. "Shut the fuck up."

"Heh, heh, heh. E'rats Captain Smiley will be disappointed." He held out a hand-woven, wicker cage to Daphne. "'Eres two fine specimens of Vamboil Beetles."

"Thank you, Whoretwang."

"S'right."

Shard looked up, blinking painfully as his brain, filled with three-day-old porridge, warmed up. "Captain Smiley?" Shard looked around for his baldric. "Fuck." He tried to rise, but Daphne again pushed him back down with her stump. "I'll fucking gack him." He moaned.

Daphne took a beetle from the cage and slipped it under her mask and quickly, mercifully, bit off its head. She dropped the decapitated bug into her boiling pot and spat out its head. "Fshquart," she hissed when she realized that the head was somewhere in her mask.

"Erah, lemme get that for ya." Ribsplitter-Jones took the second beetle, bit off its head and dropped it into the pot.

Daphne flicked the bug head out of her mask and looked up to the tall goblin. "Thank you."

Shard slowly looked up at the two of them. Daphne was slowly stirring her pot, looking up at the tall Goblin. The Sergeant Major was looking back.

Shard felt his bowels stir again, his brain refusing to work. "Sergeant Major, report."

Ribsplitter-Jones stiffened, annoyed at the intrusion. "Eah?" His expression changed as he realized who he was talking too. "Oh, uh, First Sergeant Shiro took a detail and re-secured our cannons. E'rats no worse for wear."

Shard struggled to sit up. "The fucking battle?"

"E'rats, e'rats. Called on account of dragon."

"Brilliant plan, Shard." Bark-Bite called, making his way through the scrub. "You did it! You bloody well did it!" He paused to catch his breath. "A little ballsy for my taste, calling a dragon and having it toast half your company, but if anyone could make that work, you could." He sucked something from his teeth. "That does solve your paymaster problem, doesn't it? Hah! Thinking on many levels, eh?" He started fishing around in his pocket for his chaw. "And you're alive to boot!" He glanced down at Daphne. "He is alive, right?"

Daphne only hovered over her steaming pot and let out a long, low, evil hiss.

Bark-Bite made a casual side-step, putting Ribsplitter-Jones between him and her. "I see." He turned back at Shard. "The Field Marshal's a might miffed. Says you mucked up his great plan with that bloody dragon. He's not ready to concede he was right royally screwed." He pulled out his chaw and plucked off a bit of lint. "That and your Sergeant Major's on report for being AWOL." He clamped on to his chaw and ripped off a piece. "And he's getting a medal for something." His cheeks bulged as he chewed.

Shard blinked. "And where the fuck have you been?"

A flash of annoyance crossed the Major's face. "You little fuck. I'll let your subordination slide on the account you saved our collective butts, but rest assured when you're up and walking, I'll order someone to kick your disrespectful Goblin ass." He spat. "If you must know, I was busy assassinating Elven mages," he drew Lil' Elfie which flared a brilliant blue, "which kept them from gang banging your little dragon." He looked at the glowing, magical blade, squinting at its brightness. "What? There's an Elf nearby!"

Shard quickly held up his hands. "I'm covered in Elf blood."

Bark-Bite shook his head, slowly turning. "No, Shard. This is different. I can feel Lil' Elfie throbbing in my hand. There is an Elf hiding about!"

Shard held his breath as Bark-Bite turned towards Daphne. Shard's mono-brow sagged as he cursed himself for forgetting about the Major's magic sword.

"E'rats!" Ribsplitter-Jones shoved a broken, bloody turtle shell under the Major's nose. "Maybe it smells my dead Skippy?"

"Oh, no!" Shard exclaimed. "Skippy died?"

"Wot? You know how many Skippys I've gone through?" He sniffed. "I don't think I've ever had a Skippy survive a real fight. Ahs figured this one'd make, it on account I wasn't wearing him on my head."

"Sergeant Major!" Bark-Bite barked. "Lil' Elfie doesn't detect dead turtles!"

"Howda you know?" He thrust Skippy at the Major and Skippy suddenly lunged out and snapped, missing the Major by a hair. "Fuck wot? Skippy! E'rats! You're alive! Now what am I gonna have fer me dinner?" He brandished the turtle at the Major again. "Par-haps Lil' Elfie's sniffin' out a live turtle."

"Lil' Elfie doesn't sniff turtles, live or dead!" He spat out his half chewed chaw. "Shard? I'm surprised you're not helping me."

Shard caught his breath. "Major, sir? My brain's a little addled from battling that dragon. Might the Major have a bit of rum that I might offer the Major?"

"Not now, Shard!" He hissed as he pointed Lil' Elfie at Daphne. "You..."

Shard gasped. "I can explain..."

Shard's words were trapped in his throat as he winced from the shrieking caterwaul that Daphne put up. Bark-Bite was forced back a step from the horrible noise and Skippy retreated back into his shell.

Daphne reached out slowly, smoothly, and hung a necklace of bones on the blade of Lil' Elfie.

And Lil' Elfie rang like a soft bell.

Bark-Bite peered at the necklace of Elf knucklebones. "My word! What a rare find!" He looked at her. "Who are you?"

"That is our witch," Shard said, trying to recover.

Bark-Bite lowered Lil' Elfie, letting the necklace slide off into her hand. "Well met. To whom do I have the pleasure of speaking?"

Before Shard could think of a name, Daphne answered with a voice that burned off the short hairs on the back of his neck. "I call Daf'nee." She slipped the necklace back around her neck and turned back to her pot. She tipped it into a mug and held it out to Shard. "You drinky, drinky all up. Make all goodgood."

Shard carefully clamped the steaming mug in his bandage-swathed hands. "Thank you, Daf'nee." Shard blew on it before taking a sip. It was surprisingly sweet.

"Where did you find her?" Bark Bite sheathed his cleaver.

"She found us." Shard looked up from his mug. "Said she wanted to help us kill Elves. She helped us steal the conceal-ment cloaks which enabled us to hide on the battlefield." Shard sipped his bug brew, not mentioning the reverse scrying spell which allowed him to look in on Julian's plan.

Bark-Bite fished around in his pocket and pulled out his hip flask. "Well, Shard, she came in right handy." He took a nip and gasped, then leaned over to pour a bit into Shard's mug.

Faster than a tax collector after a loose penny, Daf'nee's hand flashed and snatched the hip flask. She sniffed it, then set it on the ground. She reached up and deftly plucked the cork from Bark Bite's hand, stoppered the flask, and the whole thing vanished beneath her robes.

"See here! That is..." He shrugged. "Gone I guess." He sighed as he rummaged around in his coat pocket again and pulled out another flask.

Ribsplitter-Jones cleared his throat. "E'rats, Major, sir?"

Bark Bite looked up. "Oh, of course." He circled around Shard, giving Daf'nee a wide berth and handed Ribsplitter-Jones the flask.

"Sergeant Major!" Smiley shouted as he made his way from the battle field, carrying a human helmet. "Is that booze? Didn't I say I wanted all booze turned over to me?"

Ribsplitter-Jones tipped the flask into his mouth. "E'rats! And fine booze it is!" He handed the flask back to Bark-Bite before Smiley could grab it. "Still 'aven't fished that nad scratcher outta yer nose, ay LT?"

"That's Captain, Sergeant, and no. Damn thing's stuck good, that it is." He looked over at the Major, licking his lips. "Ah, Major? The Colonel scarfed the last of my stash, might I a sniff of yours." He set down his helmet.

Bark-Bite handed him the flask. "I have a bit of good news/bad news for you."

Smiley snatched at the flask. "What's that, sir?"

"Shard's alive."

Smiley brightened, his old smile returning. "Well, that's excellent! Where is he?"

Bark-Bite frowned. "Well that, is the bad news."

Shard rolled over and propping himself on one arm, punched Smiley in the nads.

As Smiley heaved over, Shard fought the building urge to scream as he clutched his throbbing, bandaged hand to his chest. Shard shook it off and reached up and tried grabbing his dangling baldric. "Give me that!" He hooked his arm over it and pulled, choking Smiley.

"Yes, Sir." Smiley gasped. "I was just holding it for you, that I was."

"You slimy fuck bastard!" Shard heaved at it, pulling Smiley off his feet and down to the ground. Shard tried clambering over him, but the two rolled over towards the fire.

Daf'nee let out her shriek that forced all four Goblins to clamp their hands over their ears.

In the moment of silence, she turned back to her fire, mixing up another potion.

Shard yanked the baldric free, then kicked Smiley. "You don't know what this is."

Smiley scrambled to his feet. "I found it on the battle-field, that I did, sir. You weren't wearing it and you looked very dead, that you did."

Shard attacked the baldric with his teeth. He pulled some threads and looked up, the dragon scale in his mouth. He spat it at Smiley. "The dragon sniffed these out. That's how he found us."

Smiley looked perplexed, then pulled out his lieutenant's baldric and looked at it. "I kinda liked it." He pouted.

"Next time, Smiley, you can fight the fucking dragon. Rip that scale off and give it here." Shard then motioned at the helm Smiley brought over. "What's that helmet here for?"

Smiley heaved up the heavy, steel dolman, blackened from dragon's fire and filled with punctures from the drag-on's long, razor sharp teeth. "It belonged to the Human gen-eral. I thought it might be worth something, that I did."

"Worth something? I'm sure it is!" Shard perked up. "Open it up. I want to see Julian's expression of surprise and horror."

Smiley braced the helmet against his leg and struggled with the helmet clasp until the face plate flipped open. "It's empty, sir."

Shard's mono-brow arched. The battle flashed in his mind like cards. He recalled the dragon tossing the body away, but not whether the body had a head or not. "Where the fuck is it? Have the thugs search the battlefield. The Field Marshal would want to see it. And find what the thugs are doing with the loot. Make sure they're not burning anything or breaking any stools."

Smiley smiled and punched a snappy salute. "Yes, sir!" He turned and started off.

"Lieutenant!" Bark-Bite called. "My hooch?"

Smiley turned back. "What about it, sir?"

"You still have it."

Smiley thought for a moment. "Are you sure, sir?"

Shard growled. "Sergeant Major? Kick the Lieutenant in the grapes and see if that helps him remember where the Major's flask is."

Ribsplitter-Jones lit up. "S'right!"

Smiley quickly patted his pockets and found the flask. "Oh, here it is!" He held it out to the Major.

Bark-Bite grabbed hold of it. "Let it go, lieutenant." Bark-Bite wretched it free. "Carry on, lieutenant."

Smiley saluted sharply, glanced at the flask forlornly, then ran off.

Shard sat up and looked around. He spotted two thugs. The senior was showing the junior how to break a leg off a stool.

"Lance Corporal!" Shard bellowed, although the effort made him wince.

The junior thug looked up and saluted. "Private First Class Baldwin, reporting as ordered, sir!"

Shard frowned, his sigh coming out in a hiss. "That's nice, private. I wanted the Lance Corporal."

The private turned and slugged his senior. As the Goblin swooned, Baldwin snatched his baldric and slipped it on. He then turned to Shard with a salute. "Lance Corporal Baldwin reporting as ordered, sir!"

Shard gave a sharp sigh. "Gather all the dragon scales, put 'em in a bag with a rock. Tie up the bag, with the rock and the scales in the bag, and fling it into the ocean. If you see a dragon, don't get eaten and stay far away from me."

Baldwin saluted, took the scales and headed off.

Gracefully, Daf'nee rose and hooked the handle of her steaming pot with a stick.

Shard's eyes followed her as he recovered his mug. "Where the fuck are you going?"

She hissed angrily, then spoke in her harsh voice. "Addiko hurt. Bleed black no stop." She held up her pot. "Drinky drinky, make all goodgood. Change wrappings, cleanclean." She bowed and scurried off.

Bark-Bite cast a curious eye as she made her way, then with a shrug, leaned over and tipped his flask into Shard's mug. "Meddle not in the affairs of witches, Shard." The Major took a sip from his flask. "And if I may say, that one's a bit of a bitch."

Shard swirled the dregs of his mug, then downed it, feeling the rum burn against the back of his throat. Shard set it down, then clumsily got to his feet, Ribsplitter-Jones hoisting him up. Shard then hooked his captain's baldric and draped it over his shoulder. It was crusted brown with blood. Human, Elf, Dwarf and Thug. The only clean spot was where his dragon scale had hung.

Shard sniffed.

It was his baldric, his thugs.

Shard's Thugs.

"Sergeant Major? Fall the thugs into formation. Let's get a good head count, then find a bivouac site of the field. We haven't won jack shit today. We've bought us some time, that's all. We've got a fuck load of work to do and we'd better get jack hot on it!"

Notes:

    Andrea Leshinski, Shard's Audience.

    Jack Lambert, Shard's Fan.

    Chris Holt, Shard's Encouragement.

    Tony Baldwin, Shard's Rabid Fan.

    Bernard Cornwell, Shard's Catalyst.

    Richard Sharpe, Shard's Hero.

    Steve Smith, Shard's Fire.

    Sandy Fuller and Max the Executioner, Shard's Entourage.

    Carol Karcheski, Shard's Marketing Specialist.

    Hilary Neckermann, Shard's Lover.

    Joe Schifino, Shard's Mentor.

    And

    M.D. Herron, as Major Bark-Bite.

Made in the USA
San Bernardino, CA
21 June 2017